DON'T GO STEALING MY HEART

KELLY SISKIND

 Created with Vellum

ALSO BY KELLY SISKIND

Chasing Crazy

New Orleans Rush

Over the Top Series:

My Perfect Mistake

A Fine Mess

Hooked on Trouble

One Wild Wish Series:

He's Going Down

Off-Limits Crush

36 Hour Date

Visit Kelly's website and join her newsletter for great giveaways and never miss an update:

www.kellysiskind.com

DON'T GO STEALING MY HEART

1

———————

THE DIFFERENCE between getting caught and executing a perfect heist is planning.

Clementine closed her eyes and silently repeated her mantra. Lucien's mantra, really. Her mentor's quote usually calmed her revving pulse, and they'd reviewed every inch of this job backward and forward. There would be no fumbles. But her chest felt like Mount Vesuvius about to erupt. She counted her inhales and exhales until her heart rate decelerated from Ferrari fast to Tonka Truck chug.

Ned Compton's townhome was quiet. He'd left for his Italian villa, as expected. The neighbors were snoozing. Clementine had cut the alarm. No fuss, no muss.

Eyes wide. Stay focused. Get the job done.

She clicked on her headlamp and glided down the hall, took the stairs to the upper level, and slipped into Ned's study quiet as a cloud. The Brendan Monroe painting above the wainscoting was striking, even in the dim light. It wasn't the exquisite artwork she was after, though. She'd be stealing the 8.47 carat diamond ring behind it.

According to Lucien's intel, Ned had purchased the extravagant piece of jewelry at auction—a Saudi princess's engagement ring, likely for the Italian girlfriend he regularly cheated on, or one of his mistresses. Ned's internet activity indicated he'd ordered a new safe. Something harder to crack for his precious purchase. It was due to arrive next week.

Clementine lifted the painting, relieved to find the old safe she'd been expecting. She propped it against the mahogany desk, her eyes skimming over a few framed photos: Ned fishing with a group of guys, Ned with his girlfriend (who had crappy taste in men), Ned at a country home, flanked by smiling people, probably family. Clementine's heart rate switched tactics, dulling to a sluggish thud. The only photo in her apartment was of little Nisha, and she'd only met that girl once.

But Nisha and orphans like her were the reason Clementine was dressed in black, hair in a tight bun, black gloves secured, about to steal from Ned Compton.

Working faster, she removed her small backpack and pulled out her stethoscope. She'd always enjoyed this part of the job, the simple mechanics of machinery. Black and white. Right or wrong. Stethoscope placed over the lock, she listened for the faint click of the drive-cam notch sliding under the lever arm. She twisted the dial slowly and held her breath. *There...just there.* Two distinct clicks.

A snarly bark cut through her focus, and her eyes snapped to the office window. Lucien hadn't mentioned a neighborhood dog, which meant she didn't have her tranquilizer darts. But she did have liver treats. The noise had come from her exit route out back. Her only other option was the front door, a poor choice in this populated area, no matter the late hour. That pooch better be out for a quick pee.

Attention back on target, she noted the contact point she'd found and turned the dial 180 degrees to park it in place, then spun the dial methodically, straining to hear the telltale click of another wheel being picked up. Three wheels total. All she needed now were those three numbers.

She pulled out her pad and paper and resumed her position, listening, twisting: *click...click*. She graphed the found numbers.

Most kids learned basic math to answer textbook questions. Lucien's homeschooling had held more of an edge. "If you get the x or y values wrong," he'd say, "you'll get the wrong numbers, you'll work slower, and you could wind up in jail."

She'd have taken jail back then over returning to foster hell.

Another snarl sounded. She worked faster.

She finished the graphs, recorded where the lines overlapped—23, 12, 66—and tried the three numbers. No luck. She reversed and reordered them. Nothing. One of the numbers had to be off, which meant she had to start over.

Twelve trials later, the *clack* and *thunk* of success vibrated behind the dial, and she swung the door open. The rush of adrenaline should have had her doing a silent fist-pump, but her senses felt dulled. Stacked papers filled half the safe, along with a small cream box that would house a ring—right there, for her taking. No different than the other paintings or jewels she'd lifted. Still, her determination wavered.

Ned was a creep who cheated on his girlfriend. Fencing the ring to ensure kids were fed and clothed trumped his superfluous "needs." So why was a slick of guilt coating her stomach?

She flexed her fingers and gave her head a shake. She'd been off-balance all day. All year, really. Longer if she counted the Monet Disaster, but thinking about that was a fast track to blundering this whole gig.

The difference between getting caught and executing a perfect heist is planning.

She inhaled deeply and snatched the cream box, checking its contents before securing it in her bag. Safe closed and painting returned, she hurried down the stairs and hastened for the exit. The crisp air gave her a shot of energy as she tucked her gloves and headlamp into her bag. She snuck across the sleek patio, her back pressed against the wooden fence, then stepped into the alley. Where she was greeted by a low growl.

Clementine glanced over her shoulder, and yep, a large pit bull-type dog stood a block down, giving her the evil eye. She believed all animals were inherently good, and bad dogs were raised by bad people. She had no clue who'd raised this bruiser, but now didn't seem the time to test her theory.

She slung her backpack forward, dug out a few treats, and tossed them as far as possible. The dog's nose tipped up. He found the scent and went to investigate. The second he moved, she bolted. Gravel kicked up as she ran, the pavement jarring her shins with each punishing footfall. A bark echoed. She ran faster. Too fast to notice the littered fast-food bag until it was underfoot and sliding. Her ankle twisted. She went down, awkward and hard, slamming her hip on the pavement.

Fucking hell.

She tensed a beat, sure the pit bull would be standing over her, drooly fangs glinting under the streetlamps. But she was alone. With a twisted ankle, a sore hip, and a two-hundred grand diamond ring.

CLEMENTINE HOBBLED into her apartment building, dreaming of her cushy pillow and fluffy duvet. She'd left the ring at the drop-off location. Lucien didn't have anything else lined up. Maybe she'd sleep for a week, rest up, tend to her ankle before he sprung another job on her. Avoid the world and pit bulls for a while.

"You need a hand to your apartment?"

Clementine froze. She didn't know that voice or the purple hair that was as bright as the smile directed at her. "I'm good. Just a twisted ankle."

"I twist my ankle all the time," the woman said, oblivious to Clementine's brush off. "The right one. How I have any ligaments left is beyond me. I have some frozen peas in my place, if you need. And Advil...but I should maybe introduce myself before I give you pills." She stuck out her hand. "I'm Jenny. New neighbor in 2B."

Clementine gave Jenny's hand a reluctant shake. "I'm Amy."

An easy, forgettable alias.

Aside from occasional lunches and dinners with Lucien, Clementine kept to herself. Being on her own was safe. She was consistent. She didn't even know a neighbor had moved out.

Jenny slung her arm around Clementine's waist. "At least let me help you to your door. 2C, I assume?"

She nodded, preferring silence. Jenny, however, liked the sound of her own voice. In the span of nine steps, Clementine learned she'd just moved here from LA and was a vegan hairstylist who planned to open her own salon. "A few friends moved here last year," she said. "They loved it so much, I decided what the hell. Life is short, right? Anyway, they're stopping over for drinks tomorrow. You should come."

"I don't think so."

"If you have plans, you can bring a friend."

"I'm going out."

"You can come by after."

This girl was more tenacious than that damn pit bull, and Clementine's mind drifted back to Ned's framed photographs. Friends and family. Things Clementine didn't have.

"I'll play it by ear," she said. A lie she wished was the truth.

"Awesome." Jenny fished a card from her pocket and held it out. "Text me if you can make it. And if you need to trim that stunning hair, I'm your gal."

Clementine smiled politely and escaped to her apartment, but her heart was doing some sort of erratic calisthenics. A messed-up ankle *and* a new nosy neighbor. This had turned into one hell of a night.

She dropped Jenny's card on her kitchen counter and limped to Lucy's terrarium. "How's my girl?"

Lucy stared at her favorite piece of wood.

"That good, huh?" Clementine reached in and pulled out her bearded dragon. Maybe sitting on the couch with Lucy would settle her overactive pulse. It didn't.

She surveyed her small but neat-*ish* apartment, simple with its Ikea essentials. Aside from spending cash on her beast of a car, Clementine only needed enough money to live on. Spreading the remainder around local charities and orphanages in developing countries fueled her drive to make a difference, to help those the system had let down, and make sure others didn't suffer the way she had. What it didn't do was keep her from picturing her apartment filled with friends, their laughter as lively as Jenny's purple hair.

The few times she'd made an effort with strangers, she'd broken out in cold sweats. Asking others questions meant they reciprocated. *What's your name? What do you do? Where are you from?* Lying on the job was one thing. Lying to potential friends made Clementine feel like a ghost. A non-person.

She stroked Lucy's back. Her bearded dragon pancaked her belly on Clementine's palm and closed her eyes. Her version of a cat's purr. "What should we do tomorrow, girl?"

No answer, of course. That never stopped Clementine from talking to her pet just to use her vocal cords. At this rate, she'd be jabbering to herself on street corners by forty, or she'd become one of those women whose body was discovered weeks or months after time of death, wedged between stacks of newspapers, her leg half eaten by pet reptiles.

She glanced at her kitchen counter and eyed Jenny's business card.

Maybe one night of socializing wouldn't be so bad.

She could go over for a quick visit, after her supposed "plans." Not linger too long. Drink wine and gossip about celebrities, or do whatever it was women did. They probably wouldn't want to hear about her bearded dragon or the car engine she'd finished rebuilding, and she couldn't talk about her illegal philanthropic work, but it could be fun to feel normal for a minute.

She returned Lucy to her terrarium and grabbed Jenny's card. Before overthinking, she sent her a quick text.

Clementine: **It's your neighbor Amy. Thanks for the invite. I'll stop by at ten.**

Now she couldn't back out. She'd force herself to be a non-ghost.

Hopefully the decision wouldn't bite her in the ass.

2

OF COURSE THAT STUPID GIRLS' night had bitten Clementine in the ass. She should have known better than to try and make non-reptile friends. Socializing wasn't in her DNA, especially when conversation veered to talk of foster care. If she'd known one of Jenny's friends was a foster parent, she'd never have gone. Listening to the woman praise those government services had been excruciating. Everyone else had smiled and nodded along with her effusiveness. Not Clementine, who had intimate knowledge of how wrong foster care could go. Nope. She'd lashed out at the woman's ignorance, revealing parts of herself she never shared, and had stormed from the apartment.

Four weeks later she still wanted to throat-punch herself for attending.

Tired of rehashing that horrible night, she focused on her current job and reread Lucien's text.

Lucien: **Find Elvis Presley.**

The instruction sounded simple enough. Unfortunately, it wasn't 1957, and she was en route to a town overrun with the deceased celebrity.

Clementine: **You're a real comedian.**

She pocketed her phone and pumped gas into her rental car while scanning her beige surroundings. A single tree punctuated the flat landscape, bruised grasses staggering in the faint breeze. An old man sat on a nearby rocking chair, pipe in hand, sentry to a dilapidated convenience store. And was that an actual tumbleweed blowing down the dusty road?

Yep. An honest-to-God tumbleweed.

She stowed the pump and resumed texting Lucien, hoping he'd feel her steely-eyed stare.

Clementine: **You've sent me to Lucifer's playground.**

Lucien: **It's not hell, Tangerine. It's small town Nebraska. Breathe the fresh air. Make nice with the locals. And get us that painting.**

Clementine smirked. Tangerine. Grapefruit. Kumquat. Yuzu. She couldn't remember the last time he'd used her actual name.

Clementine: **The fresh air of which you speak is stifling. Sweat is practically dripping from the sky.**

Lucien: **You hate New York winters. Quit bitching, enjoy it, and stop dragging your feet.**

She gulped at his last comment.

Clementine: **I'll secure the painting in no time.**

Lucien: **But don't rush. Rushing leads to mistakes.**

Clementine: **I won't let you down.**

Except she already had.

Without that awful girls' night, Clementine would have flown here from New York as planned. A quick flight to prepare her character and analyze last minute details. Instead she'd spent the past few weeks distracted and down, and hiding in her apartment to avoid Jenny. When the walls had felt like they'd been closing in, she'd chosen to drive to Nebraska. A quicker escape from home, only a twenty hour drive. But she'd been on the road three days now. Three freaking days, delaying her arrival, her unease growing as she neared her destination.

Annoyed with herself, she put that night and its after-effects out of her mind. She swiped a line of sweat from her neck. She needed a cold drink, something fizzy and bright to wake her up. The shoebox convenience store, with its rotting siding and worm bait advertisement, didn't look particularly convenient, but it would do. Still, she didn't move.

Her attention dragged to that lone tree. It stood tall and stoic. Strong. Resilient. *Alone.* An unnamed ache spread through her chest and she rubbed her breastbone.

"Passing through?"

She swiveled. The pipe-smoking man was intent on her, his skin as weathered as the scorched earth. The wooden sign above him hung at an angle. Thanks to the odd slant, its painted arrow pointed toward the ground. It read: *This way to Whichway.* She snickered.

"That's how the town got its name," he said, his voice like crunching snow.

"Excuse me?"

"Whichway."

"What way?"

"The town down the road." His rocking chair chewed over gravelly pebbles. "There ain't much to see there. Farms. Prairie. That big 'ol factory. No reason to stop and visit, but it's on the way to larger counties. Folks passin' through often ask directions: Which way to here? Which way to there?" He shrugged. "And the town of Whichway got slapped on a map."

Right. Whichway. The Elvis-infested town where she'd be living for a few weeks. She was always meticulous about her research. She knew exactly where the town was and how it had been named, but she felt hazy, grappling to follow their conversation.

She jerked her mind back on target.

For the next few weeks she would be Samantha Rowen, not Clementine Abernathy. She'd be a music producer and judge for the town's famed Elvis Festival—a gig somehow secured by Lucien. She'd find Maxwell David and charm the man until she'd located his family's priceless Van Gogh, a treasure the overpaid tycoon didn't deserve. Lucien would fence their prize, the money earned would help those who couldn't help themselves, then she'd be back in New York, her job done, her classic car loud, her apartment quiet, her remaining hours spent talking to a bearded dragon who couldn't talk back. There would be no *girls' nights*.

Nothing about this job should be different than her others. But that lone tree drew her attention again, muddling her thoughts.

Music cut through her stupor, a lively beat building from down the road. A car punched through the hazy heat, and Clementine's jaw dropped. Chryslers were always hip and classic, this one likely from 1955, but its porcelain green paint job was exquisite.

She eyed her rental car, the meek Prius mildly offensive. At home, she wouldn't be caught dead in that horror show. But in forty minutes, when she rolled into Whichway, she'd be a character. A show. A congenial woman who'd chat about her friends and family and how full her life was.

She gritted her teeth and focused on the sexy Chrysler. The stunner pulled up to the gas pump. A colorful man stepped out. He had a sweep of gelled black hair, thick sideburns, rhinestone-studded sunglasses, and a patterned polyester shirt with lapels large enough to take flight. His Rolex was definitely a fake, but his elaborate persona wasn't, and her on-the-job radar pricked up.

This man was an Elvis. But was he *her* Elvis?

Lucien's folder detailing her mark had been on the thin side. She knew Maxwell David went for morning runs, followed by a coffee and pastry, usually an apple turnover. Strawberry when feeling frisky. He then spent hours at his office, no doubt scheming ways to pad his wallet while overworking his employees. He was also an Elvis impersonator, one of the hundred-odd performers vying for the crown of top tribute artist.

She knew these details and others about Maxwell David, CFO of David Industries. What she didn't have was a clear picture of him. The man shied away from social media. David Industries didn't have an online presence. Whoever Lucien had hired to snap surveillance photos had had a shaky hand and an overly large thumb, always obscuring Maxwell's face.

She squinted at this particular Elvis, deducing he was too old to be her mark. When he winked at her and belched, she thanked her lucky stars.

Taking that as her cue, she bought a Pepsi, even though she hated Pepsi. The pickings at the inconvenient convenience store were on the gaunt side of slim. She hit the road and pressed the cool can to her forehead. Elvis and that lone tree faded in her rearview mirror. She drank her not-a-Coke and drove, but her foot eased off the gas pedal. Her Prius glided slowly. Too slowly. Below the speed limit, actually.

What the hell is wrong with me?

She should have had the pedal to the metal, making up for lost time, hurrying to Whichway so she could scope out the town. Yet here she was, her speedometer decelerating at a rapid rate.

When she spotted a car curbside, its hood up and its owner leaning over the engine, she yanked over to the shoulder.

I'm just doing my Good Samaritan work, she told herself. *I'm not delaying this job or my role as Samantha Rowen.*

She hopped out of her god-awful Prius and shaded her eyes, assessing the old Jaguar across the road. The car was gun-metal gray, with splashy chrome styling, but rust had taken a few bites from the fenders. Nowhere near as pretty as that Chrysler had been. Not that she could judge, considering her present vehicle.

When her gentleman in distress stood from behind the hood, her focus shifted to him, and her heart raced faster than an Aston Martin Vulcan.

Six-foot-and-then-some, with his cuffs rolled and the top buttons of his dress shirt undone, he was one hell of a man. Thanks to the heatwave, his damp white shirt clung to his broad chest, declaring its wearer a fine male specimen.

She fanned her face, but her hand created little breeze. "Car trouble?"

He dragged his wrist along his forehead. "Car disaster."

"What happened?"

He eyed the innards of his Jag's engine. "I was on the road about an hour, no issues, then there was a loud pop and I started losing power. Aside from that, your guess is as good as mine."

Clementine's guess wasn't as good as his. It was miles better. The only thing she loved more than cars was her bearded dragon. "Mind if I take a look?"

"I'll take all the help I can get. My meeting starts in"—he grimaced at his watch (a genuine Rolex)—"thirty minutes, and it's forty minutes away."

Even his grimace was sexy. She tried not to stare at his generous lips, the masculine cut of his jaw. Like with friendships, she'd given up on dating a couple of years back. Developing a relationship when you couldn't share job details or commiserate about work stress was a challenge. *My last heist almost went south when I got chased by a pit bull and twisted my ankle* wasn't typical Friday night chitchat. Tinder hookups had sufficed for a while, until the one-night stands exacerbated her loneliness, emphasizing what she didn't have.

Which left her staring at this man's large hands as they tunneled through his dark hair, leaving the strands even more askew. Sweat gathered on her clavicle. His blue eyes darted to the spot, upping her already hot temperature.

He cleared his throat. "Thanks for stopping."

"No problem. Cars are kinda my thing."

Tall, dark, and handsome was also her thing, and the urge to interact with a real, live human reared its dangerous head again. She should have learned her lesson last month, but he was easy on the eyes, and it was nice to admit she was a car junkie. Something she couldn't do in Whichway—never smart dropping clues to your true identity. But if this man had already driven an hour, he'd be from Headlow or Brandock, or one of the farther counties.

She maneuvered in front of the engine. The man didn't step back, and his long body bumped against hers. Firm. Damp. *Warm.* "Sorry," she murmured. Sweat dripped down her cleavage.

He shuffled backward. "No. *I'm* sorry. You're nice enough to stop and help, and I'm in the way, standing like an idiot."

"I don't mind."

"Me being in the way?"

"You being an idiot."

He barked out a laugh.

"Just teasing." She winked at him, feeling loose and bubbly. More herself than she'd felt in ages. "I meant I don't mind helping. I travel with emergency supplies, just in case. Nothing worse than car trouble when you're on the road." Or fleeing the scene of a crime.

"Considering this baby belonged to my granddad, and

hasn't been on the road in a while, I shouldn't be surprised she got temperamental."

That explained the rusted fenders, but it didn't tamp her rising temperature. She tore her hungry gaze from his transparent shirt. *Nothing to see here. Move along.* She focused on the car. The engine issue was easy to spot. "Your baby's vacuum hose is cracked. Too much air passed through the power brake line and the engine backfired. Turned your drive sluggish."

"Power brake line?"

Clueless men were adorable. Outsmarting them in "manly" tasks was always good fun. "The engine's intake system. You'll need a new hose."

He cursed.

"It's not that bad. Although I don't have the part, I have the world's best cure-all."

"Does it rhyme with *Shmiskey* and go down nice and slow?"

She laughed at his unexpected humor, but the steamy visual intensified her hot flashes. She wanted him to go down *nice and slow*, but that wouldn't help his Jaguar. Nor would a tumbler of *whiskey*.

She motioned to her car. "I travel prepared." He squinted at her Prius, and she barely refrained from explaining her Charger at home was hell on wheels, and that she hated her Prius almost as much she hated her khaki shorts and floral top. "I'll have you on the road in a jiff," she said. "But this is a temporary fix. You'll need to hit a garage as soon as possible."

"But you can get me moving?"

"For a short while." She popped her trunk, found the greatest invention known to humankind, and held it in the air. "Consider yourself saved."

"Duct tape?" He grinned, and the effect had her stumbling over a non-existent stone. Someone should follow him with a road sign: *Beware of dimples, shortness of breath ahead.*

She tried to fan her face again, but the duct tape and scissors offered less relief than her hand. "You can watch me work, maybe learn something."

His gaze dropped to her legs and traveled upward. The second he met her eyes, he looked away. "I could do that."

He didn't just watch, though. He talked. "You passing through Nebraska?"

"I am."

"Work or pleasure?"

"Bit of both."

She kept her answers short. Being the listener was easier. She could smile and nod and make those around her feel important. That part wasn't a role. She loved learning about others, living vicariously through them. Too much interaction could end like her girls' night fiasco.

Mr. Tall Dark and Handsome wasn't making staying quiet easy.

He leaned his hip into his Jag, and some of that haphazard hair flopped onto his forehead. "How'd you learn about cars?"

"A friend." *Lucien*, she wanted to say. The man who'd caught her stealing shoes for a shoeless friend and had seen something in her worth nurturing. She flattened her lips and focused on cutting tape strips.

"Where are you from?" he asked.

Another simple question that wasn't simple. "I move around a lot."

He made an impatient sound under his breath. Frustrated with his one-way conversation? Still, he kept at it. "It was stupid of me to take this car, but it was my granddad's pride and joy. Kind of think of it as good luck." When Clementine didn't reply, he moved alongside her and bent to watch her fasten the tape. "You're certainly good with your hands."

"Best if one of us is, or you'd be stuck waiting for a tow."

"I didn't say I wasn't good with my hands."

"You can't fix your own car."

"I'm good at other things."

"Are you now?" She smirked at him over her shoulder, and her mouth dried. His baby blues had darkened, his irises blowing wide. His gaze skipped away again, that hint of shyness upping his appeal. A sip of not-a-Coke would be heaven right now, or she could lick the moisture from his sweaty chest.

Down girl.

She turned abruptly and smoothed the tape, ensuring it was secure. He let her work in silence, but his attention kept flitting to her, his sharp blue eyes zeroing in. With the hose doctored, he test drove the Jag. It purred as it should but wouldn't last him long. At least he wasn't stranded.

Even though he was late for his meeting, he walked her to her car, lingering as she shut the trunk. She took extra-long wiping the grease from her fingers.

When she faced him, he thrust his hand forward. "I'm Jack."

She didn't move or extend her hand in reply. If she did, he'd expect her to share her name. Normal social pleasantries. Problem was, using her alias, Samantha, didn't feel right. She was far from home, and she wasn't in Whichway yet. She hadn't shed Clementine in favor of her chosen identity, but saying anything other than Samantha would be foolish. She bit down on her molars.

Jack kept his hand extended and chewed his bottom lip. When she remained silent, he said, "Is it because I'm an idiot who isn't good with his hands and fumbled when trying to flirt with you?"

She sucked in a ragged breath. God, he was sweet. And cute. And his flirting had been subtle but lovely. In another life, she'd have played up her femininity. Gone on a date. Finished that date with a toe-tingling kiss. This wasn't another life, though. This was her life, and she had a job to do.

Still, thistles invaded her throat, scratching it up. The scratchy pressure built, burning hotter until...

"Clementine," she squeaked.

His hand hadn't moved. Neither had hers.

"Clementine," he repeated, as though tasting his first chocolate cake.

He tilted his hand slightly, angling his palm upward. An invitation. One she couldn't resist. She pressed her hand against his, and *whoa*, the feel of his scorching skin. Warmer than the sultry air. It felt so good to touch him, a man who knew her name, even for this fleeting moment. A breath shuddered through her.

"Clementine," he whispered again.

They both held on, longer than was decent. Sweat slicked their palms, the heat between them intensifying, along with her fluttering pulse.

He held her gaze this time, momentarily. When he glanced away, he quickly looked back. Moisture clung to his brow. A few lines dripped down his cheek, drawing her eyes to a drop sliding along his throat, over his collarbone, toward his chest. She forced her attention up, but it didn't help. His lips were full and sensual. He had thick eyelashes, longish sideburns. Not like the belching Elvis from the gas station, but not exactly in fashion...something she should have noted. Details never escaped her, especially when heading to a job.

Elvis impersonators wore sideburns. Jack could be a fan. He could show up in Whichway for the festival. She could run into him again, this man who knew her real name.

She yanked her hand back, ignoring the sharp pang at the loss of contact. "Good luck in your meeting."

"Can I have your number?"

"I'm just traveling through."

"We could swap Twitter or Instagram handles? Or that snapping thing. Snap that Chat? I don't do social media, but I could make an exception for the woman who rescued me."

"I'd rather not."

Avoiding looking at his handsome face and seeing all she couldn't have, she turned her engine over and peeled away as quickly as her crappy Prius allowed.

3

———

DAY one as Samantha Rowen was full steam ahead. Clementine's extended drive was a thing of the past, yesterday's flirty lapse in judgment over. Straight hair secured in a demure braid and purse slung over her squared shoulder, she walked Whichway's Main Street, surprisingly charmed by the historic vibe. Brightly colored buildings lined the street, along with old-fashioned lampposts and cobbled sidewalks. A vast improvement to the highway's desolate landscape.

She pushed into the town hall and nodded at the receptionist. "I'm Samantha Rowen. Here for Jasmine Jones."

The young girl checked her computer and notified the town liaison.

Clementine stepped aside as two men entered. Two Elvi, to be precise. *Elvi* was plural for multiple Kings, not Elvises. Another tidbit she'd learned while researching the festival. Best to sound educated around this crowd. These two weren't wearing polyester jumpsuits, but their slicked black hair and rock star swagger were dead giveaways. One looked Filipino, the other Japanese. One was heavy, the other heav*ier*. One old, one young. Both winked at her.

Apparently the King came in all nationalities and sizes, and winking was a thing with them.

"Here to sign in," said the portlier fellow.

She'd have inspected them more intently, but her mark was Caucasian and fit. Neither of these Elvi were Maxwell David. She studied the hallway instead, Whichway's history splayed behind glass panels. The photo of a horse and buggy plodding down Main Street was beyond quaint. Maybe spending time here wouldn't be so bad. With the festival kicking off in ten days, she'd have over a week to get settled and find Maxwell before the town went nuts. Getting an invite to his family's estate could take longer.

"Samantha Rowen?"

"The one and only." For the next couple of weeks, at least.

Jasmine approached, her hand held out for a shake, and Clementine's mind snapped back to the last hand she'd held. Large. Masculine. *Sweaty.* Her heart gave a twist.

She shook Jasmine's hand and forced a smile. "I'm surprised contestants are already showing up."

Jasmine eyed the new arrivals. "Some like to get settled. Some love Whichway and extend their stay here. The town swells to twelve times its size during the festival."

Which would complicate Clementine's job, but she'd dealt with worse. She just had to find *her* Elvis and nab his painting while being Samantha Rowen, music producer, not Clementine Abernathy, lover of large sweaty hands. "That was my plan, too," she said. "Spend some time relaxing before the festival starts. Thought I'd let you know I was in town, in case you needed anything." And to solidify her alias.

Jasmine handed her a festival guide, then fiddled with her

diamond ring. The one carat beauty sparkled against her dark skin. "This is the festival's twenty-fourth year, and the event runs smooth as molasses. Just glad to have some young blood judging. As long as you're at the performance arena for the first show, you go on and enjoy our town. You'll fit right in."

Clementine's pink skirt and sleeveless top *did* have country girl written all over them.

After a bit more chitchat, Clementine pushed into the still-humid air and zeroed in on her next target: the Whatnot Diner. A pretty hilarious name for the town of Whichway. Beside it was the Who's It Café, like a Dr. Seuss book had come to life. But the Whatnot Diner was her focus. If her intel was correct, Maxwell David would be sauntering in there shortly for his morning coffee. The perfect time to force their meeting and follow Lucien's usual advice.

Be nice, but not too nice.

Show some vulnerability.

Insinuate a problem you have.

Make your mark think it's his idea to meet up again.

Cleavage always help.

Clementine had plenty of cleavage. She, however, never slept with her marks. Another of Lucien's rules: *too much familiarity clouds judgment.* A kiss was okay, coquettish flirting a must, but she was never to take things further and lose sight of her goals. Shaking large sweaty hands wasn't as important as giving a kid a future. She'd remain a lone tree in an empty field if it gave one child a chance.

The diner was across the road and down a block, everything here walkable. Pedestrians smiled as they passed her, some even saying hi. A sharp contrast to New York's head-down, cell-phone-obsessed commuters. The unfamiliar cheeriness unnerved her, but she found herself smiling back, each exchange draping her like a favorite coat.

She opened the diner's door and a bell chimed. Booths lined the windows, red leather stools along the counter opposite. The place was half-full, a mix of men and women in khaki and denim gossiping or reading the paper. None had black hair or wore a suit. Maxwell David wasn't here yet. Since he usually sat at the counter, she chose a stool.

A waitress—Imelda, according to her nametag—appeared with a coffee pot and mug. "How'd you like a cup, honey?"

"I'd take it intravenous if I could, but a cup will do."

Imelda lifted the pot higher as she poured, turning the simple act into an impressive show. "Our turnovers are our signature pastry, the sausages are homemade, and we only use free-range eggs. Bread's baked fresh, too."

"So basically, everything's good?"

"As sure as my daughter will flunk her next math test." Fondness bled into Imelda's joke. She looked young to have a kid taking math tests, her round face and dimpled cheeks doll-like. A picture of kindness. What would it have been like to have grown up with a mother like her?

"Sounds like I have to try the turnovers," Clementine said, squashing silly sentimental thoughts. "Apple, please." Because Maxwell ordered them, a commonality they could discuss.

"You won't be disappointed."

Imelda moved down the counter, and Clementine checked the Elvis wall clock. The rock and roll legend took up the face's center. The hands indicated 9 a.m., Maxwell David's usual coffee-and-pastry hour. So far he was a no-show.

Her phone buzzed, and her stomach dropped. *Lucien.* His text wasn't a surprise. He always kept her apprised of new details, and she never went more than a few hours without checking in, but he knew she wasn't on schedule, that her drive here had been prolonged. She pulled her phone from her purse.

Lucien: **Made contact yet?**

She could practically hear the disappointment in his words. Aside from the Monet disaster, she'd been flawless for ten years. She'd executed heists with precision, never losing a score unless a competitor had snatched it first. Mistakes were like rust bubbles, corroding a car's metal, hinting at the vehicle's eventual demise. She'd been virtually rustproof until four weeks ago. (Goddamn Jenny and her fun purple hair.) She needed to get her head in the game.

Clementine: **Today's the day. Sitting in the diner now.**

Dots bounced in reply.

Would he chastise her for delaying their plans? Warn her someone else would beat them to the painting?

The diner door chimed, but she couldn't drag her attention from her phone. The David family was clueless to their painting's worth. Lucien's exhaustive research had traced the unsigned Van Gogh over the decades, eventually learning the David family had acquired it through an estate sale, neither party aware of the artist's name. Maxwell's father owned it now. He'd hung it somewhere in their gaudy mansion, unaware of its value. But others might have sniffed out its worth and location. Her rival, Yevgen Liski, could have sniffed it out, a prospect she'd rather not contemplate.

Lucien: **Go slow. With a long con, gentle and gradual is the best way to earn trust. Once you have that, you've already won. And if you're feeling off, if you need out or need to talk, I'm just a call away.**

Of course he wouldn't chastise her. Not Lucien, the man who'd played cards with her the nights she couldn't sleep for fear nightmares would tear through her fourteen-year-old mind. He'd also taught her how to ride a skateboard and take down a man twice her size.

"You're in my seat."

Her thumbs froze, a second from typing a reassuring reply. She knew that voice. She'd heard it whisper her name and had replayed the memory on repeat all night. It was a voice that should not be here.

Tensing down to her sandaled toes, she turned and her mouth dried. Jack didn't look sweaty today. The man was dapper and clean shaven. He was close enough that she could smell his fresh scent, like spicy icicles swelled with sunshine. So crisp and so real, and he shouldn't be anywhere near this town or this diner. What the hell was he doing here?

"If I'm sitting on this seat, then it's mine." Snarkiness calmed her some.

He tilted his head slightly. "Hello, Clementine."

The end of her name smoothed into a song, and her pulse crooned in reply. "Why are you here?"

"I live here."

"In the diner?"

He chuckled. "In Whichway. But you don't. You...I'd remember."

He wasn't forgettable, either. Not the way his helter-skelter hair contrasted his tailored slacks and slim dress shirt. *Hello muscles.* Heat clawed her neck. Her armpits threatened to mutiny. The air conditioner must have crapped out, and she needed to ignore this unwelcome attraction. No matter the excuses she'd made yesterday, revealing her name had been a moment of abandon. Now Karma was giving her the middle finger. "You'd been driving for an hour when I stopped. I assumed you lived elsewhere."

He stuffed his hands into his pants pockets. The effort pulled at the expensive-looking wool, revealing strong thighs. "I had several meetings, none of them in town. And I still don't know why you're in my seat." He frowned like her occupation of his supposed seat pained him.

"Would you like me to move?"

"Definitely not." A long swallow later, he claimed the stool beside her.

Exactly where she'd hoped Maxwell David would sit. Unless...

They must be friends, probably met for coffee or drinks. Watched the odd sports game. If he was anything like the Maxwell David she had researched, Jack was an egotistical, selfish man. Considering the town's size, they probably worked together, big boss types who sat in their ivory towers while laying off long-time employees, ruining families and lives. Just to fatten their pockets.

The prospect made resisting his appeal easier, and his appearance wasn't altogether inconvenient. Making nice with Jack could ingratiate her with Maxwell. Unfortunately, the man at her right had proven he could short-circuit her wiring with nothing but a handshake. Something that couldn't happen again. If he was friends with Maxwell, she would use him to connect with her mark, then ensure they stayed out of handshake distance.

Easy as pie. Or easy as the apple turnover heading her way.

Imelda placed the pastry in front of her. "Anything else, honey?" Clementine shook her head, remaining silent as she assessed this new wrench in her plans.

Imelda smiled at Jack. "The usual?"

"I'm feeling a little wild today. Let's go with the strawberry."

"Strawberry, it is."

As Imelda left, Clementine was accosted by another familiar face: Jasmine Jones. Unfamiliar panic curled its fist around her lungs. The town's Elvis coordinator approached until the only Whichway-ian who knew her alias was sharing oxygen with the only Whichway-ian who knew her real name. Could this morning derail any faster?

Don't call me Samantha. Don't call me Samantha.

At least, not until she'd untangled this mess.

Jasmine eyed Clementine's breakfast. "I see you've made friends with Whatnot's famed apple turnovers. One bite, and you'll be hooked."

One more minute in this diner and she'd officially blow her cover. "So I've heard."

Clementine clamped her mouth shut and prayed Jasmine would move along. The quaintness of this small town was feeling more straightjacket than comfy coat.

Jasmine strolled to a nearby booth, thank God, but swiveled back. "Tell your father to fly home for the festival, Jack. It won't be the same without him. And be nice to Samantha. We'd like her to come back."

If this scene were a GIF, Clementine's turnover would detonate, showering her in apple and pastry, and a whole lotta trouble.

"Samantha?" Jack's brow crinkled.

It was a sexy look on him, but he wasn't allowed to be sexy. Not in this town, or on that seat. Anywhere near her. Especially when he was likely an asshole, his shyness yesterday probably a total act. She needed to leave and regroup, find her way in Whichway. If Maxwell walked in now, this stormy blip would torpedo into a natural disaster. "I think I'll take my pastry to go."

He opened his mouth and closed it. He fiddled with his cufflink. "Can I have a name explanation?"

She caught Imelda's attention and asked for a check and take-out bag, while mulling over her options. Only one lie made sense. "What did you expect? That I share my name with a stranger in the middle of nowhere? Any woman would have more sense than that."

He released his cufflink, but wouldn't quite meet her eyes. "And how do you know Jasmine?"

"I'm a judge for the Elvis festival."

He stared at Clementine's profile.

She stared at Imelda, willing that woman to work like the wind. It was worse than watching sloths race.

"You're a judge?" he asked slowly.

"I'm a judge," she repeated. *Again.* Was he hard of hearing?

"And your name is Samantha."

Maybe he'd been dropped on his head as a child, and she hated that name on his lips. Yesterday, when he'd whispered *Clementine,* she'd pictured forests and roots and blooming flowers, not lone trees and bruised grasses.

When Imelda *finally* handed over her check, Clementine paid and gathered her things, attempting to ignore Jack, whose delivered strawberry turnover and coffee sat untouched. His steadfast focus hadn't swayed from her, as long as she didn't seek direct eye contact, and she was doing it again, leaving him in her review mirror as quickly as possible. Creating more suspicion.

She'd meet Maxwell another way. On his morning run, maybe. She would avoid blue-eyed, large-handed Jack. Ensure their paths never crossed. But two steps away, he said, "Clementine."

She turned. A knee-jerk reaction. *Goddamn him.*

He crossed his arms awkwardly, like he didn't know what to do with his hands. "To be fair, Jack isn't my given name, either."

The Elvis clock seemed to still. Her lungs backfired worse than Jack's Jaguar. She knew his name before he said it, before those two syllables passed his lips. His appearance in the

Whatnot Diner at his predicted time should have clued her in, the "usual" turnover, strawberry when frisky, a blaring sign.

Dread corkscrewed through her, twisting far and deep.

She knew his name. That didn't limit her shock when he said, "My name's Maxwell David the Third, but my friends call me by my middle name. Jack."

4

JACK WATCHED Clementine's cinnamon eyes widen, her posture stiffen. She didn't like that he'd used her real name. And it was real. As true as the way she'd trembled when he'd held her hand yesterday. Sharing your identity with a strange man on a strange road wasn't smart, but the sparks between them had been undeniable. He had no doubt Clementine was her name. That didn't explain the Samantha twist, or why she'd fled from him yesterday.

Why she was doing the same now.

His abysmal flirting was likely the cause.

She turned on her heel and speed walked out of the diner, the chiming bell echoing as she vanished. Every molecule in him wanted to bolt from his seat and trail after her.

He'd spent most of last night reliving how she'd worked on his car, hands adept, mind focused. The sexiest thing he'd ever seen. He'd wanted her greasy fingers smearing his dress shirt and skin. The memory of her shoulder's crescent-moon scar and the sweat glistening on her long neck had thrown a stumble into his much-needed sleep.

Yeah, he wanted to follow her now, fill in her mysterious blanks, but what would he do? Fumble his words again? Demand to know why she'd occupied his usual seat, when he should have been confessing he'd thought about her all night?

Well done, Mr. Smooth.

He watched the door until an unfamiliar man with a swarthy complexion and thick beard walked in. Tattoos covered what he could see of his arms, a realistic knife and a skull the most discernable images. He was likely here for the festival, one of the thousands who descended upon Whichway. A reminder Jack had to up his rehearsing if he planned to win this year's contest. He nodded and smiled at the tourist, who sneered in return. Rudeness also descended upon Whichway this time of year. At least the interaction hadn't involved Jack repeating sentences or blabbing about seating.

He bit into his strawberry turnover, annoyed with himself for scaring off Clementine, but her departure was for the best: she was a festival judge, and he was a festival contestant.

Dating her wasn't an option.

"You look like you're arm wrestling with your mind." Marco slid onto the stool beside his.

"Something like that."

"Are you winning?"

"Far from it." Not that it mattered. Flirting may come as natural to Jack as fixing cars, but he had larger problems to solve, ones that affected more than his stagnant love life.

Marco waved to Imelda, who held up her finger to let him know she'd be a minute. "Came by your office yesterday, but you weren't around."

"I was out."

"Was it because of Wednesday? You avoiding the factory?"

It was a loaded question, but one he could manage. This conversation, although fraught with landmines, wouldn't tie his tongue in knots. "Wednesday was tough, but the severance packages were more than generous."

So generous, he'd been thanked profusely. He'd looked eight of David Industries' long-time employees in the eyes on Wednesday and had let each one go. The task could have been passed to others, but part of success included owning your mistakes. It was one of Granddad's priceless lessons, along with *mind your manners, never give up,* and *Elvis Presley is the greatest showman who ever lived.*

Unfortunately, none of Granddad's wisdoms had helped Jack see the signs that one of his employees had been sabotaging him.

Marco flexed his wrist, working his old injury in a familiar pattern. "I'm hearing talk. People are freaking out about their jobs, worried more of them will be let go."

"There's nothing to worry about."

"That's what you always say."

"Because it's always true. Everything's under control." All but the way he kept glancing at the exit, wondering where the mysterious Clementine had gone. "Times are changing, is all. More lens factories are opening up. We need to stay competitive. Costs need to be cut."

Marco stared at him, his dark eyes as intent as their factory's laser cutter. "You're not telling me something."

His best friend was astute.

As kids, they'd raced around town on their bikes, hollering into the wind. They'd shared their first beer together, both pretending it hadn't made them gag. When Marco's baseball scholarship and major league future had evaporated after his brutal car crash, Jack had kept him from drowning in puke and vodka. Marco knew each of Jack's pet reptiles by name, could probably list the songs on his iPhone. He was well aware of the night Jack had spent in jail at fifteen—a disaster Jack would rather forget.

His best friend and charity manager knew it all, but Marco couldn't know Gunther Doright had stolen company secrets, forcing Jack to fire employees so he'd have the funds to continue research and development. Marco gossiped worse than Jack's kid sister. "Times are changing," Jack said again. "It's as simple as that."

"So you're telling me nothing's going on?" Marco pushed. "You don't need me to talk with the staff, do damage control?"

"No type of control needed."

"More workers won't be fired?"

"That's what I'm saying." Years of schooling and scientific engineering had taught Jack how to attack complex formulas and experiments, but it was his granddad who'd instilled his drive. Obtaining additional bank loans yesterday hadn't been a cake walk, but he'd pulled it off. All that remained was completing his lens experiments by next weekend and securing their new technology before anyone learned David Industries was on a collision course with disaster.

"Enough about work," Jack said, ready for a topic change. "How's Lauralee?"

Marco passed his hand over his beard, pride in the grin that snuck through. "She complains all day. Barely sleeps. And you should see her when I forget the milk or bread. Damn near bleeds my eardrums with her yelling."

"It must be love."

"Something like that." The man practically glowed with it.

"Your house will be even louder soon."

"Better be soon." Marco bounced his knee restlessly. "Bed rest is killing her, and the woman's as big as a barn, but don't you dare tell her as much."

"Not sure I should take advice from a man who accidentally swallowed his fiancée's engagement ring."

"You need all the advice you can get."

He couldn't argue with that. Jack had misjudged his last girlfriend, and he'd mishandled Clementine's appearance today. Give him a research team and he could command attention. Give him a stage and he could embody the raw charisma he lacked in everyday life. Give him a beautiful woman, up close and personal, and he either talked like a stiff robot or made asinine remarks like *Shmiskey* and *Snap that Chat.*

Jack picked up a newspaper, his aggravated breaths crinkling the edges. Marco ordered breakfast and ate. They sat in companionable silence until Marco's cell vibrated. He grinned at his phone. "Lauralee needs an emergency supply of tuna."

"Tuna?"

"Don't ask. I'll meet you at work. And tell your dad to get his ass back to town. Seeing him will help employee morale."

"Will do." Another lie to his best friend. This one as pleasant as chewing crushed glass.

Marco dropped a bill on the counter and hurried from the diner, eager to get to his wife and dote on their unborn twins. Envy lassoed Jack, but he shook it off. It wasn't like he had time to entertain a relationship. He needed every second he could milk out of his day, which included keeping up appearances and maintaining his routine. He was a creature of habit. The town knew it. If he altered his morning run or coffee hour, questions would arise. Maintaining normalcy meant working longer hours and spending the remaining time rehearsing in the estate's sound room, but he could do it.

"Hello, Maxwell."

Jack's neck tensed. He knew that grating voice, hated

hearing it taint his given name. Alistair Murphy was the last person he cared to waste his seconds with. He faced the tribute artist, noting Alistair's smug grin and oily hair. "Have the winds changed so soon?"

Alistair glanced out the diner window. "Winds?"

"Seems early for garbage to be blowing into town."

"There was no garbage in—" His lips thinned, Jack's insult finally sinking in. Never quick on the draw, that one. "Don't be testy," Alistair said. "I won last year because I'm the best. And my back view is almost as nice as my front. You'll enjoy looking at it again this year."

"Especially when it's driving out of town."

"Maybe I'll stay this year. Move to this godforsaken stretch of dirt."

"There's a kennel on the outskirts. I'm sure they have room."

Alistair made a show of slicking back his immobile hair. "I doubt Ava would approve of the accommodations. Not that she doesn't like to get dirty." He smirked. "She'll be arriving next week."

Jack fisted his hands, one flared nostril away from smacking that lewd smirk from Alistair's face.

Jack hadn't seen Ava since she'd left him to hitch her star to last year's festival champion. She'd seemed genuine when they'd first met. He'd fumbled when flirting with her, as he always did. She'd pushed and pursued and made him feel as though his dating ineptitude was attractive, a tenderness some men lacked. Exactly as his mother had insisted during his awkward high school years. "You're perfect as you are," Sylvia David had told him. "Kindness and integrity are the traits of great leaders. A woman will see how special you are one day and love you for it."

Ava hadn't wanted kindness. She'd enjoyed Jack's money,

probably more than his company, but it was a Vegas ticket she'd been after. Anything to reach her popstar goals.

Aside from one very important reason to win this year's top tribute artist, Jack would relish watching Ava and Alistair choke down a pan of humble pie. "I hope you two enjoy the town. I'll go enjoy rehearsing in front of my signed gold record—the one you'll never have."

Waving his prized possession in Alistair's face was childish, but the record made the man green with envy.

Alistair's cheeks flushed. He stepped closer as his eyes darted around the diner. "My offer from last year still stands."

Unbelievable. "You mean the one where you return sweet Ava to me if I give you Elvis's last known signed record?"

Alistair ticked up his pointy chin.

Jack couldn't hold in his disgusted laugh. "I want nothing to do with Ava, and women aren't possessions. Seems to me you two are perfect for each other."

He strutted past Alistair with the confidence he wished he'd displayed around Clementine, who went by Samantha, who was judging the Elvis competition, who also didn't seem to be an upfront woman interested in a nice guy. On top of saving David Industries, making sure everyone thought his father was out of town, and beating Alistair at this year's festival, Jack added avoiding Clementine to his exhausting to-do list.

CLEMENTINE NEEDED to meet with Jack again. There was no choice. The Van Gogh wasn't hung in his home. It was housed in his family's estate, and he was her ticket in to that monstrous piece of real estate.

She barreled into her motel room and spread out her Maxwell David files on the starchy sheets. At least the starch implied they'd been washed. The first thing she'd done after arriving yesterday was toss the maroon comforter on the floor, which matched the carpet's unsettling shade of not-quite-blood.

Legs tucked under her, she pushed the surveillance photos around, livid at Lucien's contact for not noting Maxwell's commonly used name. Furious at herself for failing to recognize Jack. The blunders had obviously thrown her off, but revealing *her* name had been an epic screw-up and Lucien couldn't know, which meant she had to regroup.

She studied the photos. One shot showed Jack entering the Whatnot Diner. The swinging door obscured his face, but not the long lines of his lean frame. A second and third showed him running, part of his morning routine. One image was too blurry to decipher. The other was botched by the photographer's thumb.

The last one gave her the most pause: Jack as Elvis.

The shot had been downloaded from the internet, commemorating last year's tribute artist champion. Jack had come in second. He was off to the side, not the focus of the photo, his face less clear. She pulled it closer, looking for the shy man she'd met on the road, the slightly awkward man today, who had ferreted out her true name. She couldn't find either man. What she found was exceedingly worse: increased sex appeal.

When first scanning these photos, she hadn't noticed the allure. She had wrinkled her nose at this whole *Elvis thing*, unable to grasp why grown men dressed like a dead man and sang dated songs. Impersonators. Pretenders. A judgmental reaction that had been overhauled.

She wasn't sure if it was the sweaty, sexy handshake, or the shyness that had hit her in her heart, but looking at the Jack she now knew, dressed in a glittery top and tight pants, his helter-skelter hair tumbling over his forehead, she saw his appeal in stereo.

There was no shyness in Jack's festival photo, nothing but confidence in his cocky grin. She couldn't connect the man she'd met to the one in the picture, but she didn't have time to puzzle it out. She also couldn't let this unwelcome attraction blossom. The Maxwell *Jack* David she'd researched had recently fired a handful of workers, all long-time employees nearing the end of their working prime. They would struggle to find work elsewhere, but Jack would save cash by hiring younger blood. He was the ruthless sort who sliced and diced without caring where his blade landed.

Clementine's father had been fired by a man like Jack. Cut and tossed out without a care. Finding him dead in their garage, the car running, had been as traumatizing as Clementine thought life could get. So young and naïve she'd been. A clueless nine-year-old.

She knew better now. Men like Jack David were nothing but trust-fund brats who coasted through life. A fact she'd remember next time his baby blues struggled to meet hers. It was time to take the upper hand. She was behind on the job. Lucien would check in again soon. If she didn't get an invite inside the David family estate, she'd have to break in. A worst-case scenario.

Break-ins led to bungles like the disastrous Monet job.

That epic fail couldn't be repeated. She needed to do this job right and sweet talk Jack until she located the Van Gogh, which meant she'd have to corner him tomorrow. Not at the diner. She'd already wrecked that plan. This meeting had to appear accidental, and she'd have to go armed with a new backstory.

5

CLEMENTINE STRETCHED at the edge of the park, enjoying the more temperate heat. Last night's rain clung to the grass. Peaty scents suffused the air, the dampness more fresh than muggy. The downpour had cleared out Nebraska's heatwave. A night of mulling had cleared Clementine's mind.

In a few short minutes, she would corner Jack on his morning run, where she'd chit-chat and flirt. Since he'd seemed interested when she'd fixed his car, he'd likely reciprocate. She'd then mention her father's (fake) birthday, along with his (fake) love of Elvis, and lament the fact that she hadn't organized a gift for him—a photo with a tribute artist, specifically. Jack would hopefully offer himself up, and a date would be set.

A platonic date. A photo date. One she would suggest occurred at his family's estate.

Boom. Bang. Done.

No sexy handshakes would transpire.

The running trail wound through Wherever Park, crossing the snaking stream and bending around towering trees. Not lone trees. Sparse but clustered, like cliques of close friends. She jogged toward the bridge at a slow pace. If Jack remained punctual, he'd catch up with her in no time and she wouldn't have to lie by omission to Lucien again.

Last night's texts had been painful. Telling Lucien she'd made contact with Maxwell-slash-Jack and would see him today had not been lies, per se. She'd simply omitted that Jack knew her real name and wasn't aware of their impending not-a-date date. Thankfully, all omissions would soon be moot. She would be one step closer to that Van Gogh.

She jogged leisurely, confident in her scheme. Squirrels nattered and birds chirped. The fresh air swelled in her chest until a high-pitched yell snagged her attention. A curly-haired woman, who looked like coffee-serving Imelda, was walking four dogs. She yanked on one leash and called the Doberman a few colorful names. She switched languages three times.

Clementine eyed the bridge she'd crossed. Jack still hadn't appeared. Needing to stall for time, she enjoyed Imelda's amusing interaction. As much as Clementine loved animals, she'd take her bearded dragon over a cat or dog any day. No walks needed. No yard to clean. She also loved watching *Graveyard Carz* while feeding Lucy crickets.

Imelda noticed Clementine and waved. "Brutus thinks he's a duck. He'd live in the pond if I let him."

Clementine would have preferred to remain unnoticed, but ignoring locals drew attention. "You could sell it as a tourist attraction," she called back. "Just put up a sign: Feed the world's first Doberman duck."

Imelda cackled.

"Don't feed the ducks." The abrupt male voice snipped over Clementine's shoulder, so close it made her jump. Jack David had caught her off-guard again, setting her off kilter.

"I wasn't feeding the ducks."

"You were suggesting it."

"As a joke."

She regained her kilter and faced her mark. Jack was sweaty again, his Nike shirt and running shorts molded to his fine physique. Her temperature rose, but his friendliness seemed to have cooled, judging by the annoyed press of his lips. Not a great start to her plan.

Imelda yanked her dogs farther down the path, but yelled to Jack, "I'll pick up Colonel Blue at noon."

"I'm sure he's looking forward to it. How's Iron Man recovering?"

"Leg will be right as rain in no time, but he's not fond of his cone of shame. The other dogs are calling him names."

Jack smiled, making full eye contact with Imelda. "Glad he's doing better. Give him a cuddle for me."

A cuddle? And why was Imelda joking with a blue-blood tyrant who had fired her fellow townsfolk? Unless Imelda's niceties were rooted in fear and she chose sucking up over rudeness.

Jack continued his run on the gravel trail, not a glance spared for Clementine. She cursed under her breath. Now she was chasing him, when she needed him chasing her.

She picked up her pace and caught up to him, mirroring his quicker stride. More difficult for her, considering his longer legs, but Clementine wasn't a petite woman, and running was her jam. She could jog Central Park with her eyes closed.

"You have a dog named Colonel Blue?" she asked.

He kept his attention ahead. "No."

Wow. One word. The awkward flirty man who'd hit on her had gone AWOL. "Does Imelda walk your pet armadillo?"

He didn't crack a smile. They skirted a large willow tree and Jack powered forward, picking up the pace. "Blue is my father's dog. He's away. Imelda walks him." Each sentence was clipped and harsh. A total brush off.

It proved her initial assessment of his insolent brattiness, but it didn't help her cause. She increased her speed to match his. Small talk was needed. She had to draw him in. Make him feel interesting. "Since you live in Whichway, not the Whatnot Diner, what do you do for work?"

The steel set of his jaw bulged, as though he was angry. Because she'd turned him down on the highway? Or maybe the false name had soured him. Both reasons made sense. That didn't keep a twinge from pinching her chest. Twinging that shouldn't happen. She didn't care if not-Maxwell was interested in her. She *did* care about his family's painting.

If he didn't soften up soon, she'd have to suck up her pride and fake an injury.

"My father founded David Industries."

"The factory in town?"

"Yes."

He ran faster. She matched his speed, breathing harder. A lawnmower buzzed in the distance.

"That place is huge. And you work there?"

That place is huge. God, she sounded inane. David Industries wasn't just huge. It was the town's main artery. It employed three-quarters of the population, keeping quaint Whichway thriving. Jack was the current CFO, the brains behind their lens-tech-invention-thingy that allowed cameras and phones to autofocus. She knew all these details, hated pretending like she didn't, but men loved talking about their work accomplishments.

Jack wasn't behaving like most men.

Feet pounding the gravel, he said, "I manage the finances and run R and D."

"R and D?" There she went, sounding simple again.

"Research and development."

"So what do you develop?"

He stopped abruptly, his chest heaving as he planted his hands on his hips. His blue eyes, the same shade as his aquamarine shirt, danced around, never quite settling on her. "Why'd you give Jasmine a false name?"

Ah. There it was. The root of his stonewalling. A niggle of guilt poked her ribs. Or maybe it was just her overworked lungs. She walked a small circle, catching her breath as she mentally reviewed her backstory. "I'm sorry about that, but it's my job."

"Lying is your job?"

Oh man, if he only knew. "I produce music. I'm not a big shot with platinum records to my name, but my brand's growing and I have connections, which comes with complications."

"Complications?" He had a thing for repeating her, but it was hard to focus on that when color splotched his cheekbones. The rosiness dramatized his bone structure and made his lips look impossibly kissable.

It was her turn to glance down sharply. She continued pacing. "When people learn what I do, they can get invasive. Like with movie producers and literary agents? If people think they can get a second with you, they pounce. Once or twice it got uncomfortable. So I don't normally do festivals. My clients are all referrals. But this was a favor for a friend, and I thought hiding my name would be easier." She quit her circle walking and tried to meet his aqua eyes. "I've decided to tell Jasmine, though. It was a silly thing to do."

He rubbed the back of his neck and watched the nearby lawnmower bump along. His focus dragged to her chest, up to her face, then to the grass beside them. "Understandable," he said quietly. Followed by, "Enjoy your run."

Brush off number two.

He powered on, leaving her in his rearview mirror, like she'd done to him twice. Flustered, she ran up to him, keeping time. He snuck a look at her out of the corner of his eye.

She smiled. "You're quick on your feet. You run often?"

"Most days."

"It's great to clear the head."

"When I'm alone, it is."

Touché, Mr. Tall Dark and Handsome. And since small talk wasn't paying off, it was time to commence Operation Elvis.

She tried to give her ponytail a flirty flip. The strands slapped her cheek. "My father's a real Elvis fan, which is one of the reasons I took the gig. I was thinking it would be cool to get candid shots while I'm here, a birthday gift for him, but it's in a couple days. Do you happen to know any tribute artists in town early? I'd love to arrange something."

She didn't insinuate that Jack was one such artist. If she wanted to stay under the radar, he needed to meet her halfway and start showing signs of interest. The cocky grin he'd displayed in that one Elvis photo suggested he'd jump at the chance to strut his stuff.

He, however, did not jump. He ran and pumped his arms. "You should ask Jasmine."

Really? Ask Jasmine? Was this guy suddenly immune to her charms?

She was going to have to trip after all, sprain her ankle or skin her knee. Or find a way to shake his hand and cast that tingly spell she'd experienced on the highway, even though his large hands were off-limits. She seriously couldn't catch a break.

The lawnmower buzzing increased, competing with the argument in her head.

"Jack!" The buzzing hissed to a stop. A bald man in overalls waved their way.

Jack slowed and shaded his eyes. "Marvin?"

"Got you crickets. A bucket full. I'll bring 'em by tomorrow."

"You're too good to me."

"Nah. It's Hank I love, not your ugly mug."

Marvin's lawnmower roared back to life, and Clementine replayed that brief interaction, unsure what to make of it. Another local appeared to be friends with Jack, the exchange between them beyond basic pleasantries. First, coffee-pouring-dog-walking Imelda, now cricket-collecting-mower-riding Marvin. It was as though Jack David was not only nice, but... well liked. This wasn't the man she'd prepared to con. And the cricket comment had fresh sweat blotching her brow.

The only use she could think of for crickets could mean she and Jack had more in common than she'd bargained on.

"What's with the crickets? Are you breeding reptiles?" She laughed at her not-quite- joke, a maniacal edge to the sound. He wasn't allowed to own reptiles. Not when Clementine loved diapsids more than people. If he was feeding crickets to reptiles, it better be because he planned to slaughter and sauté them. Jack wasn't allowed to be any more attractive.

"I don't breed them," Jack said, his cheeks burning redder. "I offer them sanctuary."

Her heart stalled. The fumes of freshly cut grass stung her nose. She sneezed, taking the moment to bend forward and cover her face. This shy, apparently *nice-when-not-firing-employees* man, who looked hot as Elvis and fantastic in a damp dress shirt, owned reptiles. Plural. Not just one or two.

That twingy pinch in her chest worsened.

In her wildest dreams, she'd never have imagined him a fellow herpetoculturist. Not a man as dashing and handsome as him. Most reptile lovers were video-game fanatics who still lived with their parents and didn't look fantastic in a damp shirt. Muggles twitched their noses and cringed when faced with ectothermic cuties.

Not reptile-saving Jack. The man she needed to deceive, for good reason.

Since her surge of guilt on recent jobs, Clementine had thought about her and Lucien's trip to India, taken after a particularly lucrative heist. Spreading that much money around the United States had become risky. Lucien had wanted to show her how they could help abroad, how crucial it could be to orphanages. What she'd seen there had changed her life: sickness that could be healed with basic medicines, hunger that could be solved with a garden, fear easily cured with a sip of love. And, God, *the overcrowding*. Kids upon kids literally dying for a bed. Without Clementine and Lucien's funding, the children turned away would be used, sold, abused.

Sharing more personal details with Jack was nothing in the face of that suffering, and giving up meant breaking into his family's estate, a possibility that made her itch.

She knew the David estate's address, but the structure was massive, and she didn't have a blueprint or a clue to the painting's location. Fumbling in a mansion that size led to screw-ups. She only needed the Van Gogh's coordinates. Once she'd secured that, she'd drop off the radar, claim an emergency and leave Whichway for one of the surrounding towns. Three or four weeks later, she'd lift his painting under the cover of night—the biggest paying heist they'd ever performed. It was a longer con, but a safe one. That made her choice easy. As was her next move.

Pulling up to her full height, shoulders back and breasts out, she touched Jack's forearm, *not his hand*. "Well then, our meeting must have been fate."

JACK DIDN'T KNOW where to look. If he focused on Clementine's eyes, his mouth dried. If he caught sight of her ample cleavage, emphasized in her sports bra, his running shorts felt too snug. The sweat on her skin had his synapses misfiring, all signs pointing to trouble.

Like he was a gawky fifteen-year-old again.

"How exactly is our meeting fate?" he asked.

"Your reptiles."

"My reptiles?"

"We're both herps."

His heart pressed against his ribs. The term wasn't the sexiest of labels, but he'd never met a fellow herp, let alone a female herpetoculturist with strawberry-stained lips and a freckled nose, who could fix cars. He should step back, move so her fingers slipped from his forearm. He stepped forward. "How many reptiles do you have?"

"Just one."

"What type?"

"A bearded dragon. A girl."

"Did you travel with her?" The words thumped out of him, everything feeling thick and leaden. She stood enticingly close, this woman who loved reptiles.

Her soft breaths brushed his neck as she tilted up her chin. "No. I hate leaving her, but Lucy's in good hands while I'm gone."

A sharp pulse of blood flooded his veins. "Lucy...as in *I Love Lucy*?"

She smirked. "Indeed."

Lucy. Bearded dragon. It didn't seem possible. Another lie, maybe? Like her name? But that wouldn't explain her knowledge of the term *herps*. A troubling coincidence. His behavior had been equally as bothersome. He'd been embarrassingly rude to her. Sure, he was sometimes abrupt with women. When struggling with his childhood stutter, he'd kept his sentences as short as possible. The affliction no longer twisted his tongue, but some habits were harder to break. This wasn't about awkwardness, though. This was about keeping Clementine—festival judge and name-fabricator—at a healthy distance.

As he stood there, though, he couldn't move away or look directly at her. She was only a head shorter than him, tall for a woman. Her slender fingers drifted along his skin, lower until they slid off his arm. He ached to pull them back. *Lucy. Bearded dragon.* What were the odds?

"I think we should reintroduce ourselves," he heard himself say.

Not the thing he should have said. *Goodbye. See you around town.* Those rebuffs would have been smart. Her judging could interfere with his plan to win this year's contest, and he wasn't sure Clementine was being forthright. The fake-name/job explanation had some merit, but she seemed to be guarding secrets. He'd sensed it in her hesitancy the day they'd first met, her quick departure from the diner yesterday, her flawless name story now. He should be wary after his ex-girlfriend's lies, but there was no fighting this strange connection.

He forced his eyes on her, breathed through the need to glance down. He held out his hand in the small gap between them.

Her lips parted slowly, but she didn't reciprocate. She grazed her teeth over her lower lip and ducked her head. The same behavior as on the highway. He turned his hand up slightly, like he'd done that day. Her shoulders trembled. Was she distrustful of men? Or of him, specifically?

She finally slipped her hand into his.

His stomach hollowed at the contact, a diving swoop like a kingfisher plunging in mid-air. He couldn't be sure she felt the same sweeping rush, but he pressed the pads of his fingers to her wrist, felt the jump of her pulse. *Yes, Clementine. I feel the same.*

"I'm Jack," he said quietly, as though too much sound would send her scurrying away, "but I also go by Maxwell, and I own a bearded dragon named Ricky."

Her eyes cut to him, accusing almost. "Ricky?"

"Ricky Ricardo."

"That's not possible."

"Afraid it is."

"But..." Her breath shuddered.

"Yes?"

"I don't understand."

"Maybe we're not supposed to."

It really didn't make sense, meeting this mysterious woman out of the blue. Yet here they were, shaking—no, *holding*—hands, both with dragons named for the *I Love Lucy* duo who'd charmed a generation of TV fans. Doubt still lingered at the back of his mind, but it was less persistent.

Clementine shook her head and snatched her hand back. "I totally forgot, but I have somewhere I have to be. Can't believe it slipped my mind." She moved as she spoke, walking backward, away from him.

She couldn't go too far. Not in a town this size. But he had a way to see her sooner. He *wanted* to see her sooner. "I can help you."

She kept backing up, fast enough he worried she'd trip. "With what?"

"Anything." He cringed, unsure how that had snuck out. "Your father, I mean. Anything you need for his birthday present."

She stumbled slightly as she stopped. "How can you help?"

"I know a tribute artist. Meet me at the diner at nine tonight and we'll get that photo for him."

A white lie, considering he was the tribute artist, but showing his passion was easier than explaining it. Performing had changed his life. It connected him to his granddad and had allowed him to be someone other than a stuttering kid with lanky limbs. It made him fearless, bold, seductive. He lost himself on stage, absorbed the bass and lights and applause. When discussing it, he often mumbled and waited for ridicule.

No. He wouldn't try explaining it to Clementine, but she didn't seem keen to jump on his offer.

Marvin's mower whizzed in the distance. Imelda's dog menagerie yipped and yapped. Another man walked by the pond, enjoying the view. He wasn't a local, but his thick beard looked familiar, his dark complexion—he was the man who'd snubbed him at the diner. Not the sort he liked invading Whichway, but Elvis fans helped support businesses and filled motels.

The visitor's aggressive knife tattoo wasn't visible and he seemed pleasant enough now, busy watching the ducks, while Clementine was busy not replying.

"Okay," she finally said, but she'd returned to hurrying away, turning as she jogged. "See you at nine." She ran off, light on her feet.

He stood there, lightheaded as he watched her go.

After last year's performance loss and his breakup with Ava, he'd promised himself he'd beat Alistair Murphy at this year's festival, put that cocky weasel in his place. A small part of him also wanted to show up his ex. They'd both used each other— Jack to take a breather from work and enjoy a woman's company, Ava to further her fledgling singing career. He didn't want Ava back, but the way she'd manipulated him had left a sour taste in his mouth. It had made him feel inept and naïve. He wanted her in the audience, regret on her face as he wowed the crowd. Petty, but the hint of retribution would feel good.

As long as the win was solid.

After a contestant had seduced a judge to pad his score, they'd instilled a "no fraternization" policy. Friendships were acceptable. Intimate relationships were not. If Jack won the tribute title, but did it while dating a judge, he could be disqualified.

Then there was his father, the more important reason to be named this year's tribute king.

Every year, Maxwell David the Second beamed while watching Jack perform. Winning was something concrete he could do for his sick father, but the town thought Maxwell was gallivanting abroad, not fighting for his life at home. Jack had lied extensively the past months, ensuring their deception's success. His father's idea, but Jack had been the one misleading investors, coworkers, friends. Another sacrifice to keep David Industries afloat.

If Gunther's sabotage came to light *and* investors learned their CEO was sick, the business's stock would plummet. Hundreds would lose jobs. Unless they could announce a technological breakthrough first.

That left Jack twelve days to solve his research obstacle, so they could quit lying, and his father could attend the festival. Watch his son perform one last time before he died. All solid reasons to avoid Clementine, but his mind was thirteen hours ahead, to them at his home, wondering what she'd think of him in his Elvis attire.

6

———

CLEMENTINE NEARED the Whatnot Diner ten minutes early. She planned to use the seconds to gather herself, because she needed gathering. Her plan had worked. Jack had offered his help and his time. She should be ecstatic, ready to sleuth out the Van Gogh's location. Instead she kept reliving the jogging trail, her hand fitted into Jack's as their bizarre similarity had pretzeled her insides.

Ricky and Lucy. Matching bearded dragons.

Her pulse still trilled at the impossibility.

She needed to pause and ready herself to see Jack again, but he was early, too, leaning on a Tesla Model S. Not the vehicle she'd expect from an Elvis impersonator. Although impressive, the Tesla held no nostalgia. That baby was all innovation. Electric. Cutting edge, with its dual motor and ludicrous acceleration from 0 to 100 in less than three seconds.

Sexy in its own way, as was its owner.

Bathed in the diner's lights, Jack's slacks and dress shirt looked slightly creased, like he'd come from work. His hair was also disheveled, the effect torquing her belly. *Focus, Clementine. Remember why you're here. Remember the kids.*

Nisha had been her favorite at the Delhi orphanage. All big brown eyes and lanky limbs, she'd avoided Clementine and had hidden most of that afternoon. Until Clementine had offered her a slice of persimmon. She'd snatched the ripe fruit, the movement incredibly quick. Not too fast to miss the burns on her arms, the slashing scars. Nisha had wedged herself into a corner, smaller than small, and had eaten like she'd never see food again.

That image: a child as feral as a wild dog—distrustful, hungry, *hurt*—haunted Clementine to this day. It brought back memories of her time on the streets. More reason not to let an unexplainable coincidence and a provocative man derail her work.

She rolled down her window. "Hey there, stranger."

Jack tucked his chin, sending a few dark strands tumbling over his forehead. "We're not strangers. We've met. Three times, in fact. I know both your names."

He hadn't scratched the surface of her names. "Good point." She glanced around, playing dumb. "Where's this tribute artist?"

She wasn't sure why he hadn't admitted to his hobby upfront, but wasn't in a position to call him on it.

"You'll need to follow me. To my place. Which is..." He winced, his focus cementing to the pavement between them. "That sounded forward, and possibly unsafe, seeing as we don't know each other that well. But I can help with your father's gift, just not here, and—"

"Jack."

He glanced up sharply, the tilt of his posture slightly bowed.

Shy Jack had returned, and her resolve wavered.

She'd hooked up with cocky men in the past, could forget

herself in the face of their aloof vanity. Jack's reticence was a different beast. He'd been sweetly sincere on the highway, awkward in the diner, curt then irresistible on their run, always with those flitting blue eyes. She couldn't quite decipher him, but she wanted to unlock his secrets, offer him a wedge of persimmon to tease the real Jack out.

She tightened her grip on the steering wheel.

"Lead the way," she said, hoping he'd take her to his family's estate and hurry her reconnaissance along. More time with Shy Jack was liable to wreck her transmission, lead to grinding and other unpredictable noises. There would be no grinding with Jack.

He led her out of town, along a windy stretch of road, toward his home, not his parents' estate. An unfortunate turn of events, but the modern architecture, lit by exterior floodlights, stole her breath. The sleek angles and dark-stained wood panels stretched toward surrounding trees, as though merging with their environment.

She parked and texted Lucien quickly, letting him know she was at Jack's home. Not the home she needed to access, but it was a step closer. She was earning Jack's trust. Lucien would be pleased.

Once inside, her jaw dropped. Massive glass walls brought the exterior in, tall ceilings adding breadth to the sprawling space. The open kitchen/living space shone in tones of stainless steel and chocolate. Indoor plants added a ripe lushness.

She felt underdressed in her jeans and too-girly peach T-shirt.

"It's quite the shack you've got here," she said, a bite to her tone. She understood basic desires, the wanting of things, but so much of this money could have helped the needy.

Jack shifted on his feet. "I love architecture."

He didn't expand on this interest or show off his wealth.

Shy. Shy. Shy.

"Yeah, well, it's certainly quaint." Sarcasm helped her remember why she was there, and how recklessly he'd spent his millions. Fancy electric car. (That helped save the environment.) Expansive home. (That celebrated ingenuity and style.)

Focus, Clementine.

She stepped farther into the space and her attention snagged on an enlarged photograph, life-sized, spanning his living-room wall. Elvis with his arm around a man. "Who is that?"

"Elvis."

She shot him a scowl, but his teasing smirk mollified her.

"It's my granddad," he said. "He was a roadie for the great man."

Reverence touched his voice, for Elvis or his grandfather, she couldn't be sure. "Is that how the festival started here?"

He nodded. "Twenty-four years ago." Again, he didn't elaborate, but he moved closer to her, stood at her side as they appreciated his family photograph.

Jack had his grandfather's sharp cheekbones, proud chin and nose. Both men were elegant and handsome. "You look like him."

"Not as much as others. But I—" An impatient sound arrested his words. "You mean my granddad."

"Who did *you* mean?" She forced the question out. She was used to playing roles, pretending to be a wholesome teacher, a sales clerk, a waitress. Always virtuous. That was her gift, Lucien claimed. Her freckled nose and blondish-red hair, open smile, and soft voice painted her as innocent. A person marks would easily trust and wouldn't suspect. With Jack, playing the role felt like she'd bathed with sandpaper.

"Elvis," he said quietly. "I don't look as much like him as..."

He worked his jaw and rubbed the back of his neck. His eyes flicked to hers. "I'm part of the festival."

"An impersonator?"

"No, no..." More neck rubbing.

"Then what?" God, he was hesitant. Worried what she'd think? Which made it even worse. She could put him at ease, admit she knew he performed for crowds and found it surprisingly appealing. She wanted to see him under those hot lights, lip curled, voice crooning, tight pants accentuating his thick thighs. She curled her toes instead.

"Impersonators," he said, attention on the framed photo, "pretend to be a singer or celebrity. They want to embody that person. I'm a tribute artist. I celebrate Elvis and the life he injected into the world. I don't pretend to be him."

Right. She'd read about the difference. Jack's vehemence drove the distinction home. "So you'll perform on stage, at the festival?"

"Yes." He didn't look at her. Color rose to his cheeks.

"Do you love it?"

"Yes."

"Does this mean you'll pose for me?"

He faced her fully, one eyebrow cocked. Now she wished she were the shy one, her double entendre not far from the fantasies she'd conjured.

She cleared her throat. "I mean, for my *father's* photo."

He flicked open his dress shirt's top button, cool and casual, like the move didn't pebble her skin. "I will." He strutted past her, less hesitant in his stride. "You can visit my reptile shelter. It'll take me a bit to get changed." He motioned down a narrow hall, where another glass wall loomed.

After pointing out the bathroom and telling Clementine to make herself at home, he disappeared to his bedroom, through a door off the long hallway. Since the Van Gogh was owned by his father, there wasn't much sleuthing to do in his personal home. This not-a-date would help her gain his trust and earn an invite to his family's estate. She should pour herself a glass of wine from the bottle on his counter, strike a sexy pose of her own before he reemerged, but she was drawn to his shelter.

She tiptoed toward the glass like she might disturb a slumbering giant. The closer she got, the faster her pulse raced. If Jack had spared no expense designing his home, he'd spent a king's ransom building his reptile sanctuary. It was twice the size of her apartment, mist hovering mid-air, with rocks and logs filling the space, select trees spreading their limbs. A green button was printed with the word *Open*. She pressed it and held her breath.

Soft sounds shushed and whirred. Humidity reached for her, pulling her deeper inside. Although the room looked undivided from outside, glass separations were visible now, as was the precious cargo Jack housed. Iguanas. Savannah monitors. Chameleons. Small green anoles.

One bearded dragon named Ricky Ricardo.

The small hairs at her neck frizzed, and her lungs swelled with the briny, swampy smells. She crouched in front of each enclosure, marveled at how some reptiles had two living spaces, probably with different temperatures for them to thrive. She noticed other things as well: one chameleon was missing a foot, the monitor's tail had been amputated.

Sanctuary, Jack had said. He didn't breed reptiles or buy them for pets.

He saved them.

"What do you think?"

She startled at his voice. Too absorbed, she hadn't heard the door above the ambient sounds. When she turned, the sultry air pressed on her lungs. "I think *wow*."

Jack was in full Elvis attire, hair combed at the sides but

ruffled up top. His black slacks and dress shirt were more fitted than his work clothes. The slim white tie was a perfect throwback, but the gold jacket was the clincher. On anyone else, the gaudy shine would be garish. On Maxwell Jack David dressed as Elvis, it was mesmerizing.

He stood tall and proud as though daring her to laugh at him.

Laughing was the last thing on her mind.

"Definitely wow," she repeated. He held her gaze this time. Bold Jack. Elvis Jack. Her belly swirled. "The space, I mean," she added, diverting her attention to his reptiles. "The space is impressive."

"Not impressive enough."

Said the guy who'd spent millions on his extravagant home. The shelter was astounding, but his matter-of-fact tone cooled her too-hot blood. "You do realize how arrogant that sounds, right?"

He even had an ancient Egyptian statue in the corner. The stone cobra was weathered, a few chunks missing here and there, but its hooding was unmistakable, the flare of its neck the most distinctive feature of the poisonous snake. If the thing didn't weigh a thousand pounds, Lucien would have her nab it.

Jack slipped his hands into his front pockets and bowed his posture slightly. A familiar pose. "Hank, the savannah monitor, had his tail mutilated. He got aggressive with his owner, because he'd been mishandled and mistreated." He tipped his chin to the chameleon. "Ella was allowed to roam around a dingy apartment and her foot got crushed. The iguana was blinded by some asshole for the fun of it. So no, it's not impressive enough. I planned to enlarge the space, but I've hit a...roadblock of sorts. I'm at capacity and can't shelter more abused animals."

Something flashed in his eyes, and her self-righteousness

shriveled like a parched raisin. She was so damn quick to judge these days, criticize and condemn, even though he'd used some of his millions to rescue reptiles. Through all her years, her ups and downs, it was like she'd lost the ability to empathize, unless someone had walked precisely in her shoes. The bitterness was exhausting.

"I'm sorry, Jack. I can be a bit...judgmental."

He raised an eyebrow. "A bit?"

Busted. "Fine, a lot."

"Funny. I didn't notice."

"Smartass."

He smoldered at her. "So you think I'm smart now?"

She thought he was smart and cute and a mountain of trouble. This bantery side of Jack was new, and she liked it a whole lot. "Don't let it go to your head, but what you've done *is* remarkable. I'm just not used to so much"—she breathed in his ingenious shelter, his elegant home, his obviously caring heart —"stuff?"

"Stuff?"

She gestured vaguely around. "It's all stunning, but it's overwhelming."

He considered her a moment. "You've had to work hard for what you have."

It was a blatant observation, not a question, made with his head tipped to the side, his large hands still stashed in his pockets. Too observant for her liking. His eyes slid from hers, but they didn't stray far. His heated gaze traveled down her neck and chest, before returning to her face.

Her next breath felt like she'd inhaled fire.

He affected her, this man. She couldn't deny it, didn't want to fight it. What she fought was the pull to open her mouth and tell him about losing her father, then being torn from her mother. The foster homes. Running away. Scrounging for food. Details she'd stupidly revealed on that awful girls' night.

Accepting Jenny's invitation had pushed her out of her comfort zone, but she'd been excited to have a social evening. She hadn't expected one of the women to have opened her home to foster children. Francesca had detailed how admirable the system was, that it had given her hope for society. She'd called foster care America's answer to its rising crime rate.

Clementine had held her tongue and swallowed the acid souring her saliva. She'd bitten her cheek to forget her painful past and focus on the immediate pain. Cheek. Bite. Blood. Yes, *blood*. But the wrong blood. Past blood had invaded her thoughts. Her cut cheek. The backhand that had sent her sprawling to the ground.

"And what about foster families who use the system for money? Turn their kids into servants and punching bags?" Clementine had nearly slapped her hand over her mouth, furious with herself for referencing her past.

Francesca had rolled her eyes. "You watch too many movies."

It should have ended there. Clementine should have realized this do-gooder chose to see the world through rose-colored glasses, a luxury Clementine didn't have. Instead Clementine spewed the ugliness that had happened in her foster homes. The meanness. The disregard for human decency. Her subsequent life on the streets.

She'd rushed from the apartment afterward, leaving all four women, mouths open, pleas and apologies following in her wake. She'd fled outside and spent the evening and morning walking aimlessly. It hadn't been her past chasing her that dreary day. It had been her present. The friends and smiling photographs she didn't have. The fact that no one knew or understood her.

She was so jaded she hadn't been able to thank Francesca for her work and see that goodness for what it truly was. She'd even forgotten her one nice foster home, where she'd met Annie Ward. Annie had been a lost girl like her. Chattiest thing, always going on about *Batman* comics and scrapbooking, quick with a smile.

When tested, Clementine had forgotten the good and clung to the bad. Her growing unhappiness had led to delaying this job with her scenic drive. It could be why she felt her guard slipping around Jack now. A good man. A kind man. A man who rehabilitated reptiles others had harmed and waited patiently while she digested his too-observant statement: *You've had to work hard for what you have.*

"Yes," she said, unable to resist. "My life hasn't been easy."

"Your childhood?"

"All of it."

"But you must be close with your father. Doing this photo for him is more than a compulsory card."

"He died when I was young." Her breathing accelerated like someone had cranked her horsepower. She never spoke about her past. Ever. Yet she'd blurted it to her neighbor's friends recently, was doing the same again, her overstuffed secrets too crammed to stay contained.

Jack squinted like the answer to her deception was written in fuzzy fine print. "I don't understand."

"Ignore me. The swampy fumes are getting to my head."

He waited on her, didn't speak.

"Your astounding sanctuary momentarily confused me. I said something nonsensical."

He smirked, crossed his arms, still silent.

"You're annoying when you don't talk."

"I could say the same about you. Annoying and secretive."

"Remember when I was fixing your car and said I didn't

mind you being an idiot?" She pointed a finger at her unamused face. "This is me minding."

He pointed at his bland expression. "This is me not caring."

She laughed. She should backtrack, make another joke. Veer far from this topic. She found herself doing the opposite. "I still give my father yearly birthday gifts through his email, and I send random messages to his account all year. As a diary of sorts."

The odd ritual had begun at her first foster home. Impossibly lonely and scared, she'd written Clinton Abernathy. One message had become two. Two had rolled into thirty. Now she was a twenty-eight-year-old woman who emailed her dead dad.

"That's beautiful," he said, his tone more fascinated than pitying.

"Or just plain weird." When she'd confessed the ritual to Lucien, he'd said it was wonderfully therapeutic and had encouraged her to keep at it. The habit made her feel odd.

Jack stepped closer, his voice dropping lower. "Beautiful."

One word, spoken with ardent compassion. The heavy air continued unfurling around them, drawing them closer. Or maybe it was her need to lean toward him and touch him. Mess up his slim tie and gold jacket and run her fingers through his thick hair. Kiss his full lips.

She fought each urge. Making out with Jack wasn't part of her plan. It wouldn't hurt her strategy, per se. Getting closer to him meant getting closer to that painting. This was different, though. This kind of closeness was like driving along the edge of a cliff.

She leaned away. "Do you come here often?"

Now she was spewing moronic pick-up lines. Of course he came here often. His sanctuary was attached to his freaking house.

He either didn't notice her idiocy or kindly let it slide. "Every night."

"To feed the reptiles?"

"No. Marvin tends our family properties and comes here during the day, spends a couple of hours cleaning and feeding. Makes sure the environments are ideal."

"So you just...what? Sit and read? Talk to them? Play solitaire?"

The corner of his lips tipped up. "I sing."

Oh, Lord.

His new road sign should read: *Beware of dreaminess, loss of self-control ahead.*

"I want to hear you," she said. She wanted to get lost in his voice. Forget for a moment she was using him to get to a painting.

"You want to hear me sing?"

"Yes."

"Now?"

"Obviously."

He freed a pocketed hand and loosened his tie. Rosiness ascended his neck. Without a word, he pressed his fingertips to her eyelids and slid them closed. "Keep them shut," he murmured.

Jack hadn't intended to sing for Clementine, or to learn such intimate details about her past. He'd wanted time with her, to understand this woman who also owned a bearded dragon and seemed torn between flirting with him and running away.

He'd gotten more than he'd bargained for.

A woman who emailed a deceased parent was as complex as they came. It hinted at a deep-seated loneliness and explained some of her hesitation with him, if only a fraction. He wanted more, but his want was more of a ravenous need to know all her secrets. The desire unnerved him.

For now he would sing. He'd closed her eyes, couldn't breathe fully let alone sing with those reddish-brown beauties locked on him. Before he overthought this to death, he hummed the first note to "Can't Help Falling in Love."

Why that song, he couldn't say. A way to communicate the stirrings Clementine inspired, to say things he'd never have the courage to admit aloud. Granted, what he felt for her wasn't love. Not this early. But the storm behind his breastbone wouldn't cease. It was a stronger desire than he'd experienced with Ava, and the few women before her.

He poured his uncertainty into the song, watched as her chest rose and fell faster, deeper, her lips parting as though to inhale his words.

This could be the beginnings of love, he hoped he conveyed.

Fools do rush in, his tone implored. *I am a fool for you right now.*

I can't help it.

The last words drifted between them, seemed to wilt in the humid air. Strawberry-blonde hairs frizzed around Clementine's face, and her slender shoulders shuddered slightly. Her nose had a slight bump in the center. An almost-invisible scar notched her chin. He was a detail-oriented person and her details were very consuming. They made his blue suede shoes feel too tight, his chest tighter.

She kept her eyes closed. He wanted to kiss her fiercely.

"I can't take you on a date," he said. A silly statement, considering she hadn't asked him for a date. Or agreed to one. If anything, she'd turned him down flat.

She opened her eyes and mouthed *what*, the word barely audible.

"I want to take you out," he tried again, "but I've been rehearsing for the festival all year. Winning is important to me...for several reasons. With you being a judge, it would be a conflict of interest."

She pressed her hand over her heart and blinked rapidly. "Right. Yeah. I get it."

"Does that mean you'd have said yes?"

"To what?" She seemed dazed, cheeks flushed, equilibrium sketchy.

He steadied her elbow. "Would you have agreed to a date?"

Her body snapped taut. Ready to bolt again? Just as quickly, she softened. "Yes. I'd have said yes." A measure of stiffness returned to her joints. "Not that it matters, with the competition and all. Plus, I don't exactly live close, so there'd be no point. And we've determined you're an idiot."

He laughed. "And that you're annoying and secretive." A mix of pleasure and disappointment winded him. "Too bad we didn't meet under different circumstances."

She reached for him and touched his jaw, feathering her fingers over his skin. The sensual move reminded him of her on that bland stretch of highway, flirty one minute, speeding away the next. She peeked up at him through her lashes. "What would you do under different circumstances?"

Kissed her. Devoured her. Used the skills one kind woman had taught him oh so well. Yes, all of that and then some, but another possibility pulled at him, too tempting to keep inside. "I'd invite you on my upcoming trip to India."

Something dark crossed her face, and she dropped her hand. "India?"

"I have investors there." Potential investors. The trip was business, not pleasure, like most facets of his life. Work was his life's blood. Seeing his factory and Whichway thrive was everything. He couldn't remember the last time he'd slept in or had gone for a leisurely walk. A vacation with a woman? He'd never done that. What would it be like to have her along? To feed her *naan* while exploring the colorful city and inhaling the spice-laden air?

She lifted her hair and fanned her neck. "Now you're just being ridiculous. Going to India," she mumbled on a laugh. "But we can still be friends. Have coffee and go for runs. Talk about Ricky and Lucy and how big of an idiot you are. And I'd love to see the estate where you grew up. I've heard it's quite something." She strutted past him, toward the exit, determination in her stride. "Best we get that picture first. I'd hate to miss my father's birthday."

Her flippancy didn't hide her need to flee. A reaction he should encourage. Yes, they could have coffee and meet for runs. They could indulge their shared herpetology interest and tease each other. But she couldn't tour his estate. Not when his father was holed up there, nurses tending to him 24/7. Another reason for Jack to avoid Clementine's draw: lying to her about it would feel incredibly wrong.

7

————

Clementine kept pace with Jack, his stride less leave-her-in-his-dust than yesterday. "But I didn't think chameleons changed color to camouflage."

"They don't," he said patiently, as though he didn't mind her reptile-question barrage. "They lighten and darken according to emotion. Ella gets vividly bright when she's afraid, which happened often when I first rescued her. Now she fluctuates depending on temperature."

"It must have taken her a while to trust you."

"It did." He snuck a glance her way. "The singing helped."

It sure as hell had helped Clementine. That was some kind of voodoo he'd performed, casting her under his Elvis spell. She'd already been primed for it, had lost a bit of her sense while standing in his shelter, mesmerized by his generosity and rock-and-roll attire.

Then that song.

He'd been kind and accommodating afterward. He'd snapped photos, even holding up a paper that read, *Happy birthday, Clinton!* All the while, she couldn't stop thinking of the

Delhi Orphanage, the money they needed, the importance of acquiring that priceless Van Gogh. Another thought had blindsided her as well: the prospect of Jack discovering her deceit.

His potential look of disgust had gutted her in a surprising way, the possibility growing alongside their strange connection. Even worse, this job had been fraught with mistakes. He knew her real name and that she owned a bearded dragon named Lucy. She'd admitted her father had died. Vague details that were difficult to connect, but paranoia had her picturing a life behind bars.

She'd maintained a healthy distance afterward, offering an awkward wave when retreating to her car. Now they were running through Whichway's Wherever Park, as though her internal warning light weren't on the fritz: Heart Trouble Imminent.

Don't fall for him. Don't land in jail.

"What about the names?" she asked, keeping their conversation light. She could do light. She could do sweet. "Hank, Ella, Ray? I'm guessing they're music inspired."

"You guessed correctly."

Not surprising from a man who idolized Elvis. Her father had enjoyed old rock and roll, too. Hank Williams. Ella Fitzgerald. Ray Charles. He would have loved the names Jack had picked. "And Ricky Ricardo?" she asked. "Why that one?"

Clouds zoomed across the sky. A thick wind mussed her hair. Where he'd answered her other eleventy-million questions quick as a flash, he delayed this time. Each thump of her feet pounded in her head. Sweat dampened her neck.

Jack wiped his brow. "My granddad watched *I Love Lucy* with his father. Then he watched reruns with my dad, who carried the tradition on with me." He jogged around a fallen tree branch. "What about you? Why'd you name your dragon Lucy?"

"Also my dad." More real details shared with Jack. She'd given up evading, but it didn't change her plan. Thankfully Jack was fighting their connection, too. "One of my strongest memories is of my father watching reruns and cracking up. I never liked the show, so I'd roll my eyes and call it lame. He'd tell me I had crap taste with a teasing wink."

The treasured flashback filled her up. The memory had led to her watching that once-hated show into adulthood and naming her dragon after its main character, but it wasn't her strongest memory. That one was less pleasant. A locked car. Clinton Abernathy slumped over his wheel. Not moving. Not breathing. Her deafening scream.

She blinked the garish image away. "I love the show now."

"How'd you get into the music business?"

The sudden question felt jarring, but this was a normal conversation. People talked about life, pets, jobs. She wasn't a normal person, though. "Honestly, this is the first work break I've had in forever. I'm kind of reveling in it and would rather not talk shop."

A pained expression crossed his face. "I get that. So, why a bearded dragon?"

"Like, why'd I choose her?"

He nodded as he ran.

"A zoo came to my school as a kid, one of those 'play with the animals' presentations. Most girls screeched and wouldn't touch the snakes and lizards. I couldn't get close enough." She'd fallen half a step behind him and gave a push, meeting his longer stride. "They had an inland dragon and explained that when stressed or territorial their scales go from soft to spiky. I loved the idea of that."

"That they adapt?"

"That they change to protect themselves." A living embodiment of herself. "Also, they don't shed or have to be walked."

"So you're lazy."

"I'm running, aren't I? Idiot," she muttered, loud enough for him to hear.

He grinned.

His amusement made her strangely happy. "Lucy is adorable," she said. "She has a red ball she chases when swimming in my bathtub. My dad would have loved her."

"Mine isn't a reptile fan."

"Where *is* your father?"

"What do you mean?" Jack stopped short, so abruptly she'd gone five strides before noticing.

She faced him, breathing hard. "Isn't your father away?"

"How'd you know he's away?"

Shit. Had she heard it from a local or had she studied it in her notes? On any other job, she'd know the answer instantly. This job had been nothing but a delayed start, distracted focus, and lusty dreams. But nope, she was sure. She'd learned that tidbit publicly. "In the diner that first day, Jasmine said something about him being away, that she hoped he'd return for the festival."

As usual, his gaze skittered away from her, but this was a different avoidance. Jumpy. Nervous. He dragged an agitated hand through his hair. "He's been traveling, and I didn't realize the time. I need to head to work."

She'd fibbed enough to sniff out lies a mile away, and Not-Maxwell Jack David who performed as Elvis was telling falsehoods. She didn't push. She didn't want to distance him more than she already had. Talking dragons was a novelty, but what she needed was to get into his family estate. "Want to meet at the diner for a coffee? I can show you pictures of Lucy."

"Another time. I'm behind at work." He tipped his head to her and jogged toward his car.

Her focus stayed firmly on him. On his calves as they balled and lengthened, his shifting back muscles and delectable butt. A butt she wouldn't touch, delectable or otherwise. She had a job to do for Nisha. For Lucien. For every kid who hadn't chosen to be abandoned. She just had to work harder and ignore Jack's gravitational pull.

8

Jack loved living in Whichway. The slower pace appealed to him. There was no aggravating traffic. The small town meant he'd never fully shake his awkward teenage past, but every hill and tree was part of his DNA.

Each morning, he'd drive past the rock where he'd skinned his first knee. He'd smile at the field that housed Whichway's annual Race Into Spring weekend. His father had cheered him on there. He'd swung him in the air, even if he'd dropped his eggs while running to the finish line. They'd done the three-legged race together, falling over in hysterics.

They still attended every spring, played the same games with Jack's little sister—the surprise child his parents hadn't planned at their age, but who brought them untold joy. His father had missed his twelve-year-old daughter's smiles at this past spring's festival. If cancer beat him as predicted, he might never see another race.

Jack enjoyed passing the field these days, having these moments close. What he didn't like was how often he ran into Clementine.

We can be friends, she'd said. *Have coffee and go for runs.*

Whichway suddenly felt too small.

She'd been everywhere the past two days. Running with him. Slipping onto the stool beside his. He may have skipped his coffee and pastry one morning, a desperate move to resist Clementine's allure, but he couldn't repeat the maneuver. Status quo needed to be maintained, which meant suffering through polite conversation with Clementine when what he wanted was anything but polite.

Now it was eleven p.m., and he was holed up in his research lab, thinking about Clementine when he should be focused on work.

He forced his attention to his page. His employees had left hours ago. The only noise was the droning air conditioner and the frustrated tapping of his pen. He was so close to solving their formula and finding the secret sauce to lower their costs and increase their volume. If they could do that, it wouldn't matter that their technology had been stolen. They could compete for a chunk of market share.

"Keep that up and you'll be as bald as me."

Jack startled and dropped his pen. He hadn't realized he'd been tugging his hair, and he certainly hadn't heard his father enter. "What are you doing here?"

"Last I checked, I own this place."

"Last I checked, you should be at home in bed."

Maxwell David shrugged, the slow slump of his frail shoulders gutting Jack. "New treatment starts tomorrow. Wasn't sure when I'd get out again. Any progress?"

He should insist his father leave, rest up for whatever horrors tomorrow would bring, but he understood the need to feel vital. Useful in the face of a disease neither of them could control. "The optics keep stonewalling us. Every time we add the extra layer to the substrates, it falls apart."

Maxwell scanned the sterile room, pausing on the microscopes and customized test chambers. "Have you tried re-integrating the LCD process?"

"A million times."

"Adjusting the ITO electrodes?"

"Of course."

His father leaned heavier on his cane, his lips flattening into a grim line. "This can't be a repeat of the Ant Man Project."

As amusing as that project name was, there was nothing funny about his father's jab. Maxwell David the Second was the epitome of conservative. Always had been, always would be. His staunch focus had built their business and lens factory. Sure, Jack's first attempt to advance them and miniaturize their lenses had failed. It was part of the reason they were in financial limbo now, but Jack hadn't given up. He'd been sure their technology had been too expensive to grow with the times, so he'd worked his ass off to shrink and leverage their current lenses until they'd been efficient and cheap enough for cell phones. Jack's work had been some next-level engineering, taking David Industries global. It had been exhilarating. Ego inflating.

This project, however, was testing his patience. There was no coasting in business, only improving. "I'm close," he said. "It's dogging me, but I can feel it." He just couldn't untangle it.

"If it fails, everything falls apart."

"It won't fail."

"Time is running out."

"If you would sell the house or tap into your funds, I could hire more people and work faster, and—" He clamped his mouth shut. He hadn't meant to raise his voice. "Sorry. It's just late, and I'm stressed." And his recent bank loans wouldn't last forever. Loans that had to be repaid.

His father pulled up to his full height. Even bald with skin sagging over his frail bones, he could be formidable: the Great Wall of Maxwell David the Second. "This will be the last time you suggest using more of my money. The estate will go to your mother. My savings will support her and your sister and your sister's kids, and their goddamn kids, God willing. I won't budge on this, Jack. It's the only peace I have."

To provide for his family when he's gone. Guilt and helplessness thickened his throat. Jack understood his father's vehemence, but the bigger picture haunted him, too. A derelict town with broken windows and mangy dogs, the factory closed, unemployment sucking the life from Whichway. "I won't mention it again," he murmured, feeling boxed in.

He wouldn't suggest selling *his* assets, either, a solution he'd offered before. His father had kiboshed that as well, red faced and frustrated, telling Jack liquidation was as good as putting up a billboard, advertising their business's demise.

Maxwell nodded and smiled at his son. "How's the rehearsing going?"

His father may be formidable, but he excelled at breaking tension. Jack wasn't sure how he'd say goodbye to him one day. "Good. Hard to find the time, but good."

"I always loved it, you know. Seeing you on stage. Sorry I'll miss it this year." His rheumy eyes misted.

Jack's eyes burned. So fucking unfair, how disease felled the best of them. Made him want to punch a wall. "So don't miss it. Let's tell the board you're sick. They deserve to know, about that and what Gunther did. They'll understand and vote to put more money into my research."

"Jack—" He swallowed, the slow action looking like it pained him. "You know we can't. If Gunther backstabbed us, anyone could. I'm not willing to risk more secrets being sold off. And we don't know when our competitors will go public with their new technology. That news on its own would be destructive. That news coupled with my illness would be catastrophic."

People could panic. Their stock could drop, and every employee owned shares. Jack doubted it would go that far, but David Industries was still his father's company and he was as obstinate as ever.

"I'll work harder," Jack said, his only option. If bullfrogs went months without sleep, merely resting their eyes, surely he could do the same. "I'll finish the research by next weekend. We'll announce the breakthrough and come clean about your illness, and you'll be at the show."

So help him, God.

"Sure, son. I know you will." It was a nice sentiment, but that had been a pacifying *sure*. Not a hopeful *sure*.

Jack would prove his father wrong and show the board he could lead David Industries and Whichway to success. They didn't trust Jack the way they trusted his father. They were old bloods who preferred conservative management to projects like Ant Man that had hurt their bottom line. Jack's more recent success hadn't erased that screw-up from their minds. They wouldn't all be pleased to see him at the helm, unless he proved his worth.

"I'm going to visit my office for a bit." His father turned to leave but paused. "Promise me, Jack, when this is done, you'll make time for a life. As proud as I am of what I've built, I wish I'd spent more nights at home. More time with all of you."

Maxwell shuffled out, and Jack's mind drifted to Clementine. Spending time with her felt like a breather of sorts. Like the stirrings of a life. If only things were that simple.

THE NEXT EVENING, Marco stepped out of his truck as Jack

pulled up to their regular haunt: Whenever Bar. Friday night beers with Marco was a ritual. One he should have canceled. Working until dawn had left Jack more drained than usual, but he hadn't been able to shake his father's words last night: *Make time to have a life.*

"You look like you need more than a beer." Marco clapped him on the back, matching his stride.

"You're as astute as always." Country music spilled over them as they walked inside.

The watering hole was more saloon than hot spot, the wooden walls and tables as scarred as a gnarled oak tree. The mostly full space hummed with post-work chatter and the snap of colliding pool balls. Perpetual Christmas lights hung over the small stage, the corner used for open mic nights or karaoke. Not on Fridays, though. Fridays were for half-price beers and darts and pool. Time to unwind from the work week.

Marco fell into a chair at their usual table. "You plotting world domination?"

"Something like that." World domination seemed a less daunting task than saving David Industries and having a life.

"Word to the wise, you should rest while plotting. You look like you haven't slept in months."

"Bet I've slept more than you."

Marco chuckled. "Lauralee says if she's not sleeping, I should suffer with her." He moaned lovingly about his wife, but Jack's attention shifted to not sleeping. Specifically, not sleeping with Clementine. He hungered to not sleep with her and do a thousand things in that stretch of darkness. Love on her. Explore her. Sing songs against her skin.

Tami, who'd waitressed here for a decade, dropped off a couple of beers. No order necessary. Just a wave and a smile. "Y'all don't be getting too serious."

"It's him you gotta worry about. Not me." Marco hooked a thumb toward Jack.

Jack shrugged a shoulder, attempting indifference. "Nothing wrong with serious."

"Except when you look constipated." Tami cackled at her joke and sauntered off, ready to sass other patrons.

Marco was talking again, about a new sponsor for their Every Cent charity, how widening its scope to encompass affordable housing and traveling medical care was what the donor loved about the project. Jack offered a distracted nod, pleased their charity work was growing, but only catching key words.

Jack stared at the empty stage. It was the first place he'd sung in public, the night Aaron Axelrod's older sister had taken pity on him and dragged him out back. She'd tutored him in the ways of women, that day and many afterward. He'd studied like a man searching for the Holy Grail. *This*, he'd thought back then. *If I can master this, learn how to make a woman shake and moan, turn her boneless with pleasure, the rest will fall into place.*

It hadn't really. Not when it came to women. But he'd soaked up those lessons, refined his skills. Skills he ached to show Clementine.

Marco veered from prattling about Lauralee and their expected twins to last night's burritos that hadn't agreed with him, and Jack settled his forearms on the table. "I met a woman."

"A real live one?"

Gotta love old friends. "Has a pulse and everything."

"Does she speak English?"

"She does."

Marco smirked. "Does she have hearing loss?"

Jack refused to laugh or acknowledge his teasing. "Not to my knowledge."

Marco leaned back on his chair and squinted at the ceiling. "So you're telling me, a real live woman, who can understand and hear you, actually found your abysmal flirting skills attractive and didn't run screaming the other way?"

Jack frowned. "Not exactly."

Marco raised an eyebrow, but Jack didn't elaborate.

"Come on, man. Don't hold back now." Marco grinned wide enough to swallow his beer bottle. "Your painful love life makes you human. Otherwise you'd be this rich, smart, hot dude that even my wife drools over, and we couldn't be friends."

"We'd always be friends."

"Stop stalling."

Jack took a healthy pull on his beer and laid out the gist of it: the highway meeting...and Clementine running away, the Whatnot Diner meeting...and Clementine running away, then running *with* her and singing for her and how they both had bearded dragons named Ricky and Lucy. "She's amazing and fascinating, but her job in the festival means I can't even ask her out."

"So don't perform this year."

Jack flinched. "What?"

"Take a year off. Have fun with her instead."

Jack pictured his father, misty eyed, saying how much he loved watching his son sing. "I can't take a year off."

"Then take her out and deal with the fallout when Alistair the Asshole gets up in your face about it, because you know he will."

That was a forgone conclusion. And hiding a date or relationship in Whichway was as easy as hiding the moon. If you sneezed in this town, ten people dropped off chicken soup the next day. "Winning is important to me, and she doesn't live here anyway. There's no point pursuing her."

Marco rolled his wrist absentmindedly. "Sounds like you don't need my advice, then."

"Guess I don't."

"Yeah, you'll be way better off without a dragon-loving woman who isn't offended by your recessive seduction gene and seems attracted to an Elvis impersonator—"

"Tribute artist."

"I'm just saying, forgetting her seems like a swell idea. One you won't regret at all." Marco's sarcasm was annoyingly insightful.

Even more annoying was that Jack couldn't tell Marco the Gossip Monger about his father and explain what this year's festival really meant to him. "All I know is—"

Clementine.

All he knew was that Clementine was *here*, sauntering toward the bar, again encroaching on his life, his space, his thoughts. It was like she knew his schedule, how he filled his minutes outside of work and rehearsal. She wore tight jeans and red-as-sin cowboy boots, a soft looking cream tank top with buttons up the front. He shouldn't be happy to see her. He should curse her unshakable presence. Instead, all he could picture was her jeans off, those sinful boots hooked over his shoulders as he devoured her.

Marco waved his hand in front of Jack's face. "You still there? Did my sly reverse psychology actually work?"

"Clementine's here."

Marco swiveled and zeroed in on her immediately. "Wow. Yep. You did not lie. She's damn beautiful."

She sure was, and picking her out wasn't tough when they knew almost everyone in the bar. In Jack's attempt to not stare at Clementine, he nodded at the Smith brothers, who both had three kids in college. A reminder of how vital saving the company was. Jack couldn't even think about Marco and how much his best friend depended on his job.

His attention slid back to the woman who'd occupied his mind too often the past few days. He quickly looked away. A few tourists sat a table, and the man with the forearm knife tattoo was in a corner. He apparently enjoyed snubbing locals, feeding ducks at the park, and taking an eyeful of Clementine. He was barely visible, that corner booth always dim, but his attention on Clementine sent a wave of possessiveness through Jack.

Marco kicked Jack's boot. "Go on, Casanova. Talk to her."

"There's no point."

"She already knows you suck at chatting up hot women."

"It has nothing to do with that." Amazingly, it didn't. The past few days, running and sharing coffee and pastries with her had verged on effortless. Clementine's endless questions had helped. He could focus on those instead of his blasted self-consciousness. They'd even joked some. With friends, he didn't stumble over his words or struggle making eye contact. With her it had been an upward battle that seemed to be leveling out. Because she was becoming a friend, which is exactly what she should remain.

He caught Tami's eye and lifted his empty beer, signaling for another round. He would stay where he was, drain his beer, and forget how much he liked the girl in the red boots.

If only he could tear his gaze away from her.

9

____

Clementine could feel Jack's eyes on her, sizzling up her spine. She'd noticed him first thing but had kept her cool. She hadn't acknowledged him or stared at how his threadbare T-shirt accentuated his muscular build. Nope. It was his turn to seek her out.

She pulled out her phone.

Clementine: **I'm at the bar. He's here, and I've decided to switch gears.**

Lucien: **Why?**

Clementine: **He's being cagey. Might not be so easy to con. I'll give it a couple days. Break in if it doesn't pan out.**

Not the whole truth, but enough of it. If she didn't get into Jack's estate by sundown Sunday, she'd have to shift gears and break in. Quit cruising at this too-enjoyable speed.

She pressed her fingers to her abdomen, over the scar Yevgen Liski had given her during the Monet job. The psychopath had tattooed a knife on his forearm—a copy of the weapon he'd used on Clementine—proud of the work he'd done. He'd trailed her one day and flashed it while on a subway platform. A scare tactic, likely. Or for his insane thrills. The incident was a reminder of what happened when she failed.

Getting to know Jack and his reptile shelter was a luxury she couldn't overindulge. Mistakes on a job had consequences.

Lucien: **Your con, your rules. Call me in the morning with an update.**

She would, but something about reporting on Jack felt dirty.

"What can I get ya, honey?"

Clementine perked up at the familiar voice. "Imelda?"

"Last I checked."

"I thought you worked at the diner and walked dogs." God, this town was on the miniscule side of small.

Imelda shone her knuckles on her shirt. "I'm a woman of many talents, who gets bored and likes to keep busy."

Imelda looked less doll-like tonight, her usual powder-blue diner uniform swapped for a plaid button-down, positioned to hint at cleavage. It was the same cowgirl look worn by the other servers.

Imelda blew a wayward curl from her forehead. "Plus, my husband comes in and pretends to pick me up. Makes for good fun."

"Can't argue with that. And I'll have a stout, if you have one on tap." Anything rich and dark with a hint of bitterness. Something to pucker her tongue so she'd stop wondering what Jack tasted like.

Imelda nodded and went to work.

Clementine watched a man and woman playing pool. They brushed shoulders, giggled, and traded teasing smiles. So at ease with each other. No concern for who was watching them or hiding their feelings. Maybe they were married or flirting for the first time. No. Married. Their rings caught the light, winking secretly at each other. Such a bond, to pledge yourself to someone. Too often, people took it for granted. Vows were tossed around as readily as salutations, off the cuff, on a whim, because it felt good *now*. The world had become a culture of *right now*.

The need for immediate gratification felt diluted in Whichway. Aside from Jack's luxury automobiles, no one seemed to compete for fanciest car or trendiest clothes, the relaxed vibe of this bar proof enough. Everything moved slower, actions more meaningful. Smiles were real. Hellos were genuine. Clementine had never considered leaving New York. Now...she didn't know.

What would it be like to nest in Whichway and sip coffee at the Who's It Café and run at Wherever Park and drink beer at Whenever and eat apple turnovers at the Whatnot Diner on the fly? She rolled her eyes at the idea. It was a selfish daydream. Ridiculous.

Imelda pushed the stout toward her. "Someone's got an admirer."

"Admirer?" Clementine said, playing the innocent. But, oh yeah, she felt those aquamarine eyes all over her. The awareness came with a sting of self-rebuke. Jack had been all she'd focused on since walking in here. She'd scanned the exits, had done a half-assed sweep of the patrons and texted Lucien, but Jack's unrelenting stare had reduced her to a tingly mess while she'd gaped starry-eyed at couples playing pool.

Imelda waved her fingers playfully. "Oh, go on now. Don't tell me you haven't noticed a certain dark-haired man's attention. He can't take his eyes off you, and I've seen you two at the diner, close but not close, testing the waters like a couple lovesick teens."

"Imelda!"

"What? The tension's thick enough to carve."

"I'm here for the festival, not to date." She was also there to lie to everyone's faces while deceiving the first man in a lifetime to make her feel real. She sipped her beer, the bitterness more pronounced than usual.

Imelda harrumphed loud enough to be heard over the country tunes. "He's still a fine male specimen."

"I can't argue with that." Or with the way her body responded to his proximity. Not turning around was a Herculean effort.

"Hard to believe that tall drink of whiskey was once all elbows and knees."

Clementine nearly choked on her beer. "There's no way."

"God's honest truth."

"Like, gawky *but* handsome?"

Another waitress, with a halo of tight red curls and big green eyes, poked her head over Imelda's shoulder. "Oh, girl. Not even close. As awkward as a newborn foal. The handsome bug didn't bite his sweet ass until college." She winked at Clementine. "I'm Tami."

"Lovely to meet you, Tami. I'm Clementine, and you've got to be shitting me."

Jack wasn't just cute. He was classic and masculine, fit and tall with those damn teasing dimples. He was an immortal among men. Maybe that was taking things a tad far, but the man was universally handsome.

Tami leaned on her elbows, a conspiratorial look in her eyes. "Picture that slice of hunk pie with braces and acne and glasses, and a preppy wardrobe suited to the fifties, all wrapped up with the self-confidence of a shamed turtle."

"It doesn't seem possible." Except for the self-confidence part.

Tami sighed. "Every woman in Whichway curses herself for teasing the poor colt. But who would have guessed he'd turn into that?" She gestured angrily toward him, like his handsome pissed her off. "And if what Melissa says is true…"

"Just gossip, Tami Troublemaker." Imelda nudged her coworker's elbow. "Don't go spreading lies."

"You sayin' you ain't heard the same?"

Clementine raised her hand. "I haven't heard anything, and I'm literally dying of curiosity." She pretended to wilt off her stool.

The girls laughed.

Clementine laughed.

Actually laughed. Easily and openly, as though it were the most natural thing in the world to laugh in this bar where husbands and wives played pool and she gossiped with pseudo-friends. Unlike that terrible girls' night, this effortless reality was her *right now*: a careless stop on the highway, a foolish toss of her real name, laughter with women who misguidedly trusted her. All frivolous choices, each made because they'd felt good in the moment, no thought to the consequences.

She didn't want her *right now* to stop.

A man hollered for a beer. Another table did the same. Tami glared at them. "Y'all just bridle your horses. We're talking life changing stuff here." Attention back on Clementine, she lowered her voice. "As far as I heard it, that late bloomer is a thoroughbred between the sheets."

Clementine's belly tightened.

Imelda tutted. "Utter nonsense."

"Everyone knows it, Imelda."

"Considering he hasn't been with anyone in town but Melissa Axelrod, who moved away years back, I'd say your sources are questionable."

Clementine could barely feel her lips. She couldn't stop imagining Jack's bedroom prowess, with her as the eager participant. *Right now. I want that right now.* She pressed her hand to her belly. "You know who he's slept with in town?"

Imelda slapped the counter and laughed. "Oh, honey. We know who everyone's slept with in town."

Tami stared her friend down, still intent on proving her point. "This ain't some twattle-basket, Imelda. I heard it from Lori Mae's cousin, who knows Emma, whose sister's best friend went to college with that slab of male perfection. He dated a girl there who, and I quote: 'still ain't recovered from sleepin' with him.' Claims he's why she can't find herself a real man. So you, dear Clementine, need to claim Jack David so we can live vicariously through you."

Imelda rolled her eyes. "Shush, you. I love my husband, and you've been stupid over yours since tenth grade."

"Did I say I wasn't? And the man of the hour is intent on you," she told Clementine.

Clementine was too busy processing the notion of Sex Expert Jack, to pay attention to Tami. *Thoroughbred between the sheets.* Like she needed to find him more attractive.

When the thoroughbred in question appeared at her side, her cheeks heated.

"Mind if I take a seat?" he asked as he slipped onto the stool beside hers.

Mind if I take you home? Clementine bit her tongue before she said that or worse. "Yeah. Sure. I don't own the place." If she didn't get a grip, she'd blow this entire job. And Jack. Fresh fire scorched her face.

Imelda and Tami busied themselves with work, while Jack rested his elbows on the bar. He cradled his beer with both hands and moved his thumb up and down the side. It was a simple motion that had become anything but simple, thanks to Tami's gossip. That damn thumb was all kinds of erotic.

"You seem to be everywhere," he said.

"That would be physically impossible."

His seductive thumb-bottle rubbing persisted. "Let me rephrase: you seem to be everywhere that I am."

Once again, his acute observations cut too close to the bone. "You have seen the size of this town, right?"

He smirked. "It's not large."

"That's one way of putting it. And maybe I like running with you and sharing our morning coffee."

And hearing the slight lilt that twanged the ends of his words and how impassioned he was about his animal shelter and how liberating it was to share real details about herself. She liked a whole lot about Jack David, Tami's meddling only upping his appeal. This was no longer a role. She wasn't acting with him. All the lines were blurring, her commitment to finishing this job just as strong as her need to finish whatever she'd begun with Jack.

She leaned into him, could smell malt and hops and heat on his breath. "Tell me a secret, Not-Maxwell Jack David."

THAT WAS A DARING QUESTION, one Jack wasn't sure how to answer. Sharing that he wanted her wouldn't be new. He'd admitted that secret when serenading her in his shelter. She also knew he'd planned to keep away. And he'd tried, dammit. He'd sat there with Marco, his beer bottle close to shattering under his unforgiving grip. He'd watched, pained, as she'd joked with Imelda and Tami, as though she belonged on that stool, in this bar, in his town.

He hadn't liked Tami talking to her much. That woman meddled worse than Marco and knew about the high school dance disaster, and the arrest he'd rather forget. That two-week period of his life had been something out of a "Just Say No" school assembly. It was partly responsible for Jack's awkwardness with women now, but he didn't fixate on it or ever discuss it. Kids were cruel. Shit happened. Dwelling on setbacks didn't breed happiness. It didn't mean he'd liked Tami chattering to Clementine.

He disliked that bearded man eyeing her even more.

The stranger had texted on his phone while occasionally watching her, innocent by all accounts. But Jack kept picturing him walking over, buying her a drink, taking her home. Jack was up and out of his seat before Marco could ask where he was heading. To Clementine. To a woman who wasn't his but shouldn't be anyone else's.

Now she wanted him to share more than reptile facts and polite conversation. An urge tugged below his skin, to tell her about David Industries and his father's cancer, details he hadn't even shared with Marco. The pull was confusing and hard to fight.

"I stuttered as a child," he told her. Not the thing he wanted to say. The safe thing, though still difficult. "It got worse in my teens, made those years hard for me—which I'm guessing Tami told you about."

Clementine had the decency to look guilty. "She might have mentioned something."

"I can always count on her."

"You don't stutter now."

"Speech therapy helped, but ultimately, singing cured me. Focusing on the notes and rhythms loosened something in my brain. I've never seen my father so proud as the day I sang an Elvis song start to finish, not a stutter in sight." *Don't ever stop singing, son,* he'd said. *Hearing your voice brings me joy.* Jack hoped it would bring him that and more at this year's festival, as long as he completed his research.

Clementine angled more fully toward him. "Tell me another."

Her eyes kept flitting to his thumb, making him aware of his absentminded movements. She made him aware of the speed of his breaths—deeper and faster since sitting beside her. He'd become attuned to the chafing of his jeans along his thighs, the pressure of his laced boots. With her, all his senses heightened.

His thumb slid up and down his beer, drawing a slow circle, moving the condensation around. Was that a whimper from dear Clementine?

He smiled to himself. "I'll give you another secret if you give me one of yours."

The tiniest flinch darkened her face. "Who says I have secrets?"

A shaky question from a woman who'd lied about her name. "Here I was, just starting to like you, and you go being annoying again."

She glanced around dramatically. "Who, *me*?"

"No. The other mysterious woman with strawberry-blonde hair and a bearded dragon named Lucy."

"Does this kind of flattery get you far with the ladies?"

"If you listened to Tami, you'd know the answer to that."

A covert smile tilted her lips. "Want a tip?"

"I'm all ears." He was curious where Clementine was going with that sultry look of hers, the intimate drop in her tone.

She leaned in close, her warm breath ghosting against his lips. "From one idiot to another: when a girl avoids a question, calling her annoying won't help your cause."

He nodded sagely. "Who said I had a cause?"

She shrugged a shoulder, nursed a slow sip of her beer.

He mirrored her pose, facing the bar. Their thighs brushed slightly, and he continued dragging his thumb up and down his bottle. She passed her beer back and forth between her hands, leaving a wet streak on the bar. They snuck a look at each other at the same moment. He raised an eyebrow.

She rolled her eyes, then sighed. "I'm the reason my mother died of an overdose."

It was his turn to flinch. She'd offered her startling truth pragmatically, no more emotion than if she'd said *I don't step on sidewalk cracks* or *I've never eaten an oyster.*

"How was it your fault?"

"My father died the year before," she said, still matter-of-fact. Emotionless. "My mother worked two jobs, barely keeping up with bills. We'd moved to an apartment and our rent was behind. I was ten and fending for myself."

"Did you have siblings?"

She shook her head. "An only child, and not a very smart one. All the idiot awards belong to me."

"I find that impossible to believe." He wanted to fold her in his arms, let his warmth dull the bite of her painful memories.

A sad smile cracked her stoic façade. "I fucked up heating pasta sauce, so, yeah—idiot of the century. I forgot that I put the pot on the stove to reheat. Got busy reading one of my father's old car magazines. I pored over them like him, desperate to learn everything I could about classic cars, learn what he knew. It wasn't until smoke filled my room and the fire alarm blared that I remembered. Then our landlady came banging on the door. When she realized I was home alone, about to start a fire, she called child services."

"They took you from your mother?"

She stared dead ahead. "They didn't care that she was the only family I had. Just ripped me out and tossed me in the foster system. Six or so months later, I got the news. She'd OD'd. Couldn't handle life without me. All because I burned pasta sauce." Although her voice had remained impassive,

Clementine was all hard lines and edges, as though readying herself to withstand a blast of wind.

He couldn't fathom what she'd endured, but her resilience was as fierce as her posture, and gratitude swamped him. Sharing this brittle piece of herself had taken trust. "I could tell you it's not your fault, that a ten-year-old shouldn't have to remember to stir her pasta sauce, but that won't change the past." When she remained impassive, he leaned toward her ear. "I don't know what you're like at work or how you live your life, but I see a strong woman who fixes cars and keeps pace with my superior jogging and who loves her bearded dragon unselfishly, even if she's annoyingly secretive at times. If I had to guess, I'd say you're not a woman who's risen above her past. I'd say you've risen *because* of it."

She closed her eyes and exhaled.

He frowned. Had he said the wrong thing? Of course he'd said the wrong thing. It was in his DNA to say the wrong thing to women. But when she faced him and opened her eyes, the glassiness and lift of her brow told him that *just maybe* this time he'd said something right.

"Tell me another secret," she whispered.

This one left before he could contain it. "I want to kiss you."

10

———

CLEMENTINE ALMOST SLID off her stool. Boneless. He'd turned her boneless with nothing but five words. No, not five. Every word he'd just offered had loosened the bitter hold she kept on her past. Lucien, the only other person who knew her story, had never given her that kind of salve. He'd told her to forget it, that it wasn't her fault. That the system was to blame. Yet here was Jack, telling her to embrace her awful, not bury it. Accept what had happened, her fault or not, the system's fault or not. Accept it and live with it and let it shape you.

Now he wanted to kiss her.

God, she wanted that, and so much more. To experience sex with someone who knew pieces of her puzzle, who didn't pity her but lifted her up. If he got his skilled hands on her, she feared and thrilled at what could happen.

The burning desire shot her back in time, to them standing over his stalled Jaguar.

"You're certainly good with your hands," he'd said.

"Best if one of us is, or you'd be stuck waiting for a tow."

"I didn't say I wasn't good with my hands."

"You can't fix your own car."

"I'm good at other things."

Other things. What things? All the things? Some things? Which damn things? "You said you couldn't ask me on a date," she said, voice shaky. A pitiful attempt to force their distance.

She'd kissed marks on a job before. She would play up her prude innocence and nothing more would happen. Rich men, she'd learned, found a hard-to-get woman enticing. A change from gold-diggers hunting for prey. After locating her targeted loot, she'd then feign illness and thank her dates, never to return their calls. A week or month or two later, she'd sneak in and secure her score.

No residual guilt. No longing for what could have been.

Kissing Not-Maxwell Elvis Jack David would wreck her. She knew it. She wasn't sure she could avoid it, or even worse, fight it.

"I did say that, didn't I?" Jack mused, unaware of her turmoil. Or maybe he was aware. It was impossible to hide her trembling limbs. "But kissing isn't dating, is it?"

"You're suddenly forward." As hard as Shy Jack was to resist, Bold Jack was proving more challenging.

"Thing is," he said, back to drawing sexy bottle circles, not meeting her eyes. "I'm painfully awkward around beautiful women, which is why I've been curt with you at times and generally artless. But when I get comfortable with someone, when trust takes over the nerves"—he looked at her then, right into her eyes—"when that happens, the confidence I feel as Elvis on stage bleeds into my life."

He continued staring at her, unabashed, no wobble or skittishness in sight. Shivers erupted along her arms.

This is who I am, his piercing blue eyes said.

I like you. I trust you. I want to kiss you.

Exactly how she felt—accepted. Maybe because she'd

shared more details of herself with him than she had with any other man. Maybe it was Tami and Imelda's meddling and the desire it had stirred. Or maybe it was learning Jack's handsomeness hadn't been bestowed upon him flippantly, like those kids who were placed on pedestals, told time and again: *this one will break hearts.* Jack's devastating looks had been earned through humility, his strong body probably honed to forget his knobby limbs had once let him down.

She couldn't, for the life of her, contemplate letting him down. "I think it depends on the kissing," she said, breathless.

"Excellent point." He hummed, still focused on her.

She struggled to fill her lungs.

He smirked knowingly. "Let's say, for argument's sake, that I kiss your cheek. Would that be considered acceptable? A non-date kiss?"

The mentioned spot tingled with anticipation. "I believe that would be allowed."

"And the crescent-moon scar on your shoulder?"

A shaky "yes" was all she managed.

"And the three freckles on your nose, and the birthmark just below your right collarbone, and the one on the back of your neck, that lines up with your spine?" He said all of this with his eyes locked on hers, confident in his seduction. He'd been studying her body without doing so overtly. No different than the way she'd snuck glances of his strapping physique while they'd been running or when emphasized in his tailored suits. Both of them had been lusting from the sidelines.

She shifted closer to him. "Only if I can kiss your jaw and the soft spot below your ear, where your skin meets your hair."

He grunted, rough and low. Their staring game continued until he wrenched his gaze away and pulled out his wallet. Money slapped on the bar, he grabbed Clementine's hand and hauled her off her stool. She heard a lewd comment from Tami or Imelda, but she didn't care. She followed Jack willingly, around the tables and through the doors, into the unexpectedly thrilling night.

Gravel crunched under their hurried steps. A car exited the lot, the bass of a rock song fading as it disappeared. Jack guided her toward the side of the bar and stopped in a darkened spot. An outdoor light cast the tiniest sliver of light. She inhaled woodsy scents from the adjacent forest.

She inhaled all things Jack. Cold, spicy, icicles. "You always smell so fresh," she said as he pressed her back against Whenever's wooden exterior.

He released her hand to cup her face, brushed his thumbs along her cheeks. "Not when we're running."

"Even better then. Fresh and dirty at once."

His eyes darkened at that. He traced a spot below her collarbone. "Here," he murmured as though lost in a fog. He lowered his head and ran his nose where his fingers had feathered. His lips followed, an erotic press of his mouth to her skin.

Her breasts felt heavy and full, the ache spreading south.

"Here," he repeated, moving to her shoulder. His tongue came out to play this time, tracing her crescent-moon scar. An unpleasant memory surfaced: the edge of a car lighter held against her skin. But his lips painted her scar with tenderness. A kiss to her neck. A kiss to the top of her breast. One to the bridge of her nose, his warm breath excruciating as it teased her lips. She needed to breathe his breath. Inhale him and his kindness. His whole heart. She needed to breathe him in and never exhale.

He flipped her around, pressed her front into the rough wood, his chest heavy against her back. The feel of his hard length nestled against the top of her ass had her seeing stars.

"Jack." His name was a plea. For what, she wasn't sure. *Right now. I want this right now forever.*

"Hush, my dear Clementine." He brushed her hair to the side, found the birthmark he'd mentioned, now tingling under his light touch.

Tears sprung to her eyes. She was sad, happy, turned on, overwhelmed to have this caring man treat her with such reverence. Her throat clogged with emotion. Her skin was on fire. When he finally kissed the apex of her spine, the rest of his body moved back, pulling away so his mouth could reach her skin, and a tear slipped out, the loss of his body and feel of his wet lips too conflicting. *I'm losing him. I'm gaining him. I'm lying to him.*

He flipped her back around and wiped the tear that had escaped. He spread the saltiness on her lips. "I think you need one here, too."

She nodded, too terrified to speak and break this spell.

His breath faltered as he neared, the swell of his chest expanding into hers. He slipped a hand into the hair at her nape and swiftly claimed her, lips on lips, tongue against tongue. A sweet kiss that turned disrespectful quickly. She hadn't expected his aggressive taking or how his hands and body moved as though controlled by their lips. He rocked into her, his hands everywhere, kneading and groping, then coasting up to her neck, anything he could grasp. She was no less demanding. She dug her fingers into the meaty muscles of his back, practically tearing at his soft T-shirt.

Kissing Jack was a new kind of adrenaline rush, better than the thrill of cutting an alarm or slipping past security or nabbing a Picasso or Rembrandt or Jackson Pollock.

He wedged his thigh between hers, lifting her slightly, an anchor of lust pinning her to the wall. *Pin me. Take me. Keep me.*

Another surprising tear slipped out.

He slowed then, lowered his thigh and hands. He gave her one more luxurious kiss, then stepped back. "I got carried away."

Judging by the sharp angle behind his fly, he was as overworked as her. "I wanted you to get carried away." She dried her cheeks, embarrassed by the wetness. "I'm not one of those girls, by the way. I never get all emotional and cry."

He tipped his head to the side. "With the right person, it feels good to let go."

It felt better than good, especially since he always knew the right thing to say. "That wasn't a non-date kiss." Her lips would tingle all night.

"No, it wasn't."

He didn't offer more, and she didn't initiate. How could she when she'd been tailing him and reporting his actions to Lucien, intent on stealing from his family? A fact she needed to rethink. Supporting poverty-stricken orphans and charities no longer felt like it excused her illicit activity. Everything once certain now felt very uncertain. Jack seemed hesitant, too. This festival performance was obviously a big deal to him. Performing on stage, stutter free, must be a yearly milestone. That left them thoroughly kissed and turned on, no release in sight.

The daunting task of explaining her wavering to Lucien—that she might not be able to complete this job—curbed her desire further.

"I should get home," she said. "Back to my motel."

Jack didn't move, only licked his lips. "I don't run on Saturdays, but I do on Sundays. Later, at ten."

She already knew this. She'd studied the ins and outs of his weekly schedule. The knowledge was another hefty blow. "You still want my company?" *Say no. Please say no.*

"More than I should."

Exactly her predicament. "I'll try to meet you."

She straightened her shirt and walked toward her car, unease hurrying her steps. Sunday morning was in a day and a half. Not long to figure out her next move. Unravel her confusion, because this distraction was a harsh reminder of how south a job could go. Last time she'd been this conflicted over a heist, it had gotten a man killed, and she had nearly died.

11

—————

FIVE YEARS ago Clementine had come to a proverbial fork in the road. The criminality of her work had weighed on her, the isolation of her life turning her into Mrs. Grinch. On her worst day, she wandered through Central Park as families lounged and couples walked, envy a fierce tug on her heart. It was like the world was only inhabited by pairs and sums. Answers to equations. *One plus one equals happy.*

She was supposed to scout her mark that day, implementing Lucien's plan for a local heist—the incognito sort where she'd wear a prosthetic nose, makeup, and a wig. She'd been tasked with charming Eddie Cohen and acquiring his stunning Monet. Instead of insinuating herself into the wealthy prosecutor's life, she'd been perfecting her Grinch scowl.

Lucien, always attuned to her behavior, invited her for dinner. "I'm making lasagna and garlic bread."

She never said no to lasagna.

His apartment was small but nice. Sinatra played on the stereo as he poured her wine and dished out food. He asked about her Charger's rebuild, the way he used to grill her on math and history, but he wore reading glasses when looking at pictures on her phone. His sight had been deteriorating recently, his cropped hair more silver than auburn, the top thinner than ever. He was still fit and lean, his staunch diet and exercise regime maintained with military precision, when not spoiling Clementine with yummy Italian food, but his age was showing.

Lucien would die eventually. She'd be less than an integer then. Just a fraction of a fraction.

Lucien removed his glasses and leaned his elbows on his thighs. "What's bothering you, Kumquat?"

"The fact that you call me Kumquat."

"Better than Nanfeng-Miju. And you're evading. What's wrong?"

She snuggled into the corner of his plush couch and sighed. "I don't know."

"I think you do."

He knew her too well, and she was being a coward. She sat straighter and took a fortifying breath. "Is what we do really making the world better? We're feeding America's criminal underbelly. The people who fence our art make cash off us. It keeps them in business, which means criminals who wouldn't think twice about killing to make a score use their services. We're perpetuating the system. And we steal, for God's sake. Wrap it up in whatever pretty picture you want, paint our victims as degenerate, millionaire assholes—we still steal."

Her last words vibrated in the airy space, clanging with her need to purge the stresses invading her recent sleepless nights.

Lucien didn't flinch, only tipped his head slightly. "What would happen to Nisha if we quit funding that orphanage?"

She pictured Nisha's scarred arms, the overcrowded

building the little girl had called home. "She would land back on the streets."

"And where is she now?"

Clementine glanced at the mantel above his fireplace, at the framed photos depicting their successes. Nisha held a fat tomato in one shot, big smile on her face. "She works at the orphanage's greenhouse."

"And how did that greenhouse get built?"

"With our money."

"And you still think our work is meaningless?"

"We could do it legally. Start a charity, get donations."

He waved his hand as though swatting flies. "You know very well I've tried that."

He didn't explain again. He'd gone over it a thousand times. Lucien had headed corporate charities, pulling in millions for Fortune 500 companies, so they could say they contributed to society. It was there Lucien had learned money often went unaccounted for. Even if the charities were on the up-and-up, huge percentages paid staff and overhead before a dime made it to their end goal. Red tape meant progress was slowed and often kyboshed. Aggravation had pushed him to take matters into his own hands. She knew the stories. It didn't frustrate her any less.

"I'm just so tired," she said.

"I understand, but there's another issue to consider. Yevgen Liski is in town."

Oh, hell no. "Are you sure?"

Lucien rubbed the bridge of his nose. "Rumbles have drifted from the streets. If he's here for the same Monet, you know how that will go."

Bloody was how it would go. Yevgen Liski may have been ten years older than Clementine, but his maturity hovered around twelve-year-old psychopath. To him, torturing victims was as exciting as an all-expenses-paid, all-inclusive vacation. Pets were dismembered for shits and giggles. Toes and fingers were left in jewelry boxes. He wore a string of teeth around his neck. *Human fucking teeth.* Twice now, Yevgen had lost scores to Clementine, and rumor had it he was pissed.

All that Yevgen represented had Clementine hugging her knees tighter.

"You are perfection at what you do, Tangerine."

She didn't answer.

"With your finesse, no one will get hurt. The money will save lives."

Shallow breaths tightened her chest.

When her silence continued, Lucien scooted closer and took her hands in his. "If this really is too much for you, if you can't continue, it's okay. I'll find someone else to work with, another protégé to train."

Those shallow breaths roughened. Her attention flicked between his thinning hair and his reading glasses on the table. If he cut her loose and found someone else, their dinners would dwindle. His calls would decrease. They wouldn't lose touch exactly, but like any family, blood related or not, life would get in the way. The work check-ins would cease. He'd be busy with a new partner and new heists, and he wouldn't discuss illegal dealings with Clementine. They'd go from communicating daily to weekly or less. Where would that leave her?

"Yes," she said quickly. "I've just been feeling off lately—not myself. Of course I'll do it."

He smiled and patted her hand. "That's my girl."

By then her window to seduce their mark had come and gone. That left breaking in. Eddie Cohen would be out of town for the night. One evening to execute the heist. They didn't know on which of the three floors the Monet was hung, so she'd have to wing it.

Unease edged her movements as she dressed in her burgling uniform: black clothing that wouldn't catch on anything, hair secured in a tight bun. Just another day at the office. Feeling skittish, she did some shadow boxing, but her punches lacked conviction and nerves continued buzzing through her. She wasn't sure if her lingering ambivalence had sparked her anxiety, or maybe talk of Yevgen and his grizzly ways had infected her.

She waited a bit longer, hoping it would pass.

It didn't.

Her head mostly in the game, she drove to the brownstone and checked for signs of life. Eddie Cohen's car was gone. There wasn't a flicker of movement in those pre-dawn hours. She picked his lock and slipped inside, tools ready to disengage his alarm, her tranquilizer secured on her hip for his dog. But the alarm didn't sound. Something sharp and coppery stung her nostrils. She studied the room and slapped her hand over her mouth.

Eddie's poodle was on the floor, bleeding all over the expensive oak.

Goddamn Yevgen.

The bastard had beaten her to the punch, sacrificing the dog *just because*. She would have used the tranquilizer if need be, quick, efficient, safe. But she'd delayed the entire plan and tonight's work. Now there was a dead dog and the painting was likely gone.

Disgusted with herself and her failure, she turned to leave, but heard a scream.

The Monet's owner?

Eddie Cohen was supposed to be out. She'd double checked his car was gone, hadn't she? Yes. Fuck, *yes*. She was sure she had, but there was no mistaking that terrified cry. Before she thought better of it, she bolted up the stairs...to do what? Help the man she'd planned to rob? Fight off Yevgen, who was three times her size? Her heart thrashed as she ran.

Then she was falling.

Something had hit her head. Hard. Crunching. A blinding blow. The stairs skidded from under her, the world tipping upside down. Her ankle crunched. Her shoulder snapped from its socket. The landing knocked the wind out of her, a deafening *smack* on the hardwood floor. She couldn't move. Spots flared in her vision.

"Stupid little girl." The accented words sounded fuzzy.

She tried to breathe and clawed at her throat. Had something punctured her lung? *Run,* she mentally screamed. *Run, run, run.* She barely twitched, and pain sliced through her.

Yevgen lowered to her side, his foul breath hot on her cheek. She tried to relax and access her self-defense training. She imagined her hand striking out, her fingers gouging Yevgen's eyes. All she managed was to clutch his shirt. She heard a rip, at least. Her nails bit into flesh.

He snarled. "Still so much fight, but not enough. This is what happens when you try to steal what's mine."

A sharp pain—new and deeper—tore across her abdomen, and a feral sound escaped her lips. Jesus Christ. The asshole had jammed a knife into her stomach, stabbed her without a thought, and she couldn't catch her breath or fight back. Her saliva gurgled in her throat.

Yevgen leaned down real close. "Next time I'll finish the job...and finish your handler. Lucien? Is that his name?" At her whimper, he grinned. "No one you love will ever be safe."

She lost consciousness there, didn't rouse until much later, in Lucien's home, tended by his private doctor. "Don't scare me like that, Grapefruit," he said, his voice wobbly.

Lucien never wobbled. He was her rock.

"How?" she croaked, tears gathering in her eyes. *Did you find me,* she tried to finish but the pain stole her words.

He stroked her hair. "I followed you. You still seemed off and I was worried. With the Yevgen rumors and your state of mind, I needed to be cautious."

She forced saliva down her throat. If felt like swallowing battery acid. "The man? Eddie?"

Lucien dropped his gaze. "Eddie Cohen is dead."

Because of her. Because she'd gotten distracted and had delayed.

Bruised and battered and throbbing with pain, she closed her eyes and cried for a man she didn't know. She cried for the girl who'd wanted to grow up and fix cars to impress her dad.

Clementine made a promise to herself that day never to let personal issues interfere with her work. She was a burglar. It was what she'd become. She did it safer than most and helped better the world with her earnings. A small piece of plaid was her token—Yevgen's torn shirt dirtied with both their blood. A reminder to never again let Lucien down, or have another person's blood on her hands.

Yet here she was, in Whichway, five years later, her personal life eclipsing her job.

After kissing Jack, she'd reverted to giggly teenager status. She'd stayed up half the night, alternating between touching her lips and smiling and cursing herself for being soft. She'd woken once, hot and sweaty, sure Jack's hard body was on top of hers. She'd even fantasized about quitting her work and moving to Whichway to live with Jack and their reptiles. Clementine *David* did have a nice ring to it.

She watched the digital clock on her nightstand now, unsure how she'd last until she saw Jack again tomorrow morning, unable to curb the desire. *Only thirty hours to go!*

Restless, she did sit-ups and push-ups and practiced yoga. She maybe did a *Flashdance* stationary run. She wrote her dad a pathetically gushy email, detailing Jack's singing voice, his whispering voice, his shy voice, his teasing voice, his bold voice. Jack's obvious affection for her.

She refolded all her clothing, spending extra time on the tank top she'd worn the night before. She stuck her face in it. *Giggly teenager status.* It smelled faintly of Jack, fresh yet woodsy from the wall he'd had her up against.

She needed to get a grip. He was her mark, not her teenage crush. She was well aware of consequences when distracted on a job. And she'd promised Lucien she'd call.

Unless she didn't check in. Unless she walked away from it all.

If she told Lucien she wanted out, that she was done with their life of crime, he'd wish her well. He'd move on, as he'd promised he would five years ago. She was stronger now, but it would mean abandoning girls like Nisha, and the notion of quitting Lucien still pained her. Especially with so many uncertainties. If she pursued Jack and their fledgling feelings fizzled, or he realized she was more damaged than a salvage yard of crushed cars, *or* if he learned she'd been a criminal *these past ten years*, he'd probably run the other way or turn her in.

If their connection and attraction turned into love and he didn't suspect anything about her past, could she, in good conscience, continue her lies? Never tell him what she was?

Her mind knotted tighter.

Until she untangled it all, she'd keep her options open. She'd tell Lucien about tomorrow's running date and that the plan was moving ahead. She'd spend time with Jack and get to know him and maybe kiss his kissable lips. She'd find the elusive Van Gogh, just to be safe. Somehow, she'd figure out what to do.

12

─────────

Clementine pulled on her socks and running shoes, like it was a normal morning. She cleared her laptop's history and tucked it in her briefcase, then she laid a fine thread over the bag—a precaution Lucien had drilled in. She may have been unfocused this job, but some habits were ingrained: leave a pen sticking up, a business card pressed between the leather. Anything to indicate if someone had touched her belongings.

Her incriminating folders were hidden and locked in her car. Nothing here would set off red flags, but she'd been using the Do Not Disturb sign anyway. She'd fetched her own towels and toilet paper. She would know if someone was snooping around.

Precautions in place, she drove to meet her running date and tried not to get too excited. She failed miserably.

She stretched her quads by Wherever Park's bridge, adjusted her sports bra and pink tank top. Ten a.m. came and went. Clouds darkened the sky as she stretched some more. She replayed Jack's last words to her, how he had wanted her company more than he should. It had been the sentiment of a man who'd keep their date.

Nerves took a bite out of her happy.

He could have panicked and decided he couldn't jog with a festival judge. He could have found out who she really was. He could be talking to the cops now, and orange was so not her color. Or something important could have come up—unrelated to her because she was clearly narcissistic—and he'd had no choice but to bail. They hadn't even exchanged phone numbers for him to call. No need when she conveniently appeared wherever he was, eager to hang out.

"Clementine!" Imelda waved at her, only one dog on a leash today. The ancient Labrador Retriever dragged his feet, his coat more gray than black. His thick middle suggested Imelda didn't walk him enough. "You, honey, owe me big time," Imelda said as they walked her way.

"How's that?"

"Tami just about died when Jack dragged you from the bar Friday night. Almost busted my ear drum with her squawking. Please tell me my hearing loss was worth it."

Considering Jack hadn't shown for their morning run, she wasn't sure. "I don't kiss and tell."

"Does that mean there was a kiss?"

Dammit. The stupid saying had just slipped off her tongue. Now Imelda scented fresh blood, her and Tami their own breed of canines: Gossip Hounds. "There's nothing to tell. He's sweet, is all."

"And hot as Lou Anne Baker's award-winning chili."

Clementine snorted. "I think we established that Friday night."

Imelda unclipped the dog's leash and clucked at him. "Go on, Colonel Blue. Take a drink from the pond." Colonel Blue did as asked, lumbering his lumpy body to the water. Ducks quacked and slapped the surface in their retreat. Imelda zipped up her windbreaker. "Rains are about to break."

They sure were, judging by the dropping temperature. Clementine had expected to be running by now, working up a sweat. Instead she was shivering in her shorts and tank top, wondering where Jack was. She'd planned to work on him while jogging, finagle an invite to the estate. Keeping her options open meant continuing with her plan. She shivered harder.

Imelda called to Colonel Blue again, warning him not to terrorize the ducks. Clementine stared at the dog and narrowed her eyes, something about the pup's name familiar. *Blue. Blue. Colonel Blue.* She knew that name. She'd heard it somewhere...

Her pulse sped up. "Is that Jack's father's dog?"

Imelda nodded. "I've walked him since Mr. David left the country. His wife's busy with their younger daughter, and Blue's arthritis means he needs slower solo walks. I take him three days a week."

Jack had a sister? He'd never mentioned her before, nor any details of his family members. Oddly enough, Clementine had shared more about her family than he'd divulged about his. That fact wedged itself beside the knowledge that he'd kind of stood her up. At least she now had a way into his family estate, her breakthrough in the form of an arthritic black Lab.

She smiled at Imelda. "I can finish the walk with you, if you don't mind company."

"Am I allowed to ask you about Jack?"

"Nope." She mimed locking her lips and tossing the key.

"You're a tough nut to crack, Clementine. Must be why I like you."

Warmth fizzed through her. First joking at the bar, now offering offhand compliments. If Clementine didn't know better, Imelda was becoming an actual friend.

"My husband forced me to watch *Pet Sematary* last night," Imelda said as they walked. "Now I can't look at Colonel Blue without seeing yellow eyes and sharp fangs."

"That old dog is harmless."

"Until someone brings him back from the dead."

Clementine laughed. "I stick to mechanic and car auction shows. Less nightmare inducing."

They also reminded her of her father. As an only child, before his depression had hit, Clementine had owned her father's affections. She'd sit on their driveway, legs crossed, sun-scorched asphalt burning her thighs while he'd worked on his car. Torque wrench. Ratchet extender. Nut splitter. She'd learned every tool used, passing them without hesitation, not a care to the grease on her hands. The memory made her smile.

"Don't tell my husband you watch those shows," Imelda said. "It will give him ideas, and car auctions sound worse than half-dead cats."

They walked and talked and joked, Imelda stopping periodically to scratch Colonel Blue's ears. They chatted about movies and books, easy impersonal topics. That didn't make the time any less meaningful.

By the time their walk ended, the sky was crazy dark, and Jack hadn't showed. There was nothing to do but follow her plan. "I'm heading toward the David estate. I could drop the Colonel for you."

Imelda waved her hand. "I couldn't ask you to do that."

"You didn't, and I don't mind." Clementine Abernathy, con artist, had returned. She was never far, after all, but this cloying guilt was new. Still, she persisted. "It's Sunday. Your family must be at home, waiting on you."

A large oak tree swayed in the rising winds. A few leaves drifted downward as Imelda glanced at her car. "You sure it wouldn't be a bother?"

"None at all. As long as the Davids wouldn't mind."

"That family's as kind as kittens. I just don't wanna put you out. Unless..." She smirked and planted her fist on her hip. "Are you hoping for a run-in with handsome Jack?"

Clementine rolled her eyes. "You're incorrigible." And kind of right. Jack David. Van Gogh. She had two works of art on her mind.

Imelda was all smiles now, pushing the leash into Clementine's hand. "Go on, then. Take Colonel Blue home, where you won't be looking for his human brother. And I expect details this time, honey. None of this locked mouth nonsense." She blew Clementine a kiss as she jogged to her car. "And do it before it pours. The sky's gonna rip open."

A rumble sounded, confirming Imelda's prediction.

Hunched to fight off the chill, Clementine coaxed the Colonel to her Prius and helped lift the old pup inside. This was it. She'd finally secured her ticket into the David estate. Excitement should've been coursing through her. Confusion abounded instead. She wasn't sure what she'd do once she located that Van Gogh. She wasn't sure what she'd do when she saw Jack again.

The rains held off, but the clouds hung lower. Shadows pressed on her car as she drove. Clementine navigated the winding drive into the David estate and gawked at the sheer size of it. The sprawling lawn was immaculate, normally tended by Marvin the Mower, who also fed Jack's reptiles. She liked knowing these details, little nothings that made her feel like she was on the inside: Imelda's daughter struggled with math, Jack's grandfather had been a roadie for Elvis, Tami had loved her husband since tenth grade. To her, those nothings felt like a whole lot of somethings.

She drove around a central fountain and parked in front of the entrance's stone steps. Where Jack's stunning bungalow was understated in its design, blending with its landscape, this mansion was designed to impress. Old-world stone and brick dominated the grounds, the prominent windows rising into triangular peaks. The front shrubbery was low, never distracting from the estate's power and wealth. The building was wide enough to house a football field.

She hadn't asked Jack why David Industries had recently fired employees. Admitting that knowledge might have prompted questions. Sitting here, though, absorbing the obscene property in all its ornate glory, she couldn't help the distaste that surfaced. Sell this monstrosity, and his family could have saved those jobs, quadrupled everyone's salaries.

"You live quite the charmed life. Don't you, Blue?" The old dog's stinky breath drifted from her backseat. Spoiled pup didn't know how good he had it. "Come on, then. You're my ticket in."

She helped him from the car and grimaced at the dog hairs sticking to her clothes. It was a treat that Lucy didn't shed. No cars lined the drive, anyone here likely having parked in the massive four-car garage. She led the Colonel up the front steps, unsure what would greet her. A butler? A maid? This place probably employed ten of each.

She stood in front of the massive wooden doors and searched for a doorbell. She rang it and gripped Blue's leash. The sky went from dark to foreboding. Another grumble rolled from the clouds. She rubbed her arms and rang the bell again.

Footsteps thumped from the opposite side, followed by a "coming." She rolled her shoulders back and plastered a smile on her face. The door creaked open a fraction. Jack filled her field of vision, sending her heart into pitter-patter land, until he frowned.

Her smile slipped.

He didn't open the door wider. "Why are you here?"

Seriously? He had ditched her and that was all he had? "Nice to see you, too."

He winced, rightfully so. "Sorry. I wasn't expecting you." He reverted to limited eye contact, his shifty gaze dropping to her not-warm-enough jogging attire. "I missed our run, didn't I?"

She shrugged, pretending the slight didn't sting. "No biggie. I met Imelda and Colonel Blue." She lifted the leash. "She had family stuff today, so I offered to drop him home." A raindrop smacked the stone step, punctuating her not-quite lie.

Jack didn't reply. He didn't explain this morning's absence or open the door and invite her in. If anything, he seemed bothered she was there. His dismissal shouldn't hurt. She shouldn't long for a man this careless with her feelings. They'd only kissed, after all. And she'd done nothing but lie to him. She had no right to feel scorned.

Yet here she was, hurt and scorned.

Well, screw him and her stupidity. His behavior proved it had been smart to keep her options open, not get carried away with fantasies of them falling in love and living happily ever after in this charming town. Ever Afters weren't meant for girls like her.

She glanced at the somber sky, prepared to see her heist through. "Mind if I come in? It's about to get ugly out here."

Jack didn't budge. "It's not a good time."

More rain fell. The door stayed wedged in place.

"It's not a good time to get me out of the rain?" She narrowed her eyes at him, only now noticing the dark circles under his eyes. He hadn't shaved, either. This was the first time she'd seen stubble on his usually clean-shaven cheeks. There was no denying the roughness increased his sex appeal, but his obvious exhaustion spun her irritation into worry. His unmoving stance didn't help. "Is everything okay, Jack?"

He swallowed and glanced behind him, into the house. He

scratched the back of his neck. "Fine. Just a long night." He held out his hand. For a moment her heart lifted. Was he finally softening and inviting her in? Then he said, "Thanks for bringing Blue home."

The leash. He wanted the leash, not her hand.

The next crack of thunder felt like a punch to her gut. She didn't try to get inside again. He obviously didn't want her there. He didn't want her, period.

More rain fell. The damp chill settled into her bones. He didn't even offer her a coat. Disgusted with herself for her ridiculous fantasies, she shoved the leash into his hand and ran toward her car, but the sky opened. The downpour soaked her hair and clothes in seconds. She thought she heard him call her name, but she didn't bother checking.

Get in the car.

Get to the motel.

Plan the break in.

That was all that was left to do.

By the time she jumped into her car, she was drenched and out of breath. Everything felt wet and ruined. She wiped at her face and wrung out her hair, but it didn't do any good. She turned the ignition with a hard flip of her wrist.

Banging made her jump.

Jack was at her window, miming for her to roll it down. She just stared at him. He probably wanted to set things straight, ask her to stop running with him and meeting him for coffee. She debated peeling away in her crappy Prius, but he looked pained standing there, hunched in the pouring rain. A glutton for punishment, she did as he asked.

He crouched lower, so they were face-to-face. Determination poured from him as wildly as the rain from the sky. "I'm sorry. I'm an asshole. You just caught me off guard, and there are things I haven't told you. Things no one in town knows. But I think you need to know, because I…" Streams pummeled the windshield. He raised his voice. "You just need to know. If you'll give me another chance, I'd like you to come in."

She shifted on her seat, her wet clothes squelching with the move. Jack was wetter than a drowned rat, not even bothering to wipe his face or hide his pleading. Humble Jack. Why couldn't he stay an asshole? She reached for him, tried to clear the water from his brow. He gripped her wrist and kissed the inside of her palm. "Please," he said. "Will you come in?"

"Yes," she replied. Not to get into his estate. Not to find that Van Gogh. *Yes, I'll help ease that troubled look from your eyes.*

13

———

JACK PRACTICALLY CARRIED Clementine inside the house. He did his best to shield her from the unrelenting rain, all the while cursing himself. So concerned for his father, he'd forgotten about their running date. He'd stood and paced and asked the nurse again and again what could be done. Forgetting his running date was one thing, but leaving Clementine standing in the rain?

That was unforgiveable.

He slammed the door behind them and smoothed the sopping hair from her face. "Stay here. I'll be right back."

She nodded while shivering. *Unforgiveable.*

He ran to the main floor linen closet, a trail of puddles left in his wake. His mother would give him hell. None of it mattered. He returned to Clementine, whose strawberry lips were tinged blue. *Unforgiveable.* He wrapped her in a large towel and led her to the bathroom.

"Jesus," she said, as they stepped inside. "Does someone live in here?"

The bathroom's two sinks, glassed-in shower, claw-foot tub,

and stacked laundry machines were normal to him. Clementine had grown up in the foster system, shuffled from house to house. He couldn't imagine how excessive it all looked to her.

"Take a hot shower," he said. "You can use the dryer for your things. I'll find you some clothes to wear and drop them inside." He motioned to the bench.

Still trembling, she nodded.

Jack ran upstairs and made quick work of drying himself off and changing, then raided his mother's closet for clean clothes. The shower was still running when he returned. He edged the door open, just far enough to drop the linen pants and T-shirt he'd brought. Music stopped him short. Humming. Clementine was humming "Can't Help Falling in Love"—the song he'd sung to her in his shelter. He closed his eyes and exhaled. Maybe she'd forgive his behavior after all.

He gripped the door to close it, but she said, "Jack?"

"Just leaving you clothes. There's a library down the hall. Head there when you're ready. I'll meet you as soon as I can." As soon as he explained to his mother why he had to tell Clementine the truth.

He could see Clementine's outline through the foggy glass. Head. Shoulders. Hips. She pressed her hand to the glass and dragged it down. The steamy heat slipped through his bloodstream.

"See you in the library," she said softly.

"The library," he murmured and escaped before he blurted how badly he'd like to join her in the shower.

He found his mother where he'd left her, curled up in a chair in his father's room. She rubbed her eyes. "Was that Imelda?"

"No. It's a friend."

"Marco?"

His father moaned in his sleep, and both their heads snapped toward him. Eric, their day nurse, lowered his *Billboard* magazine but didn't move. "You folks need to quit with the hovering. The new treatment is tough, but he's strong. He'll pull through."

It didn't feel that way when Jack's sister had called him, frantic, at three a.m., whispering things like *vomit* and *shaking* and *I'm so scared.* He'd tested his Tesla's power, driving faster than he should, only for his mother to berate him for coming. The night nurse had shooed them from Maxwell's room with tough love. "The effects are nasty, but necessary," she'd said. "Gotta kill the poison in him."

None of it made Jack feel any better.

Jack had offered to move in months ago, his proposal met by two glaring parents. Neither of them wanted him to change his life. He needed to sleep, they had claimed. To focus on work. He did need those things, but getting middle-of-the-night calls from his frantic sister made him rethink his priorities.

Lying to a beautiful woman standing in the rain had done the same.

He caught his mother's eye. "Can we talk?"

After another steady look at her husband, Sylvia David pushed her blanket aside, stretched, and joined Jack in the hall.

She pressed her hand to his cheek. "You look tired."

No matter how much he blinked, he still felt foggy. "I am tired, but it's you I'm worried about."

Her shoulder-length curly hair was usually styled, her outfits always pressed and elegant. Today her dark hair was haphazard, the back flattened from sleeping on the chair. She fluffed it, but it didn't do much. "Just a rough night. Chloe shouldn't have called you."

"Yes, she should have. Actually, no. She shouldn't have because I should have been here. It's too much for—"

"Enough of that, Maxwell Jack David." She three-named him like he was still seven years old, coming home from exploring with Marco, covered in muck and grass. "We have twenty-four-hour nursing, the best doctors money can buy. Being here won't help your father. In fact, it will stress him more. It will stress *me* more. So enough of this moving nonsense. Come by and visit, stay for dinner tonight, but please make a life for yourself. For your father. For me. It all..." Tears sprang to her eyes. "It all goes so fast."

He slumped forward, helpless and frustrated. What could he say to that? He understood their wishes. Stage Four pancreatic cancer couldn't be cured, but this new aggressive treatment could prolong his life. For years, maybe. Sitting vigil now would hinder Dad's fight, not boost it.

All Maxwell David the Second asked was that his kids kept living their lives. He wanted them to visit and share their troubles, not pretend all was swell. "Just because I'm dying, doesn't make your problems any less real," he'd said the other day. "Talk to me about your troubles, and find yourself a good woman." Again with the love and life advice.

Advice Jack should heed. When Jack sang, music vibrated through his feet. The beat filled his chest, the rawness of Elvis —man, myth, and legend—bursting from his lungs. Kissing Clementine had blasted through him like that, louder than a song, wilder than the thrill of performing. She was more than just *good*.

"I'm telling someone about Dad," he told his mother.

She wrung her hands. "Is it Marco? Has he figured it out?"

"Not Marco."

She straightened her spine. "Then the answer is no. You know your father won't be happy. If the investors find out—"

"The investors won't find out."

"If Gunther Doright's betrayal breaks and our Chinese

competitors put their lenses out at half our price, we may as well roll over and play dead." She cringed. "Not my best choice of words, but you know how serious this is. The town depends on that factory. We can't give investors any reason to question our position, and your father's poor health would do just that. We don't like you lying, but there's no other way."

He didn't need the lecture. The stakes if he failed kept him up most nights. "I won't be doing a CNN interview. There's just this...girl. She's the one who came by."

His mother leaned back, giving him her famous side-eye. "A girl?"

His neck heated. "We met on the road. She helped me with granddad's Jag, and she's in town for a couple of weeks." A timeline that pitted his gut. "I like her and not telling her is causing problems."

She sighed, everything in her posture softening. "You never excelled at lying. We're impressed you've managed this long."

"I didn't have a choice."

"You still don't have a choice, but this girl—she's important to you?"

He rubbed his chest and nodded.

Sylvia David, a romantic at heart who'd gotten married eight weeks after falling for his father, got teary eyed again. So emotional these days. "Then tell her, sweetheart. Make sure she knows she can't breathe a word, but tell her and invite her to stay for dinner."

He kissed her cheek. "I'll ask her to stay."

Jack found Clementine in the library. She was running her finger along a row of bound spines. The room smelled of resin and lemon floor cleaner, mingling with her freshly showered scent. His mother's linen pants hung loosely on her, the blue T-shirt snug enough to emphasize her lack of bra. He swallowed a groan. "Find something you like?"

She spun and faced him, eyes wide. "It's a tad overwhelming."

"You say that a lot around me."

"You're overwhelming."

He could say the same about her. "The room doesn't get used much."

She tipped her head back and scanned the upper shelves. "I've never seen anything like this. Except in movies."

Like with the bathroom, he tried to see the library from her perspective: thousands of books no one read, a piano that gathered dust, velvet couches and ornate curtains better suited to a Baroque era, brash in their extravagance. "My father wasn't wealthy as a kid. He built David Industries from the ground up, and all he wanted was to give my mother a palace. It's excessive, but it came from his heart."

She walked behind a couch and traced the gold-trimmed detailing. "Right. The heart."

Her judgmental tone cut. There was a time when his wealth had embarrassed him. On top of his stutter and awkwardness, he'd also been ostracized for his posh upbringing. They'd called him Caviar and Richie Rich and other inventive slurs. That was then. This was now. His confidence wasn't top notch with the opposite sex, unless they were in bed, but he wouldn't apologize for his money or how it was spent. Or how it *wasn't* spent, as was the case these days, too worried he'd need to liquidate his assets eventually.

Those facts didn't change her judgment. "My father likes to spoil my mother. He likes nice things, as do I. It's all been hard earned."

"Do you give to charity?"

"Several." He didn't elaborate on Marco's work.

At Jack's urging, his best friend had grown their philanthropy tenfold the last five years, always looking for new ways to give back locally and abroad...before David Industries was faced with economic disaster. If Jack failed, the charity work would suffer. Marco's job security would vanish. He quickly silenced those thoughts. Failure wasn't an option, and if Clementine liked him, she'd have to like him as he was. High school had taught him pretending to be something you weren't was a fast track to misery...and jail.

She didn't push him or ask other questions. She gathered her wet hair over her shoulder, waiting on the explanation he'd promised.

"Do you want to sit?" he asked.

"Think I'll stand, thanks."

She was either worried about wetting the couches or spending too much time with him. Probably the latter.

He leaned against the mahogany desk and gripped the edge. "I'm sorry I missed our running date."

She shrugged one shoulder, still quiet. All he could do was look at her head on and hope she saw sincerity in his openness. "My father isn't traveling. He's here, and he's very sick."

She made a tiny sound, the sucking in of a shocked breath. "I didn't know."

"No one knows."

"Like, *no one*?"

He shook his head. "You're the first person I've told. Our former floor manager stole company secrets. I have no clue if he decided to do it on his own or if our competitors baited him with cash. Either way, with the setup they have, they're able to use our formulas to increase their productivity at massively reduced costs. Once they're up and running, they'll undercut us so spectacularly our customers will flock to them. Luckily, I started working on a new technology over a year ago, before this shit storm."

"Because you knew something like this would happen?"

He wished he'd known Gunther Doright would do wrong and stab him in the back. He'd been utterly clueless. "Because I'm always striving to better our business. And I'm close. Unbelievably close, but I messed up a project a few years back, and our board of directors limited the funds for this research. They're conservative, and the issue wasn't pressing at the time. So I raised money through investors and got some recent bank loans. But if they get a whiff of my father's illness *and* learn our current technology is about to be undercut, they'll get spooked. They could pull funding. If we lose that and it takes longer to complete our experiments, we're screwed, and the board will have to cover those losses."

He explained how much the town relied on them to maintain their living conditions and support their families, how tough it had been keeping the secret, and how helpless he'd felt when his much younger sister had called him last night, frantic with worry. "It's also why the festival is a bigger deal than usual. There's one tribute artist I'd very much like to squash, but this could be my father's last year, and my singing always meant so much to him. So I set myself this deadline, to complete our research by the festival's final performance, so we could quit lying and my father could attend the show. I can't cure his cancer or make his treatments less horrific, but I can do this. I can control this one silly thing."

He wasn't sure when Clementine had moved in front him, or when he'd dropped his focus to the ground. She pressed two fingers under his chin and lifted his head. "It's not silly. It's beautiful."

"Or I'm acting like a child hoping to impress his father."

"Beautiful," she whispered, the same word he'd used when he'd learned she wrote emails to her late father. He liked the feel of her fingers on his face and the fact that he wouldn't have to lie to her any longer. Still, sharing the burden made him feel both lighter and heavier.

Her fingers drifted off his chin and lowered to her side. "Why tell me these secrets and not a friend?"

It was an excellent question, one he didn't quite comprehend. All he knew was he'd hated saying goodbye to her Friday night, had despised sleeping in his bed alone. He'd been excited for their run until his sister's worrying call. He'd begun to feel more comfortable around Clementine, and life was short and some chances were worth taking. "There's something about you, Clementine. And I can't date you with lies between us. It's why I froze when you showed up here."

Again with that sweet little sound, the hissing of her breath. "Now I'm really overwhelmed."

"Why?"

She backed away slightly, creating space between them. "I'm only here a short while."

"I know."

"And there's the judging."

"We'll figure something out."

"It was supposed to be a non-date kiss." Panic was written all over her beautiful face, her freckles bright on her flushed skin.

He wanted her face flushed for different reasons. "It never was and you know it. So I'll ask what I should have asked that night. Will you go on a date with me? A proper one."

"I can't."

"You can't what?"

She curled her hands into fists and pressed her lips together. She marched past him, aiming for the door. To leave? Bail again? She was as skittish as a leopard gecko.

"Clementine."

She stopped and slumped forward. She shook her head

slightly, then turned, defiance in her cinnamon eyes. "There are things I haven't told you, things I haven't been honest about."

"What things?"

"Scary things. Bad things. Things you won't like."

He'd assumed as much, based on her behavior. Her lie about her name and avoidance of work topics were troubling, her difficult childhood hinting at trauma. Maybe she'd been treated as poorly as his reptiles, taunted, ignored, abused.

"Tell me," he said softly.

"I can't."

"Then tell me this—do you like me?"

Her face crumpled. "So much."

His heart gave a painful thump. That admission was all he needed. "It's settled, then."

She sputtered, probably about to toss out more excuses, but he closed the distance between them and pressed a finger to her lips. "I like you so much, too. So we're going to take this slow. One day at time. Just focus on right now."

"Right now?" Those two words seemed to relax her.

"I won't push you to open up before you're ready, or worry about the day you leave, under one condition."

Her confidence returned, the lift of her shoulders accentuating the soft curves of her breasts, free to roam beneath that light cotton T-shirt. "Only one."

"Stop judging me for how I spend my money."

She rocked on her feet, then nodded. "Seems like a fair trade."

He was on the losing end of it, that much he knew. Clementine's secrets were big enough to have her running from him since they'd met. But she'd opened up to him at the bar, nothing but bitter truth in her family history. She'd trusted him then. She would trust him more, if he worked at it. And their connection made the work effortless.

Plus, striking the bargain meant he could buy her gifts and she couldn't complain. He would have some fun with that.

"Are you free tonight?" he asked.

She twirled a wet strand of hair around her finger. "I am."

"Then you'll stay for dinner."

She gawked. "Excuse me?"

He cornered her against the baroque couch. "You said you'd agree to a date."

"That must have been the other girl you tricked into thinking you're a nice guy."

"Back to being annoying, are we?"

"What did I tell you about seducing women by calling them names?"

"That it's an excellent way to declare my adoration?"

She snorted. "You're trouble, Elvis. No way am I meeting your entire family on our first date."

He clasped her hips and pinned her in place. "I've already told my mother. Saying no now would be rude."

She clutched his shoulders. "I think I liked you better when you were awkward and shy."

"Oh, Clementine." He leaned down, brushed his lips against her ear. "You'll like me confident just fine."

Her breath hitched, and he moved to capture her mouth with his.

"Jack? Is that you?"

He groaned. His little sister really needed to work on her timing.

CLEMENTINE PUSHED JACK AWAY, hard enough that she rolled over the couch arm and landed with an ungraceful *oof*. Perfect. Not only had she been caught getting cozy with Jack, she'd gone and rubbed her wet hair all over their gazillion-dollar sofa. She pushed herself to sitting and crossed her legs, like she wasn't braless and makeup-less and a general mess.

"Hi." She waved at the tough-looking girl hanging off the door frame.

"This is Clementine," Jack said, completing the introduction. "A friend of mine who's staying for dinner."

"I'm Chloe," the fierce girl replied. Her gaze darted between her brother and his *date*.

Clementine still wasn't sure how that had happened. An actual date, with this wonderful man (and his family!), who'd confided his deepest secrets because he couldn't handle lying to her. A freaking con-woman. If her guilt were any thicker, she'd drown in it.

He walked over to his sister and smoothed her hair. "How you holding up? Nap okay?"

"Not bad." She fiddled with the hem of her T-shirt. Her outfit was hardcore. Ripped jeans. *Game of Thrones* T-shirt. Boots too warm for the weather. Her wavy brown hair was long and loose, lighter than Jack's, her nose petite and feminine, but she had his aquamarine eyes.

Jack nudged Chloe's shoulder. "Rain's stopped. What do you say we explore the woods?"

She rolled her eyes. A barely-there effort as her lips twitched, fighting a smile. "I'm too old for that."

"Yeah, you're right. Twelve is ancient. Maybe Clementine and I will go on our own. Check out the new jump I built last week."

Chloe scratched her cheek, the skin already inflamed with teenage acne. She fidgeted with her hands—made him wait for it—then she grinned. "Race you to the treehouse? Loser has to eat Mom's overcooked carrots."

Jack shivered. "Those aren't touching my tongue." He

glanced at Clementine, eyebrow raised. "A walk in the woods sound good to you?"

It sounded fine, but he was oblivious to her uncomfortable attire. She jerked her chin downward, toward her braless breasts. A state of undress she'd rather not share with his sister.

The clueless man mouthed, *What?*

She mouthed, *Bra.*

Him: *What?*

Her: *BRA*, but shouting in silence didn't work.

She finally pointed at her boobs.

He cringed and patted Chloe's shoulder. "We'll meet you at the forest edge, Ladybug."

Chloe side-eyed the two of them, a move that looked beyond her years, then she punched her big brother's arm. "Be prepared to lose."

Chloe darted from the room and Clementine slumped. "That wasn't awkward at all."

"Not sure what you're talking about." His eyelids fell heavy, clearly enamored with her sparse wardrobe.

"Stop looking at me like that. I'm in your mother's clothes."

"It doesn't matter what you wear. You're always sexy."

Her heart gave a flutter. She still had no intention of traipsing around, boobs willy-nilly, all afternoon. "I'll see if my sports bra's dry. And I have a change of clothes in my car." Because her getaway bag was always close. "Then we'll go for a nice walk in the woods and check out this jump you built." It would give her time to adjust to these new "dating" circumstances.

She moved to pass him, but he grabbed her upper arm. "You don't mind spending the day with us?"

She was in his estate, could easily use the time to tour its expanse, find the Van Gogh. Nothing could be further from her mind. Especially when she'd been so close to telling him exactly what had brought her to Whichway. Instead bone-deep fear had seized her lungs. If this went much further, she'd have no choice. She'd have to risk him calling the cops and tossing her out of his house. But he'd offered her *right now*, and right now sounded pretty darn good. "I'd love to spend the day with you."

14

THE LEISURELY ESTATE walk Clementine had pictured was anything but. Jack and his father had built an honest to God obstacle course in the woods bordering their property: planks to jump on, logs to duck under, secured knobs for climbing. Clementine wasn't as adept as Jack and Chloe, who obviously knew the course as well as Clementine knew her Charger's engine, but she ran and slid and jumped, her jeans slick with mud in minutes.

"Your girlfriend's slow," Chloe called to Jack as she bent her knees and launched herself into a suspended net. The taut fabric bounced with her weight but held firm. She rolled off the side, hurdled over a stack of tree trunks, then ran across a narrow log raised a couple of feet off the ground. Damn, she was agile.

Clementine, however, skidded to a stop. *Girlfriend.*

Jack didn't notice. He kept on his sister's heels, his dark hair flopping with his athletic stride, knee-weakening grin on his face. They disappeared ahead, Chloe's giggles mingling with his rumbling laugh. All Clementine could think was, *Girlfriend.*

Of all the roles she'd played, all the names she'd assumed, she'd never been one of those.

She leaned into a tree and fixed her now-dirty T-shirt, which had ridden up. Her fingertips grazed the puckered skin beneath. If a one-night stand asked about her scar, her pat reply had always been the same: "I fell through a coffee table. Sliced myself on the glass." An easy lie, but she couldn't imagine lying to Jack about that. He'd probably see right through her anyway, always so darn observant when together.

A loud *crack* snapped her attention to the right. Chloe was barreling toward her. She grabbed Clementine's hand and yanked.

Clementine jogged to keep pace. "Where's Jack?"

"Shut up and run."

Okay, then. Still unsure where she stood with Jack's little sister, she did as she was told. Hands linked, they bolted through the trees, onto the manicured part of the lawn. Chloe tugged her back into a denser section of forest, finally skidding in the mud and falling to her knees.

She pointed at what looked like an on-land beaver dam. "In here."

That would be a hard no. Clementine had no issues with confined spaces, but her belly seesawed as she watched Chloe cover their footprints and shove herself into a barely visible den. Running around with Jack's kid sister was one thing. Shoving into a confined space with her, where they'd have to *talk*, was another.

"I don't think I'll fit," Clementine said.

Chloe squished herself farther in. "Just do it. He won't be far behind."

Crawling in there meant alone time with Chloe. *Girl time.* Minutes to chat and gossip. Time for Clementine to ruin this fun outing.

Chloe's fierce expression softened. "Please. Come on, just...*hurry.*"

Dammit. How could she say no when those eyes, so much like Jack's, pleaded with her? She sucked in a large breath, then scrunched her frame as small as possible and wriggled into the Hobbit hole. She flattened her back against the "wall" opposite Chloe.

A rotting leaf fell onto Clementine's face. "Where'd you say Jack was?"

Chloe grinned. "He fell. And he doesn't know I built this. He'll never find us."

He better find them. "I may have a limit on how long my body can stay folded this small."

A white lie. She was skilled at staying still and small, but she couldn't discuss those talents with Chloe. She opened her mouth to make small talk about music, school, food? All basic generalities, but no conversation starter came to mind. Their heavy breaths warmed the hovel. Clementine's heartbeat echoed in her head. The longer they waited, the more suffocating the silence became. What did people say to teenagers?

"You and your brother play out here often?" Hopefully most people said smarter things than that.

Chloe didn't seem to mind. "Not as much as we used to. Jack's really busy." She picked at the rip in her jeans. "But his job's really important. Lots of people count on him."

Including one little girl who wasn't hiding her disappointment well, and the honesty had Clementine breathing easier. "He's a pretty great guy."

Chloe's jean picking intensified. She progressed to her nails. "His last girlfriend didn't play with us. She didn't like to get dirty."

The girlfriend label threw Clementine for a loop again, but

the mention of another woman trumped that shock. "Who was his girlfriend?" Tami and Imelda had only mentioned one girl he'd slept with years ago.

Chloe scrunched her nose. "Ava. Not from around here. Totally dicked him over. Lied to him and stuff, I think."

Imagining Shy Jack taken advantage of made her want to claw this Ava chick, but hearing the evil ex had been deceitful hit too close to home. Jack had been so accommodating when Clementine had admitted her secrets were too ugly to share. If his ex had also hurt him through lies, he wouldn't be so quick to forgive. "What happened with—"

"Chloe!" They both jumped at Jack's booming voice. "You can't hide forever. And tell Clementine defectors get punished."

Chloe giggled.

Clementine forced a smile. "He's gonna find us."

"I like your shirt."

The whiplashy comment turned Clementine's smile genuine. She glanced at her filthy top. Since her change of clothing had been from her getaway bag, they were real Clementine clothes, not disguise clothes. Her gray T-shirt read: *Be yourself unless you can be a lizard.* Jack had smirked when reading it.

"Thanks," she said, gratitude making her feel light and airy in this dark confined space that reeked of decaying bark. "I like your boots."

Chloe mumbled, "Thanks." It was a bashful thanks, not a *whatever* thanks.

Clementine had expected a twelve-year-old to be sullen and moody. Emo with a side of fuck off. Chloe, a girl whose father was dying and who dressed like a badass, was including and complimenting her. Maybe asking her not to dick over her brother in her subtle way? Hopefully it wasn't too late for that, and Clementine suddenly didn't want to be found. She wanted to hang out with Chloe and learn more about her adoring brother.

"I see footprints," Jack shouted, closer now.

Clementine held her breath.

"Where the heck are you two?" Closer still.

Chloe gripped Clementine's knee, excitement shining in her eyes.

"I can smell you," he whispered. His muddy boots were visible from their angle. "I can smell traitor blood."

Clementine struggled to fight her laugh. Silly Jack was a hoot.

Chloe pressed a finger to her lips, a warning to stay quiet, then contorted her body until she lay on her belly. She slithered toward the entrance, as stealthily as Clementine slipping into someone's back door. The clever girl inched forward. When Jack's boot was in grabbing distance, Chloe swiped at his ankle.

Jack yelped and stumbled, landing on his ass. "Jesus fucking hell." He was prone on the ground, clutching his chest. "Fucking Christ."

Chloe squealed and popped out of her ingenious hideout. Clementine dragged herself out and onto her feet, while Chloe sat on Jack's stomach and pumped her fist in the air. "I got you so good."

"Nearly gave me a heart attack."

She played his chest like a drum. "You had no clue I was there."

"Because you're a feral child who should live in the woods." He tried to shove her off, but Chloe wouldn't budge. She dug in deeper, poking and tickling Jack. He howled, a roar of a laugh that came deep from his belly.

Finally, he cried, "Okay—off, off, off."

"Winner and still champion!" Chloe crowed.

Jack lay sprawled on the ground, panting. "She's evil, that one." He tipped his head and caught Clementine's eye. "Remind me to punish you for helping her."

An image of Jack tying her to a bedpost sent a rush of heat south. For a woman who'd only ever kissed a mark, thinking of crossing that line should've tossed red flags her way. The only red flag she could see was Jack's face if he discovered all the lies she'd told.

Before she could reply to Jack, Chloe nabbed Clementine's hand and started walking. "She's coming to my room for a bit. We'll see you later."

Chloe's giddy grin was infectious, and warmth spread through Clementine's chest, forcing her Jack worries to the background. There wasn't enough room for all these new emotions.

She spent the next couple of hours on a twelve-year-old's four-poster bed, actually talking with her, never once reverting to her guarded self. They looked through magazines, listened to screamer music, scoured the internet for cool boots, as though Chloe cared what Clementine thought. As though Clementine had a little sister and roots and soil and enough water to grow.

Jack hunkered down in the estate's lower level sound room and sang until his throat burned. The festival kicked off in earnest this Wednesday. That gave him three days to perfect his act and seven days to solve his lens quandary. Then he'd announce their innovation to the world, and his father could attend the finale show.

He hadn't seen Alistair since the diner altercation, but there was no doubt he'd been rehearsing more than Jack. As much as that imposter irked him, Alistair's voice was good. Jack didn't relish the thought of losing to him again, or seeing his ex, who would be in the audience cheering for her man of the hour.

Jack was pleased not to be that man. Hanging out with Clementine emphasized how wrong Ava had been for him. When they'd dated, Ava had barely spared his sister a smile, let alone her time. Getting muddy and crowding herself into Chloe's filthy hidey-hole? Not on her life. She'd adored the sound room, though, had loved lounging in the library and marveling at his mother's floral arrangements and the foyer's crystal chandelier.

All surface interests. As had been her affection. Lies to get what she wanted. He wasn't sure how it would feel to see her again.

It was much more enjoyable to focus on Clementine, a woman who seemed to prefer getting dirty in the woods to gawking at his wealth. Unless she was locked in his sister's room, silently cursing him for letting Chloe kidnap her.

He stood outside their door now, listening for a clue to Clementine's state of mind. She hadn't surfaced for two hours. Not so much as a peep. What did girls do locked in a room that long? Frustrated, he pressed his ear to the door. Low voices grew in pitch. They were too quiet to make out the words, but the tone worried him. He simultaneously knocked and opened the door.

The laughter and talk halted. The girls stared at him like he was an intruder.

"Think I can steal Clementine away?" He wanted to say *my girlfriend*. He'd loved hearing Chloe use that term, but it was too soon and Clementine didn't look pleased to see him right now. He should have interrupted sooner, rescued her from Chloe, but his sister had latched onto Clementine like she was the older sister she'd never had.

Clementine held up a finger, hinting at Jack to wait, and turned to Chloe. "Did you message him?"

Chloe cheeks burned pink. "Yep."

"If he replies, text me. Tell me exactly what he says."

Jack narrowed his eyes. "If who replies?"

Chloe giggled, ignoring him. "I'll text you if you buy the flower combat boots."

Jack's eyes felt twitchy. "Who's messaging you?"

Neither girl glanced his way. "They'll look better on you," Clementine told Chloe. "With that funky skirt of yours."

"Which skirt?" Chloe asked.

"The purple one."

Chloe rolled the corner of her comforter through her fingers. "I don't know."

"I do. Toss on black leggings, and it'll look hot."

Jack choked on nothing and coughed. He banged his chest to ease the burn. "She's not supposed to look hot."

Clementine smiled sweetly at him. "Sorry, did you say something?"

Had he entered the *Twilight Zone*? "She's twelve. There are no boys and there is no looking hot."

Clementine squeezed Chloe's thigh. "Message me."

His sister sighed a dreamy sigh, Jack fumed, and Clementine stood, grabbing his hand as she passed him. "Come on, Elvis. Show me your old room."

Chloe cackled.

He never should have left those two alone together.

As soon as they were down the hall, he yanked Clementine close. "Please tell me she isn't dating."

She patted his arm. "She isn't dating. She's crushing."

"Crushing is worse. She's too young to have her heart broken." He knew how that felt. He'd lived it in a high school bathroom, complete with his pants undone, heart shattered, his embarrassment spread throughout Whichway.

"Crushing is what kids do, and you're being overprotective."

Exactly what *he* should be doing. He'd have to barricade Chloe inside the estate. Homeschool her. Arrange her marriage. "She's too young."

"She's not a baby, Jack. May as well embrace it or she'll shut you out. Now show me your impossibly large, over-the-top, cool childhood bedroom."

Her description was correct on one account: his old room was large. The rest? She'd learn what a pitiful kid he'd been soon enough. No point fighting that, just like there was no point fighting how quickly his sister was becoming a woman.

Brooding over that unwelcome revelation, he led Clementine into his teenage bedroom. She wandered through the space, stopping to touch his Mathletes trophy, the model airplanes he'd built. There were no photos of friends on bulletin boards or football jersey in the closet. Nothing about the space was "cool."

"There's a sound room in the lower level," he said. "It's got a full stage and instruments. I could show you." It was definitely cool. Amazing at thirty-one, the need to impress a woman hadn't vanished.

She shook her head. "I like *this*. I like seeing who you were."

"There's nothing interesting here."

"Everything about you interests me."

The tips of his ears heated. "What else were you and Chloe whispering about for two hours?"

She picked up his Lizard Lover mug and put it down, then fiddled with his pink yo-yo. "Nothing."

"Nothing doesn't fill two hours."

"Girl stuff." The softest smile touched her lips. It was subtle, but tenderness rounded her cheeks and gentled her eyes.

"You like her." The fact surprised him. His much younger sister had always seemed a nuisance to the few women he'd dated.

Clementine, however, looked at him like he'd sprouted a third eye. "Your sister is super cool, and she cracks me up. Great sense of humor. You should hear her impression of you."

Okay. *Not* cool. Chloe wasn't as loose-lipped as Tami and other Whichway gossip junkies, but she knew his worst moments. One in particular, thanks to the miniaturized size of this town. But Clementine's obvious affection for his sister hit him square in his chest.

Chloe's moods had been more down than up in recent months. She'd been happy today, though, because she'd had a woman to hang out with. Clementine seemed more at ease, too. She may be hiding things from her past, but it didn't feel deceitful and personal like it had with Ava. Not when the rest—Clementine's happiness with him and his family—was undeniably genuine.

Clementine finished picking through his things and sat on the edge of his bed. "I like your room."

She lay back and clasped her hands over her belly. He sat beside her, close enough that the bed dipped, pushing their thighs together. The minimal contact thickened his blood, but she'd been cagey with him from day one. If he moved too fast, she could run again. He forced himself to stay still. Wait.

She spider-walked her fingers up his thigh until she'd threaded her fingers through his. A small tug later, he was lying on his back, too, their feet planted on the floor.

He ached to roll toward her and kiss her thoroughly. He also wanted to thank her for making his sister smile, even though they should never discuss boys or crushes. He wanted to understand this woman who watched *I Love Lucy* and found his reptiles beautiful. "How did your father die?"

She stiffened, and the soft puffs of her breaths ceased. Had he pushed her too far? "Suicide," she finally said. "I found him in our garage, in his car, with the exhaust running."

Jesus. Was there no end to the trauma she'd suffered? He held her hand tighter. "When you were nine?"

She tensed even more. "How'd you know that?"

"At the bar—you said you went into foster care at ten, a year after your dad died." Her breathing evened out. She inched closer and laid her head on his shoulder. Jack liked that a whole lot. "Do you know why he did it? Did he leave a note?"

"No, and I was so young at the time. He did it on my birthday, which was pretty fucking awful. I didn't understand mental health issues or even know they existed, but he was fired the year before and could have been upset he couldn't buy me something. He'd spent most of his last days in front of the TV, and my mother was hard on him, I think. If I try to piece through it now, I see signs of depression: he lost weight, didn't sleep well, would get angry at stupid stuff. Near the end, the only times he was his old self was when we worked on his car together. He's why I love the classics and learned how to rebuild engines. The Prius I rented hurts my eyes."

"The car doesn't suit you."

Clementine lifted to her elbow and looked down at him. Something he couldn't pinpoint arrested her expression. "What does suit me?"

"Fast and dangerous." He didn't have to consider his reply. Clementine's clothing was as conflicting as her car. This afternoon, grimy in her T-shirt and jeans, she'd looked at home, but her usual prim skirts and pastel colors didn't fit with the woman who'd greased up her hands under the hood of his Jaguar, who carried herself with a bold, athletic stride and sassed him with her sarcastic humor. Her outfits often seemed as rented as her Prius. A personality to emulate, the way his sister moved through fashion styles—hippy, goth, emo, rocker—trying on different personalities, hoping one stuck.

Clementine was dressed in his mother's clothes again, waiting for hers from the dryer. Just thin linen pants over strong legs. Their thighs pressed more heavily together, so much heat concentrated along his quad.

He lifted his torso and leaned toward her until she lay back down. He traced a line from her clavicle, over her shoulder, to the hard knot of her wrist bone. "I'm sorry about your father."

"I'm sorry about yours."

Mutual understanding. No false platitudes. She moved to reach for him, but he held her down. "I'd like a moment with your body."

She bit her lip, but didn't say yes. She didn't say no, either. They were three-quarters on his bed, both their legs hanging over the side, feet still tethered to the floor. To security. He wanted her vulnerable and unleashed. He also knew himself. If he got her naked, he'd be more demanding, and she wasn't ready for that.

He moved his hand to the drawstring at her waist, splayed his palm over her abdomen, and eased two fingers under her T-shirt. Air hissed through her teeth, but her stomach stayed flat. Like she couldn't inhale. She was either nervous about messing around with him, or men in general.

He could stand, not push things further, but he wanted her to know she could trust him. "No matter what I do or how I act, if you ask me to stop, I will."

He might desire control in the bedroom, but those lines never blurred. He glided his hand up an inch. She trembled, but didn't protest. Her lips parted in longing, and when she mouthed *more*, his willpower snapped. He bent forward, kissed her fiercely, coaxing her lips open with his tongue as he pressed his hand against her hipbone, reveling in the softness of her skin. Fire shot to his groin, the intense throb tensing his thighs.

She tipped up her chin, opening her mouth more fully. He kissed her deeper, swallowed her moans as he curled his fingers around her ribs, ready to lift her toward the center of his bed, somewhere he could have better access.

His fingers met hard, puckered skin.

She froze.

Head hazy with lust, he lifted her shirt and brushed his thumb over the angry scar on her abdomen. "What happened?"

Her belly rose and fell faster. More color flushed her face. She looked at the ceiling, then at his chest, then down at her stiffening body. "Just an accident. A coffee table that—" She winced and went to curl away from him, then she grabbed his hand and held it right there, over her scar. "That's a lie." Pleading eyes met his, but he had no clue what she was asking. "That was going to be a lie."

Unease slowly cooled his desire. "Do you want to tell me the truth?"

"I was stabbed."

A flash of a blade filled his mind, pressing against her sensitive skin, pushing in. Jack wasn't the fighting sort. He'd never punched a man or brawled in a bar. He wanted to punish someone now. "Who hurt you?"

She held his hand in place but kept her mouth closed. She wasn't ready to trust him. Could he fault her? She'd found her father dead and had been shuffled through the foster system. She blamed herself for her mother's overdose. Then, somewhere along the line, she'd been *stabbed*. Those experiences didn't nurture faith in others. When she looked at Jack, she probably only saw a past filled with chandeliers and libraries and bathrooms large enough to live in. Idyllic perfection.

His shitty teenage years had been far from perfect. Nothing comparable to what she'd endured, but he could offer her a part of himself he'd never offered anyone.

"I went through a rough time in high school," he said. He wouldn't describe his worst moment, what he'd done to land in jail, but sharing his vulnerability might help her share hers.

She released a stilted laugh and raised her eyebrows. "Did I miss the segue into this conversation?"

He smirked. "Kissing beautiful women messes with my head."

She eyed his crotch. "Is that what it does to you?"

"I plead the fifth. But I would like to talk."

Her shirt now covered the scar, but her eyes darted there. She nibbled her lip. "About the situation in your pants?"

Always evading. "About me, yes. But not the *very large* situation in my pants."

Amusement sparked in her eyes. "How modest of you, Jack."

"I do excel at modesty," he said, matching her sarcasm. "But this topic's embarrassing, not ego building. My model airplanes and favorite yo-yo might have you fooled, but I wasn't the hippest kid in high school. Some experiences changed me."

Her delight faded. "You don't have to say."

He settled himself against his headboard and beckoned her to follow. She crawled over and cuddled into his side, turned her face into his neck.

"I don't have to tell you," he said, "but I want to."

It wasn't like she hadn't seen him at his most awkward, and she would see him confident and bold between the sheets, if he had anything to say about it. But he knew what he was like during sex: controlling, demanding. It suddenly seemed important she know what had shaped him.

"When I was fifteen," he said, closing his eyes as those unpleasant memories resurfaced, "I was a mess when it came to girls."

15

Jack had been more than a mess with girls. He'd been fifteen with braces, acne, and a stutter, and he'd been in love with Charlotte Aaron. Even in science, one of Jack's favorite classes, he'd watched her instead of scribbling notes as Mrs. Eschenbaum expounded on seed germination rates. Normally a fascinating subject.

All Jack could hear was the beating of his heart as Charlotte passed a note to Stella, both girls suppressing laughter. Stella was pretty enough. Boys in the locker room, when not picking on him, often made rude remarks about her big breasts and full lips. She was magazine pretty.

Charlotte was fairy-tale pretty.

If Cinderella took human form, she'd be Charlotte Aaron. The sun refracted through the classroom windows, blinking off her blonde hair. Her rosy cheeks looked like ripe apples, her eyes so large and blue his often-misfiring tongue would shrivel and dry around her.

Mrs. Eschenbaum turned to write on the board. Stella took advantage of the lack of supervision and leaned toward

Charlotte. She whispered in her ear. Both girls giggled. Then looked at him.

Crap.

He'd been caught staring. Again. Mortification swamped him. The state of his erection was even worse. His body had a mind of its own these days, a girl's laugh or smile acting like his own personal magnetic field. When Charlotte looked at him? His penis strained like it was pumped full of iron, reaching for her magnetic force. He crossed his hands over his lap.

The girls giggled harder.

Marco poked him from behind. "The archery stand's almost done. Come over Friday. We'll put up pictures of the D Squad and shoot their faces."

The D Squad, aka the Douche Squad, encompassed the three Ds: Derek, Darrin, and Dale—all assholes who tripped Jack and Marco in the cafeteria, knocked books out of their hands, and there was that time they held Jack down in the Phys-ed locker room while Derek farted on Jack's face. Their female entourage was a different kind of mean. They used dramatic coughs to barely disguise insults like *loser* and *gross* when passing Jack's locker, a subtler brand of nasty.

All but Charlotte. Charlotte would glance back after Stella or Meredith cough-shamed him, an apologetic smile on her beautiful lips.

Charlotte, Charlotte, Charlotte. Dammit. He was staring again. His groin throbbed.

Another giggle from the girls. Another poke from Marco.

"Yeah, okay," Jack told Marco. "Archery s-s-sounds cool." Anything away from the D squad and Charlotte's penis mind control.

He focused the rest of the class, got his body under control. He packed his books methodically, careful not to damage the Elvis record his granddad had given him. He planned to use the school's music room to record the classic songs as they were meant to be heard. Scratchy. Raw. Load them on his iPod so he could sing along while riding his bike. He sang daily now, morning and night, and hummed in between. His stutter was getting better, and he couldn't get enough. When he sang, his tongue was loose and fluid, not skittish and uncooperative.

Backpack on, he pushed his glasses up his nose. Marco fell into stride with him. Marco may have been a pitcher who'd have scouts salivating before high school was done, but he drifted in Jack's orbit, inhabiting the outer rim of Planet Cool. Marco's single eyebrow and mullet drew a hefty amount of cough-shaming, too. But where Jack would hunch and try to disappear around the D Squad, Marco would lift his chin and tell them to fuck a duck.

They moved with the student flood toward their next class. The hallways looked like a candy store had exploded, colorful streamers and balloons fighting for space with empty candy boxes—next week's Candyland dance theme in full force. The artsy kids were working on Double Bubble papier-mâché sculptures and fake Hershey bars. Girls were making jewelry and hair clips with excess candy wrappers. Guys joked about wearing candy ties. When Jack overheard boys asking girls to be their dates, envy burned through him worse than a sip of his dad's Scotch.

Jack ignored the decorations and trudged toward math class.

Marco hopped as he walked, always a bounce to his step. "My mom got me a new fishing rod. You keen to boat this weekend?"

"Yeah."

"And we're due for another *Star Wars*-athon. Thinking the night of the dance. Do something fun while these asshats step on each other's feet."

"Okay." But he wouldn't mind if Charlotte stepped on his feet. He also kept his answers short. No stuttering with those words. Marco got it, never ragged on him to show more enthusiasm or use a whole sentence. He wanted to. Man, did he want to tell him about the model X-wing fighter he'd built and how they should act out the scenes while watching *Star Wars*. Totally geek out together, but whatever. It was something to look forward to, besides wondering how much fun everyone else was having at the dance.

Charlotte was ahead of them, her blonde waves springing with her steps. A weird sigh-groan escaped him. Marco snickered. When she tipped her head back and laughed, Jack's body zinged liked he'd inhaled all the candy from the empty boxes.

Marco prattled on about his archery setup.

Jack dropped his hands. Erection barricade.

Charlotte moved to the side and waved her friends along. She swung her backpack forward and opened it to get at something. Jack diverted his eyes. He tried to think of Mrs. Eschenbaum's hairy mole and tuna-tainted breath.

"Fucking asshole," Charlotte blurted.

Jack's attention whipped her way. Her bag and books had toppled, while one of the football guys bounded in the other direction, probably after knocking into her. She mumbled under her breath and bent to gather her things. Jack should have left. He should have kept his head down, his feet moving, his mind on hairy moles and halitosis. But his granddad always told him to treat girls nice, to help when they were in trouble.

He told Marco he'd meet him in class, then hurried to Charlotte's side and grabbed her bag. He held it out for her to fill, but couldn't meet her Cinderella eyes.

"Thanks," she said.

He nodded.

"No, really." She placed her hand on his wrist, and holy fucking magnetic field. The situation in his jeans became a problem. A very big problem. He stayed crouched. She kept her hand on his arm. "Seriously, Maxwell. It was nice of you to help."

She'd never said his name before, even if she hadn't used his preferred name. He wasn't even sure she'd known he existed. Stomach swooping like an X-wing fighter, he chanced a glance up. "Sorry." One word was easier than two.

"Why are *you* sorry? That prick"—she nodded down the hall—"is the one with shoulders too big for his body. You're the one who stopped to help."

He half-smiled, hiding his braces best he could, and silently thanked his granddad for his top-notch advice. They packed the rest of her things, hands brushing a few times. He'd never felt anything so soft. When they were done, she stood, and he was forced to do the same, with more difficulty. He maneuvered his bag in front of his groin.

"So," she said.

He offered a tight-lipped smile.

"You don't talk much."

He shook his head.

"Is it the stutter?"

There was only so long he could play the silent card. Sighing, he said, "Yeah."

Charlotte's big eyes went soft. "I had a lisp as a kid. Not as bad as your stutter, but it was embarrassing. Kids made fun of me."

"I w-w-wouldn't have." He wished he'd known her then, but she'd moved here a couple of years ago. Swept in with her red-apple cheeks and Cinderella eyes, upending his life without even knowing it.

"Thing is," she said, "I still talked. I didn't let it stop me."

Because you're nice and beautiful and your hair looks like a bed of sunshine.

The hall emptied out. She sassed out her hip and raised an eyebrow.

He diverted his eyes to the ground. "The guys are d-d-dicks. And you can c-c-call me Jack."

"Okay, *Jack*. They can be douches, but they're not all bad. And they're not here now."

No, they weren't. The hall was almost empty. Jack should head to math. He'd never skipped a class before. He didn't want to miss today's geometry lesson, but he was standing in a candy hallway with a sunshine girl, who wasn't cough-shaming him.

Charlotte tapped her heels, then her toes, doing an impromptu dance. "I took tap classes until it wasn't cool anymore, but I loved it."

"You're good."

"Whatever. I'm fine. Now tell me one thing about yourself, Jack David." He opened his mouth, but she held up her hand. "And you have to use actual sentences. I won't tease you."

Five minutes ago he would have given his model airplane collection to get Charlotte alone, be allowed to watch her pink lips form her consonants and vowels. Now he wanted to disappear. He eyed the fire alarm. Could he pull it without her knowing?

"Times a tickin', Jack. Tell me something. Ask me a question. I'm not moving 'til you do."

Sweat slicked his armpits. The fluorescent lights felt like blasts of heat radiation. Why did she even care? She'd never said a word to him, let alone waved hello. Yet here she was, wide stance, arms crossed, staring him down.

His eyes flicked to the fire alarm again, to the sheet tacked beside it. A promotion for the dance, which was a week and a half away. They planned to play old fifties tunes at it, the type of music Jack loved. Elvis Presley. The Everly Brothers. Dean Martin. He liked dancing, too, moving and singing, his body and tongue loosened by the beats. He'd rather swing Charlotte around the gymnasium than string together three words for her.

She waved in front of his face. "I've heard you talk, Jack. Just ask me a stupid question."

A door slammed shut. His saliva was practically glue. When she huffed and moved to leave, he blurted, "Will you go to the d-d-dance with me?"

Her mouth dropped open. He almost reached for that damn alarm. Go to the dance with him? He couldn't look at her without his dick hitting warp speed. Dance with her? Yeah, right. Not like she'd say yes anyway. All he'd done was invite ridicule and rejection when she was just being nice.

"Sorry. Forget it." He turned, bag still guarding his crotch, and hurried toward the stairwell, needing to get away and inhale fresh air. He'd skip math after all. Get notes from Marco. He leaned his shoulder into the door, gave it shove.

A quiet "Yes" stopped him cold.

He glanced back. Charlotte hadn't moved. She chewed her lip and bounced her knee and rolled her eyes. "Yes," she said louder. "I'll go with you. It'll be fun. But don't wear that preppy stuff. It does you no favors."

She strutted the opposite way, like she hadn't just changed his life. Like she hadn't elated and terrified him with equal measure. Jack was taking Charlotte Aaron to the Candyland dance. Alone. Just her and him. He would also never wear his khaki pants, loafers, and collared T-shirt again.

It wasn't just his clothes that changed that day. Everything changed.

For the next week and half Jack David was cool. The D Squad invited him to sit with them at lunch. No one teased his stutter or farted on his face. The cough-shaming ceased. Charlotte was tense around him and seemed kind of down. Post-dance-date-acceptance regret, likely. Jack tried to care. He tried to care when he ditched Marco on the weekend, choosing to sit in a parked car with the D Squad instead, hacking as they prodded him to smoke. He tried *not* to care when Darrin hip-checked Marco into the lockers. Marco's books fell. The Squad laughed. Jack forced a chuckle while Marco shook his head.

Stickiness coated his insides at Marco's disappointment, but it seeped out when Darrin pounded Jack's back. He was accepted. Cool. *This is what it feels like.* One day a loser, the next he was *in*. He should have known something was off. Basic instincts—*self-preservation*—should have kicked in. He was too high on acceptance to care.

So when he was at the dance—the corners of his lips stained red from the punch, slacks and button-down on instead of khakis and a Polo shirt—and Charlotte asked him to go for a walk, he said yes. They had danced a bit. His tongue had somewhat obeyed him, his stutter less severe as he'd relaxed. He wanted to walk with Charlotte and be alone with her and kiss her. But the second they left the gym, Elvis's "The Wonder of You" fading as they walked farther away, the obeying ceased. His braces felt more cumbersome than usual, his saliva nonexistent. His vital organs all pumped too fast.

"Let's go to the bathroom." She didn't look at him. Just kept walking.

"B-b-bathroom?"

"For privacy."

Yeah. Right. Privacy. He wanted privacy, right? To be alone with fairy-tale Charlotte and her sunshine hair.

Her nails and dress were candy-floss pink, her lips plump and shiny. She licked them. The wetter her lips looked, the drier his mouth became. He stopped once, ached to adjust his pants. She would for sure see how turned on he was, and thoughts of hairy moles didn't help. Each shift of his fly over his erection made it worse. Oblivious to his discomfort and mild panic, she took his hand and led him into the girl's bathroom, right into the handicapped stall.

She closed the door and faced him. "Undo your pants."

Pants? Wasn't there supposed to be kissing? "Wh-wh-what?"

She rolled her wrist as impatiently as she often rolled her eyes. "I want to see it."

"My..."

"Yes, Jack. Your dick. Don't be such a prude."

He forced a swallow, couldn't stop looking at her lips.

She focused on the stall door, like she didn't want to look at him. Her chin trembled. "Just hurry up already. I don't wanna miss the last dance."

Something felt off—her chin wobble, her rushing. He sensed her discomfort, wanted to ask about it, but talking would ruin the moment and so much blood was flowing south, away from his brain. Penis. Charlotte. Touching. These were the only sureties he could grasp, and he wanted the grasping to occur. He'd pictured this moment enough to blind himself. There was always kissing first, but there'd been skin, too—hers, his, theirs. He'd dirtied many a sock in the imagining.

Now it was here. It was happening.

Too shocked to coordinate his hands, he fumbled with his zipper, shaking like a pathetic leaf.

Charlotte made an aggravated sound. "Just...stop. Let me."

She reached for him as a squeak and shuffle came from outside their stall, then running water. A girl must be there, doing her makeup or washing her hands. Charlotte didn't pause, and his body shuddered. He couldn't think beyond how good she felt. Those soft hands on his boxers. The smallest brush made his penis jump, more blood rushed. She pulled his cotton waistband down, barely grazed him, more sounds invaded...then he blacked out.

No. *Fuck.* Not blacked out. Worse than blacked out. He came in a rush all over Charlotte's hands and dress, the length of him spasming with the release. That was when he heard the laughter, the *holy fucks* not even covered with a cough.

Then a rat fell.

Charlotte yelped and spread the cum in her hands all over his shirt, smearing it as she tried to get away from him and the rat. She looked as shocked as he felt, except she didn't have a dick hanging out of her pants while someone above cackled.

16

———

"CHARLOTTE RAN SCREAMING FOR THE EXIT," Jack said, his voice hard and quiet. "I stood there, filthy, pants undone, while the D Squad hooted and whistled and high-fived each other. I was mortified, and so pissed I didn't realize it was a prank from the start. I should've known Charlotte wouldn't go for a guy like me."

Jack was quiet awhile, his dreadful story lingering between them. Clementine wasn't sure what he was thinking, but she looked at his teenage room with new eyes. She pictured a skinny boy with hunched shoulders and flayed self-esteem hiding under his covers, mortified to leave his room. His model airplane collection had probably grown. He'd probably aced every test, studied instead of socializing. Her heart pinched.

She maneuvered so she was cross-legged facing him. "What they did was beyond horrible."

He released a long, slow exhale. "It was, and it hurts to talk about it, but it was sixteen years ago. I've moved on. And if it had been a bunch of friends, it wouldn't have been a big deal."

She squinted, replayed his words, but nope...he still

sounded like he was excusing his bullies. "I hope you're kidding me right now."

He shrugged. "Guys play pranks. Dropping a rat on a friend while someone's giving him a hand job could be funny."

"But they weren't your friends, Jack. They were assholes and that Charlotte bitch should be sent to colonize Mars."

His lips twitched. "Or Uranus."

She barked out a laugh.

He frowned. "That sounded better in my head."

"Like when we met and you asked if I wanted to connect on Snap that Chat?"

His smile was self-deprecating. "Just like that."

"You're such a dork. In the best way." One of his sweetest attributes. "But seriously, what they did was inexcusable."

Bullies in general deserved corporal punishment. Her last foster home had been bully central. The man of the house had been the ringleader, but he'd had accomplices. They'd taken in four foster kids. Two had been spawns of Satan. She'd never laugh off their reign of terror as harmless pranks.

"Totally inexcusable," she repeated.

Jack's legs were stretched out, his ankles lazily crossed. A contradiction to his upsetting story. "I'm not denying that. But Charlotte left a few weeks after, disappeared from town. She sent me a letter, like four or five months later, explaining the girls made her life hell because she fooled around with one of their exes. Claimed she said yes to the dance because she wanted to, but when they found out, it spiraled out of control."

"That doesn't make it right, and I'm guessing the guys didn't apologize."

"Not formally. A few nicknames followed me. Jack-off. Rat Jack. One-Second Jack was popular for a while, and other creative slurs. Everyone in town knew what happened, but it all eventually faded. I just kept to myself, pleaded with Marco to forgive me for ditching him, which he thankfully did. Then came college and growing my father's business. Dale and Darrin even work for me now."

"Seriously? You hired them?" She'd have sent them packing. With bloody noses.

Jack reached behind him and grabbed the top of the headboard. If Charlotte and her posse could see the sharp cut of his triceps stretching his T-shirt, the sliver of happy trail teasing from below the hiked-up cotton, they'd curse themselves. Clementine bit off a breathless sigh.

"One thing that mess taught me," he said, "was we're all willing to do mean things to fit in." His mood darkened for the first time since reliving his humiliation. Like there was more to the story. He adjusted his grip. The muscles in his arms flexed. "I understand it enough to not hold a grudge. But they've never apologized, and I don't want them to. It's a subject I don't discuss and would rather forget."

Clementine pressed her hand to his thigh, spreading her fingers on his firm quad. It was nowhere near as strong as his empathy. "Then why discuss it with me?"

He released the headboard and anchored his hand on top of hers. "Because I've never told anyone."

"But you said everyone in town knows."

"They do. And I mean *everyone*. I had to listen to my mother explain that premature ejaculation is normal." Clementine half-snorted a muffled laugh. He shot her a playful scowl. "Which is no longer a problem. But I've never spoken about that incident. Not once. Not with anyone. Not until you."

After he'd felt her scar, and she'd refused to explain how it had happened.

It was him in the end, holding out a juicy piece of persimmon, hoping to coax out the real Clementine. She wanted to accept his offer. Roll the dice and watch Jack's face transform as he learned who she really was. Sink or swim. All or nothing. Empathy or disgust.

But his languid body moved and rose until he'd settled on his knees beside her. He stroked her cheek. "You don't have to tell me who hurt you today or tomorrow, but I hope you'll tell me eventually. For now, I'd like to erase the geeky image of me you're imagining by kissing the hell out of you."

"But I like you geeky. And shy. And—"

With the know-how of a man who didn't prematurely ejaculate, he overpowered her, swallowed her words, and rocked into her as he laid her out on his bed. His soft-wet lips skimmed her jaw. He nipped her ear, moved and sipped and tasted, taking, taking, *taking*, but giving as voraciously. She arched toward him, tipped her head back, eyes closed, lost in the glory of Jack. He pressed a hungry kiss to her breastbone, above her sports bra. She'd never hated clothing so much. "I want you, Jack. I'm burning up."

He chuckled, deep and predatory. "I'm not having sex with you here. When that happens, we'll be in my home and I'll be taking my time. But I know just the thing to soothe you."

He pulled her V-neck lower, tried to yank her sports bra down. The thick material barely budged, and Jack growled. He pushed up her T-shirt instead, maneuvered his hand under the tight band cinching her ribs. "These contraptions are evil."

"I usually dislocate my shoulder taking it off, but it keeps my girls from bouncing."

"It's keeping your girls from my mouth." He wiggled his hand a fraction higher. The tips of his fingers grazed her breast. "I also might be stuck like this for the rest of my life."

She'd laugh if her body wasn't a firecracker about to be lit. "I could think of worse things. Why don't I—*wow*." Whatever he was doing with his hips, rolling his hard-on between her thighs, he needed to do more of that. She could come just from that. "You better not—"

"Clementine, dear." A knock on the door turned them both to (horny) stone. "Your clothes are dry."

Now she'd never hated clothing so much. She'd rather burn her clean clothes than leave this spot and lose Jack's weight from her body. She kept thinking about Tami's salacious gossip, how proficient Jack was between the sheets. Damn his polite mother. "Thanks, Mrs. David," she called. "I'll be down shortly."

"It's Sylvia, and I'll leave the pile by the door."

Jack collapsed on top of her, laughing into her neck.

Clementine grabbed handfuls of his thick hair. "What's so funny?"

His fading laughter tickled her collarbone. "I'm thirty-one and this is the first time my mother's interrupted me fooling around with a girl."

She snorted, both of them cackling now. Jack was supremely adorable, but her amusement faded. Clementine was twenty-eight and this was the first time she'd fooled around with a boy who knew her real name.

CLEMENTINE HAD ASSUMED rich people were cold and harsh, tough on their kids and judgmental. Easier than believing they had money *and* happiness. The belief had made stealing from the upper class easier and erased her guilt if it snuck up. She'd never expected such fondness at Jack's dinner table.

"You should have seen him as a child," Sylvia gushed to Clementine. "The Pied Piper of Whichway, always humming. He attracted every hurt animal in a five-mile radius, turned half our kitchen into an infirmary."

Jack swallowed a forkful of mashed potatoes. "You're exaggerating."

"You had three in there one day, that bird with its damaged wing, the blind frog that hopped into the walls, and that awful lizard."

"If I didn't take them in, they would have died."

"Feeding that slimy thing worms on my kitchen counter almost killed *me*." Affection punctuated her chiding.

"So dramatic, Mother. And salamanders aren't slimy. They're beautiful." Jack placed his hand on Clementine's knee and leaned closer, feigning a whisper everyone could hear. "She refuses to go inside my shelter."

Sylvia wrinkled her nose. "I've tried. Really, I have. I just can't do scaly creatures."

"I love it," Chloe boasted. "They don't scare me."

Jack grinned across the table at his sister. "As long as none of them dress like clowns."

Chloe scowled at him, their mother laughed, and Clementine absorbed as much of this normal family banter as she could.

Maxwell David the Second hadn't been well enough to join them for dinner, but everyone seemed in good spirits. Used to the hand they'd been dealt, at least. Clementine hadn't fully acclimated to the tall ceilings and elegant china, but the Davids couldn't have been further from the money hungry tyrants she'd imagined.

"How long are you in Whichway?" Sylvia asked her.

A clump of chewed carrots lodged in Clementine's throat. She glanced at Jack. It was a reflex. Look at him. Search him out. *How long do you want me here?* The way his eyes shone, she wondered if he could read her mind. "At least until the festival is over," she said.

Sylvia's face brightened. "At least?"

"Things are up in the air."

"Is your job flexible?" Sylvia placed her knife and fork on her empty plate, the ends lined up neatly. Lucien had taught Clementine to do that. Keep her cutlery tidy. Big fork for the main course. Little fork for salad. All other spoons and forks memorized in case a mark took her to a fancy restaurant.

He hadn't taught her how to navigate affections for a man, though. How to discuss her fictitious job with her date's parents.

Colonel Blue retched by Jack's feet, probably because Jack had been feeding the old dog chicken. He pushed his chair back to comfort the pup, while Chloe and Sylvia cooed from their seats. Clementine exhaled during the distraction, searched the room for a plausible job reply, but all she saw was artwork accenting the maroon walls: a Chagall, a prehistoric mask, and something modern with bold slashes of yellow she didn't recognize. No Van Gogh, thank God.

She hadn't seen it yet, hoped she wouldn't encounter the painting before she'd decided what to do. Right now she was happy. Right now she had Jack and the memory of his kisses.

Right now she didn't want to lie to his mother about her job.

When old Blue settled by Jack's feet, Sylvia returned her attention to Clementine. "You were saying about your work?"

The chicken she'd eaten churned. She fisted the napkin on her lap.

"She can work remotely," Jack said as he stood. "And I'd like to show her the sound room, if you'll excuse us."

"Can I come?" Chloe's words rushed out as she tossed her napkin on her plate.

"Not this time, Ladybug."

"But I wanna show Clementine the gold record."

"And I'd like an hour alone with my date."

His sister slumped and noisily flipped her fork.

"Leave them be, Chloe." Sylvia's no-nonsense tone suggested she was accustomed to laying down their family laws. "Your brother's free time is valuable." She turned to Jack. "Best if you make it an early night. We need you sharp for work. Your father needs that breakthrough."

Tension edged Jack's movements. "I'm aware."

"Then you shouldn't have come over last night."

"Seriously? You think I should have told Chloe—" He cut his rant short.

Chloe paled. Sylvia pursed her lips.

"I have to check my phone," Clementine said, breaking the tense silence. No need to partake in this family tête-à-tête.

"It was lovely to meet you," Sylvia said. "Jack will be along shortly."

He nodded. "I'll meet you in the library."

She left as their butler, Walter—who she'd learned cooked and cleaned and chauffeured the family around—floated in to clear the table. They really did have a manservant, and a maid, in a mansion that could go toe-to-toe with Wayne Manor. But she was no Rachel Dawes in this Bat World. She was Catwoman, and her Bruce Wayne had no clue to her secret identity.

She settled in the library, relieved to be away from job questions, and pulled out her phone. She hadn't checked in since this morning, an eternity for her, but unplugging had been surprisingly exhilarating. She'd experienced real moments today, with real live people, instead of talking to her bearded dragon or texting Lucien.

On cue, a message from Lucien lit her screen. The first line sent her heart into her throat. By the time she'd finished reading, she'd almost bitten through her lip.

Lucien: **We have a problem in Delhi. The orphanage**

contacted me. They're being squeezed by some thugs. If we don't send cash within the week, they'll be shut down.

Clementine: **Our last score. The diamond ring money? Is it gone?**

Lucien: **You asked me to spread as much around locally as I could. The rest went to the Cambodia project.**

She *had* wanted to help out in New York, not just abroad, as much as possible without drawing attention. And the Cambodia project funded schools. All worthy causes. None of those facts dimmed her panic. If the Delhi orphanage was shut down, Nisha and the rest of the children there would have nowhere to go.

Lucien: **You mentioned moving up the timeline. Get the job done and I'll see if I can stall for a few days.**

She looked across the foyer, in the direction of the dining room, where she'd had a lovely meal with a lovely family who trusted her. Could she really steal from them? Just the thought of it made her sick. She closed her eyes and pictured Nisha's scarred arm as she'd snatched the persimmon from Clementine. There were no other jobs lined up. Clementine had no savings to pinch from. It was this or nothing.

Clementine: **I'll get it done.**

She sent the reply, unsure how she'd pull this off, or if she could live with herself afterward.

"Everything okay?" Jack appeared, looking calmer than in the dining room.

That made one of them.

She stashed her phone in her purse. "Yeah. Fine. Thanks."

"Shall we?" He turned toward the marble-floored foyer, expecting her to follow.

She could make an excuse about not feeling well, escape to plan her heist, but she didn't know where the painting was, and she didn't want to leave yet. If she went through with this, this could be the last time she ever saw Jack. A sharp pang twisted her gut.

He led her down the spiral staircase. She kept up while trying to compartmentalize her job from her life. She'd done this hundreds of times, but it felt like her first con. They passed a massive television and games area, complete with ping pong and pool tables. He remained quiet and didn't glance at her, swinging his arms faster as he walked. His family discussion had obviously stressed him, but he seemed more agitated the farther they got from the main floor.

Could he sense her betrayal? Did her panic have a smell?

He kept moving across the large living area. "You're not a music producer, are you?"

If she really were Catwoman, she'd use this moment to transform into costume and plaster herself to the ceiling. Did Catwoman actually have ceiling-walking powers? Could she walk up walls like Spider-Man? Clementine knew basic *Batman* details, thanks to Annie in her nice foster home, but she didn't even know if Catwoman was a superhero or a villain, or why she was pondering ridiculous thoughts when her mark, who she was falling for—*and would probably steal from*—had busted her cover.

Jack's stride didn't slow.

She hurried to keep up. "It's complicated," she said. The vague answer was easier facing his back.

He stayed his course, still strutting ahead. "Were you honest earlier, when my mother asked how long you'd be in town?"

"Which part?"

"You said you'd stay in town at least until the festival's over, which implies you might stay longer. Was that true?"

"It was." Past tense. Unless she could figure out a way to have her cake and inhale it, too. God, she wanted to inhale Jack.

He turned down a long hall and paused by a doorway, then he faced her. "Why?"

He'd thankfully quit pursuing the job questions, but this topic shift was as daunting as splaying her heart on a chopping block. His face was impassive, unreadable. Evasion was an option, but he'd confided in her too much today to reciprocate with another lie.

"Because of you," she whispered.

His stoic face relaxed. "Good."

She wobbled, feeling breathless...and unhinged. Fantasizing about staying in Whichway was a stupid hypothetical game. It meant leaving Lucien and starting life from scratch. It meant abandoning Nisha to a beggar's fate.

"Looks like I have some convincing to do." Jack leaned down and brushed his lips against hers. He kissed her deeper until she moaned, then pulled away with a mischievous smirk. "Want to see my playroom?"

"Sure" was as witty a reply as she could muster. It was tough to focus when her future was barreling toward her at an alarming rate.

Jack took her hand and led her in.

She blinked at her surroundings. "It's purple." Like really purple. Purple carpet. Purple walls. Purple ceiling. A felt-like fabric covered the entire sound room.

"My granddad had my father build it. Bought a killer sound system, set up all the instruments on stage. He played in a band and would jam with the guys. I never picked up the whole instrument thing, but I'd come in here when I was upset or frustrated and blast music. Tune out the world."

She eased her fingers from his grasp and stepped on stage. The ceiling was low, adding cocooned warmth to the funky room. She dragged her hand over the mic stand, the bass guitar's strings, made a row of chimes trill with her index finger.

Behind the drum kit, on the wall, hung a framed gold record. "Is that Elvis's signature?"

Jack's footsteps thumped quietly as he approached. He gripped her hips and pulled her back into his chest. "It was Granddad's prized possession—Elvis's last known signed record. He left it to me in his will. I brought it to the festival last year and put it on display. You should have seen the fuss. The tribute artists kept posing with it and snapping pictures."

"I've never seen an actual gold record," she said.

One that was undoubtedly worth a bucket of cash. Lucien would drool over it, could probably earn a mint selling it off. She immediately bit down on her tongue. This wasn't a thing to be sold for money. This was a precious memento, and she was a guest in this house. *A house she planned to rob.*

The room suddenly felt too small.

Jack's hands wandered around her hips, securing her in a tight hold. "I want to thank you," he murmured. "Chloe may have pouted when we left the dining room, but I haven't seen her this happy in ages."

"It was nothing." She leaned her head back onto his shoulder, tried to elongate her neck, allow more oxygen into her lungs.

"It wasn't nothing. Things have been rough with her the past year."

"Because of your father?"

"My mother, too. She's been more distracted. I think the older Chloe gets, the more alone she feels. With our age difference and my work schedule, she's pretty much an only child. All our aunts and uncles and cousins live in different states. And our mother isn't exactly young and hip." Jack rubbed his thumb along Clementine's belly in a slow pattern. It wasn't soothing her much, but it seemed to calm him. "She needs a woman to look up to," he said.

Nope. The thumb rubbing definitely wasn't soothing. "She has teachers, and she talked about friends."

"She got in trouble recently, spray painting graffiti in town. Just to fit in, like a typical teen, but I think she's lost. Isn't sure who she is. Spending time with a woman like you could really help her."

Forget stretching her neck, Clementine needed an oxygen mask. "You give me too much credit."

"You don't give yourself enough."

He didn't have a clue. Clementine was as good a role model as Al Capone. She was a criminal. She had no friends. The hours gossiping in Chloe's room had been selfish time to pretend *she* was normal, to swoon over Chloe's crush and just be a freaking *girl*. Not a con-woman. Another reason to quit procrastinating.

Agitated, she shrugged off Jack's hold and banged into a cymbal. The clang vibrated in her chest. "Chloe's smart enough to scare you in the woods. She'll be fine."

Better than fine if she didn't hang around Clementine. Still, Jack's declaration gave her pause: *I haven't seen her this happy in ages.* He would know. They really had had fun together.

None of it changed Lucien's text.

Clementine needed to gather herself, create space to choose the less horrible option: steal from the best man she'd ever known or abandon Nisha. She swiveled for the door and stopped breathing. There, across the room, was the whole reason she'd traveled to Whichway.

The reason she'd met Jack.

Since the Van Gogh had originally been owned by Jack's grandfather, it made sense to be hung in a room Maxwell the First had loved.

Shades of green whirled and eddied, bringing the landscape to life. A sunny day. Fields. Grass. Trees. Bushes.

Simple in its serenity. It wasn't as stylized as Van Gogh's better-known works. It had been a study, one of five that hadn't been signed, exactly why it had gone undetected, sold and resold, its true value undiscovered. Now it hung in a basement room on a purple wall, mocking her.

Her and Jack's mutual attraction was undeniable, but envisioning their happily ever after had been nothing more than a teasing lottery ticket you scratched, only to be disappointed by a predictable *womp, womp*. Clementine ached to date Jack, maybe stay in Whichway, but he had a family to care for, an entire factory and town depending on him. He deserved an honest partner who could love his perfectly shy self. He deserved Rachel Dawes, not Catwoman.

The Van Gogh was Clementine's life. Little Nisha and the orphans in India—they were real. Helping them was the one true thing she'd accomplished in her twenty-eight years. A fact she should remember.

"Your mother was right," she said. "I should get going."

His brow furrowed. "My mother is overreacting about work. I have it under control."

"You barely slept last night, and you've concocted an elaborate lie about your father's traveling because your business is in trouble. So no, I'd say she isn't overreacting. And I'm tired as well." She touched his arm, savored the feel of his steadiness one last time. "Are you staying here again tonight?"

If he said yes, she'd slip in tomorrow night, steal the painting then and leave these conflicting feelings in her Prius's rearview mirror. Disappear before she hurt someone else besides herself. If he said no, she would steal it tonight and get it over with. Burgling the estate while Jack was here wasn't an option. It would induce mistakes.

She pressed her nails into her palm, focused on the sharp sting.

"I wanted to stay," he said, "but my folks forbade it. Told me to go home and get some rest."

That was that, then. She'd steal the Van Gogh tonight and complete this job like all the others. She'd save the Delhi orphanage from ruin. She'd return to New York and the life she knew. Maybe move to a new apartment, away from Jenny and her friends. So why did her chest feel like it was caving in?

The creases in Jack's forehead sunk deeper. He ran his thumb down her cheek. "Everything okay with you?"

"Yeah. Fine." It would be tomorrow, at least. After she'd done the heist.

17

Jack stared at his ceiling, his sheets bunched around his knees. *Hot.* His parents kept the house so damn hot. He should have listened to them, slept at home like they'd asked, but Chloe, who often shut him out of her room these days, had looked at him with her big blue eyes and asked him to stay. She'd claimed her window had been opened, that she hadn't done it and she was scared. A move she'd often pulled as a kid. Back then, it had been more of a sobbing plea, and the culprit had been a boogeyman who'd threatened to eat her. This reeked of a different fear.

She hadn't admitted she was worried Dad would get violently sick again. She didn't have to.

Now it was two a.m., and Jack was in nothing but his briefs, sweaty, awake, in his teenage room, wishing Clementine was still on his bed.

He kicked the covers lower, scrubbed his hands over his face. Clementine. There was that folk song about her name: "Oh My Darling, Clementine." He closed his eyes, tried to remember the lyrics. Something about Clementine drowning, her man unable to swim and save her. One of those depressing old tunes about losing the woman you loved.

It struck a chord in his gut, mimicking how he'd felt with *his* Clementine in the sound room, when her eyes had shifted—kind to hard—shutting him out. She had kissed him sweetly when leaving, after agreeing to meet the next day for their run, but there had been coolness in her tight-lipped smile. Like she was slipping through his fingers. It could have been the dinner and his mother's prodding. More likely it had been him. He shouldn't have cornered her afterward, asked outright if her job had been a lie, after promising he wouldn't demand answers. His promise had lasted half a day.

Oh My Darling, Clementine.

How little I know you.

He'd been as open with her as he could be. He hadn't confessed he'd stolen Mr. Hawthorn's oxygen tank during Jack's week of being "cool." The rat hand job was an embarrassment. His brush with crime and moment in jail shamed him to his core. It still baffled him that fitting in had been important enough to him that he'd dropped his morals and had hurt an old man just to feel part of a group. Clementine had marveled that Jack had forgiven and hired Darrin and Dale. How could he judge others when he'd been just as heartless?

No. He didn't want to tell Clementine about that. But he wanted *her*, more acutely than he'd ever wanted a woman. A normal, no-strings affair would be tough to fit into his unforgiving schedule. And nothing about Clementine would be no-strings. She affected him, deeply. Every real detail she'd shared about her past had felt like a hard-earned reward. If he had to guess, he'd say she didn't reveal herself often, if ever.

He closed his eyes and tried to relax into his mattress. A muffled clang sounded, and he tensed.

The nurse? His father? Chloe awake and scared? Anxiety

tightened his stomach. It wouldn't be Colonel Blue. That old boy never left his bed, his arthritic joints happier pillowed by the cushioning. Jack's overtired brain could be the cause, but his chance of sleeping would be nil without checking on his father.

Too sweaty to bother with a shirt or socks, he padded out of his room and down the hall. Chloe's room was quiet except for a song drifting out. He'd suggested she sleep to music, a trick he'd used as a teen, to focus on the notes and lyrics instead of upsetting thoughts. He hoped it lulled her the way it had him.

Their parents' room was silent. His mother still slept there often, but after the previous night's drama, with the nurse coming for her and waking Chloe, she'd decided to stay with her husband in the nanny's old suite. It was on the main floor, at least. No stairs for his father to climb, but it was sequestered from the rest of the house. If Chloe woke up scared, no one would be close by. Probably why she'd concocted the window story.

He'd just make sure his father was okay...and maybe pour himself a finger of whiskey. A nip to take off his edge, quit worrying about random sounds and the nagging thought that today was the last he'd see of Clementine, who had a habit of running away from him.

He held the banister as he descended the stairs. Moonlight filtered through the windows. The chandelier absorbed it, refracting blue-black diamonds across the foyer. The cool, polished marble felt refreshing on his bare feet. He held his breath, listened for sounds. Nothing. He passed through the kitchen and den, down the long hall that led into the former nanny's quarters.

He poked his head into the room and exhaled. His father was sound asleep, as was his mother, who was on the floor. On a *mattress* on the floor, but she was sleeping beside Blue. Jack had ordered another bed for the room. It wouldn't arrive for a week.

Their night nurse noticed him and startled, pressing her hand over her heart. Agatha mumbled something about Jesus and shuffled toward him. She dragged him out of the room. "Almost scared me half to death."

He crossed his arms, suddenly wishing he'd put on a T-shirt. "I heard a noise. Wanted to make sure he was all right."

"He's fine as long as he doesn't catch you in here. You know he didn't want you staying over." Even whispering, Agatha's tone commanded attention. At five-foot-nothing, thin as a rail, she could intimidate. Exactly the type of nurse he wanted caring for his father.

He hunched lower and quieted his voice further. "So you didn't hear anything?"

"Not unless you count your worrying. Think they heard that in Canada."

He chuckled softly. His mind really was getting away from him. Lack of sleep wasn't helping. Listening to his father puke his guts out last night had also taken its toll. There was no way he'd have heard his father tonight, across the estate from this section of the house. The nanny's wing had been designed for privacy.

He scratched his chest. "Guess I'll be on my way."

Agatha patted his shoulder and resumed her reading position by Maxwell's bed. Jack watched his father a moment, happy to see him peaceful. He dragged himself away and headed for the library, drawn by the whiskey in their wet bar.

OUTSIDE OF THE MONET DISASTER, Clementine had never

fumbled a job. Not even her first heist. Lucien had been with her that day, watching that she followed his instructions.

Glide, don't walk.

Stop and listen.

Move as quietly as a whisper.

If the Hulk busted into the David's home, he'd be more whisper-like than Clementine.

Breaking into the estate had been child's play. She'd parked in a deserted barn a mile away, then hiked up to the house. Thanks to Whichway's nonexistent crime rate, the Davids didn't set their alarm. Clementine had used their massive bathroom earlier, ensuring the window was ajar. Unfortunately, she'd neglected to move the scale that sat nearby.

She may have been dressed in black, "sneak socks" fastened over her shoes, gloves on, hair tightly secured. The uniform didn't keep her from stepping on the scale's corner. A loud *crack* had rung as it slammed back to the floor. Silent as the Hulk.

She waited long enough to ensure no one stirred, then slipped into the foyer and down the spiral staircase. Although dark, her headlamp illuminated her way. No need to stop and get her bearings. Exactly why she didn't break into homes without scoping them first. She knew where she was going. She wouldn't fumble again.

She reached the last stair, strode toward her target, and her light skimmed over a photograph. She hadn't noticed it while following Jack to his sound room earlier. She'd been too busy freaking out. The image stopped her in her tracks now. It was a harmless photo—one of Jack dressed as Elvis, performing on stage. He looked younger, his shoulders not as broad, the cut of his jaw softer, but the devilish look in his eyes was all Jack.

Bold Jack. *Good with his hands* Jack.

Uncharacteristic tears sprung to her eyes.

Heists were never personal. She might date a man, make

small talk and get to know him, but a barrier always existed. The past week with Jack: running, talking, meeting his reptiles in his fabulous shelter, spending today kissing, talking with his sister and mother and learning about his tough teen years...it had gotten very personal.

The awareness gave her heart a fierce tug. Thank God she'd ensured Jack was at his own home this evening. If he was here, she'd be tempted to slip into his room, strip out of her sneaky clothing, and crawl into his bed. Learn him. Touch him. Feel real and known.

Unrelenting desire shook her, and those tears threatened to fall. Pretty much the worst timing to cry. Clenching her jaw, she adjusted the long tube latched over her shoulder. The forged canvas was rolled inside. That was why she was here. Not to fantasize about impossible things. She swiveled away from the picture. Too fast.

Smack went her tube into the photo. Down it tumbled.

Shit. Shit. Shit.

The carpet absorbed most of the sound, but she stared at the cracked glass, razor-like air nicking her throat. She strained her ears and listened. No sounds replied. Sweating like a rabbit at a wolf gathering—*why was this house so damn hot?*—she rehung the picture. They would notice the two cracks. Nothing to be done about that. But they wouldn't notice the forgery she planned to slip into the Van Gogh's frame.

The sound room wasn't far. She had to get there and take her time swapping paintings. Half an hour tops. She needed to stop shaking and just *breathe*.

She'd done this hundreds of times. It was just a painting. Jack was just a man.

She hurried to her target.

JACK RESTED his hip on the library desk, exactly as he had this past afternoon. This time he was only in underwear, holding a glass of whiskey, and Clementine wasn't on the couch opposite him. Braless Clementine. The memory stirred his body. When he recalled them in his room this afternoon, her sports bra trapping his hand, he laughed softly.

He wasn't used to joking in bed. When things got heated, something always switched in him, a need to take charge and direct. Control the scene. He wasn't into pain and role play, as far as he knew, but having his dignity stripped as a teen had branded him. He'd fought the urge to overpower Clementine, letting her humor lead them instead. He wasn't sure he'd be able to do the same again, but the thoughts inspired images of her skin and body. He adjusted himself in his briefs, feeling too awake for his own good.

He should go for a run. Tire himself out. Or head to work. Lord knew he had a mountain to climb in the next week. He nursed his whiskey instead, let the amber liquid burn down his throat. The house was still too hot. His father couldn't keep warm these days, kept the AC off at night, even shivering under blankets. Painful effects Jack couldn't control. He stretched his neck, each sip of whiskey loosening his muscles. Drowsiness finally tugged at his eyelids.

A dull thud had his eyes snapping wide.

That sound hadn't been imagined. It had come from the lower level, unless he really was going insane. It could be the furnace room. Maybe his folks had jacked up the temperature on top of turning off the air conditioner. Or the thing could be on the fritz. Or an animal could have scampered in. Chloe's habit of leaving doors ajar *had* invited a bat in that one time. Maybe that was why she'd lied about her window. She didn't want to admit she'd allowed something to sneak in.

He downed the rest of his whiskey and headed for the

stairs, the too-hot temperature easing off as he descended. He paused partway down, waited for his eyes to adjust to the dark. When the outlines of the sofa and pool table defined, he finished his descent. All seemed quiet.

He headed for the furnace room, snapped on the light and blinked until the brightness quit searing his vision. The furnace hadn't been turned on. Nothing was amiss, except for evidence of a resident mouse. The insanity theory was beginning to hold water.

He returned to the basement living area and rubbed his eyes, the light still too bright at this hour. Turning on the TV could help. He could lie on the massive sectional and fall asleep to an infomercial or old movie. Yeah. That sounded like heaven. But Chloe was on the second floor, the whole reason he'd stayed tonight. He needed to get back up there. First he'd check the sound room, just to be sure. A flying bat could do some damage in there.

CLEMENTINE WAS FROZEN. Not cold frozen. More like *What the hell am I doing* frozen. She was on her knees, the framed Van Gogh carefully placed on the floor in front of her, its back face up. All systems were full steam ahead. But she hadn't touched her tool kit or tried to unscrew the frame. She had looked up once, her headlamp slicing across Jack's prized gold record... and that was it.

Frozen city.

The room, with its instruments and gaudy purple walls, vibrated with Jack's family history. All of it was precious to him. Even the painting she was about to steal. Jack hadn't talked about it or pointed it out. That didn't mean it lacked sentimental value.

Who was she to tarnish his history?

Robin Hood, that was who. Steal from the rich and give to the poor. The silly moniker had been a badge of honor in her early days, successful heists celebrated with Lucien, champagne bubbles as effervescent as her glee. She wasn't gleeful now.

The adrenaline rush that usually fizzed through her on a job was more of a nauseating lurch. Way worse than at the diamond ring heist. She didn't want to be this woman. To do this job. To leave Jack in her rearview mirror. She'd built her world methodically, a life where she was clothed and fed, and loved by the one man who'd given her a home. She'd spent a decade helping others through her work. A self-made saint, she'd thought. What a crock of shit. The rightness of it suddenly seemed so wrong. But it wasn't sudden. Not really.

She'd begun questioning her choices five years ago. All her screw-ups this job were proof of her ambivalence, like each mistake was her subconscious way of asking for help.

The frantic beat of her heart slowed, relief sagging her body. Was that it? Was that what she craved? An end to it all?

What would happen to Nisha?

Her stomach kept churning, but she moved. Legs. Arms. Hands. Her extremities seemed to behave on automatic, simple instructions coming from her brain. *Out. I want out.* She wanted to laugh with a man while making out, have gossipy friends, and enjoy dinners where she could discuss her *real* job. Make a difference in the world legally. She wanted to hang out with girls like Chloe and not worry about being a shitty role model.

With or without Jack, she wanted it all. But she craved him in that life: a new beginning in Whichway. The ramifications of that fantasy were as harsh as a New York winter. If she told him about her past, that new life may involve an orange jumpsuit and rationed meals. For now, she'd return the Van Gogh to its rightful home and figure out how to tell Lucien she couldn't finish this job, or any others. She'd find a way to live knowing she'd let Nisha down. Then the reinvention of Clementine Abernathy, hopefully *non*-incarcerated criminal, could begin.

But a quiet shuffling had her freezing again.

JACK REACHED the sound room and blinked at the closed door. He usually left it open, didn't like the space getting musty. He'd have to remind Walter and Marie about it. At least there wouldn't be a bat or critter inside. Unless one had gotten stuck in there? A ridiculous possibility. He turned to return upstairs and forget whatever noises were going bump in the night, but his sleep-deprived brain wouldn't let him. He'd probably lie in bed second-guessing himself.

He pushed the door open, felt along the wall for the light switch, and flicked it on.

The lighting wasn't as bright in here, the purple tone and softer hue easier on his eyes. He stepped inside and scanned the room. Everything was as he'd left it, except for the landscape painting he'd never liked. His grandfather had loved the piece. He'd told Jack it made him feel calm. It was tilted slightly, probably from being dusted. Jack stared at it, searching for his calm. He rubbed his eyes, no calmer than before, and he wasn't asleep.

He flicked off the light and headed for his bed.

JACK CLOSED the door as he left, but Clementine still held her breath. Jack was here. Jack, who was supposed to be at his house, had almost caught her red handed. Or black handed, considering her gloves. He probably had stayed to care for his family, and if he'd taken one more step inside the sound room, or had angled his body slightly to the right, he'd have seen Clementine shoved behind the open door.

She crouched forward, elbows on her knees, as air whooshed out of her. She gulped in ragged breaths and waited long enough for Jack to return upstairs, assuming he would. What if he didn't? What if he decided to lie on the couch? Watch TV? She'd have to slip behind him and up the stairs because the lower level exit was in the games room, right by that couch.

She really was one fumble from getting caught.

The notion should have had the ache in her ribs intensifying, but resignation turned her body leaden. She'd already made her decision, knew she couldn't keep this up. If she left Jack and Whichway now, he'd be none the wiser. She could still break the news to Lucien and not have to watch Jack's face harden as he realized what she was. She could start fresh in another small town. Maybe one that hosted a Dracula festival. She could get down with that.

As long as she didn't wimp out like she had five years ago. She'd been close to walking away then. So close to shedding her skin. The Monet Job fallout and notion of losing Lucien had silenced those thoughts. The same could happen again. She was weak where Lucien was concerned, and he was good at talking her down. But if she marched upstairs now, told Jack who she was and why she was here, there would be no turning back. The wheels of fate would come for her.

She rolled out her neck and took one last look at the Van Gogh.

Time to let the chips fall where they may.

18

———————

Jack settled back into bed. He stretched and yawned and focused on his breathing, slow inhales and exhales. His eyelids grew heavy, his mind fuzzy around the edges. Sleep, glorious sleep.

Thump, thump, thump.

What in the actual hell?

The pestering noise was muffled but rhythmic. Footsteps? His mother returning to her room? Or an intruder. He got up —*again*—snapped on his light and searched his room for a weapon, just in case. All he saw was a pink yo-yo and model airplanes. He didn't even have a baseball bat. The models were pointy at least. He grabbed his B25J Mitchell Bomber and moved toward his open door. The footsteps grew louder. Chloe's room was too far to reach quickly. If someone *had* entered through that window...

Fuck. His pulse rattled.

He walked into the hallway. A person approached, too tall for the nurse or his mother, too far away to see clearly. He raised the bomber.

Clementine stepped forward and yelped.

He startled and bit back a curse. "What are you doing here?" He winced at his volume, worried he'd wake Chloe.

Clementine clutched her chest, then glanced at his torso. "You're not wearing a shirt." Her gaze dipped lower, to his briefs. She released a needy sound.

"You didn't answer me." And why was she wearing tight black clothes and black gloves in his parents' house at way-too-late a.m., staring at his goddamn briefs?

"Is that a weapon?" she asked.

"Excuse me?" Disbelief edged his tone, until he realized she was talking about the plastic plane in his hand, not his crotch. Using the model as a bludgeoning tool made as much sense as Clementine standing in his hallway at this hour. "What are you doing here?" he asked again, more guardedly.

She didn't reply.

He gripped her elbow, steered her into his room, and closed the door. Whatever had brought her here, he wasn't about to wake Chloe while finding out. He stood back, still clutching the stupid plane. "So?"

Clementine worked her jaw. "I was here to steal from you, but I couldn't do it."

He dipped his head and squinted, sure he'd heard her wrong. "To steal from me?"

"The Van Gogh in the sound room."

"We have a Van Gogh?"

She nodded, her jaw still bunching. She folded her arms, but her hands kept moving, her fingers fidgeting by her elbows. "I'm a burglar. It's why I came to Whichway. To find you and case the estate and steal the painting, but then I met you and your reptile shelter, and your family isn't what I thought. Chloe is amazing, and I didn't know your dad was sick, not that it matters. I just can't do this anymore. Not to you. Not to anyone.

But really not to you and..." Longing and desperation twisted her features. "I'm so sorry, Jack. You can call the cops or whatever. I'm prepared to deal with the consequences."

Clementine.

Burglar.

Van Gogh?

He stared at her, unblinking. He opened and closed his mouth, confusion growing as he tried to assemble this unfathomable puzzle. With her skittishness and all she'd been hiding, he'd known she'd had skeletons in her closet. Dark secrets. He'd never imagined they resembled this. "Do you have a weapon on you? A gun or anything?"

She recoiled. "No. God, *no*. I've taken a knife to jobs since"—she glanced at her abdomen—"the stabbing. But I'd never bring something dangerous into your home."

His shoulders lowered. He believed her. He wasn't sure why in the face of her confession, but if Clementine wanted to do him or his family harm, she wouldn't be standing here, telling him to call the cops.

Clementine.

Burglar.

Van Gogh.

The stabbing she wouldn't discuss earlier.

He kept blinking, puzzling. It didn't help. He just felt... numb. He put his model back on its shelf, crossed his room, and sat on the edge of his bed. "Why?"

She chewed on her lip. "Why what?"

"Why do you do it?"

She tipped up her chin, a hint of pride in the move. "The money funds orphanages and schools. We—*I* can't use most of the cash here. I keep it untraceable, spend it overseas and spread it around where it does the most good, with a focus on a couple of places. I try to make a difference for these kids."

"By stealing?"

"Yes."

"You don't keep any of it?"

"Enough to live comfortably and work on my car. I don't need much."

He clenched and released his hands. "Why should I believe you?"

She huffed out a bitter laugh. "I guess you shouldn't."

"And all of this with me..." He motioned to the bed, aggressive now. Pissed off. "Was all of this a lie, too? Was everything with me a way to get into my parents' home?"

Like Ava had used him for his connections. The shock was wearing off, anger replacing his numbness.

Tears shimmered in her eyes. "Not the first time we met, when I helped with your car. I didn't know who you were then. My attraction to you was as real as real gets. It's why I gave you my actual name, something I never normally do. But at the diner the next day and meeting you on runs...that was on purpose, to get invited here. Then it got complicated."

The heat felt freshly oppressive, the air in the room thick and stifling. She focused on her feet. He closed his eyes.

"I fell a little for you when you sang for me in your shelter," she whispered, her pleading tone slipping over him, forcing his eyes open. "Then a little more each day after. Or maybe it was before that, the first day we met. I couldn't explain it then and I can't now. It was so unexpected. *You* were so unexpected. And I've never told anyone about my past. Those stories were true, all of them—about my parents. But I used you, so..." She blinked and a tear slipped out. She dashed it away, looking appalled. "It's okay to call the cops. I'm ready. I just want it done."

He didn't move for his cell phone. She'd lied and used him,

but those tears yanked at his chest. Her admission did the same and worse to his heart.

He pictured her as a kid, walking in on her father dead in his car, being torn from her mother, tossed into the foster system. Clementine was a strong woman. She had overcome, but at what cost? She hadn't become a burglar on her own. Someone would have schooled her. "You said we."

"What?"

"Before, when explaining, you said *we*, then you switched to *I*. Who do you work with?"

Her fidgeting ceased. "No one. I work alone."

The hard lines of her face said otherwise. "If you want me to believe you, you need to stop lying."

She flinched like she'd been slapped and mouthed *fuck*. He waited. If she shut down and didn't give him the full story, he was done. He wasn't sure he'd rat her out, but he'd make sure she left Whichway and never came back. The thought alone did painful things to his insides. He'd fallen for her, harder than he'd realized, but could he forgive her? Animal or human, Jack believed in change. Rehabilitation. Easier said than done when the betrayal was personal.

"My handler," Clementine finally said. "I work with a handler. He took me in when I was fourteen, cared for me when my choices were living on the streets or foster hell. He researches and chooses the jobs and does the business end of things. I do the heists."

Heists. He'd only ever heard that word in movies. *Ocean's Eleven. The Sting.* He couldn't wrap his brain around it all. "Is he in town?"

She shook her head. "But don't ask for his name. I love him like a father and won't implicate him."

Jack dragged his hand through his hair, tried to untangle

his thoughts. It all coiled tighter. Clementine hiked a large tube over her shoulder. He'd only just noticed it.

"Are you calling the cops?" she asked tentatively.

"Not yet."

She stepped closer and dropped her voice. "Why not?"

There was no answering that question tonight, not while his mind was more reactive than his middle school volcano project, but he believed she hadn't known him when they'd first met on the road. She had been looking for Maxwell, not Jack. She had seemed cornered in the Whatnot Diner the next morning, when her cover and fake name had been blown. "Do you really want to change?"

She dropped the tube and lowered to her knees. A position of supplication? "So much. It's gone on too long. And I didn't dare hope you'd forgive me, but if you would. God, Jack—*if you would?* I want that more than anything. I want you."

Another twisting in his chest, stronger this time. He didn't like seeing her like this, beaten and pleading. He liked her sure and sassy, hands dirty from a broken-down car. He liked her on his body, laughing and kissing him. "I won't call the cops," he said, "but I need time. I'm not sure how I feel or what I want. Even without this, there's a lot on my plate right now."

"I can give you time." Her words rushed out. "Whatever you need."

He needed a cure for cancer, a magic wand to fix his company, and forty-eight hours of sleep. For now, he'd make do with space. "Will you stay in Whichway?"

She seemed to hold her breath. "Do you want me to?"

The hard thump of his heart answered before he did. "Don't leave. Let me process this. But you need to walk away from judging the Elvis festival. Tell them we've become close friends and you wouldn't be impartial. A replacement won't be hard to find. And I'm not promising anything."

"Yes. Of course. I'll speak with Jasmine first thing tomorrow." She looked at the tube by her knees and pushed it toward him. "I won't be needing this."

She hurried from his room and didn't glance back. Worried he'd change his mind? He might, if she stayed. His anger had returned, burning a line up his throat. He wasn't sure how she planned to leave, through a window or the front door. Clementine the cat burglar. A woman who stole from the rich and gave to the poor. As a kid, he'd cheered for Robin Hood in movies. He'd imagined himself a bow slinger with a gift for thievery and an eye for archery. Marco's love of the sport had led to many weekends shooting targets and playing make-believe.

Now here he was, ensnared by that reality.

Existing in a daze, he opened the tube Clementine had brought and pulled out a rolled canvas. It was a duplicate of the painting in the sound room, the one his granddad had said provided a sense of calm. Jack stared at it for a long while. He was still anything but calm.

19

———

THREE DAYS. Clementine hadn't heard from Jack in three excruciating days. She'd remained in Whichway as he'd asked. She'd avoided his regular haunts. She was giving him the space he'd requested, while simultaneously developing an ulcer and gnawing her fingernails to shit. She kept expecting a brush-off text from him, or ringing sirens coming for her. The fact that she'd avoided talking with Lucien was partly to blame.

Ulcer city.

She'd emailed her father every night, lamenting her fears of starting over. She never mentioned Lucien specifically, or her illegal work. Just vague worries and stress. The idea of him knowing how far outside the law she lived soured her stomach. She wasn't sure why, considering he couldn't get mad or reprimand her, but her shame reinforced her decision to quit burgling.

All that remained was telling Lucien.

She sat in her motel room, legs crossed on her bed. It was mid-afternoon, the sun shining, but she was indoors. Her phone was clutched in a death grip. She'd dialed Lucien's number ten minutes ago, intent on making her decision final. She hadn't had the guts to send the call.

Grow a backbone, girlie. Slightly nauseated, she pressed Send.

Lucien answered swiftly. "Thought you'd gone underground on me."

"You always tell me to be slow and thorough."

"And you always listen. Time is ticking. How are you making out?"

Screwed. Hanging by a thread. Missing a man who probably wanted nothing to do with her. "Oh, you know, living the life in Nowhere, USA." If she made Whichway sound dull and simple, maybe she'd quit picturing herself living here.

"Told you driving out was a bad idea. Never good to know just how far you are from civilization." Rustling crinkled through the line. It was early. Lucien was probably on his couch, feet propped on his ottoman as he skimmed the paper, reading glasses in place. "I've bought us an extra week. What's your time frame looking like?"

"Funny you should ask." The words she'd rehearsed during her sleepless night slipped from her mind. All brainwaves went blank. Fan-freaking-tastic. "There's been a complication."

She could practically hear his spine snap straight. "What kind of complication?"

A prince of a man who sang like Elvis and kissed like a seductive king. Jack was a huge complication, but it was more than that. "Remember during the Monet job, when I procrastinated and delayed and struggled with my role in our business?"

"Of course, Orangelo. I'll never forget that job." The gravity of his voice hung between them. It was how he'd sounded when he'd sat vigil by her bedside, fresh stiches healing her stab wound. Neither of them would ever forget that.

"Thing is, I think I want out." She cursed herself for saying *I think*. So wishy-washy. Cowardly.

His pause felt weighted. "What's brought this on?"

She bunched her knees to her chest. "I don't think I ever fully settled into things after that job. I did the work. I stayed focused, but it was because I felt...cornered? Like this work was my life raft and without it I'd sink." With no one to keep her afloat or call her sweet citrus names. "There's also a guy."

A small laugh drifted through the line. "You fell for your mark."

She'd become a cliché. "I did."

"Does he know who you are? Why you're there?"

"No." She'd rehearsed this answer. If Jack sent her packing, she'd have to tell Lucien, in case her confession came to bite them in the ass one day. If Jack offered her a second chance—God, she hoped he offered her a second chance—Lucien never needed to know.

He sighed. "It happens, sweetheart. It likely won't last, and changing your life because of it isn't smart. Rash decisions lead to regret."

Her only regret was not getting out sooner. "Even if Jack and I don't work out"—if he decided he hated her or called the cops—"I still want out."

"You're willing to walk away from our work? Let the Delhi orphanage fall apart?"

A sucker punch below the belt. "If I don't do it now, there will always be another emergency. Another kid who needs our help. Stepping away is gutting me, but I want a life. I want friends and a proper job. I want to plant roots." In a forest, surrounded by all sorts of trees.

"Okay."

He hadn't skipped a beat, but her hammering heart had. "Okay?"

"What choice do I have, Tangerine? Your happiness has always been my priority. Yes, I'd rather we continued our work, but we both know what happens when you're not focused." The Monet disaster happened. "It'll take me time to replace you, but I will. And it's not like I haven't sensed this brewing. Selfishly, I didn't say anything. What we have works. But if this is what you need, I support you one-hundred percent."

She flopped on her back, adrenaline leaching out of her. "I'm sorry."

"Don't be, sweet girl."

"I'll still find a way to do charity work. Maybe not at first, but I'll figure something out."

"As will I. I'll do my best to cover the Delhi extortion."

"We'll still have dinners?" She tried not to wilt, but her voice sounded so small. "And can you keep Lucy until I figure things out here?"

"Of course on both accounts."

"I also need to ask you another favor. A big one."

"Anything for my Clementine."

His use of her actual name inflamed the heat behind her eyes. "Don't steal the Van Gogh. I know you need the cash, but it's important to Jack's family. Having it or anything taken from them would crush him and me."

"I have a line on something else. Consider the matter closed."

"And..." She swallowed roughly. "Is anyone else after the piece?"

A soft thumping sounded followed by a hiss and whir. Lucien loved his coffee machine. "As far as I know that Van Gogh is under the radar. It took me years to find it. But you know how things have been."

Yevgen Liski was how things had been. The man had popped up occasionally the past year: a sighting here, a sighting there, always with him flashing his knife tattoo from a distance. He'd swiped a ruby necklace from under her and Lucien a day before they could execute their planned heist. In the past, losing a score to another burglar would push her to work harder and faster. Competition lit a fire in her gut. That time it had been a relief, a job she wouldn't have to complete.

Yevgen, on the other hand, thrived on risky jobs, newspaper-worthy thefts. The ruby necklace had been notorious, owned by one of Chicago's elite. Right up his alley. If Lucien said the Van Gogh was under the radar, no one else would have tracked it, and Yevgen wouldn't give it the time of day. Still, Clementine's mind snagged on one of her worst memories, the moment Yevgen had pushed his knife into her gut, followed by his ominous words: *No one you love will ever be safe.*

She loved Lucien, but Lucien could handle himself. What would happen if she fell fully in love with Jack? She was halfway there already. Did that mean Yevgen would find her and hurt Jack for his psychotic thrills? Hurt Chloe or Jack's family?

A chill swept through her, and she glanced at her purse. Yevgen's bloodied shirt shred was in there. She'd kept it as a reminder. It was also insurance—she had his DNA. If he pushed, she'd break the burglar code: Thou Shalt Not Snitch. The odds of ever needing it were minimal. She had driven to a nondescript town, so small you couldn't find it on a map. She'd broken professional ties with Lucien. But having it made her feel better.

She chatted with Lucien a bit longer, then said goodbye. Not a forever goodbye. A *see you very soon* goodbye. A lump of sadness sat in her throat afterward, for him and the children she'd let down, but nerves and excitement pushed and pulled her in a million directions. Her body vibrated with the thrill of the unknown. She had cut herself loose and had saved the painting. With or without Jack, she'd learn to sink or swim, like that song written about her name...except she'd never learned to swim. A small technicality.

Her lack of résumé or school diploma would be an issue, but if Lucien had taught her anything, it was how to use her best assets. She excelled and focusing when stressed, finding weaknesses to exploit. In the work world, that meant finding where a business was struggling and proving you could fix it. She could eventually source a charitable organization that needed her skillset. First she'd get a job in a garage, make an honest living. If Jack didn't turn her in.

He was performing at the festival's opening concert this evening. She shouldn't go. He wouldn't want her there. She hurried to the shower anyway.

***

CLEMENTINE WALKED through Whichway's main street, flabbergasted. She'd never had call to use the word *flabbergasted*, but the situation warranted the term. Thousands of people filled the road and cobbled sidewalks. Vendors were crammed into side streets—booths selling lemonade and souvlaki and corndogs. Kids skipped happily, fingers and mouths pink with cotton candy. There were lineups to buy fake sideburns and Elvis wigs. Posters of the King filled other kiosks. Several Elvi mingled, stopping to pose for photos and sign autographs.

It was like stepping into an Elvis snow globe.

She bought a peanut butter and banana sandwich—one of the King's favorite foods—and munched while she walked. She didn't have anywhere she needed to be, no mark to seduce. She was even in jean shorts and her *I like it hard and fast* muscle car tank top. There was no role to play. She couldn't quit smiling.

"My daughter ditched me." Imelda appeared out of nowhere and matched Clementine's lazy stride. "She's thirteen and already too cool for her momma."

Clementine finished her sandwich and licked peanut butter from her fingers. "How is it possible your daughter's thirteen? You barely look thirty."

"I knew I liked you for a reason." She bumped her hip into Clementine's. "And I had her young because of hormones. I got knocked up at eighteen."

Clementine had been robbing penthouses at eighteen. "Did you marry right away?"

It was a direct question, but Clementine had seen Imelda three times the past few days, in Wherever park (after Jack's running hour), in the Whatnot Diner (after Jack's morning coffee), at Whenever Bar (on Jack's off night). They'd chatted at length, more about movies and music, and Imelda had gossiped about this customer's pain-in-the-butt dog or that person's horrible lawn. Clementine had even shared that she'd been in the foster system. She hadn't mentioned her mother and father's deaths like she had with Jack, but it had felt *good* and *real* to be honest with a friend. Imelda had replied with a fierce hug.

"Lawson proposed the second I told him I was pregnant," Imelda said. "But it wasn't obligation. We were silly for each other. I still love the idiot, even when he drives me batty."

A blush highlighted her rounded cheeks, and jealousy careened into Clementine. She wanted an idiot to love. She wanted Jack to drive her nuts. "So you two were happy just having one child?"

Imelda moved her hand to her belly. "We tried for more,

but it wasn't in the cards for us. We're blessed with what we have."

They sure were.

Music strummed from a main stage a block down, and Clementine stopped. The sun wouldn't set for another couple of hours, the temperature fresh and breezy. Still, sweat slicked her palms. Jack would be performing shortly, like any minute. She shouldn't have come. She eyed the crowd vaguely, unsure if she should move forward or retreat. A kid wearing fake sideburns did an Elvis hip sway, delighting his parents. A young couple walked arm-in-arm as a man in a sparkly Elvis hat passed behind them.

Suddenly, the back of Clementine's neck prickled. As though someone was watching her. She spun around, scanned the tourists, searching for anything odd. Ridiculous when everything about an Elvis festival was odd. Still, her intuition flared.

"Jack's on soon!" Imelda called. She was several strides ahead, frowning, probably wondering why Clementine was impersonating an obsessive prairie dog.

She scanned the smiling tourists again, searched faces, postures, clothes, and came up empty. She ground her teeth. This was because of her life, the choices she'd made. She was insane to think she could just walk away from burgling unaffected. She'd probably spend the rest of her life neurotic, looking over her shoulder, waiting for the rug to be swept from under her feet. Still, she should message Lucien later, ask him again to send out feelers, make sure no one else was in town.

"Did you hear me?" Imelda said, now at her side. "Jack's on soon."

"Yeah, sorry. I know." Clementine knew exactly when Jack was on. She had memorized his schedule. A more immediate dilemma than her overactive imagination.

"He'll want you there."

She laughed. "He won't."

"Isn't this the same man who dragged you, panting, from the bar?"

The very same one who knew her history and hadn't called in three days. She chewed her cheek.

Tami waved from behind a portly Elvis, her halo of red curls a beacon through the crowd. She pushed her way toward them. "Y'all are slower than dirt. Jack'll be shaking his fine hips in no time."

"There's something she's not telling us," Imelda said, joining Tami for an impromptu interrogation.

Clementine stayed quiet.

Tami planted her hands on her hips. "We ain't budgin' 'til you spill the beans, and you don't want me missin' Jack's performance. I have a perfect attendance record."

There was no way in hell she'd be detailing her criminal history with these women, but she could offer a partial truth. "I've fallen for him."

Tami rolled her eyes. "Tell us somethin' we don't know."

"Okay—he's not interested. He said he's too busy for a relationship." The latter statement may have been a lie, but the ache in her heart was as real as real got.

Tami's reply: "So just bang him."

Imelda's: "Do it for us."

Clementine snorted. These ladies really were good fun... until they flanked either side of her, linked their elbows with hers, and dragged Clementine toward the stage.

She tried to slam on the brakes without causing a scene. "Seriously, he doesn't want me there."

Tami yanked her forward. "That sinfully sexy man has a stick stuck up his fine behind. He works too much and needs to have fun. It's practically a prescription. Any doctor would tell him as much."

"He wants you as much as you want him," Imelda said. "His eyes devour you whenever he's in spitting distance. He'll come around."

They didn't understand. How could they? But Clementine wasn't strong enough to resist their meddling. They led her through the crowd, jostling elbows and shoulders, persistent as ants on the march. The music got louder, the stage nearer. Sweat migrated to Clementine's armpits and brow. People sat in rows of lawn chairs, tapping their toes and singing along. A kid was on stage, dressed as a young Elvis, wearing a shiny red shirt and patent leather shoes. His voice was astounding. If she weren't a moment from hyperventilating, she'd enjoy the show.

They stopped at the side of the crowd, close enough to the stage that Jack might see her, and Imelda released her right elbow.

Tami didn't budge. "He'll be on in a sec," she whisper-yelled in Clementine's ear. "He always sings an upbeat number for the openin' show. Lots of hip action."

Clementine might instantaneously combust.

The young Elvis belted out his last chorus. The girls jigged to the beat, while Clementine turned perspiring into an Olympic sport. When the music ended and the audience erupted, she just about passed out. For a woman who'd spent over a decade evading authorities and invading homes, she should've been impervious to a case of sweaty nerves. She was out of her depth.

Jack sauntered on stage.

Elvis Jack. Bold Jack. *Good with his hands* Jack.

She whimpered.

Tami tipped her head back and cackled. "You have it so bad."

She was an absolute goner.

Jack's swagger was all class. He wore the same costume as the night he'd sung for her in his shelter: black slacks and shirt, slim tie, gold dinner jacket. He'd chosen "Can't Help Falling in Love" that night. If they were in his shelter now, just the two of them alone, would he sing "Heartbreak Hotel" or "Love me Tender"?

The band struck up the opening notes to "All Shook Up," and the crowd went wild. Imelda whooped. Tami whistled on her fingers, finally releasing Clementine so she could shimmy and shake. Exactly what Clementine wanted to do. What she should do.

She was an independent woman for the first time in her life. Every day would be as exciting or boring as she made it.

Determined to forget her neurosis from moments ago and stop worrying about Jack's decision, she closed her eyes and moved. Heels, knees, shoulders—she tapped and bopped. Her mind and body gradually loosened. She wouldn't be cast in *Dancing with the Stars*, but with Jack's voice dipping and diving around the funky beats, the moves felt effortless, as long as she kept her eyes closed. If he spotted her and frowned or glared, she wasn't sure what she'd do.

20

———

THE DRUM BEAT THROBBED in Jack's veins, each pulse moving his limbs as if by rote. He performed as always, smiling and living it up for the crowd, but the growl in his voice had dimmed. The joy of the stage felt muted. His father's absence was partly to blame, as was the fact that his lens research had taken a step back today, not forward as he'd planned. His life was far from easy, but the depths of his funk had a more specific source: he missed Clementine.

Theirs hadn't been a long affair. Not much of an affair at all, physically. And her deceit had cut. He'd nursed his resentment these past few days, but the missing had never faded. If anything, it had magnified, like a guitar plugged into an amplifier growing into an echo that reverberated through him. *Move on*, he'd told himself. *A woman with her complications is only trouble. She's just like Ava.*

But she wasn't. Deep down, he knew it, and he couldn't let go.

She was still in town. He'd driven by her motel on his way home, to check for her car. Finding her there had surprised him. She may have said she'd wanted to change, but that type of reinvention looked a lot less appealing when reality hit home. A real job. The nine-to-five treadmill. It might sound novel now, but what would happen in a day, a week, a month? Still, she hadn't left.

He hadn't knocked on her door, the exercise in restraint nearly killing him. Not calling or texting had been worse. He wanted to be with her and help her through this upheaval. She had been inducted into her life of crime as a child. It hadn't been by choice. None of that erased his hurt, but missing her overshadowed it.

He tried to focus on the song now, the *ba-da-bum* of the backbeat. Not the dull thump of his heart. He made eye contact with an older woman wearing an *I Love Elvis* T-shirt. He winked at her and curled his lip, giving her the full star treatment. She blushed and cheered. It should have made him feel ten feet tall. Then his sights locked on Clementine, and he almost fumbled a lyric.

Her eyes were closed, but she swayed to the beat, a smile on her lips. Lips he'd kissed. Lips that had invaded his dreams. He couldn't tear his gaze away.

His baritone deepened. He threw an extra snarl into his lip and a hint of aggression into his tone. *You screwed up*, he wanted to convey. *You hurt me, but I miss you so damn much.*

Clementine's eyes popped wide, and she pressed her hand over her heart. *His* heart felt like it was beating outside of his chest. Their connection was as strong as ever, stronger than he'd ever experienced. Around her, no awkwardness remained. None of his usual relationship fumblings ensued. She'd done dark deeds in her life. Darker than most. That didn't mean she couldn't start fresh, with him at her side. *Make time for a life*, his father had said.

Could he risk Clementine filling that void?

He performed the rest of the song for her, rolling on his toes and rocking his hips. The stage lights seared his scalp. The front of his hair flopped as he put his soul into the number. For a beat there was nothing but the music and his non-stuttering voice, and a stunning strawberry-blonde who only had eyes for him. For a beat, his pressures lessened.

He belted out the last lyrics, and the crowd roared. Tami and Imelda screamed and whistled with their fingers. The adulation always rocketed his adrenaline, but it was the way Clementine bit her lip and stared at him with restrained longing that fevered his pulse. He wanted off that stage, to talk to her and figure this out. She had stayed as requested, hadn't forced his hand or changed her mind. Showing up here meant something.

This show was an exhibition only. A way to welcome the crowd. No need to linger and impress the judges. He exited stage left and dashed down the stairs, rounding to the audience at a clipped pace. He nearly plowed into Alistair and Ava.

"Fancy meeting you here," Alistair said as he swung his arm around Ava's shoulder. Jack's ex snuggled into the imbecile's side, the way she used to cozy up to him.

"Fancy implies a level of class, which you lack." Jack waited for his gut to sour around his ex, to relive the distaste when he'd realized her affection had been lies. He waited for the memory to reinforce Clementine's deceits. All he felt was restless.

Alistair crowded his space. "If that performance was anything to go by, you'll slide into last place with ease."

He couldn't rebut the insult. The first two thirds of his number *had* been weak. But he couldn't focus on much besides searching for Clementine. If he could talk to her face-to-face, he'd know how he felt, decide if he could forgive her. Something told him if he gave her another chance, there'd be no holding back the strut from his voice. Unless she had come to say goodbye. Offer closure. She could have changed her mind, unable to give up her life. He didn't like that possibility at all, his visceral reaction confirming what he'd suspected: he wasn't ready to lose her.

"Whichway seems as exciting as always." Ava's disdain was as thick as her makeup. "Do you even have a Starbucks yet?"

The town council had stopped one from breaking ground a few years back, the victory a point of pride with Jack. Ava, however, had preferred big box to home grown. He tried to think of something to say, a brush off that would show he was over Ava, or even a basic conversation starter, but nothing came to mind. Conversation with Ava had often been an effort. He'd assumed it had just been him—his struggle to act normal with women.

Clementine had proved the right person could improve his confidence and help his words flow easily.

"I hope you're happy," he told Ava. True words. It was time to let his bitterness go.

The corners of her pink lips tipped down.

Alistair puffed out his chest. "Since she's with me, the answer to that is clear."

The only thing that was clear was how desperately Jack wanted to find Clementine. He also wouldn't mind punching Alistair in the throat.

"Go congratulate him." Imelda not-so-gently nudged Clementine.

"He's talking to people. And he might not want to see me."

Tami grabbed Clementine's shoulders and stared her down. "He ain't talkin' to people. He's talkin' to Alistair, his Elvis nemesis, and his skanky ex. And he just eye-banged you from the stage, so stop your worryin'. That boy's moonshine drunk for you."

She was bottle-of-tequila drunk for him, and she didn't like him talking to his ex, a woman who had *dicked him over*, according to Chloe. Ava's curves were stuffed into a strappy pink dress. Next to her, Jack had morphed from swagger-confident to stiff and broody, and compassion cut through Clementine's nerves. She excelled at playing roles, and she knew one that would help Jack deal with his ex.

She moved before she could talk herself out of it. Fallen popcorn crunched under her sneakers as she dodged dancing bodies. The band played "Jail House Rock." A song Jack could make a reality of if he chose. Not even that prospect deterred her. Jack's attention was mostly on his nemesis, but he kept craning his neck, checking the crowd. Looking for her? A bubble of hope rose through her chest.

Inhaling a lungful of courage, she snuck up to his side, pressed to her tiptoes, and kissed his cheek. Jack flinched—for a millisecond—then wrapped a strong arm around her shoulder. Like he wanted her there.

She scooched in closer. Might as well take what she could get. "You were unreal, sweetheart. Half the women in the audience damn near fainted."

He tipped his head down, burning intent in his blue eyes. "I was only singing to you."

Her pulse surged. "I heard every word." She hoped she'd understood his riveted attention while he'd sung, the hungry nip in his searing gaze now. Unless he was following her lead and putting on a show for his ex. "I love when you sing to me," she said, playing her part, toes crossed this role wouldn't expire. "It's my favorite thing."

"I'll have to do it more often."

"You won't hear me complaining."

Jack rubbed his thumb along her upper arm in slow, purposeful strokes.

Ava cleared her throat and tugged on Alistair. "Take me to the carnival. I want one of those big stuffed bears."

"Sure, babe," he said, and turned to Jack. "See you at tomorrow's show. Or maybe I won't since you'll be eating my dust."

"I don't attend the dog show, but I do hope you win."

"What? No. The *show*, show. The concert."

Jack ignored Alistair's sputtering. "Colonel Blue's in fine shape, so you'll have your work cut out for you. That old pup tends to win crowds."

Alistair glowered at Jack. Jack smirked in return. His rival tossed a dirty look Clementine's way as he hauled his girlfriend off, Ava scrambling to keep up in her too-high heels.

With Clementine's performance unfortunately done, she moved to give Jack space.

He held her closer. "Why did you stay in town?"

"For you, Jack. Because I hoped we could try again, start over. Anything to—"

"Come home with me."

Her belly swiveled as wildly as his hips had on stage, but she wasn't sure if he meant for the night or longer. "I don't know."

It was his turn to give her space, but he kept his hand on her arm. Hesitancy carved a line between his eyebrows. "Have you changed your mind about us?"

"Far from it." She'd take Jack over the crown jewels, but offering someone the key to her heart was light-years beyond acquiring priceless baubles. Sex with Jack would be everything. Aside from Lucien, those she'd loved had only ever left her. "I've fallen for you, Jack. Harder than I realized. These last few days really hit that home. So I need to know that you believe I want to change, that I won't hurt you or your family. I need to know where your head's at...otherwise this risk—I'm not sure I can do it."

His fingers pressed into her upper arms. "I'm a bit wary, if I'm honest, but I've tried to stop thinking about you, and it only makes the missing worse. There's something strong between us I can't explain, but I think that's why it's special. Why you're special." He pulled her in front of him, latched both his arms around her back. "We have some serious talks ahead of us, but I'm willing to risk my heart if you are. Come home with me."

He held eye contact and she melted against him, unsure how she'd found herself in Elvis's arms. "My Prius is here."

"We'll get it later."

"I'm still scared."

"That makes two of us."

"You also think I'm annoying."

"True." The sweetest smile softened his face. "And you think I'm an idiot."

She laughed. He was such a dorky idiot. He shifted slightly, enough for her to feel his intentions. The hard length of him turned her insides liquid. "Okay," she whispered.

With a possessive grunt, he led her to his car.

They didn't speak for the drive. Jack moved her hand to his thigh and held it in place, his palm heavy on hers. At his house, he opened her car door and laced their fingers together, keeping her close as they walked inside. She felt like she'd swallowed a pound of jumping beans.

He paused inside his entryway and cupped her cheeks. "I need you, Clementine." There was more rasp in his voice than when he sang. "We can talk later, but I need you right now. Tonight you're mine."

God, she hoped it was longer than tonight, but she was too

needy to think beyond the tightening in her belly and dampness between her thighs. "I'm yours," she whispered.

His answering kiss wasn't slow and sweet. There were no soft brushes and little nips. He devoured her, a starving man savoring his last meal. No, not last. The first in a long while. The first of many, hopefully. She grabbed fistfuls of his hair, dragged her fingernails along his scalp, eliciting a delicious moan from him. She tried to show him how sorry she was, that abusing his trust was the worst thing she'd ever done. Their tongues danced, his lips forceful and skilled. Every sensation heightened until a shiver wracked her body.

He scooped her up, one arm under her legs and one behind her back, cradling her to his chest like she was a precious thing. His long strides moved them toward his bedroom, the heavy thud of his heart beating against her. She nosed his neck, kissed the vein running its length. She bit his collarbone. A deeply male sound rumbled from him.

She hadn't seen his bedroom during her last visit. Not while she'd been busy gawking at his reptile shelter. The space was sensual yet masculine, decorated with grays and charcoals and warm browns. Large and elegant. Perfectly Jack.

He laid her on the bed, then stood and consumed her with nothing but his heavy-lidded eyes. "Mine," he murmured.

Yes. His. She only wanted to be his. As long as he was hers.

His dark hair was messy from her busy fingers, his neck red from her teeth and lips. It wasn't enough. She needed to see him naked, to touch every inch of his body. She scrambled off the bed and lunged for him. Smirking, he caught her and slowed her progress, his hands moving possessively, squeezing and tugging. He trailed wet kisses along her ear and neck. More dampness. More belly-curling need.

"Your clothes," she said. "Off now." Sentences eluded her.

"Gonna feast on you," he gritted out.

He tugged down his tie and yanked it off. Desperate, she fumbled with his shirt buttons, while he wrestled himself from his gold jacket and removed his socks and blue suede shoes. His black slacks hit the floor in a rush, then she was on her knees, fingers clawing at his black briefs, her breaths short and sharp.

He stilled her hands. "Stop and stand."

Her core clenched at his dominance. Shy Jack had left the building, and she liked it. "But I need these off."

"They will be off, but I'm going to strip you nice and slow. Take my time with you."

Said the man previously known as One-Second Jack. She eyed the bulge in his briefs and licked her parched lips. "Slow can wait. I need you hard and fast."

He released a satisfying grunt. "We do this my way. And I want slow."

He yanked her up and stepped out of grabbing distance, then dropped his briefs, not a bashful bone in his toned body. Proof of his desire sprang free, rigid flesh that made her ache and squirm. Her eyes gobbled up his wide shoulders and defined chest, the smattering of dark hairs that curled over his olive skin. Ridged abs led her gaze down to his hip bones and all that male perfection standing at attention for her. His strong thighs tensed.

"You're beautiful," she said. Words for a woman, maybe, but handsome wasn't enough for Jack. Beautiful was bigger. Beautiful was inside and out. "But you're too far away."

She was on fire. She wanted him in her mouth, filling her body. She pressed her thighs together, but it didn't help. This was new for her, being the one clothed, the man before her baring himself. The men she'd been with had been quick to remove her shirt and bra, work their hands into her underwear. Jack was offering her something different, like when sharing his awful teen story, giving a piece of himself first so she'd feel comfortable doing the same.

A knot formed in her throat.

He stroked himself once, roughly, his eyes so intent she felt naked, too. "Don't touch me," he said. A command.

Then he was on her, his mouth and hands caressing as he lifted her arms and removed shirt. Her bra landed on the floor. He kneaded her breasts, his knuckles skimming her inner thighs as her shorts and thong dropped. His hot breath puckered her nipples as he explored her body.

Don't touch. Don't touch. She fisted her hands.

Not touching him was the hardest thing she'd ever done, and he was everywhere, gliding along her skin, his teeth on her hips, his fingers caressing her backside, dipping into her crease, teasing, teasing, *teasing*.

"Get on the bed, on your knees. Face the headboard and wait."

She was dizzy with desire, her body a live wire primed to spark at the faintest touch. She knew sex with Jack would be life altering. She hadn't been prepared for his electrifying control. "Are you always this demanding in bed?"

"Yes."

Tami's gossip hadn't done him justice.

Trembling, she crawled onto his bed, lifted up to her knees, and waited. Her body throbbed, cold and warm at once. What was taking him so long?

The bed finally dipped and Jack's body fitted behind hers as he tossed a condom beside them. His length nestled against her, hot and hard and silky. She wiggled to feel more, but he held her firm...and explored. One hand massaged her breast, the other gliding to the apex of her thighs. He cupped her, spread her wetness around while pressing open-mouthed kisses to the sensitive parts of her neck. She bucked. Couldn't control herself. He was behind her, but she was utterly open to him. Vulnerable. He rutted against her back while murmuring throaty endearments.

Mine. Gorgeous. Perfect.

And his *fingers*. They filled her and rocked, his thumb pressing and rubbing just right. She had never been so wet, so ready, so under someone else's control. "Don't stop, Jack. It's so good. I'm so close."

"You're clenching my fingers so damn tight. Can't wait until it's my cock in there."

His inner angle changed, or maybe it was his dirty words, but pleasure burst through her. She cried out and shook. Her vision blurred. She knocked her head back and arched as the aftershocks blinded her. "What did you do to me?"

"That was for me, love."

Oh, this man. She was ruined. She would never feel this good with someone else.

He eased her to her stomach and rolled her to her back. The sight of him had her desperate for more. His wild hair tumbled over his forehead, his cheeks hollowing as he stared at her hungrily.

"I need to touch you," she said, begging.

"Not yet." The words seemed to pain him. He hovered above her, chest expanding with his heavy breaths, but he didn't move to kiss her or connect their bodies. She was about ready to tell him where to shove his control, when he whispered, "You're the most amazing person I've ever met."

With the tenderness of a man in more than lust with a woman, he inched down and kissed her scar.

She flinched, fire fisting her throat. She twisted slightly, hoping he'd move lower, higher—anywhere but near that scar. He held her in place and kissed the puckered skin again.

Part of her wanted to jump off the bed and run back to

Lucien and the familiar life she knew. One where her heart only beat for her and zero friends and zero lovers meant zero hurt. But Jack's lips, his affection—she shuddered with the joy of it...and surrendered.

She tunneled her fingers through his hair and held him to her abdomen. He kissed her scar again, each press like fresh stitches healing her wound. His lips traveled to her ribs, over her breasts, tugged at her sensitive nipples. More exploration. More devotion. "Touch me," he commanded.

It was about time. She kneaded the muscles of his back, dug her fingers into the deep grooves. She arched her spine for him.

"Yes," he murmured. "Bend for me, love."

Bend, don't break. *Contort myself into this man's world.* His erection slid against her thigh. He rocked his hips, the heavy length of him so close yet so far. She tried to wriggle lower, anchor him between her thighs. He stayed in control. Kissing. Worshipping. *Bend for me, love.*

When he finally lowered his bare chest against hers, a sob almost burst past her teeth. She clamped her molars tight. Flexed every muscle in her body.

Don't cry. Don't cry. Why the hell am I about to cry?

"Clementine," he said softly. "You need to let go. I'm not going anywhere."

Fear of abandonment. Her issues were basically tattooed on her forehead. She wasn't blind to them. Didn't mean she'd dealt with that mess or had ever cared to try. Jack cared. She wanted to care, too.

"I don't know how," she whispered.

He held her head between his large hands and gazed at her. His mouth was full and lush, softening the serious lines of his face. "Be here with me. Nowhere else. Just here, right now."

Right now. The best *right now* she'd ever known.

His eyes didn't shift, the steadiness making her feel safe.

And God, the fervor in his eyes. He looked at her with so much —warmth, compassion...*love*?—so much *something* that it stole her breath. She couldn't suck air in or let it out. Out would mean tears. In would open her heart further. Both moves could get her hurt. But oxygen was as integral to life as affection. Living without either turned a person hard and cold.

She chose exhaling, a whoosh of air that brought with it that terrifying sob.

Jack's chest swelled wider, his eye contact solid and sure. "I've got you. I'm not letting go."

But she did—she let go. He was naked on top of her, holding his body up enough not to crush her, his remaining weight offering comfort. A blanket of skin and bones and trust and hope. It was too much and not enough. She yanked his head lower, forced his mouth on hers. He swallowed her fears and gave her a promise of more. Another sob. Wet, hungry lips.

His body heat intensified, everywhere their skin met scorching. "Need to be inside you," he gritted out.

"Yes. Now. Please."

He nudged her legs apart and knelt between her thighs, using his fingers to drive her mad again. She canted her hips, asking for him, while wiping at another escaping tear.

His fingers stilled. "Don't touch your face. Don't hide from me."

So this was what he needed from her, to see her vulnerable and trust her after the lies she'd told. Clementine wasn't normally a crier, unless she was intimate with Jack, apparently. She rarely succumbed to emotion. Crying was weakness. In foster care it painted you as a target.

Jack demanded her submission.

She let her next tear fall and despised the wet slide of it down her skin. She hated who she'd allowed herself to become. Fake and distant. Isolated. Jack kissed her jaw, and the hate lessened. He kissed her neck, and the self-reproach fled. Most of it, at least. Desire to prove herself to him flared, so he could fully forgive her lies.

He grabbed the condom, but she pulled it from his hands. "Don't use it."

He stilled, but his erection twitched. "What?"

"I'm on the pill and I've been tested."

"You didn't ask if I'm clean."

"You won't hurt me."

"How do you know?"

"I know you, Jack." She hoped that included believing he wouldn't rat her out to the cops, but it didn't matter anymore, not right now with what they were about to do. "I trust you. I want you to come inside me." *Feel the trust I'm putting in you.*

His eyes flashed, primal with a dash of recklessness. "You're sure?"

She spread her legs.

A growl rumbled from him, but he didn't move his hips. He slid down her body, eyes and tongue and lips devouring her on his descent. "Need this."

No. Not this. She craved him inside her, filling her, leaving no room for her worries. "You said we needed sex now."

"I lied." He paused and quirked a dark eyebrow at her. "I think I'm entitled to one or two white lies with you."

She laughed, the sound slipping into a moan as he reached her inner thigh. "We're joking about this already, are we?"

He gave her a long, slow lick, right beside where she ached. He glanced up and smiled, eyelids weighted with lust. "Laughter is the best medicine."

"I heard orgasms are."

"I heard demanding girls get spanked."

Whoa now. She had only ever been hit out of anger or just plain cruelty. Jack's threat was wicked and playful, and her excitement hit light speed. She couldn't speak again. Not with his focus on her body, licking, sucking, stroking. He controlled her like a Nascar champion, revving her engine just enough, pulling back, reacting and adjusting to her moans and moves. Smooth yet aggressive. He knew her. In five seconds flat, he was reading her needs. Predicting them.

The force of her release stunned her, the quick snap of her hips out of her control. She didn't mean to squash Jack's head between her knees. "If you keep this up, we're never leaving this room."

He looked up from between her legs, his lecherous grin sending fresh waves of pleasure through her. "Don't tempt me."

Her body felt sated yet alive, still hovering on the edge of release. She wasn't prepared for his big frame to loom over her, his thighs to nudge hers wider as he positioned himself at her entrance. "You're sure?" he asked again.

His tenderness only proved how right she was to trust him. "I am."

He sank into her in one smooth stroke.

She gasped. "Jack."

His shoulders pitched forward, a rugged grunt ripping from his throat. "Clementine. So good. You feel so fucking good."

She wasn't prepared to feel this *full*. So why did it also feel like she was teetering near the brink of a cliff? Like she was about to shatter so spectacularly there would be no putting herself back together?

21

Clementine's eyes shimmered. "I'm so sorry," she whispered. She bent her knees and pressed them into his sides, forcing him deeper.

Jack's moan was dredged from the soles of his feet. "We're done with apologies."

Talking needed to happen, but not now. He only needed her eyes on him, the same trust pouring out as when she'd asked him to forgo the condom. If she didn't trust him, she would lie again. He would question her. The cycle would undermine their progress, and this: the hot-wet melt of their bodies moving as one. He was no longer the boy who'd suffered humiliation. He wasn't the kid who'd stuttered through his words. He was this guy now, capable of earning his woman's faith and giving her pleasure, more pleasure. Drowning her in it.

The craving sent a punch of lust to his groin.

He gathered her wrists and pinned them above her head, shifting so just the tip of him rubbed her opening. In and out, kindling her flame. She choked out a muffled curse. "Faster, Jack. Deeper."

"My room. My rules."

"When I get you in my motel, the game will change."

"It won't." It never had in the past, at least. With Clementine, he wondered if he could let go. For now he reveled in her every moan and twitch. He wanted to watch greedily again as she fell apart because of him.

She tried to thrust up to him, but he moved in time, keeping just his tip inside her. Torture. For them both. He altered his angle and dragged himself along her opening. "You telling me you don't like when I do this?"

Her inner walls squeezed. "Okay, yeah. I like that. A lot. Your stamina has improved, Jack."

He laughed. *Laughed* about that horrible time in his life. Laughed while making love to this woman with strawberry hair and freckled skin. "You can call me Marathon Jack now."

"I call you Sweaty Hands Jack."

Still moving in her. Still laughing. "Explain yourself."

"The first day we met—I fell for your large sweaty hands."

He surged forward, a sharp thrust that moved her up the bed. She cried out. Molten lava flooded his veins. "I fell for your greasy hands, so we're even."

The way she'd leaned over his Jag's engine, sweet yet flirty, confident in her car diagnostics, had distracted him from the bank meetings that had kept him up the night prior. Other things would keep him up now. Clementine things. Moving inside her things. His heart feeling too big for his chest things.

Desire tugged at his gut. The coiling burn flooded his bloodstream, fiercer than anything he'd known. A stronger pull. A need to claim her.

He released her wrists. "Grab my ass. Pull me deep."

Her nails bit into his flesh, and he slammed into her,

harder, faster. She was getting closer, arching her back, pushing up her breasts and trying to rub herself against him. His own need clawed for release. He used his thumb on her, tight little circles that elicited a glorious cry. The second she screamed his name and clamped down on him, he detonated.

Fire. Shaking. An endless storm.

Reality returned slowly, the fuzzy edges of his room sharpening. She latched her ankles around his back and pressed her face into his sweaty chest. A lump moved to his throat. He wasn't sure why.

"I'm all for locking us in here for eternity," he said.

She didn't reply or laugh. She kind of froze beneath him, and alarm bells clouded his head. He pushed up slightly, not enough to slip out of her, but he forced her to show her face. More tears. These ones sliced right through him. "What is it?"

She shook her head. "I don't know."

"Talk to me." Jesus. He was inside her and had just experienced the best sex of his life.

This was not okay.

He had replayed their first meeting the past few days, how real it had been. No agenda. No role playing. Just them on a dusty road, attracted to each other. Tonight had been just as real: the clench of her inner muscles around his hard flesh, the openness of her gaze, a hint of fear mixing with her trust as he'd dragged in and out of her.

The fear stood out now, both hers and his. A slight premonition that she'd panic and decide she'd chosen wrong. Life was hard. Living by the rules made it harder.

"I'm feeling...things," she said. She bit her lip, a hitch to her breath.

They were both feeling plenty of *things*. Fear things. *Too big* things. But her affection for him was written all over her flushed cheeks. Her rigid limbs were just as easy to interpret. Not far from the anxiety he felt, too.

He was pretty sure he was in love with Clementine, a complicated woman he'd known less than two weeks. The time didn't matter. His parents had gotten married after two months. There were no rules when it came to love, and if she was feeling a fraction of this overwhelming pressure on her heart, the need to lock them in this house, this room, this bed for fear the outside world would taint this perfection, then they would be okay. That kind of worry was surmountable.

He pressed in deeper, a nudge that made her gasp. "I hope you're feeling things," he said. "If not, I have a problem."

Her answering laugh had him slipping out of her, but that was okay. For now. The laugh was what he'd been after.

She pinched his hip. "You know what I mean."

"I do. Let's clean up and have that talk of ours."

Her next swallow took so long, it pained him.

He lay down beside her and pressed his hand over her hammering heart. God, the speed of it. A terrified bird. "I don't sleep around, Clementine."

She flinched and moved to sit up. "That's not why I'm... It's not because—"

"I know." He eased her down and leaned over her. "You trusted that I'm clean, and it means more than you know, but I don't take sex lightly, with or without a condom. I never have. I wouldn't sleep with you as a fling or a way to work you out of my system. I slept with you to get closer to you. To show you how much I care. But we also need to talk. It's the only way for us to move forward—an honest, open talk."

Her racing heart didn't slow, but she rolled toward him and kissed his chest. "Okay. Let's get less naked for our talk."

Twenty minutes later they were back on his bed, him in his briefs, Clementine looking way too sexy in one of his dress shirts, cuffs rolled, most buttons undone. He had fetched Ricky from the shelter and a few leaves of endive to feed him. His bearded dragon navigated the bed, the familiar reptile relaxing Clementine as he'd hoped. She rested her hand near Ricky and waited until he showed interest and approached. She petted his back, knowing just how much pressure to apply. When Ricky moved closer, she held out a piece of endive and let him nibble.

"You're good with him," he said.

"I miss Lucy." Her pout was endearing.

"Who's looking after her?"

She didn't reply. Her mentor, he assumed. The father figure she refused to name. Jack hunched farther over his crossed legs. "Tell me how you got into your business." He didn't know what to call it. Burglary? Con-womaning? Criminal philanthropy?

She kept feeding Ricky. "A friend needed a pair of shoes."

"So you stole them?" No judgment. He truly wanted to understand her.

Her attention stayed fixed on his bearded dragon. "My second foster home was actually nice. There was a girl there— Annie Ward, younger than me, but she always seemed older. She'd brush my hair and tell the most ridiculous stories just to make me smile, and she was an encyclopedia of all things *Batman*. So random and I kind of loved her. But our foster mother got pregnant and they decided to quit fostering. We got separated and never saw each other again, and the next house was...unpleasant."

She paused. Jack waited, throat tight, for her to go on.

"They took in four kids. One girl was the sweetest thing. Her name was Nyomi and she still sucked her thumb at eight years old, didn't speak much. Her last home had been a bad scene. I tried to take care of her like Annie had taken care of me, but the two other foster kids—one boy and one girl—could have starred in *Nightmare on Elm Street*. They terrorized Nyomi."

"Physically?"

"Yes."

"Did they hurt you, too?" The tendons in his neck strained. He wasn't sure when he'd fisted his hands.

She shrugged. "As much as I could goad them into it. Anything to take the focus off Nyomi."

Kids. Just a bunch of kids, who should have been cared for, not left to defend themselves against violent bullies. Yeah, he wanted to punch something. "And where were the foster parents during all this?"

"Eileen ordered us around. Had us doing chores nonstop—cleaning, cooking, gardening. Greg liked to wear his rings when he backhanded us."

She didn't flinch or shudder. She fed Ricky and spoke of her mental and physical abuse, not a wobble to her voice, but Jack's anger flared. Taking in foster kids was a responsibility a thousand times more precious than giving abused reptiles shelter. Yet his enclosures were more a safe haven than Clementine's foster homes had been.

"The shoes," he said hoarsely. "Tell me about them."

"One day they cornered Nyomi when I wasn't home. By the time I got back, Nyomi was bleeding from cuts on her arms, like someone had attacked her with a razor. I tried to tell Eileen, who just got pissed I'd dirtied a towel cleaning Nyomi up. The next day I realized Nyomi's shoes had been stolen. Both pairs. And it was wet and cold out. Mine were too big for her, so I did something about it."

"You stole for her." To help a friend and step in when others wouldn't.

"My first day on the job," she said. Her sarcasm didn't mask her discomfort, or the fact that she wouldn't look at him. "Not that I had much finesse. There was an outdoor display of kid's and women's shoes. I chatted up the sales lady and moved the sneakers I wanted closer to the edge, but didn't take them. I mean, I was terrified. I actually thought I was having a heart attack, but I wouldn't leave. Nyomi needed shoes. So I lingered long enough that the lady ignored me, then I snatched the sneakers and ran. Couldn't believe I got away with it. At least I thought I did."

"She caught you?"

"No. But Lucien, my handler, watched the whole thing go down. He cut me off a few streets over and scared the shit out of me, but he didn't call the cops. He asked if I was okay and had somewhere safe to go. When I avoided the topic, he praised my skill, then kind of cut himself short. He gave me fifty bucks before he left and a business card. Told me to call him if I ever needed help."

She let Ricky pick at the endive on his own, while she picked at her nails. "I kept the card. Figured if he had fifties in his wallet, there was more where that came from. That if I hit a snag, I could prey on his decency. Not the noblest thought, but I was fourteen and scared. Then things got worse in the house. I tried to tell the social worker, but when the others found out I snitched, it got really bad."

Her face paled slightly, her first sign of emotional trauma. "I woke up in the middle of the night with a switchblade pressed to my throat, and a promise that I'd be killed if I ratted out our lovely foster siblings again. I ran away the next morning. Tried to take Nyomi with me, but she wouldn't leave. Tried living on the streets until that became scarier than foster care. So..." Her next swallow took so long *his* throat ached. "I eventually called Lucien."

"And he took you in, just like that?"

"Not at first. He said he'd let me stay with him while he

tried to find me a better foster home, but I freaked out and told him I'd call the cops and claim he kidnapped me. That ended his attempts to deal with the system. He even admitted he had a record and couldn't afford a police visit. Having that power over him boosted my confidence, and he was so nice. I felt safe for the first time in a long time. So I worked my ass off to do things for him—dumb things like get him coffee, clean the bathrooms and kitchen, stay as quiet as possible when he read or watched TV."

The desperation of a child crept into her tone: to be loved and protected. The simplest of needs. "You tried to make him like you so he'd let you stay."

She finally looked up, fastened her uncertain gaze on him. "Pathetic, right?"

"Pathetic is playing with your yo-yo instead of socializing with other kids." The highlight of his teen years.

A watery laugh escaped her. "Such a dork. But I do love the color of it. Hot pink suits you."

"You should see me in my pink Elvis jacket."

Her eyes dipped down his bare chest, lingered on the waistband of his briefs. "I prefer you without it."

He'd loved her naked and surrounding him earlier, but he also loved her like this, open and honest. "Did Lucien legally adopt you?"

She shook her head, her amusement draining. "Not possible with his line of work, which I didn't clue into at first. I begged him to let me stay. He flat out refused and gave me a month to figure things out. When I asked why I had to leave, he told me I wouldn't understand what he did for a living, that he didn't feel right bringing a child into his world. I'd been on my own long enough to sense something shady, and my instincts went on high alert, so I followed him. Did it for three weeks. I never saw him steal. He was too good for that. But once a week, he'd go to different homeless shelters or charities and drop off anonymous gifts."

She described how she'd watched people open his donations and cry and hug each other, so overcome with joy, how Lucien had finally admitted what he'd been doing and how he'd acquired the money, and that his father had died homeless and alone, the two of them estranged, his work a way to staunch that failure. "I was hooked," she said, resignation weighting her words. "I wanted to impact people like that. I was so enthralled by the end results I didn't care about the stealing."

Meeting a caring man willing to raise Clementine when she'd been scared and alone had been a lucky stroke by all accounts, or had it been? He might have homeschooled her and provided food and clothing, but he'd taught her the tricks of the trade: breaking and entering, stealing jewels, paintings, priceless artifacts. Nothing a kid should learn. When Clementine spilled the story of her vicious stabbing, how her ambivalence in their work had led to it, and that she'd continued to steal for another *five years* afterward, Jack was livid.

"He shouldn't have let you risk yourself."

"He gave me the choice to leave, but I couldn't handle it."

"It shouldn't have been a choice. He should have insisted."

"He needed me as much as I needed him. We were both selfish in our own way."

She squared her shoulders, unapologetic in her choices. His torso was pitched forward, as though itching for a fight. He was angry, all right—*for* her, not *at* her. Sick for what she'd endured. But he couldn't explain that from where he sat in his extravagant home, nothing but love and support in his childhood. Dealing with taunts and ridicule from teens didn't compare to fighting for survival.

He lifted Ricky from between them and placed him on his

favorite pillow. Jack lay on his side and spooned Clementine against his chest. "And now? What's changed that you want a fresh start?"

She didn't relax into him. "It's been brewing awhile. I have no real friends. I hate lying about what I do, and the pride I used to feel is getting...tainted."

"Pride in the philanthropy?"

She nodded. "When it came to burgling, I was a stellar pupil. Our heists got bigger. I wasn't working solo yet, but we did this crazy job in New Orleans. A friend of Lucien's told him about a collection of diamonds. Massive, acquired by a real shady guy. We worked with Lucien's friend, a total eccentric—a magician named the Marvelous Max Marlow. And the score was huge, even after we gave him his cut."

Her body flexed against him, and he tightened his hold on her. "What did you do with the money?"

"We were funding area shelters at the time, kids programs and stuff like that, but Lucien got nervous. It was too much money to spend solely in the U.S. So he did research and took me to India. He showed me what else our scores could fund. And God, if you saw what it was like, how awful the conditions were, maybe you'd understand. It spurred me on and was enough for a while, but I'm finding it harder for the end to justify the means. The orphanage might close soon because I didn't do this heist, but I just couldn't follow through," she said more quietly.

She traced slow circles on his hand. "I want to like who I see when I look in the mirror. I want to do things legally, even if the results aren't as dramatic. I want to plant roots and grow."

He'd been to India and had a business trip scheduled there soon. He'd been to Africa and Asia and had seen his fair share of malnourishment and struggle. Through Marco, David Industries had spearheaded amazing philanthropic work, abroad and at home. He didn't need to see those things to understand Clementine, though. He only had to feel the rapid flutter of her pulse, hear the passion in her voice, try to imagine her devastating childhood. He couldn't fault her for what she'd become.

He faulted the man who'd taken her in, who could have altered the course of her life. For now, all he wanted was to move forward with this fascinating woman.

He hooked a leg over hers. "Can our roots co-mingle?"

She went from stiff to rigid. "Don't do that."

"Do what?"

"Pretend like this is easy for you. In the light of day, when we aren't in bed, my past won't be so easy to ignore."

Easy wasn't the word he'd use. He'd spent the last few days stewing, looking for reasons to cut Clementine off, hoping she'd give him an excuse to forget her. The second he saw her at the festival he only wanted a reason for her to stay. Yes, she'd lied to him, had targeted him and his family to steal a painting. But her confessions now had been devastatingly real. If there was one thing Jack understood, it was the importance of forgiveness.

He kept her pinned against him and moved his lips by her ear. "The week before I went to the school dance, when Derek, Darrin, and Dale hung out with me, they dared me to do something bad."

"Did you toilet paper someone's house?"

"Much worse."

"Knock a mailbox off its stand?"

He'd laugh if the memory didn't still bite. "It was bad enough that I spent the night in jail."

She rolled onto her back and gaped at him. "Say that again."

"At fifteen, I spent the night in jail."

"One more time."

He couldn't help chuckling, and she smiled. An awed smile. A sweet smile. He kissed her forehead, her eyelids, her nose. "You're dating a felon."

CLEMENTINE SOFTENED AGAINST HIM, too amused to worry that this night was a fleeting glimpse of perfection. Not-Maxwell Elvis Jack had a dark side. "I need details."

He leaned his weight on one elbow and stroked her hair. "It's not a nice story, part of my past I'm ashamed of."

"Then we have something in common." Sort of.

He tipped his head in acknowledgment. "As you know, when that shit-show went down, I was obsessed with being cool for a minute. Ditching Marco was an awful thing to do, but I also worked one day a week for a local veteran. I volunteered to hang out with him and play Scrabble or Boggle or read to him. Mr. Hawthorn would talk about the women he'd picked up when in the Navy, go on about the bands he loved and how he danced better than Fred Astaire. He was probably full of shit, but I always liked listening to him, and he'd let me sit in the old Corvette he kept in his garage."

"Sounds like my kind of guy."

"You would have liked him." Jack kept playing with her hair.

She purred and nudged his side. "What did you do?"

"Hawthorn used an oxygen mask. The guys asked me to sneak in one night and steal the mask and tank. They said we'd put it back by morning, that it would be fun to use it."

"Assholes."

"I was the asshole who said yes. I had a key to get in but didn't count on Hawthorn waking up. He'd always been such a deep sleeper. I figured I could slip in and out, do the same after. No harm. No one would know."

She scrunched her face. "He caught you and called the cops?"

Shadows darkened his eyes. "He saw me and screamed. It was the middle of the night, and he didn't recognize me. He got up too fast, tripped and fell and smacked his head on his dresser as he went down. Completely passed out. So I called 9-1-1. Couldn't even lie when the cops came, blurted that I broke in to steal the oxygen tank and mask. I never implicated the other guys, but my sense of self-preservation just flat-out fled." He shook his head like he wished he could fly back in time and scold his younger self. "Turned out Mr. Hawthorn also broke his hip. And later, like six months or so, he died." He winced on the last part.

She reached up and traced his broody cheekbone. "That's not your fault, Jack."

"Yeah, it kind of was. The hip break weakened his body. His immune system slowly worsened after that. It was the root cause."

All because of stupid kids being stupid. "It must have devastated you."

He frowned for several beats. "Thing is, he wouldn't press charges against me. The cops urged him to, even with my family name, but he refused. He made me sit with him in the hospital instead, bring games. Listen to his stories while I choked on my shame. He only mentioned what I did once. He looked me dead on and told me screwing up happens, that we all make bad choices to please others or fit in. What defines us is rising above and forgiving ourselves. Forgiving others."

The code Jack lived by. Mr. Hawthorn's legacy. Jack had forgiven the D Squad, even hiring a couple of them at David Industries. He'd forgiven Charlotte for her evil prank. He was forgiving Clementine now. This man lived and breathed integrity.

"I'm not good enough for you, Jack."

He didn't seem to hear her quiet words, but he slid down so they were face-to-face. "Have you told your handler you're leaving? That you're done with your work?"

Her stomach still seesawed when she replayed the conversation. "This morning."

"Did he try to convince you to stay?"

"He said he'd sensed it coming for a while and that he understood."

His brow lifted with...awe? "You've made a huge decision, without me or anyone in your life to cushion that change. You didn't know how I felt, never pressured me to decide. Still, you took that leap and challenged yourself to start over. At..." He squinted and paused. The corner of his lips quirked up. "I don't know how old you are, Clementine. And I don't know your last name."

She shouldn't feel light and fizzy from that question. Not while her future with this man lay in the balance. Yet here she was, a fizzy, bubbly, normal girl. "I'm twenty-eight and my last name is Abernathy."

He unleashed his Elvis smolder. "I slept with a younger woman."

"Newsflash: so do most men."

"Most men don't have the luxury of staring into your gorgeous eyes. But where were we?"

They were nearing uncomfortable territory. "I'm not good enough for you."

"Ah." He brushed his lips against hers. "At twenty-eight, you, Clementine Abernathy, are taking a leap of faith. Staying the course is easier than admitting wrong or changing. I'd be proud to call you mine."

There he was with that hypothetical persimmon again, teasing her out, offering her the roots she craved. "You should also know I read the newspaper backwards."

"Upside down?"

"That would be cool, but no. Last story to first."

He narrowed his eyes. "I always knew you were a weirdo."

She fought a laugh. "I also lick off the potato chip flavoring before I eat the chip."

"Now you're just gross. But this idiot doesn't care."

"You have problems, Elvis." She wanted to shake him, list all her strange habits and quirks until he tossed up his hands and tapped out. Believing he could truly forgive her and move on was the scarier option. "How can you be sure about us —about me?"

"I just am." No hint of hesitation.

"It might take me time to find work."

"Good thing I made you promise to quit judging how I spend my money."

Oh, right, that agreement. Sneaky devil. "No one can know about my past."

He shrugged a shoulder, still pressed tight to her side. "Thanks to my father, I've become skilled at evading questions."

"I'm not sure it's smart for me to be around Chloe. Not the best role model and all..." Her weak laughter faltered under her nerves.

Jack's playfulness vanished. "That's bullshit. She was the happiest I've seen her in ages with you. You weren't acting. Your past mistakes aren't your future choices. So if you're done trying to convince me to break up with you, I'd like to explore that hard and fast sex you were after."

Hard and fast sounded amazing, but the breaking up part made her feel soft and gooey. Only couples could break up. She wanted her and Jack to be a couple, like Imelda and Lawson, annoying each other, quibbling, making up, doing it all over again.

For that to happen, she had to quit waiting for this bottom to drop out. She'd broken the news to Lucien. Jack had forgiven her. There was no reason to keep riding this second-guessing train. Especially after the Sex of the Century. When Jack had moved inside her, it hadn't just been thrusting, pursuit of pleasure. That type of sex she knew: find the sweet spot and chase your release. Jack had moved his whole body when making love, a wave from the tip of his spine to his toes, turning every spot sweet.

Clementine snuck her head under his chin and kissed his Adam's apple. Loved how his rumbling groan vibrated against her lips. "Hard and fast sounds perfect, but we have a visitor in bed." Adorable Ricky dozing on a pillow.

Jack rolled his weight onto her, nipped her ear, and slapped her hip. "Be right back." But he paused before getting up and frowned at something over her shoulder.

"What is it?" All she saw was a sleek lamp and digital clock.

"Nothing. I just always move the alarm cord so it's tucked behind the nightstand. Ricky got tangled in it once, and I'm always careful. My cleaning lady is, too."

"I guess one of you forgot?" They better have forgotten. Minor details like that could indicate an intruder. Lucien had harped on details. *Anything that moves goes back. Disturbing a speck of dust can cause suspicion.*

Jack was rich. Anyone could target him. Steal from him. Hurt him. Or maybe she really had been tailed at that concert and someone had broken into his house...*or* she was losing it. Half a minute into her new life, she was imagining break-ins and gun-wielding burglars, still so entrenched in that life. Because an alarm cord had been moved. Because she'd felt jumpy at a festival shortly after altering her entire life. Of course she'd been jumpy!

Jack gave his head a deprecating shake and gathered Ricky. "It was probably me. My mind's been more than a little occupied the past few days." He winked at Clementine.

Her head would take longer than a few days to quit undermining her. Messaging Lucien soon would help. "Hurry back."

"Don't you dare move."

She had no plans to move from his bed. His home. His life.

As long as her past didn't find a way to suck her back in.

22

———————

CLEMENTINE STRETCHED AND YAWNED, her body and senses slowly waking up. Soft sheets. Cushy pillow. Fluffy duvet. Faint scents of man and sex tickled her nose. This was definitely not her mildew-smelling motel, and she was not the same Clementine Abernathy. For the first time in her memory, she felt pure happiness. There was no trepidation about an upcoming job, no second-guessing her choices. However her life panned out from here, she'd always remember this peace.

She cracked an eye open and reached out for Jack. She came in contact with empty sheets. In place of his body was a note:

Find my blue suede shoes.

Come again?

Had he really left her in his king-size bed, alone, with a note to do his bidding? Lucky for him, her body still felt floaty and satiated, her best parts sore and well used. He'd still be getting an earful about morning-after etiquette.

Their clothes were scattered on his floor, igniting delicious memories of peeling them off. She poked through his drawers and pulled out a white T-shirt, long enough to cover her bum. She spotted his blue suede shoes by her jean shorts and stared at them. Following instructions when in bed had turned her on like nothing she'd ever felt. If she had to guess, she'd say his need for control stemmed from his awful teenage experience. This demand, although mundane, wasn't so understandable.

The new Clementine Abernathy was an independent woman, who wouldn't kowtow to any man, even Jack. But this was one favor. Grabbing something for him wasn't changing who she was, as long as it didn't become a pattern.

She snatched up the shoes, but felt something inside the right one. Another piece of paper. With more instructions. A slow smile spread as she read it: *Find my shampoo.*

These weren't demands. He was playing with her.

She beelined for the bathroom and spied her next clue: *Find my car keys.* So absorbed in him last night, she didn't remember him dropping his keys, but most people left them by the front door. She brushed her teeth with his toothbrush—to avoid killing him with her morning breath—then headed to her target, her bare feet slapping the floor as she hurried. Her guess had been spot on. She snatched the newest paper and read greedily: *Find my biggest addiction.*

She didn't know the answer to that one, which irked her. She wanted to know all of Jack's addictions and hates and hobbies and the noises that had scared him as a kid. Without him here to question, she headed for the kitchen and the addiction that cursed most people in the morning.

Jackpot.

Not-Maxwell Elvis Jack grinned at her, coffee cup poised at his lips. "Took you long enough."

God, he was sexy as hell, standing there in black briefs and a blue T-shirt. "Are you the prize at the end of this scavenger hunt?"

"One of them."

"What's with the game?"

His shrug was anything but nonchalant. "Just having fun."

Liar. "Is there coffee for me?"

He jutted his chin toward the coffee maker. "The pods go in the top."

Okayyyyy. He could have made her a cup, but he stepped away, his cheekbones rosier than they should be. If he'd filled those pods with dirt as a practical joke, hellfire would rain.

She approached the pods warily, narrowing her eyes as she neared them. One sat higher than the others. It had a sticky note on top that read *Open Me.* She tried not to grin. She tried to scowl and pretend this game wasn't the best morning-after fun she'd ever had.

Bottom lip trapped between her teeth, she peeled back the tab and gasped. "What is this?"

"A gift." Jack was suddenly behind her, his hands brushing her hair over her shoulder.

"I can't accept it."

"You can and you will."

"It must have cost a fortune." The teardrop chocolate diamond wasn't a fake. Six carats, easy. Its gold chain and the small clear diamonds surrounding the stone were real, too. Fortune was an understatement.

Jack reached over her and tipped the delicate necklace out of the pod. "It belonged to my grandmother and was left to me, so it didn't cost me anything. But even if it did, you promised not to judge my spending."

She'd also promised herself to never get greedy with her money, to always use the excess to help others. "Really, Jack. I can't. It's too much."

Ignoring her, he laid the stone over her sternum and

fastened the clasp at her nape. Goosebumps erupted along her neck.

"The chocolate diamond reminds me of the darker flecks in your eyes," he whispered. "I decided to give it to you before our encounter at the estate. It means more to give it to you now. I hope the necklace reminds you of me."

She was in his T-shirt, in his house, wearing his family's invaluable jewelry against her thudding heart, even though he knew all her secrets. She didn't need baubles to make her think of Jack, but the gesture clearly meant something to him. Maybe one teensy, excessive gift wasn't so bad.

She turned and flattened her palms on his chest. "I hated waking up without you next to me, but I loved your game, and this"—she pressed her fingers into the diamond—"is beautiful."

He kissed her nose. "You're beautiful. How about some breakfast?"

She definitely needed something to soak up the soppy feelings filling her belly.

They moved around each other in his kitchen, like a regular couple, while they gathered fruit and she learned his space. He kissed and touched her at every chance. She kept fingering her new necklace, couldn't believe Jack cared enough to gift it to her.

She held his kitchen knife and attempted to focus on slicing melon for their yogurt bowls. "Do you always eat this healthy?"

He sipped his coffee, one hand on his mug, the other tracing circles on her shoulder. "As often as I can, but I'm not strict about it. You know I love Whatnot's turnovers."

"Apple," she said. "Strawberry when frisky." She smiled to herself, then she remembered she'd first learned that fact from Lucien's file on Maxwell David the Third. Her smile slipped.

"What's your favorite color?" The softness of his voice turned the mundane question intimate.

"Green." She looked up at him. "Where's your favorite place you've ever traveled?" She needed new details. New likes. Things she discovered for herself.

"Paris. Yours?"

"Outside of the States, I've only ever been to India. Just that once to see the orphanage, but I fell in love with it."

He tilted his head, a spark of something lighting his eyes. "It's a fascinating country."

"Why Elvis?" she asked, eager for more. "Did you fall in love with his music because of your grandfather, or was it more than that?"

Jack left her briefly and returned with two bowls of yogurt. He placed them on the counter. As soon as his hands were free, he stroked one down her back, eliciting a contented sigh from her.

"My granddad introduced me to the music and encouraged me to sing, along with my speech therapist. I also had lots of free time, seeing as I didn't have a full social calendar. I spent a lot of those hours building models and mucking around outside, and playing with that super cool yo-yo, but I'd also research Elvis on the internet. I learned he'd never taken a guitar lesson, couldn't even read or write music, and I think that stuck with me, how a man could do something great with nothing. He made rock and roll an international language, brought people together. He made *me* feel whole and invincible when I listened and sang his songs, not like a loser who couldn't form a sentence."

Elvis had rehabilitated him, the way Jack yearned to rehabilitate others: birds and frogs as a kid, his beautiful reptiles now. Clementine. Maybe that was where his compassion came from, wishing to banish that damaged feeling from his youth. Helping others see the best in themselves. "You make a wonderful Elvis," she said, hoping he saw her understanding and how hard she'd fallen for him.

He stared at her so long her cheeks heated. Then his brow furrowed. "Do you know how to swim?"

She sputtered out a laugh. "Why would you ask that?"

"That song about your name. It terrifies me."

The sudden pressure on Clementine's chest terrified her. "I never learned."

"I'll have to teach you. We'll use my parents' pool."

She hadn't seen the pool. She wasn't prepared to feel this much this soon. The same fears Jack just voiced swirled through her, the idea of him hurt in any way unthinkable. Her mind flashed to Yevgen, the madman's knife piercing her skin, his creepy tattoo and threat to hurt those she loved.

Jack couldn't get hurt.

"What foods do you hate?" she asked before she panicked. *Silly. I'm being silly.* The mundane question was also easier than blurting *I love you.* But those words were there, balancing on the tip of her tongue. *You better not get hurt. I love you too much.*

She resumed her chopping, wasn't sure when she'd stopped. The repetitive movements calmed her and drove home her need to quit overthinking.

Jack pressed his nose to her hair and breathed her in. "Not a fan of Brussels sprouts. You?"

She wrinkled her nose. "Shellfish and bacon."

He froze. "Everyone loves bacon."

"Not this girl."

"But it's the best food."

She turned toward him, loving the feel of her hip sliding against his. "Are you arguing with a knife-wielding woman who's trained in basic combat?"

He set his coffee down, removed the utensil from her hand,

then caged her against his granite counter. "I'm arguing with a sexy cat burglar." He hummed a tune and pressed his lips to Clementine's ear. "Don't go stealing my heart," he sang.

She knew the melody— Elton John's "Don't Go Breaking My Heart." The play on words was cute, but wariness undermined her mood. "Are you sure you're not having second thoughts?" she asked tentatively.

Cat burglar. Stealing hearts. Jokes were often rooted in truth.

He rolled his hips forward, the hard length of him stating his desire. "Does it feel like I'm having second thoughts?"

Naughty boy. She coasted her hands around his shoulders and down the hard muscles of his back. She squeezed his fine behind. "You're sure?"

He kissed her lips, once, twice, a third time. "I know we can't talk about your past in public, but I don't want it to be an avoided topic between us. Doing that could turn it into something bigger. It could hurt us. So if I ask about your work or make a joke, that's why." He glanced down and gnawed on his bottom lip. "And I want you to be patient. Don't expect everything to fall into place—friends, work, life in general. Don't freak out if you have setbacks."

"Okay," she said, touched he cared so much.

His smolder returned. "Okay, meaning I can fuck you on this counter?"

That would so be happening, but she wanted more details. Every last one. "First tell me something that scares you."

He kept her pinned to the counter, his brow puckering as he thought. With enough gravity to have her holding her breath, he said, "People who don't eat bacon."

She rolled her eyes. "Something that makes you angry."

"People who don't eat bacon."

She flicked his ribs. "You're not playing fair."

"You asked and I answered. What makes you angry?"

"Men who get angry at people for not eating bacon. What if I was kosher?"

"Not the same thing."

"Your idiot light is on the fritz again."

He was full on smirking now, his dimples winking at her. "As bad as the first day we met?"

"So much worse."

His current road sign would read: *Beware of sexy idiot, life-changing words like* love *ahead.* Could a person even fall in love this quickly? Or was this intensity her inexperience? The overwhelming feelings of basking in all things Jack, the first man to know her name and age and that she hated bacon? She gave her head a small shake and focused on what was real. What she wanted *right now.* "I recall you saying something about fucking me on this counter."

"I did, didn't I? I'm also rethinking my breakfast. There's something else I'd like to eat."

They forgot about fruit and yogurt. They forgot about the world as they dropped their clothes and Jack dropped to his knees. He spread her legs and turned her boneless in minutes, his skilled tongue and hands shredding her sense. Then he was in her, his hips unrelenting. He took charge again, telling her where and how to move, his end game always her. Her pleasure. Her release. Like her satisfaction was his foreplay.

Clementine floated through the rest of her morning until they were in Jack's car, holding hands as he drove her to pick up her Prius.

"Move in with me," he said abruptly, dropping the atomic bomb, like it was an ordinary conversation on any ordinary day.

The man had lost his marbles. "Did you hit your head during sex?"

"I did not."

"Did you hold your breath too long when doing that thing with your tongue and now you've lost a few too many brain cells?"

Eyes on the road, he grinned a devilish grin. "You liked that thing?"

"It's my new favorite thing."

"Noted." His phone chimed with a message. He ignored it and signaled a turn, humming while he drove. "So you'll move in?"

"That would be insane."

He yanked his car to the side of the road and parked. Someone honked and waved. Smallest town in the world.

Jack crowded her. "Insane is how badly I want to be inside you right now—*again*—but I have to work, then rehearse, then perform, then maybe work some more. If you're not sleeping in my bed, I'm not sure when I'll see you. And I need to see you."

To reassure himself he'd made the right decision? Her insecurity resurfaced, and she mentally chastised herself. Their night and morning had been amazing. Because of their talk or in spite of it, she couldn't say. Either way, each round between the sheets and in the kitchen had gotten better, more intimate. She'd be crazy to say no.

"Okay, but I'll—"

He kissed her before she could demand to pay her way. Whatever. She'd check out the surrounding mechanic shops, get a job and contribute where she could. Use her small savings to buy groceries and such. In a few weeks, she'd return to New York, pick up Lucy and organize her belongings, then drive her hard-and-fast Charger back to Whichway.

Another honk and wave. Her cheeks heated. "Does the whole town know about us already?"

"Guaranteed." His phone buzzed again. He ignored it.

"It's like living in a fishbowl."

"Does it bother you?"

It would have terrified the old Clementine. Now... "I kind of love it." *And you*, she didn't say, those three words still hovering.

The next honk blasted for a couple of seconds, followed by Imelda's head hanging out the car's passenger window. "Check your phone, Jack! Marco and Lauralee have two girls!"

Jack froze, then fumbled for his phone. He smiled as he read the message, his brightening glow seeping into Clementine. "Two perfect girls," he murmured and showed her the photo.

She only wanted to look at Jack. Watching him swoon over baby pictures was a sight to behold.

He typed a message back, then returned to the road, but his mood dimmed as he drove, a gradual despondence she didn't understand. They'd had a great night. His best friend had just had twins. He'd been ecstatic a second ago. She fiddled with her precious necklace.

He stopped at her car and rubbed his jaw. "Key," he said distractedly. "I'll give you mine and grab an extra from Marvin."

He reached for his set from the cup holder, but she stilled his hand and tilted his face toward her. The dark circles under his eyes were partly due to their lack of sleep, but she wasn't the only cause. With all they'd discussed, she hadn't asked about his family, his challenging job. So many burdens. "How's your dad?"

He swallowed hard. "No better, but no worse. He's holding strong."

"And the business? The tech stuff you're working on?"

"Fine. Everything will be fine." The same platitudes he'd

offered his mother. False bravado. He searched her face, then deflated slightly. "Not fine, actually. I hit a speedbump yesterday morning. I thought we were going to have a breakthrough, but it might be a setback."

"I'd ask for details, but I wouldn't be much help."

"Knowing I'm coming home to you is a help." Still, a muscle in his jaw bunched.

"Who can you talk to about work?"

His next pause lasted longer. "I discuss the project with my team, but they don't understand the time constraints and pressure, the repercussions if we fail. I don't want to add extra worry to my family, and I was sure I'd have this done by the festival so I could announce the new technology and stop lying about my father. I was so sure it would be settled."

His frustration seemed to sit heavy on his slumping shoulders. She was no engineer, had no clue how to solve this for him, but his openness? Sharing the concerns he often hid? It meant everything. "You still have a few more days."

"It's not even about that anymore. Don't get me wrong—I want nothing more than to have my father out and enjoying the show, so he can watch me one last time, if that's what this is for him. But there's more at stake."

More employees could be fired. Marco's good news flashed through her mind, Jack's slipping mood. "What does Marco do for you?"

He blinked a few times, then blew out a rough breath. "He runs our charities. Researches where to spend the money, does fundraising and disperses funds."

Non-essential work. Her heart clenched. "He's next on the pink-slip list, isn't he?"

Jack twisted his hands around the steering wheel. "He should have been on the last round, but I couldn't do it. I mean,

Jesus—he just had twins. He needs this job. How can I look my best friend in the face and ruin his life?"

She'd heard enough to know how close he was with Marco. The pressure must be killing him. Even still, he'd given her last night and this morning, was determined to work her into his hectic world. "Maybe I should go back to New York. Spend a few weeks there to get organized before returning. Give you time to focus."

He released the steering wheel and laced their fingers together. "Not having you around the past three days was painful and distracting. After last night, it'll be worse. This is so fresh. Too fresh." He winced slightly. "I want more time together before you go back."

Tension rolled off him, more than seemed right. He couldn't seriously believe she'd change her mind now, could he? "You're worried I won't come back."

"Of course."

His honesty bowled her over, but the man was a fool. A sentimental, perfect fool. She undid her seatbelt and crawled toward him, wedging herself sideways onto his lap. "But no one else does that thing you do with your tongue."

He smiled, thank God, and palmed her bottom. "No one else has cinnamon eyes quite like yours. Or calms me like you do," he said more quietly.

If she weren't pinned between his lap and the steering wheel, she'd probably float away. "Guess I better stay, then. For the calming factor. And to cheer for you when you perform and boo that Alistair character."

He glowered. "Alistair is the worst."

This, however, was the best: feeling part of Team Jack. He had confided in her, sharing his worries, just as she had with him.

He dropped her off and she drove her car to her motel, her

inner giggly teen resurfacing as she neared. Her fingers twitched, eager to pull out her laptop and email her father. She pushed inside her room quickly and picked up her briefcase, then jerked to a stop. There was a thread on the floor, the thin string she'd placed over the zipper, one of her meticulous fail-safes, to catch an intruder.

The thread falling would mean someone had touched her bag, but she didn't know if it had fallen off before or after she'd picked her bag up. She'd been too distracted to notice.

She braced her legs and studied the room. The maroon comforter was still piled on the carpet. The bed was unmade. The bible was still ninety degrees with the nightstand edge. The Do Not Disturb sign had been hung on her plywood door. Nothing was amiss and no one should have been in here, but she went through everything anyway. The bathroom. Her drawers. Her suitcase. All was well, but paranoia prickled like it had before Jack's performance and when he'd questioned the moved electrical cord. Three times now.

Still, nothing else *had* been touched. The thread had probably been hanging over the zipper, as she'd left it, and she'd knocked it off when picking up the bag.

Just to be safe, she texted Lucien as planned.

Clementine: **Anyone in town I should know about?**

She watched her phone and bounced her knee until his reply came through.

Lucien: **As far as I know, all's clear. Something up?**

She nibbled the inside of her lip while eyeing the fallen thread. Aside from being jumpy, Clementine hadn't actually seen anything concerning at the Elvis show, and Jack had said he'd probably moved the electrical cord. She could easily explain the thread. Her instincts still tingled, but she was probably overreacting.

Clementine: **Nothing's up. Just being cautious. If you hear anything, let me know.**

She almost added that she missed him and couldn't wait to go for dinner or meet for coffee or watch him brush his teeth. Needy Nelly. At least he'd replied swiftly. Not that she was surprised. He wouldn't play hot potato and drop her just because they weren't partners. Something else she should accept. Every shift and change wasn't a sign of the apocalypse. Lucien would always be in her life.

Emailing her father was the best way to regain her sanity. The second her fingers hit the keyboard, her worries began to fade. A swarm of butterflies filled the nervous cracks the fallen thread had left.

She gushed for two pages about her very own Elvis Presley. Nothing felt real until she'd emailed her dad, even though he'd never read the messages. A wish sent into the wind. But writing the words solidified this newfound relationship. She'd be there for Jack as much as possible and hate on whoever gave him trouble—Alistair and Ava would be getting some serious stink eye. She would do her best to integrate into this life and get to know Marco and Jack's friends.

Her fingers paused, hovering over the keypad as a different worry sparked. Firing your best friend who'd just had twins could lead to regret and resentment. If Clementine became a distraction, she could wind up in that line of fire. She would be an easy target to hit. Residual nerves blossomed, reminding her how fragile their new beginning was. Then she replayed their night and morning, the hungry look in his blue-suede eyes as he pushed inside her.

I love him, she wrote to her father. *I already love him so much it hurts. If I lose him, it will devastate me.*

23

———

Jack shouldn't be happy. He shouldn't find himself smiling for no reason. His father was fighting for his life. His family business could be weeks from imploding, but here he was, his pen poised over his scribbled notes, a goofy smile on his face, like he was thirty-one going on thirteen.

Clementine Abernathy was to blame.

If he could sequester her in his house for a week, to talk and make love day and night, it wouldn't satisfy his cravings. He had enjoyed his few girlfriends. Three women in his life were enough to know how happiness felt. Clementine was happiness to the tenth power. She was adrenaline. She was better than an adoring crowd whistling and cheering for him. He couldn't wait to spoil her, show her how full life could be. How good they would be together, and he knew exactly where to start.

Another perfect gift for his little cat burglar.

A knock on the door was followed by Marco's head popping in. "How was your night? Anything you wish to share?"

"Why are you here?" He should be with his girls. All three of them. Not nosing around for gossip.

"Left a few loose ends on the Every Cent project that needed tying up. Thought I'd sneak in while Lauralee slept."

"And harass me?"

"The town is buzzing, my friend. I heard you were making out on the side of the road."

Jack really did live in a fishbowl, but the making out had been too good to be annoyed with the gossip. As was the trust he was building with Clementine. He hadn't realized how badly he'd needed to discuss his business difficulties until she'd ferreted out his troubles. With everyone else, he had to be careful. With everyone else, there were reasons to keep secrets. Not with her. They knew each other's deepest and darkest.

"Clementine is staying in town," Jack said. "She's moving in."

Marco a weird whooshing sound effect and pretended to pitch an invisible baseball. "Isn't that kind of fast?"

"Didn't you profess your love to Lauralee after two dates?"

"Point taken, but she was the first good thing to happen to me after I lost my scholarship." He flexed his wrist, as though the memory brought with it physical pain. "I owe her my life."

"Pretty sure I was the one who forced you to sober up and got punched for the effort."

"I owe you, too, man. For everything. Including this job."

Not the reminder he needed. "You earned it."

"I begged for this job, and you know it. Who else was gonna hire an injured pitcher without a college degree?"

"You excel at what you do. You've made a difference in the world." Like Clementine had, although her methods had been questionable. He still worried leaving that life was easier said than done. Once the realities of regular work kicked in, she could have second thoughts and disappear from his life as quickly as she'd appeared. A smart man would keep his heart protected, but if he wanted her to open up and be honest with him, he had to do the same.

"I am good at my job," Marco said. "Unfortunately most people don't look past a résumé. But I didn't stop by to worship your overpaid ass or needle you about your love life, or gush about my perfect wife and perfect baby girls, who are absolutely perfect, by the way."

They shared a grin. "I'm thrilled for you both. Can't wait to meet them."

"We look forward to it, which brings me to my point." He sat in the chair opposite Jack's glass desk.

The corner-office windows looked out over a forest, trails, and streams. A constant reminder of Whichway's beauty, the land and people he helped support through his business, including the man opposite him, who needed this job and paycheck. And Jack was so damn close, on the verge of their next leap of progress. Day in and day out, he turned over his experiments, tried to solve the unsolvable. Even in bed, his brain never rested.

Except for last night. And this morning.

"We want you to be the girls' godfather," Marco said.

Jack's mind snapped on target. Twin girls. Godfather. A sting burned behind his eyes. He passed his hand over his mouth until his emotions settled. "You sure I'm the right choice?"

Marco leaned back and shrugged. "It was either you or one of the D Squad. Figured you could at least teach them how to use a yo-yo."

Chuckling, Jack tossed his pen at Marco's face. Marco batted it away, and Jack relaxed into his leather chair for what felt like the first time in months. Years, maybe. He smiled at his best friend, full of love for him and his new family. He smiled about Clementine Abernathy, who would be receiving an airline ticket to India so she could join him on his upcoming trip. An extravagance, considering how tightly he spent his money these days. But travel points earned through his business made the majority of this gift easy on his pocketbook.

He smiled wider, picturing Clementine walking off the plane, excitement in her steps. Touring the city together, learning each other's travel quirks.

His vision blurred at the edges, filled with so much goodness. Love for his friend's blessings and this amazing woman crowded out his anxieties until something shaped in his mind: the lens issue he'd been grappling with. A change. A tweak to the extra layer of substrates.

The possibilities teased him. Foggy at first, but no...*no*. It was there. So fucking there. How had he missed this for months?

He'd known the optics were the issue, had understood the problem, but he hadn't been able to pinpoint the exact complication. He saw it clearly now, because he'd given his brain a break. Because Clementine had forced him to focus on something else, like remembering that movie title or word after you'd quit obsessing over it.

He shot to his feet. "I have to get to the research team, but tell Lauralee I'm beyond honored. I'll swing by tomorrow. Might bring a gift or seven." He might be able to save the job Marco didn't know he could lose.

Marco stood and pulled Jack into a hug. "Thanks, man. And just bring your girl. We'd love to meet her."

He'd love that, too, slotting Clementine more permanently in his life. He also couldn't wait to thank her for indirectly helping with his breakthrough.

24

———

ALTHOUGH JACK'S extravagant home was as foreign to Clementine as living in the North Pole, she couldn't imagine being anywhere else.

She lounged in his shelter, a habit she'd come to enjoy the past two days of cohabitation. The only thing missing was Lucy. Her bearded dragon would be right at home here, too. Lucy *would* be here in a few weeks, sharing Ricky's enclosure, enjoying the humidity and foliage. A luxury compared to her small terrarium. Clementine would visit often, like she did now. It was so easy to lose track of hours in here. Too easy, and Jack would be dressed soon, leaving to get ready for tonight's performance. His second-to-last Elvis concert.

She lay on her side and faced Ella. "He's being sneaky," she told the chameleon.

Jack had a particular fondness for the sweet thing, sang to her softly at times. Ella would settle near the glass, her color its natural shades of light green, proving her calmness. "I think he bought me something," Clementine said. "And he knows it's going to piss me off."

Ella stared dead ahead.

Clementine sighed. "If it's excessive, I'll rip him a new one. I don't even have a job yet and he's already put a roof over my head."

Unless her fortunes changed soon. This morning's hands-on interview had gone well. Ray's Auto Body was as much an old boy's club as any mechanic shop, but they'd tested her diagnostic skills. After Ray had described the Volkswagen's laments—engine light on, exhaust smoke, shrieking noise—she'd maneuvered an endoscope down the Golf's turbine, and bingo! Turbocharger failure. Ray had grudgingly praised her diagnosis. The win didn't mean he'd offer her the job. "But maybe, right?" she said to Ella. "He might take pity on me."

The chameleon continued staring.

Clementine flopped onto her back. This one-way conversation wasn't so different from emailing her father or talking to Lucy at home. No, not home. New York wasn't home any longer. Whichway was home. Jack was home.

Knocking sounded from the entrance—Jack signaling his departure.

She dragged herself up and met him in the entryway. The second he saw her, he dropped his phone on the side table, like it had burned his hand.

"You're up to something, mister." Being a super sneak. The past two days he'd jumped when she'd entered a room, quick to hide his phone. "Are you having an affair?"

He glowered playfully and stalked toward her. "How would I have stamina for an affair? You keep me up all night."

"You're Marathon Jack, remember? Maybe all your time at work is a ruse."

"Not a chance in hell." He dropped an open-mouthed kiss on her neck and worked lower. "I'm going to take you from behind tonight. Go so deep. Come so hard in you."

She might fall apart from his words alone, but she pushed him away. "You can't kiss me and talk dirty when you're dressed like that."

Like Elvis Presley. He wore a bedazzled powder-blue jumpsuit with huge lapels, the front V-neck dipping mid-chest. Full tribute-artist mode. She'd never have thought she had an Elvis kink. She was too turned on to stand still. "Seriously. You need to leave or I'll maul you and you'll be late and lose to Alistair, and I won't get to gloat and toss popcorn at him like I planned."

In character, he winked at her and snarled his lip. "Just 'cuz you asked so nice, doll. But don't miss my performance. I've got a surprise for you after."

She eyed the bulge in his tight pants. "Can I put this surprise in my mouth?"

He groaned. "You could, but I wouldn't recommend it."

The sneak had definitely done something for her, and it wasn't cool. "If you bought me a gift, Jack, I reserve the right to turn it down."

"Not possible when you promised to quit judging how I spend my money."

She knew she'd live to regret that promise. "It better not be over the top."

He grinned wider. "I owe you. You're the reason David Industries will have a big announcement to make."

"I didn't do anything."

"Nonsense. I wouldn't have solved the lens problem without you in my life. The team is thrilled. All systems are go, and that new patent means we'll weather any storm Gunther's stolen technology sparks. David Industries will grow. The factory and town will thrive. You're my muse."

She shrugged off the compliment, but felt tingly and warm. Any success was all Jack's. He was clever and creative and would have solved his lens problem in time. Just like she was responsible for the one-eighty her life had taken. Jack had been a catalyst, but she'd been the one to pull the trigger, like his brilliant brain had done all the heavy lifting.

They were good for each other. The best.

She followed him to the door. "How soon until you can announce?"

"Still a few days, if not more. Dad's being extra cautious, refuses to tell the board about his illness yet, but the pressure's off." A few locks of his dark hair hung over his forehead, crossing the crease settling on his brow. The pressure was off, but his father wouldn't watch Jack perform.

"I can video tomorrow's final show for him," she offered. "I know it's not the same, but we can watch it on that massive TV, or Chloe can do her impression of you doing *your* Elvis impression."

He fought a laugh. "I don't do impressions. I'm a tribute—"

"Artist," she finished. "I know, and you're the best. And I'm not just saying that. When you perform, I get swept away. The audience does, too. You're magic on stage. I can't imagine how proud your father is. How proud your grandfather would be. You're just..." Perfect. Amazing. The best man she'd ever known.

She clamped her mouth shut before she blurted out her heart.

Jack stared at her so intently, goosebumps cascaded down her spine. He closed the gap between them and pressed her against his sparkly suit. He was so solid and warm, made her feel small and feminine. She had never expected to meet a man who could light her up like this, make her world feel bountiful, the ground beneath her firm and fertile.

Emotion flared in his eyes as he leaned down. "I love you, Clementine."

The room spun. Her hands shook as an unexpected ache lanced through her. Had her heart actually exploded? Except she hadn't exploded. She was frozen, so epically stiff he probably thought she didn't feel the same.

But she did. She so did. Why couldn't she say the stupid words?

He kissed her before she could reply or cry or pass out. She lost herself against his lips. *I love you so much*, she thought. *I love you to the moon and back.*

Jack pulled away and pressed his forehead to hers. "Don't say it. Not because I did. Say it when you're ready, when it gets too hard to keep it in."

It *was* too hard. Painfully so. Those words had been teasing her tongue with their sweetness for days, but saying them was scarier than picking a lock and stealing a priceless painting.

He gave her another meaningful look, Elvis persona in place, then swaggered to his car. She barely moved. She watched his Tesla disappear down the long road, unease growing. She fiddled with her necklace as regret swamped her. She should have said it back. She wanted to reverse time and breathe the words into his mouth, fill his lungs and chest with them. She hadn't reinvented herself to become a coward.

Her phone buzzed and she snatched it, hoping it was him. A chance to right her wrong and pull up her big-girl panties. The sight of a message from Ray's Auto Body only upped her anxiety. *Get a grip, girl.* If this job didn't work out, there'd be another. But there wouldn't be another Jack. She'd tell him how she felt first thing after his show, jump into his arms and confess her love. For now she didn't want to be alone while learning her job news.

She returned to the shelter and sat cross-legged, facing Ella. "If I didn't get it, it's no big deal, right?"

Ella stared blandly. Clementine nodded, fortified.

She read Ray's short note and punched the air. "Goddamn right, I got it. I swear, this place is destiny. I'm meant to be here."

Everything was somehow, magically, falling into place. She'd get to work on cars and make an honest living. She wouldn't be a lone tree on a bleak landscape. She couldn't wait to tell Jack.

AN HOUR later she stood in front of the town's main stage, a bouncing Imelda at her side. Imelda's husband and daughter jigged to their right. Alistair was on stage, and Clementine refused to dance. She glared at him.

"If you keep making that face," Imelda hollered, "it'll stay that way."

"The guy's an a—" Imelda's daughter glanced her way, and Clementine had the good sense to switch tactics. "He's a loser."

"He won last year. And Lawson swears plenty, honey. Don't worry about offending young sensibilities."

Thanks to their spot near the stage, Alistair looked directly at Clementine. He gyrated his hips and winked at her. Yep. Total asshole. His voice *maybe* wasn't half bad, and the cheering crowd was enthralled, but where Alistair was pomp and peacock, Jack was charisma and class. The two didn't compare.

If the concert were outside, she'd give him the finger and wander through the stalls and stuff her face with candy during this impersonator's—*not* tribute artist's—two-song set. But this venue was indoors, affording fewer options.

The Maxwell David Arena had been funded by Jack's father, the name less inventive than those of other local businesses. The space was used for ice hockey and skating year round, and hosted the odd concert and this festival. Pretty cool for a town of Whichway's size, and another reason the David family was held in high regard. The space was packed, even at the sixty-dollar ticket price.

She touched her purse, prepared to tap through her phone, hoping Alistair noticed her lack of interest, then she remembered she'd left her cell at home. She'd need it to video Jack's final performance tomorrow, but leaving it behind tonight had been a conscious choice. She no longer needed her link to Lucien. Disconnecting was therapeutic. The only connection she craved would be performing on stage shortly.

Instead of suffering through Alistair's effusive hip thrusts, she nudged Imelda. "I'm gonna get a beer. You want anything?"

Imelda shook her head and shimmied her shoulders. "Too hard to dance with beer, but thanks for asking."

She smacked a kiss on Clementine's cheek, the upbeat drum line taking up song in Clementine's chest. Love from Jack, affection from Imelda. She already felt tipsy on happiness, but a beer would hit the spot, too.

She pushed through the all-ages crowd and plucked at the front of her tank top, hoping to cool down. The material might have been thin and loose, but excessive dancing bodies created heat. And energy. She couldn't fight her smile or the bop of her head. She shouldn't bop. Not when Jack's nemesis, who was maybe kind of awesome, was performing. His rendition of "Blue Suede Shoes" was infectious, dammit.

"Clementine!"

She searched for the source of her name and spotted Chloe. She waved to Jack's sister and fought her way over. "What are you doing back here?"

Chloe's goofy grin was aimed at a boy her age. The boy's cool factor was more calculated than effortless, with a sweep of blond hair covering his eyes, but he was cute and smiled at Chloe while chatting with his friends.

Well done, girl. "Is that who I think it is?"

"He asked me out this morning. I was too frantic figuring out what to wear to text you."

The combat boots, ripped black jeans, and vintage Goo Goo Dolls tank top were perfect. No micro-mini skirt that would send Jack into a panic. "He definitely likes you."

"Really?" Her desperation was adorable. "How do you know?"

"When he looked over here, his eyes lingered. Plus you're funny and smart and beautiful, and he'd be an idiot not to notice."

Chloe's cheeks blushed crimson. "He's so cute."

"You're so cute. You should meet us by the stage, get a better view of your brother. Imelda's holding my spot."

Chloe's gaze flitted to her boy of the moment. No doubt there would be others in the coming years. "Nah. We'll stay back here."

Away from her overprotective brother. Smart cookie. "Any chance you'll hang with me tomorrow? I told Jack I'd video his final performance for your dad."

"Yeah, sure. Sounds great!" Chloe moved as she talked, lured by the awe of newborn hormones, but her easy agreement turned Clementine's tipsy happy into a drunk happy.

Two steps later, Tami caught Clementine's eye through the crowd and hollered, "Heard you changed living arrangements. I need details."

Tami was, *thankfully*, too far to ambush her for those details, but the yelling had turned heads. If the whole town hadn't known she was living with Jack, they sure did now. She should be embarrassed, horrified these folks knew the minutia of her life. Instead, her drunk happy veered toward sloshed.

Beaming like she had her first Halloween with Lucien, before she'd puked on his floor from eating all her candy in one sitting, she continued on her way. Marvin—Jack's gardener and the keeper of his shelter—patted her shoulder as she passed. The town's Elvis festival liaison, Jasmine, stopped her when she finally reached the bar.

"Sorry the judging didn't work out," Jasmine said. "But I hear you'll be staying in Whichway. Call me for a coffee sometime."

Jasmine hurried off to meet friends, and Clementine gawked at...everything.

Somehow she'd fallen madly in love. She'd met friends, with more of them on the horizon. She had a reptile shelter to lounge in, a job doing what she loved. She had a cool twelve-year-old girl asking her advice and willing to hang out like sisters. This wasn't normal. Her new world couldn't be this nice and welcoming and full of Elvis goodness.

Whichway must truly be a Dr. Seuss creation.

The crowd roared behind her, a familiar voice rumbling through the sound system. Jack. She should be at the front, cheering for her man. Not that she'd minded this jaunt to the bar and chatting with her new friends. All she wanted now was to be closer to Jack.

Plastic cup of beer in hand, she began her march back. No distractions this time. Not when the sexiest Elvis she'd ever seen was strutting his stuff in a bedazzled jumpsuit.

He sang the opening lyrics to "Are You Lonesome Tonight," and her feet faltered. His voice was velvet. Shivers slipped over her skin. She pictured them in bed this morning, couldn't believe they had endless mornings and days and nights ahead of them. He was hers. He was too far away, but she couldn't move. *Love.* All she could think was love.

I love him so much.

He seduced the audience with his haunting voice and

glanced at where she should be standing. He frowned. Just a second, but the reaction hit her in the heart.

She hurried closer, but got caught behind an Everest-sized biker, his tattooed neck the width of her thigh. Grumbling, she maneuvered around him, beer clutched to keep from spilling. She was halfway to her spot, but Jack was halfway through his song, and he kept glancing at Imelda, that frown sinking deeper. Did he think she hadn't come? That his *I love you* had scared her off?

She'd really screwed up, not saying it when she'd had the chance. A mistake she could fix right now, because she was drunk on happiness and tipsy on wonderful Whichway. The band quieted, Jack's voice turning silky as the lyrics transformed into a tender poem, and she whistled on her fingers. Loud. Piercing. Lucien had taught her that move, much to his chagrin.

Jack's attention snapped her way. He didn't miss a beat, but his eyes scoured the crowd and found her. His frown spread into a grin.

Her poor little heart hiccupped. Holding her beer to her fluttery chest, she mouthed *I love you.*

Jack kept singing, eyes on her. She wasn't sure if he'd read her lips, but his tone turned even silkier, his movements more soulful. She could drown in that voice. She searched for a better path to Imelda, and closer to Jack, her sights skimming over swaying heads. One head caught her eye, something familiar about the bearded man. She squinted, leaned forward...and her knees locked.

She dropped her beer. Someone cursed her. The music and crowd faded into white noise.

Yevgen Liski had never worn a beard, but there was no mistaking the dark slash of the man's eyebrows, his menacing scowl. *He couldn't be here.* Lucien had said the Van Gogh hadn't flagged attention. He hadn't reported any concerns, and it wasn't the sort of heist Yevgen favored. Why the hell was he here?

Her lungs seized, the beer-tinged air solidifying in her chest. She blinked, hoping he was a mirage. When she looked again, he wasn't there. Gone. Just gone. An apparition? Her happy drunk messing with her mind?

She shoved her hand into her purse, only to remember leaving her cell at home. Shit. She plowed her way to Imelda, praying her friend had a phone. She'd call Lucien. He'd know if this was real or a mirage. She elbowed an older man and cringed, apologizing as she pushed ahead.

She nearly fell into Imelda as she grasped her arm. "Do you have your phone?"

Imelda's attention was fastened on stage, on Jack, who'd just finished his first number. "I do."

"I need to borrow it."

"Gotta cheer for your man first."

Clementine couldn't look at him, not if Yevgen was here. Not if she'd brought that dangerous criminal to his town. "I can't wait. It's an emergency. A work thing in New York."

Imelda fished her cell from her purse and gave Clementine a pointed stare. "You city folk need to learn to turn off."

That was the problem. Clementine *had* shut off, way before tonight. Her brain had switched to standby on her drive from New York and the whole extended route here. It had fried when shaking sweaty hands with a handsome man on the side of the road. It had floated away when Jack had confessed his love. Now Yevgen could be in town.

Jack's next song began, more fun and upbeat: "Burning Love."

She scanned the crowd, didn't see Yevgen anywhere. She speed-walked to the arena's edge as Jack's powerful voice chased her heels. *Please tell me I was seeing things.* She dialed Lucien's number and waited. He didn't pick up. She sent a quick text, but no reply came. His phone could be dead. Or he could be out. He had no "partner" to keep track of any longer and this wasn't a recognizable number, because she'd thought disconnecting from her life would be smart. Dumbest con-woman alive.

She scanned the dimly lit arena again. Nothing. She clicked on the phone's internet icon. If the number was the issue, Lucien would at least answer an email from her account. She would take a breath afterward, figure out what to do. Tell Jack first thing. Make sure the estate used its alarms. She'd get rid of the Van Gogh and the temptation it held. Yes. They could secure his family, ensure nothing went wrong.

That the Monet Disaster didn't repeat.

Thumbs shaking, she fumbled her email password three times. When she finally opened her account, she yelped.

She had one message. From her dead father.

What in the actual fuck?

No matter how much she blinked, the message was still there. From a deceased man. She opened it, her stomach lurching. Just as quickly, her confusion spun into horror.

Daddy loved you, Clementine. And he's dead. No one you love will ever be safe.

That last line. She knew it. Yevgen had spat those words while his blade had twisted in her gut, and all the strange happenings the past week roared back: feeling like she was being watched, the moved alarm cord, the fallen thread in her motel. It hadn't been her who'd knocked off that thread, after all. Yevgen had been stalking them.

He must have hacked into her email and found her letters to her father, details about her affections for Jack and

Whichway. She didn't do tech jobs, but hacking wasn't a stretch, and that unforgettable line made this invasion personal.

Heart in her throat, she scoured the audience. When she didn't find Yevgen, her eyes landed on Jack. So confident. No stutter in sight. He was handsome and kind and had forgiven her for her deceits. And this was how she repaid him? Bringing danger to his town, his family?

No. No way would she put him at risk. Not now, or ever. This wasn't even about the painting for Yevgen. He'd hated her since the first prize she'd stolen out from under him, and he wanted to hurt her where it counted. She still couldn't wrap her head around his obsession, but dissecting his motivations wouldn't help her. Only one thing would. The hardest thing.

She had to leave Jack.

She choked on a sob, but what did she expect? Criminals didn't ride off into the sunset. Getting everything she wanted wasn't in the cards for her. If Yevgen wasn't a threat, someone else would be. She'd stolen from people. Those actions came with consequences. Hers was losing Jack.

Frantic, she checked if Lucien answered her text. Nothing. She sent him a quick email, then typed a reply to Yevgen, using Lucien's teachings about long cons as she went, how the aftercare was as important as the initial lure. *Make yourself inculpable*, Lucien would say. *Give them what they need. Fill the emotional void they crave and they'll never suspect you.*

She'd done it often, would spend a couple of weeks with her marks after a heist, as a friend or confidant. Go on the occasional date. Disappearing as soon as a job was performed raised suspicion, so she'd flirt expertly, avoid intimacy, and string them along until the coast was clear.

She knew this game. She just had to convince Yevgen this was a long con and she wasn't soul-deep in love with Jack. Once she and the painting were away from here, there'd be no reason for Yevgen to stay.

She controlled her breaths as she reread her reply.

You're as gullible as my mark, Yevgen. Not that I should be surprised. Nabbed the painting a week ago. Lucien has it. Had a slipup and had to take the con deeper, but when I "accidentally" leave these emails open for Jack to read, gushing about my love for him, he'll believe my tears when I break up with him to take a job overseas. If they discover the forgery, he'll never suspect me. You, however, are an easy suspect. I could drop that torn piece of your shirt in the house as evidence. Place a call. Quit stalking me, or I'll sing.

The last line made her think of Jack's knee-weakening voice and everything she'd be leaving. The pain was hard to breathe through, but she didn't have a choice. She had to focus on facing a madman.

Just to be safe, she did a directory search and called Jack's mother, who answered swiftly.

"Hi, Sylvia. It's Clementine." She stuck her finger in her other ear to drown the arena noise. "Jack wanted me to let you know there was a break-in outside of town, one of the tourists likely. Nothing to worry about, but he wants you to put on your alarm and make sure all doors are locked."

Sylvia tutted. "What a shame. Seems like the festival draws unsavory sorts these days. Are you at the concert? How was Jack?"

Clementine couldn't talk about Jack. One word about him, and she'd break. "It's loud and I'm having trouble hearing you. Just make sure you set the alarm."

She barely listened as Sylvia agreed and hung up. Yevgen hadn't replied yet. He could be heading to the estate now. Her thumb hovered over the number nine. Calling the cops and alerting them to Yevgen would be smart, an extra step to ensure protection, but her throat dried. She'd be implicated. Yevgen would disappear as usual, evade detection, and she'd wind up in the slammer.

Sicker than before, she lowered the phone with a shaky hand.

Best thing she could do was disappear from Whichway and never come back. Start over somewhere new. Be a lone tree. Living in a forest as lush as this meant forest fires could strike.

Jack's performance was nearing its end. He'd be off stage soon. Her cue to get her shit together. The fact that he didn't know she'd gotten that mechanic job would help her con him one last time, but the prospect of lying to him had her nauseated again. She swallowed and gritted her teeth. Time to find out how good of an actress Clementine Abernathy, con-woman and cat burglar, could be.

25

JACK'S SKULL POUNDED. His hands itched. Clementine had peeled off from Imelda, looking rattled. Now she was hunched over her phone, oblivious to his performance, and he couldn't shake the feeling that something was wrong. He wanted to leap off stage and ask what was worrying her. Or maybe it was his ego talking, the desire to have his girl's attention messing with him.

He powered on, played to the audience. Kept time with the band. He flicked his hair and deepened his voice, found his rhythm. *Sing. Just sing. Win this thing for Dad.*

But a man's profile slid into his vision, the tattooed creep who'd been curt with Jack at the diner and had eyed Clementine the night they'd first kissed. The lurker had seemed dodgy at Whenever Bar, nursing his beer in that dark booth, eyes constantly flicking to Clementine. He was part of the reason Jack had joined her for a drink. Jack should feel gratitude for that push, but the man wasn't watching the stage. He was a distance from Clementine, arms crossed, eyes locked on her again.

Somehow Jack sang and performed, more by rote than anything. He'd rehearsed plenty, could sing "Burning Love" backward. The only thought looping through his mind was *get to Clementine.*

The number finally ended. He smiled and bowed, then hurried off stage, but people slowed his progress, clapping his back and trying to shake his hand. *Get to Clementine.* When he could extricate himself, he strode into the auditorium and was hit by another wall of people. Some tried to congratulate him. Others held their phones up for a photo. Flashes blared. The band kicked up, the crowd's hoots and hollers disorientating.

Get to Clementine.

He found Imelda first and grabbed her shoulders. "Where is she?"

Imelda startled and didn't brandish her usual smile. She looked downright disturbed. "You okay, Jack?"

His eyes must look as wild as he felt. "Where's Clementine?"

"She borrowed my phone. Something about a work emergency."

Jack growled.

"What's going on? Do you need Lawson's help?"

Her husband was a good man, but Jack couldn't discuss Clementine's "work" with anyone. "I'm good. Just want to see my girl." Make sure she was safe.

And the work comment ate at him. Clementine could be having second thoughts about her life-changing decision. His fear from the start could be real: that she'd eventually resent a normal day-to-day existence, and him.

Imelda tipped her head toward the arena's edge, where he'd spotted Clementine while performing. "Last I saw her was over there."

Which is exactly where she wasn't. The bearded man wasn't around, either. The two likely weren't linked, but Jack's pulse wouldn't slow. He was still kicking himself for his confession at his house. He shouldn't have told her he loved her. She needed time to acclimate and dig her heels into their new life. Find a job. She'd been stressed about it. Only a few days into their new living arrangements and she'd been at loose ends, hanging out in his shelter, even falling asleep in there. Probably bored out of her mind. Her muscle car wasn't here to tinker with. Her days were aimless.

If he'd told her about her surprise, instead of making a big deal of it, she could've been focused on that. But, nope. The imbecile he was, he'd admitted he loved her. Classic no-game Jack. At thirty-one, he still couldn't play it cool.

"Jack?"

Clementine's voice had relief rushing him. He turned and crushed her to his chest. "Couldn't find you," he murmured into her hair. Safe. She was safe. Why did he feel so unhinged?

Instead of hugging him back, she shook free of his hold and returned Imelda's phone. He wasn't sure why she'd borrowed it, but it didn't matter. What mattered was making sure she knew a man had been eyeing her and that Jack had something worthwhile for her to work on while job hunting. A reason for her to stay.

"Come with me." He grabbed her hand, not giving her a chance to reply.

He maneuvered them through the crowd, to the backstage office where he'd stored his belongings. Two items in particular.

Once inside, he faced her and tried not to wince when her gaze darted away. "What happened during the show? Imelda said you had a work emergency."

"Something like that." Vague answer. Flitting gaze. Edgy movements.

Not okay.

He was dressed as Elvis, wearing his most ornate costume, a contrast to her jean shorts and breezy tank top, but she'd loved him in this earlier, had shuddered while held against him. Now she was more awkward than he'd been when they'd first met.

He had ammunition, at least, a meaningful gift that would hopefully overshadow his "I love you" fumble. *So uncool, Jack.*

He pulled two envelopes from the briefcase he'd brought and held them out to her. "This is my surprise. I should have given it to you earlier."

She dragged her teeth over her bottom lip and crossed her arms. "Whatever it is, I can't accept that."

"I thought we were past your money issues."

"It's not about excessive spending. I have to go."

His neck prickled. "Go where?"

"Home—back to New York. I've tried, Jack, but this life isn't right for me."

"It was right for you in bed this morning." Bitterness laced his tone, but he fought for control. He opened the first envelope and showed her the plane ticket. "I have a trip to India coming up—I think I mentioned it a while back. I'd like you to come. I'd love us to visit your orphanage together."

Her chin quivered, but she didn't take his gift, and his gut bottomed out. Jack had never known love. He understood that now. With Clementine in his life, the lyrics he sang held more meaning, the angst of them—pleasure laced with pain. This was why songs of heartbreak were achingly beautiful and why he couldn't catch his breath on stage these days, performing affecting him more than usual. Love was everything, and he didn't want to lose it.

More agitated, he slapped the ticket on the cluttered desk and ripped open the other envelope. A part of his brain rebelled, yelled at him that money wouldn't lure Clementine to stay, but his heart beat wildly, drowning his sense.

He shoved the check toward her crossed arms. "I sold the Van Gogh. I spoke to my parents about it, after explaining I read an article online about the missing studies. The painting was more important to my granddad than to us. With my work research done, they agreed using the money for charity would be smarter. So this is for you, to continue your work. Help the kids who need you, Clementine."

She backed up, one step, then two, hands held up like the check was on fire. "You... You can't do that, Jack."

"I can and I did."

"It's too much."

"It makes perfect sense. This is who you are, a philanthropist. Put your skills to use."

"I never dealt with the money."

"You'll learn."

"No." She shook her head, a whiplashy movement. She covered her mouth, but couldn't hide the tortured look in her eyes.

He could barely swallow. "You're happy here, Clementine. Happy with me. I know it. I also know this change can't be easy, but it's only been a few days. Please, give yourself time. Give *us* time."

She lowered her hand from her face, any trace of distress gone. "I have been happy, but not in the way you think. This has been like a vacation, but vacations get tedious. I got carried away and lost in the moment. And when you told me you loved me, I realized how different we are, how far from that kind of commitment I am. I'm not built like you, Jack. This town has felt smaller each day. Suffocating. I can't even find work."

She glared at the check in his hand. "And throwing money at me is the last thing that'll help. I'm not your charity case. I'm not a broken bird or chameleon you can fix. Which is exactly how that makes me feel. How *you* make me feel. I'm just..."

Her gaze dropped to the floor between them, and he chucked the check next to the airline ticket. So this was it. Exactly what he knew would happen. Predicting it didn't stem the pain. He wasn't sure what would cure this unrelenting ache, and it didn't fully make sense. It felt sudden and unjustified.

"You said *I love you*," he murmured, the memory jarring him.

"Pretty sure I said nothing."

He stood taller, searched her brown eyes. "While I performed, you whistled. Then you mouthed something from where you were. You said *I love you*."

For the first time since this awful conversation began, she looked unsure and a little afraid. Was she lying?

Just as quickly, her face shuttered. "I was singing along, Jack. I know you want to believe I said that, but the audience lights were dim and I was far from the stage. No matter where things stand with us, I was excited to watch you perform."

Lies. Truth. Lies. Truth. He could no longer tell his head from his ass with her. Maybe he never could. She did excel at falsehoods, after all. It didn't mean he was ready to give up. "I love you, Clementine. More than I thought possible. And I know you feel it, too. Some of it, at least. Tell me you don't feel it—right now, right here. Say it to my face, and I'll let you go."

If she could look him in the eye and admit that, he'd have no choice. He'd live with this pain...unless he tied her to his bed and forced her to ride out this rough patch like a detoxing junkie. Jesus. He didn't even dismiss the idea outright. He was that far gone.

She blinked and touched the necklace he'd given her, feeding him a kernel of hope. If she remembered how she'd cried the first time they'd made love, she'd stay. If she recalled how attuned they were to each other, in and out of bed, she'd fall into his arms. He sure as hell remembered. But he couldn't *make* her remember or stay if she wanted to run again.

She met his pleading gaze, and said, "I don't."

He grabbed the edge of the desk, gripped it until it bit into his palm. "So that's it? You're just leaving?"

"I never meant to hurt you. I care more about you than I ever have about anyone, but I'm not built to love you the way you deserve to be loved. You're busy. I'm at loose ends. I can't live in a town this small, with everybody knowing everything. But it's more than that. Little things I can't describe. In the end, I'm not ready to give up the life I know."

Her eyes darted to his gifts, desolation eclipsing her face for a beat. Then she swiveled and stepped toward the door.

"Wait."

She turned at his desperate plea, but the move seemed to pain her. Was he that distasteful to her already? Could she not stand to look at him? The regret on her face just now had likely been pity, the *I love you* he'd thought she'd mouthed from the crowd wishful thinking. The dismissal was a bitter pill to swallow, but he'd gotten over Ava's betrayal. He'd move on from this.

Rubbing the twinge in his chest, a twinge he'd never felt with Ava, he said, "You need to be careful."

She narrowed her eyes. "Why?"

"There's been a man around town. A guy with dark hair and a beard. He has tattoos on his arm—a knife and skull. He was watching you tonight."

"WHEN DID YOU SEE HIM?" Clementine forced a casual tone, like she hadn't broken Jack's heart and hers in the process. Like she wasn't desperate for this information.

"While I performed."

"Had you seen him before?"

Jack massaged the bridge of his nose. "The first time was in the diner, after we met there, when Jasmine called you Samantha, but you'd already left. Then at the park, but he was feeding the ducks. Nothing seemed off. But he was at Wherever the night we…kissed. I'd noticed him watching you, which was one of the reasons I joined you at the bar. Then again tonight—he was in the crowd. He didn't glance at the stage. Only watched you."

Fuck, fuck, fuck. She'd assumed Yevgen had been here four or five days tops, not two weeks. If he'd been here longer, her email might have no effect. He could have tapped her room early on. She had called Lucien from there to quit. If Yevgen had heard that, her claim the emails to her father had been used to lull Jack into submission would be moot.

She pressed her nails into her palm and refused to look at Jack's amazing gifts. He understood her better than she'd thought: her love of India, the orphanage, her need to help kids and make amends for her choices. None of it mattered.

Her only option was baiting Yevgen out of town.

She forced herself to relax and waved her hand, a dismissive gesture she hoped was believable. "I'm sure that guy's harmless."

"It didn't feel harmless. I'm worried about you."

"That's the thing, Jack. I'm not yours to worry about." If she told him the truth, he'd tear out of there to protect her and his family. This man who'd never been in a fight or punched a guy would go up against the likes of Yevgen. If she weren't bone-cold scared, she'd laugh at the prospect. No way could she tell Jack. He'd find out eventually, when she was in jail or miles from here. For now she had to fix this, make sure he stayed safe, which meant putting herself at risk.

First thing on her agenda: calling the cops.

"Thanks for the heads up," she said, her voice shakier than she'd like, "but I'm fine. I'll be out of town in no time. Speaking of which, can you give me a couple hours at your house? Time to get my things and go?"

Jack flinched, the sharp move gutting her. She was talking too fast, and hurting him was worse than getting stabbed.

His lip curled. Not his sexy Elvis curl. A disgusted with her curl. "Sure, Clementine. Whatever you need. Have a nice life."

She'd never hated herself so much, but she didn't have time to wallow.

The second she was out of the office, she ran away from Jack and barreled into the auditorium. The music blared. A plastic cup crunched under her feet. She elbowed at least three people, the drumline ringing in her ears as she craned her neck.

There. Imelda was where she'd left her by the stage.

Breathing hard, she gripped Imelda's upper arm. "I need your phone again."

Imelda pulled it out slowly, keeping it out of reach. "What's going on with you? Is everything okay with Jack?"

"I'm so sorry, but I don't have time for this." She snatched the phone and hunched away from Imelda, far enough not to be overheard. She dialed 9-1-1 and held one hand over her other ear.

"9-1-1, what's your emergency?"

"Someone's breaking into the David estate, the huge mansion off Red Creek Road."

She expected the operator to ask questions or calm her down. To say anything but, "I've had about enough of these calls, ma'am. We've checked that house twice now. You and whatever boy is calling are on thin ice. One more call like this, and charges will be pressed. You're wasting the sheriff's time."

Goddamn, Yevgen. He was one step ahead of her, goading the sheriff's department, pranking them to check the estate so they'd quit when it counted. He'd probably already cut the alarm system, her call to Sylvia not worth a damn. The man was cocky, psychotic, and clever. A dangerous combination that left her high and dry. She had to outsmart him at his own game. She pulled up her email again, not surprised to find a reply.

The only gullible one here is you. And you fell for your mark? That's pathetic. I don't care if Lucien has the Van Gogh. I'm after something shinier and legendary. Hope no one gets in my way. Wouldn't want a repeat of the Monet job...

A hand touched her shoulder, and she jumped, practically hyperventilating.

Imelda stroked her arm. "Seriously, Clem, I'm worried about you. What's going on?"

The sky was falling. The ocean was overflowing. The Earth's crust was cracking.

Jack was hurting.

"I'm so sorry," was all she managed, repeating her platitudes.

She pushed the phone at Imelda and tore off. No time for explanations or goodbyes. She knew the shiny, legendary score Yevgen was after: Elvis's last known signed gold record. He always went for the notorious scores, heists that would land him in the news, increase the risk. And the record was at the estate. Jack's parents were in trouble, their night nurse as well. Colonel Blue. And...*oh shit*, Chloe. What if she went home early?

Clementine busted out of the exit, gravel flying under her sandals as she ran. She slammed her car door and pushed her Prius to its max. *Go, go, go.* She still had her knife under the floor mat, thank God. It would have to do. If Yevgen hurt anyone, even one hair on that old dog, she'd gut him. She wouldn't think twice about it...she hoped. She'd never harmed anyone during her heists. A tranquilizer here or there to temporarily disable pets, but nothing damaging.

Could she come through when it counted?

She flattened the pedal to the floor, hoping the cops found her and gave chase. She'd lead them to the estate happily. The sun was beginning to set, the sky still incredibly blue. A blinding shock of perfection against the ugliness swimming through her mind. Her car skidded briefly, sending her pulse into overdrive. The damn thing vibrated as she booked it.

It didn't feel safe. Nothing felt safe.

A mile from the estate's long drive, a car approached. It slowed down, but she sped along. Too fast. She knew she was driving too fast. An animal darted, small and furry—a squirrel crossing the road. She braked and her tires bit into the gravel. She fishtailed. A horn blared as she braced for impact, but somehow skidded to a stop.

Her hands shook on the steering wheel, her breath rattling in her chest. So close. She'd almost caused an accident. She clutched her necklace, only to remember she hadn't returned it to Jack. An unconscious plea for their romance not to end? It was time she stopped believing in fairy-tales. She'd have to leave it for him at the house.

When the billowing dust cleared and she saw Marco in the car she'd almost smashed, she gasped. His daughters were strapped in the back. She could have hit them. Tears tracked her cheeks, but she didn't stick around to apologize or fall apart. There was no time.

26

———

WHEN CHLOE WAS LITTLE, Jack and their parents would entertain her with the Statue Game. Chloe had loved calling the shots, but Jack didn't believe in handing over fake wins. No matter how loud or often she'd yelled *red light* or *green light*, she'd rarely caught him moving out of turn.

He felt like he was playing the game now.

He hadn't budged since Clementine had fled. He stood and stared, one hand still clutching the desk. He wasn't sure how long had passed. His mind had been stuck in a loop, replaying every detail between them: her confidence at their first meeting, that dusty road kicking up the chemistry between them, her trust when confiding about her past, the lies in between.

She may have seemed shocked when he'd confessed his love, but he was sure she'd mouthed *I love you* tonight. She'd looked proud and starry-eyed then. A contrast to the woman who'd brushed him off and claimed she couldn't leave her old life.

Yeah, he'd worried about exactly that, but something didn't add up. It was all too sudden. Was she just scared to trust?

His phone rang, the shrill sound slicing through his confusion. Hope sparked with it. Maybe she'd changed her mind, realized how wrong she'd been. Marco's name on the screen sapped his energy.

"What's up?" Jack couldn't hide his disappointment.

"Is something wrong at the estate? With your family?"

His knuckles whitened on the desk "Why? Is my father all right?"

"I thought your father was out of town?"

Shit. That stupid lie. He was tired of it, couldn't think straight enough to keep it up. "He's here and he's sick. He's been here the whole time. Tell me what happened."

"What do you mean he's sick?"

Jack speared his hand through his hair. Tried to, at least. His hair gel crunched against his fingers. "We'll discuss this later. Just tell me why you called."

"It's Clementine."

A boulder lodged in his gut. "Start talking."

Crying filled the line, one or both of his daughters stretching their vocal cords. Marco groaned. "The girls were fussy and not sleeping, and I thought driving would lull them. So I was out near the estate and a car came barreling down the road, nearly careened into me when it avoided a squirrel. It was Clementine, and she did not look okay."

"Are *you* okay? The girls?" What had Clementine been thinking, driving like that? Had she needed to get away from him that desperately?

"Yeah, yeah—we're fine. But Clementine looked...spooked as all hell. She was crying. Then she took off for the estate."

The crying comment worsened his turmoil, but the estate? Driving there didn't make sense, but neither had her sudden shift in behavior. Unless she'd left something at the house when she'd visited, or went to return the necklace he'd given her. Or steal another painting...

He massaged his temple while promising Marco he'd explain about his father tomorrow. He hung up and focused on his good moments with Clementine. The real ones. She'd been excited to come tonight. She'd planned to record his show tomorrow, spend time with his family next week to watch it. It wasn't the same as his father watching the show live, but knowing they'd been in Clementine's thoughts had meant the world. Her about-face tonight—dodgy behavior and edgy movements—stood out as the lies.

If that was true, it didn't explain the why of them.

"Can I talk to you, Jack?" Imelda stood at the door.

"Of course." It would give him time to question her, see if she found Clementine's behavior off.

She held her phone in one hand and scratched her neck with the other, her usually upbeat demeanor subdued. "I think Clementine's in trouble."

First Marco, now Imelda. Worry whipped through him. "What happened?"

She glanced at her phone like it might leap up and bite her. "She left her cell at home and used mine. Aside from the fact that she basically yanked it out of my hand and ignored my questions, she bolted from the auditorium faster than Lawson when I ask him to clean the garage. Didn't bother logging out of her email." Tentatively, she held it toward him. "I think you should read this."

Reading Clementine's email was an invasion of privacy, and he wasn't sure getting in deeper with her was smart. He loved her, found it tough to breathe through the unrelenting heartache, but she'd point blank said her life wasn't Jack's concern. Too much felt wrong, though. She could be in trouble.

Speeding and crying didn't jive with the woman who'd coldly brushed him off.

He took the phone and read the first message.

The only gullible one here is you. And you fell for your mark? That's pathetic. I don't care if Lucien has the Van Gogh. I'm after something shinier and legendary. Hope no one gets in my way. Wouldn't want a repeat of the Monet job...

He squinted and rubbed his brow. The email was from Clinton Abernathy, and the only Clinton Clementine had mentioned had been her deceased father. Unless she'd lied about his death. The mention of the Monet rang an ominous bell, too. He paced as he strained his brain for the connection. The Monet job—the job Clementine had described where she'd been stabbed. His own gut pitted at the memory, her father's name only confusing him more.

He scanned the message again, desperate for a clue. Lucien didn't have the Van Gogh. That much he knew. Jack had sold it. He'd parted with the forgery as well, bringing both along to validate the original. There were lots of shiny things at the estate. But legendary?

He pushed that message up, read the next one.

Daddy loved you, Clementine. And he's dead. No one you love will ever be safe.

Fear fisted his lungs. Not a subtle threat. He wanted to drop the phone and race to find her, but the random notes muddled with tonight's seesawing emotions, leaving it all unclear.

Mind running faster than a spiny-tailed iguana, he scrolled down farther, needing something to grasp. The next message was clearly one of Clementine's notes to her father. The few sections he scanned—*I hate that you're gone, I wish you could tell me what to do*—indicated that he was, in fact, deceased and unable to email.

Had the account been accessed by someone else?

He read more slowly. Confessions about Jack and her life filled the lines, like the diary-style emails she'd admitted to writing. She wrote of her fears of falling for him, how much she loved making friends in Whichway, how she felt like she'd finally found a real home.

I love Jack, it said at the end of one message. *I already love him so much it hurts. If I lose him, it will devastate me.*

Emotion stung his eyes. She loved him. He fucking knew it. Their whole conversation had been a charade, but his relief was bittersweet. The realization didn't explain her lies.

He reread the messages and pieced through what he'd learned:

She'd been crying and had sped to the estate.

Someone threatened those she loved.

She loved Jack.

Mention of something shiny worth stealing. Something legendary.

It clicked like the moment his lens breakthrough had struck, and the burn moved to his throat: she was protecting him...and someone was after the gold record.

His mind slammed back to that man in the arena—the tattooed creep eyeing her. That was when everything had changed. When Clementine had changed.

"Christ." He pulled up the keypad and started dialing.

"Jack, you're scaring me."

God, he'd forgotten Imelda was here. He silenced her with a raised hand.

The other end clicked through. "9-1-1, what's your emergency?"

"Call the sheriff and tell him there's an emergency at the David Estate."

"That's it," the operator barked. "This number has been traced. Charges will be laid."

"Excuse me?" The phone bit into his clenched palm.

"Pranking the department comes with consequences, kid. The sheriff and his deputies are busy. Fourth strike and you're out."

Kid? Prank? He held the phone away, gaped at it, then shoved it back against his ear. "Listen here, lady. I don't know who you are, but I'm Maxwell David the Third, and if you don't send Sheriff Moray and his deputies to the David Estate, you'll never work in this town again."

He stabbed the End button and almost upended the office desk. Samuel Moray and his deputies were at the midway, the carnival always set up on the far side of town, in the opposite direction of the estate. He had no clue why the operator had given him lip, but help might not be on its way.

He dialed the estate next, but got a busy signal, which was odd. He tried his mother's cell and the damn thing rang and rang, each passing second escalating his panic. Of course she wouldn't answer. She wasn't like Chloe, practically glued to her cell phone. He closed his eyes, tried to think. If they were in the nanny's wing as expected, they should be safe. Only someone with intimate knowledge of their home would stumble upon that. But if his mother went to the kitchen or her room at the wrong time she could be in danger, and God knew what Clementine was doing, if she was placing herself in harm's way.

He pushed the phone at Imelda harder than he should have. "Keep calling the last two numbers I dialed—for the estate and my mother. If someone picks up, tell them to stay in the nanny's suite and lock the door."

He snatched his keys from his briefcase and lunged for the door, but Imelda grabbed his arm. "What's going on?"

"I don't have time to explain. Just know that Clementine adores you and your friendship."

She bit her lip and nodded.

Two steps out the door, Alistair blocked his way. "Your set lost momentum. You're practically giving me the win."

He wasn't wrong. His performance had nosedived toward the end. "Don't care," Jack said, maneuvering to the right.

Alistair mirrored the move. "You think you're so much better than me, with all that money of yours, your fancy degrees. But which of us has Ava, huh? Which of us is gonna win top tribute artist? There are hundreds of hopefuls, but only one winner. Only one King."

Jack clenched his fist, ready to deck the guy, but he needed to get to his car, get to the estate...and do what? Fight a criminal with his bare hands? He didn't own a gun. He had less than zero combat skills. Sweat slicked his spine, his heart beating wildly as his mind whirred. Then it stalled. *There are hundreds of hopefuls.* Damn straight there were hundreds. Enough Elvi in this auditorium to fill five platoons. And they would be willing to fight for one thing.

The notion sinking in was ridiculous. Insane.

His options were limited.

He faced Alistair. "You still want that gold record?"

27

———

CLEMENTINE SLAMMED her car into park. She fished her hidden knife from under her seat and flew out the door without bothering to close it. The estate was deathly still, no hint of Yevgen or anyone having broken in. She could be wrong about him being here. Yevgen could just be playing a game of cat and mouse to taunt her. Her chest still felt like it was holding in a scream.

Please be okay. Please be okay.

Jack's family had to be okay.

She tried the front door first, but it was locked. If Yevgen was here, he must have snuck in another way. She scrambled around the grounds, to the bathroom window she'd used on her break-in. Her belly curdled. The fact that she'd done that was despicable, but Jack had forgiven her, the good man he was. A reminder she'd never deserved him. Just like his family didn't deserve to be caught in Yevgen's crosshairs.

The bathroom window was closed, but not locked, saving her from smashing the glass. She lifted it and checked for the scale she'd landed on last time before slipping in. Once inside, she wavered. No alarm had sounded. Sylvia had either ignored Clementine's instruction or Yevgen was here and had cut the power, maybe the phone lines, too.

Working faster, she tucked her knife into the back of her jean shorts and ditched her sandals, opting for quieter bare feet. She dashed across the foyer and through the kitchen, heart racing faster as she neared Maxwell David's room.

Please be okay.

The door was closed, but muffled grunts and curses had her panic rising. What had she done? Heart in her throat, she pulled the knife from its sheath, busted into the room, and the air whooshed from her lungs.

The nurse, Sylvia, and Maxwell stared at her, slack jawed. Even Colonel Blue gave her some serious side-eye. The TV was playing a Robert DeNiro movie she didn't recognize, the source of the commotion. She almost sagged to the floor.

"Clementine, dear. Why do you have a knife?" Sylvia moved to stand.

Clementine held up her palm, fighting the urge to hug the woman and never let go. "Stay here and don't make a sound. Turn off the TV. When I leave, push something against the door. And no matter what happens, what you think you hear, do not open the door for anyone. Do you understand?"

Thank God they'd been in this sequestered wing. If they'd been in their upstairs room, and Yevgen was here, he would've found them easily.

Maxwell pushed his upper body forward, looking frail and weak in the large bed. "What's going on?"

"If this is about the break-ins," Sylvia said, nonplussed, "the sheriff stopped by twice. He walked the perimeter and said some kids have been pranking their dispatch."

The nurse stood and studied Clementine, lips pursed as she

lifted the phone, likely to call the cops, but frowned. "The line's dead."

Dammit. There went any hope of this being a hoax. "Block the door," Clementine repeated. "I have reason to believe a dangerous man's in the house. Do not leave this room."

The nurse nodded and Clementine turned to leave, but paused. "I'm so sorry," she told Jack's parents, the same meaningless words she'd uttered to Imelda, pathetic attempts to ease her conscience. There was no apologizing for this.

She rushed from the room, Sylvia's concerned voice drifting after her. At least they were safe. That left saving the gold record and ending Yevgen's threats once and for all.

Clementine's only chance with him was the element of surprise. Lucien had trained her in hand-to-hand combat. They'd practiced weekly until his knee had started acting up. Elbow strikes to the back of the neck, the eye gouge, throat punch, nutcracker choke—she'd mastered it all. Her expertise hadn't helped on the Monet job, but she was prepared this time. She knew what Yevgen was capable of, and she was expecting him.

She slipped down the stairs to the lower level, blood rushing in her ears. She paused, controlled her breaths. *Steady, girl.* She resumed her slow prowl. The early evening sun glowed through the patio doors, casting gold beams over the pool table and TV area. Nothing was amiss. Jack's Elvis picture was still on the wall, still with the crack running through it. She'd planned to fix it for him. Instead she'd cracked his heart.

She fisted the knife handle and padded toward the hall while straining her hearing, listening for a noise, a clue... anything. A faint *clunk* sounded. Her adrenaline spiked. The noise had come from the sound room. Of course Yevgen was already there.

She snuck up to the closed door and adjusted her grip on

the knife. Firm and steady. Time to end this maniac's obsession with her.

But an arm circled her waist, a blade pressed to her neck. "Nice to see you, Clementine."

JACK CRAMMED five Elvi into his Tesla. Another twenty-odd followed in a few cars. He hadn't gathered the platoons he'd hoped in his timeframe, but they'd found enough to make a stand against an intruder.

Alistair sat in Jack's passenger seat, bouncing his knee. "You better not renege."

"You better make sure nothing happens to Clementine or my family."

Their deal had been simple. Alistair would help him mobilize as many Elvi as possible, explain that the gold record was being stolen from its rightful owner. Tribute artists were purists at heart. They wouldn't tolerate disrespecting the King, or Jack's granddad, who was responsible for the festival. In turn, Jack would give Alistair the gold record.

Not what the artists had signed up for, technically, but desperate times and all that, and Jack prayed he'd be handing his prized possession over to Alistair.

One of their traveling companions grunted. "Watch your hand, Ernie."

"Your elbow's lodged in my ribs."

"I'm choking on your aftershave, man."

"I'll choke *you* if your hand moves another inch."

Jack glanced in his rearview mirror and bit back a laugh, the maniacal kind. His Tesla had become a version of a clown car, crammed with bedazzled polyester, gelled hair, sideburns, and enough cologne to get high. He was in a fucking jumpsuit, too, all of them racing to save the people Jack loved. Definitely maniacal.

At least he'd reached Chloe before leaving. She'd promised to steer clear of the estate. The rest better go as smoothly.

His Tesla whizzed down the road, the train of Elvi-packed cars speeding in his wake. Trees and farmland zipped by.

Alistair's heel bounced incessantly. "Ava ever disappear on you?"

Jesus. The last thing he needed was a heart-to-heart with the man dating his ex. "Does ditching me to sleep with you count?"

"I was always the better man," Alistair said, less taunt in his voice than usual. He played with a loose thread dangling from his thigh seam. "But that was a shitty thing to do."

If Jack wasn't racing to the estate, he'd slam on the brakes. Alistair apologizing was as rare as a ploughshare tortoise. "It's forgotten. When it comes to underhanded dealings, I expect nothing less from you."

"True. Overshadowing you is my calling."

That was better. Their familiar jousting he could do. But Alistair slumped and knocked his head into the headrest. "I think she's seeing someone."

With her history, Jack wouldn't be surprised. He could sneer, tell Alistair he deserved everything Ava dished out, but he'd been on the receiving end of her whims, knew how it felt to be deceived. "She'll always gravitate toward the brightest star in the sky. There's no loyalty with a woman like that."

Clementine, however, was loyal to a fault. She was willing to break her own heart, if it meant saving Jack. She could be giving her *life* for his family's right now. Fire singed his lungs. He couldn't stop picturing that bearded man at the concert, the way he'd scowled at Clementine, unrelenting in his attention. Same at the bar the night they'd kissed, with enough time in between for Jack to have warned her he was in town. If something happened to her, he'd never forgive himself for missing the signs.

Alistair sighed. "Should never have fallen for Ava."

Eyes stinging from horrifying visuals, Jack forced his focus on their conversation. "Stealing her from me was too enticing for you."

"I do love beating you."

"Letting you win is my good deed for the year."

"Hey—no way did you throw last year's concert."

He hadn't. But it was so easy working up the man. "You'll never know."

"Jesus," barked one of the guys from the back. "I'm gonna chop off that fucking hand."

Alistair ignored the grumbling and glared at Jack. Jack smirked in return, the distraction calming his rattling pulse. No matter why Alistair was in his car, Jack's nemesis was helping protect his family and was getting enough grief from Ava. "Thanks for coming," Jack said quietly.

"Anything for that gold record." The cocky comment was typical Alistair. The way Alistair reached over and squeezed Jack's shoulder was not.

YEVGEN PRESSED his chest to Clementine's back, his foul breath wafting against her cheek. "Drop the knife, doll."

Her hand slackened, but she didn't let go. Jack had called her doll tonight, a way to lighten the mood after he'd said *I love you* and Clementine had gaped. She'd never get to explain her lack of reaction and confess that she loved him so much it felt like her organs had atrophied. Lying to him tonight had been the toughest con she'd ever performed.

Yevgen pressed his blade into her neck, and warm liquid dripped from the pressure point. She let her knife fall to the carpet.

"Well now, isn't that better? I really have missed you. Think about you all time."

"Funny. I haven't given you a thought."

"No? Not even when you see your scar?" He pressed his thumb into the blood trailing down her neck and smeared it around. "I'd love to see it for myself. Proud of my work."

If Tami were here, she'd say Yevgen was nuttier than a porta-potty at a peanut festival. The man was beyond insane, and Clementine's options were limited. Still, her survival instincts flared. She let her body get heavy, moved her weight to the balls of her feet.

Stay agile. Prepare to fight. Lucien was always in the back of her mind.

She judged the leverage it would take to twist her head and bite Yevgen's ear. He'd for sure slice her neck before she succeeded. She could bite his forearm, though. Yank on it enough to loosen his hold and chomp down. Yeah, she could do that. She'd have to grab him before he sensed her move, give an explosive push. Her fingers tingled. She clacked her teeth together.

She would not die today.

Yevgen adjusted the knife—just a millimeter—enough for Clementine to surge. She clawed his forearm and wrenched it down, then bit his skin and stomped on his toe. His holler ripped through her eardrums and his knife jerked away from her neck, giving her the space she needed to crouch and grab her weapon. She stood, ready to rush him and drive her blade into his gut. His dark eyes widened, the first time she'd seen fear on his face, and she wavered.

She was about to sink a blade into someone's flesh. Take a

human life. Her knees shook with the implication, then she noticed her bite mark on Yevgen's forearm, right over the tattoo he'd inked to commemorate her stabbing. This was do or die.

Her muscles contracted, ready to pounce.

"Drop the knife, Tangerine."

She faltered and choked on air. The voice had come from behind her, but she'd recognize it anywhere. Lucien was here. He'd come for her, like he had on the Monet job, because he knew she'd been distracted and off her game.

Yevgen straightened as though accepting his fate. Did Lucien have a gun on him?

She dropped her knife in a rush, relieved she wouldn't have to kill Yevgen herself. Lucien would always protect her. He'd *always* protected her. Gratitude made her dizzy, or maybe it was the adrenaline crash. She turned to hug the man who'd raised her like the daughter he'd never had and blinked in confusion. It almost looked like his gun was aimed at her.

28

CLEMENTINE TOOK A STEP AWAY, then remembered Yevgen at her back and stopped.

"What's going on, Lucien?" She laughed nervously, unable to reset her brain from attack mode to unthreatened. Lucien was the last person who'd hurt her. He was here to help.

He tipped his chin to Yevgen. "Take down the record. Wrap it carefully and meet me at the extraction point."

"And miss all this fun?"

Lucien ran his tongue over his teeth, a move he did when impatient. "You've had enough fun. Get on with it."

Lead settled in her stomach. They were talking like a team, and Lucien was dressed in black heist clothes. *Because he's here to save me*, her mind protested.

Yevgen lingered, something unspoken passing between them, and Clementine's wishful thinking plummeted. There was no animosity between them. They were implementing a plan, one she'd asked Lucien to avoid. She may not have mentioned the gold record, but she'd asked him to leave Jack's family in peace, and here he was, robbing them with the man who'd stabbed her.

She rounded on Lucien. "I know my leaving left you in the lurch and training someone from scratch is rough, but Yevgen is a loose cannon, and you know it. He's a fucking lunatic."

Yevgen chuckled. "That's no way to speak of your kin."

She snarled at the bastard. "Working in the same circles doesn't make us kin."

He waggled his dark eyebrows, his smugness unsettling. She'd seen him boastful and predatory, hostile and off-kilter. She'd never seen him like this, giddy with delight.

"No, it doesn't," he said, his accent thickening as he spoke. "Personality wise, we are nothing alike. If I were as naïve as you, I'd kill myself. But we are kin, Clementine. We were raised by the same man."

Ridiculous. Yevgen must be toying with her. Clementine and Lucien had lived together on their own. He'd leave for days at a time, busy with his research and fencing stolen goods, visiting charities and orphanages overseas. He would set her up at home with food and money, call her every day. Yevgen may be ten years older than her, but she'd have known if Lucien had raised another surrogate child.

She faced Lucien, expecting annoyance on his face—irritation with his new partner for trying to get under her skin. Instead she saw pity. "Bag the record," he told Yevgen. "I'll meet you shortly."

Lucien hadn't contradicted him. Not so much as an eye roll at the idiocy of Yevgen's claim. Numbness tingled through her limbs.

"Sure thing, boss." Yevgen sneered at Clementine and disappeared into the sound room, doing Lucien's bidding like it was the most natural thing in the world.

She curled her toes, didn't know why she couldn't feel her feet. "He's lying, right?"

He had to be lying. Lucien raising Yevgen made as much sense as Clementine walking on water.

Lucien's gun stayed on her, but his eyes crinkled with a fondness she used to love. "My darling, Yuzu, you were always so easy to sway."

The numbness spread to her chest. "It can't be true."

"But it is."

He didn't hesitate. Not so much as a pause, and blood flow returned to her veins, growing hotter by the second. "He's worked in competition with us for years, even sabotaging our heists, getting there first. He stabbed me, Lucien! Jammed a knife into my stomach. If you raised us both, how could you forgive him for that?"

"Nothing to forgive when it was done under my orders."

She stumbled back and braced herself against the hallway wall.

A flicker of madness flared in his eyes. "You needed the competition, sweetheart. The push to succeed. And you were always better than him, which he knew. So when you started second-guessing our work, threatening to quit, I had him up the stakes."

"You had me *stabbed*?"

"It was a wounding blow, easily healed."

"No. No. *No*." This couldn't be happening. "You cried that day, sat with me every night. You said you'd support me if I quit." Like he had this time, but her voice shrunk as she spoke, her world spinning off its axis.

He shook his head, condescension in the emphatic movement. "I gave you what you needed. I've always given you what you needed."

The long con. The longest she'd ever known. *Make yourself*

inculpable, Lucien would say. *Give them what they need. Fill the emotional void they crave and they'll never suspect you.*

Clementine had needed affection, security, food, shelter. A father. Love.

His other lessons flipped through her mind, each making her queasier.

Be nice, but not too nice.

Show some vulnerability.

Make your mark think it's his idea to meet up again.

He'd brushed her off plenty in those early days, claiming he had a police record, that if she called the cops he'd be in trouble. You didn't get more vulnerable than that. She had *begged* Lucien to keep her. She'd followed him, thinking he'd been clueless. Their first contact may have been luck, her follow-up phone call not a guarantee, but Lucien had orchestrated every subsequent note.

Naïve didn't begin to describe her.

She squeezed her eyes closed and pressed her body into the wall. "Why tell me now? Why have Yevgen follow me and show his face and entice me here? He could have done the heist on his own, been in and out of the estate without me ever knowing."

She wished she didn't know this truth. She wished she hadn't hesitated with her knife and gutted Yevgen when she'd had the chance. Ached to do it now. He was still in the sound room, behind the closed door. Still wrapping up their prize.

"I couldn't resist." Arrogance radiated from Lucien's cocked head and squared shoulders. "You're my greatest triumph."

Betrayal clouded her vision at his admission, along with self-disgust. She'd been duped and deceived, hadn't suspected him for a beat, and he wanted to revel in his mastery. Her entire life had been a lie.

Everything but Jack.

He had been real—his love for her, and hers for him. For the first time in her life she'd felt whole, and she'd ruined that as spectacularly as Lucien had ruined her. All she had left was the work she'd done, the kids she'd helped. But the second she opened her mouth to ask about the orphanages, she snapped it shut. Nausea rocked her. "You kept the money."

A villainous smile contorted his face. "I did."

"You encouraged me to keep emailing my father. Why? So you could hack into my email? Keep tabs on my state of mind?"

"Yes and yes."

The extent of his deceit unfurled in its horrific glory. She'd never had emotional privacy. Little Nisha's picture on Lucien's mantle was a lie, somehow forged or purchased. She had probably been sold into child labor after their visit, to panhandle on the streets or worse. "You took me to India, gave me something to work toward, then let those kids suffer."

"Finally catching on."

"There was no extortion to shut them down. The... the orphanage doesn't even exist." Her mind spun with his audacity. "Why spend that kind of money on a long con when the whole thing might go bust?"

"I saw your potential."

The scope and dedication of his con was astounding. If she hadn't been the victim, she could almost appreciate his commitment, but Clementine had spent her entire adult life funding a madman who'd had her stabbed.

She stared at the stranger before her, feeling detached. Like an observer trying to puzzle out these past weeks. "I still don't get why Yevgen was here from the onset."

"Insurance. I clued into the record while you were driving down and didn't want to add that to your job just yet. I knew you were delaying, having second thoughts, and you work best when heists go as planned. Yevgen was here to tail you and step in if needed, and I wasn't ready to give up on you."

Not on *her*. On his investment. One no longer bringing in returns. "Are you going to kill me?"

"If it makes you feel better, it won't be easy for me."

Only because he'd be killing his greatest success, not for any sentimental reasons. His ego was visible now, practically glowing through his smugness, and her haze began to clear.

Part of her welcomed the prospect of a shot to the chest, rather than exist with the knowledge that she'd lived a lie and had hurt the only man who'd ever mattered. Jack's shattered expression would haunt her forever, but Lucien had taught her too well. A ferocious desire to live flared. She may not have Jack or Nisha or Lucien, but she'd sampled freedom these past weeks. She wanted more of it, to know how it felt to work a full day and use that money to buy groceries and pay her bills. To groan when her alarm clock woke her for a job and feel relief when the weekend rolled around. Habits most people detested. She'd trade her Charger for that simple life.

She also wouldn't mind drop-kicking Lucien in the groin. And he still had Lucy. Her sweet girl was in his care.

If she was going to overpower him, she'd have to stall for time, distract him with his ego. Wait for Yevgen to leave the sound room and the estate, secure her footing, then pounce.

She stood from the wall and faced him as though ready for his bullet to end her heartache. "I knew you were good, Lucien, but this is..." She whistled a low note. "Did it ever bother you, lying to me?"

His finger teased the trigger but didn't pull. "I've always been fond of you. I'm fond of all my children."

Children *plural*? How many had he used? She wanted him to choke on his tongue, but she schooled her expression.

Talking. She needed to keep him talking, while slowly shifting her stance, angling her body. "Did the others not last?"

"They served purposes, but none were as moldable as you."

High praise on his lips, but a repugnant insult to her. "You always did know how to make me feel special." Cared for and safe. There was no denying that. "I did love you, not that it matters now. Fake or real, you changed my life."

Living with him had beaten scrounging for food on the streets, dodging fists and switchblades in foster hell. That truth twisted with his lies, but neither changed her current circumstance. His gun was still aimed at her. Lucky for her, it had shifted a hair lower. He should know better than to let his guard down with a mark, but the gleam in his eyes made him look high. Like the success of this long con had pumped him full of heroin.

Yevgen exited the sound room, a flat pack on his back. The signed gold record secured, no doubt. He curled his lip at Lucien. "Why is she still alive?"

"Since when do you question me?"

Yevgen's attention shifted to her neck. "That necklace is a knockout. Could get a pretty penny for it."

Her hand jerked, but she didn't touch the teardrop diamond. Like the gold record, this was a family heirloom. Irreplaceable. Worth more than money. She cursed herself again for not returning it. "Guess you've lost your touch. Can't recognize costume jewelry from the real deal."

He slinked toward her, vile and mocking, aware of her desperate lie. "Sentimental, huh? Or playing your man? Fucking him for the money. Yeah, that sounds about right."

"Take it and go." Lucien's patience was wearing thin.

Clementine clenched her jaw to stem the rising tears as Yevgen slowly unclasped the necklace. It dragged along the cut on her neck, a stinging pinch she felt in her heart. She would not cry. She refused to shudder at Yevgen's nearness. Any reaction from her would prolong his presence, and getting him out of here was her only chance to take Lucien down and find a way to get that necklace and signed record back.

Jewelry clasped in his hand, Yevgen blew her a kiss. "I'll miss you, sweet Clementine."

Total psycho. But he'd be out of the house shortly, probably through the lower level patio doors. As long as he didn't return and distract Lucien, she'd have that gun in no time, and she'd point the barrel at Lucien's temple. Then at Yevgen's.

She'd be the one in control.

JACK PEELED into the estate grounds and careened along the winding driveway, unsure how the wheels were still on the road.

Alistair braced his hand on the dashboard. "Mind not killing us before we get there?"

Curses grumbled from the guys in the back. The estate loomed ahead, and there were no cops, as he'd feared. Clementine's rental was in front, the only sign of trouble her still-open door. She could be in the house, another stab wound in her gut.

He slammed on the brakes and skidded to a stop.

Alistair grunted. "I think my kidneys landed in my lungs."

Jack's body still vibrated from the engine, every nerve ending on high alert. He wanted to race into the estate, check on his family and Clementine, but if an intruder was in there, if he had a gun, things could go south fast. "Let's wait for the others and make a plan."

They piled from the car and motioned for their backup to

pull up by the garages. Jack kept glancing at the house and shifting his feet. Could these men move any slower?

As the last few joined him by Clementine's car, Alistair squinted toward the lawn. "Is that the guy we're after?"

The sun had begun setting, but there was enough light to see the bearded man coming around the back of the estate, a flat backpack hooked over his shoulders. The man paused, likely shocked to see an Elvis gathering, then he ran the opposite way.

"The record's on his back," Jack called as he sprinted after him.

The other men surged. Jack upped his speed, pushing his thighs to their limit. If the intruder got away, he'd continue terrorizing Clementine. She'd live in fear, and Jack and his family would remain a target, because there was no way he was letting Clementine go.

The man glanced over his shoulder and stumbled slightly, the scene behind no doubt mind boggling: glitz and hair gel galore. The thief found his footing and aimed for the trees.

Jack increased his pace, but it wasn't fast enough. A tribute artist blasted past him, and Jack gawked at Alistair's back. His nemesis flew across the lawn, closing the gap to their mark. He was either a closet track star, or that gold record brought out his inner Captain America.

Ten strides later, Alistair launched himself at the burglar and latched his arms around the man's shins, taking him down —face first, thankfully. But a blade flashed in the criminal's hand. Alistair grabbed his forearm and tried to force it away. The man overpowered him, the knife jerking toward Alistair's throat.

A deafening *bang* blasted from behind Jack, and he ducked.

Alistair gained the upper hand, forcing the burglar to drop the knife as Jack slammed to a stop. One of the Elvi stood with his legs apart, a gun aimed at the intruder. The multicolored sky made it look like a ridiculous movie scene.

By the time Jack made it over, Alistair had the gold record in his possession and the man flat on the grass, hands behind his back. Jack should be thrilled they'd thwarted his scheme and would prosecute this man within the full extent of the law —if the goddamn cops ever showed up—but he'd been foolish chasing him. His adrenaline had kicked in, sending him after the intruder when he should have sped to the estate.

He was about to jog away when something shiny sparkled in the grass. The chocolate diamond. The one Clementine had been wearing. Feeling ill, he picked it up only to see red streaks on the chain. Ruby red streaks. *Blood.* "Where is she?"

The bearded man twisted his head and spat out dirt and grass. "She's where she deserves to be."

Cryptic bullshit. He started running, but shouted over his shoulder, "If you hurt my family or Clementine, you'll be wishing that bullet hit you."

"Your family's lucky they were out tonight," he called back. "Clementine wasn't so lucky. Her game should be up any second now."

JACK SPRINTED, signaling to guys as he went. "Five of you stay with Alistair and keep that man contained. If you have a phone, call an ambulance. The operator will give you shit, but if enough of you make a fuss, they'll have to comply. The rest come with me."

Hearing his family was safe barely made a dent in Jack's fear. Clementine's game couldn't be up. He didn't know exactly what that meant, but there was blood on the necklace she'd been wearing, the possibilities revving his pulse. She could have been hurt before the burglar left, bleeding out while Jack had given the man chase. Sweat gathered under his polyester suit.

"Where to once we're in?" The Elvis at his side had forty pounds on Jack, but he matched his pace.

"There's a spiral staircase to the lower level. She might be down there."

The Elvis nodded and pumped his arms. "No one messes with the David family on my watch."

Jack silently thanked his granddad for launching the

festival and giving him an Elvis army. He passed off the necklace and explained where the nanny's quarters were, panting between instructions. Two would head there once inside.

All breathing hard, they piled into the estate. The two ran toward the kitchen and his father's room. Jack led the rest down the stairs, motioning to keep quiet, but voices stopped him cold. Two people. Clementine and another man. Hearing her meant she was alive, but he hadn't counted on another intruder.

He halted the guys and spoke low. "I'm going to check things out. If I yell *Elvis*, that means I need you." Too much commotion could endanger Clementine more.

He crept down the steps toward the sound room, flattened his back against the wall and peeked down the hall. His heart lurched. Clementine didn't look harmed, but an older man stood before her, his gun pointed at her chest.

"I homeschooled you because you needed to be educated," he said. "Our cons involved high society. They required a level of book and street smarts. And, if you recall, you begged me not to send you to public school, which saved me from forbidding it."

"Because I was terrified of being discovered and put back into the system. Another weakness of mine you exploited." She let out a disgusted laugh. "Wow, Lucien. You really did a number on me."

Jack reeled at the man's name. Lucien had raised her, hadn't he? He had clothed and fed her while training Clementine to steal. A fact that hadn't sat well with Jack, but she'd only ever mentioned Lucien with fondness, no hint of bad blood.

She kept asking questions, his replies almost eager. The more he heard, the more it sounded like Lucien had been lying to Clementine, raising her under false pretenses. The conversation didn't fully make sense, but there was no misunderstanding the weapon aimed at the woman he loved. A woman trained in combat. If he distracted Lucien and gave her an edge, she'd take it. She'd understand. Anything else, including an Elvis horde, could increase her danger.

CLEMENTINE PULLED her right elbow back, just a smidge, ready to land a punch to Lucien's kidneys. His weak spot. Over the years, landing a kick or punch there had always ended with them on the floor, sweaty and laughing. She'd never put her muscle into it back then.

She'd throw her entire body into it now.

"If I needed normalcy in my life," she asked him, "what did Yevgen need? A puppy to mutilate?"

Lucien smirked, still happy to divulge his secrets, boast about his brilliance. Now was her chance, while he relived those glory days. She fisted her hand, but his pupils flared and his jaw hardened. His attention darted over her shoulder.

Oh, God.

She'd told Jack's parents to stay put. Not to leave the room. She swiveled, dread rising with the move, and horror winched her chest. Why was Jack here? He couldn't be here.

"When I envisioned meeting you, Lucien," Jack said with his Elvis voice, deep and confident, "I never expected it to be like this."

His eyes darted to Clementine, intensity in their depths, like he was trying to communicate with her. She wasn't sure how he knew she'd be here or what he was doing, but she knew an opening when she saw one. Lucien was distracted.

She lunged and punched Lucien where it counted, but he didn't hunch as expected, didn't so much as wince. He *always* winced when hit in the kidneys.

The man who had used and corrupted her laughed. "I knew insinuating a weakness would help me one day."

He backhanded her, his ring cutting into her cheek. She stumbled, too shocked by his latest revelation to keep her footing, and he raised the gun. Not at her. He pointed it at Jack and smiled. "Never fall for a con-woman."

No, no, no.

Clementine launched herself as Lucien squeezed the trigger. *Save Jack. He can't hurt Jack.* The prayer looped as pain shot through her chest. The floor rushed to meet her.

JACK ROARED. One second Clementine had the upper hand, the next she was on the floor, her blood seeping into the carpet, exactly as he'd imagined but worse. Agony ripped through his chest, like the bullet had hit him.

"Elvis!" he shouted and charged, no thought to guns or bullets or consequences.

Fury had never clouded his sense before. Nothing in life had been worth inciting violence, or so he'd thought. Clementine was hurt. His girl was bleeding out and moaning, and his self-preservation flew out the window. All that remained was vengeance.

The second Jack yelled *Elvis*, Lucien frowned. Then his eyes widened as men in jeweled jumpsuits flooded the stairs and lower level. Lucien aimed his gun and shot. The air by Jack's face whizzed, the bullet just missing him. Jack was too close and enraged to slow his assault.

He pulled back his arm as he reached Lucien and put his whole body into the punch. His fist connected with Lucien's face, a sickening crunch sounding. Lucien reared back, but didn't go down. He was a tough son of a bitch, and Jack couldn't quite re-fist his hand, wasn't sure why it wouldn't obey. Instead of exploiting Jack's weakness, Lucien cut his losses and ran, bolting toward the guest room at the end of the hall. Five Elvi rushed after him.

Jack spun and crumpled next to Clementine, scared to touch or move her. Her eyes kept fluttering closed. Her breathing wasn't right. He wasn't right. He'd never be right again if she died.

He lay beside her and stroked her hair. His hand throbbed. The pain didn't compare to the ache overtaking his heart. "Stay with me, baby."

"Jack?"

God, she was pale. Why was she so pale? "I'm here," he said, his voice breaking. "Not going anywhere."

"My life is a lie," she mumbled. "All for nothing." A tear slipped down her cheek.

"Oh my darling, Clementine." Jack didn't know the turn of events that had led to Lucien shooting the girl he'd raised, but Jack wanted to punch the man again. Over and over until Jack's already-mangled hand was a bloody pulp. So much for not believing in violence.

The Elvi who'd given chase jogged from the guest room.

"He escaped through a window," one of them said. "Couldn't shove myself through if I rolled in Crisco. We'll notify them out front."

All the men were on the hefty side of husky, and that window was damn small. Jack wasn't even sure how Lucien had managed the feat, but it wasn't his priority.

A distant ringing registered, tough to decipher from the basement, but it sounded like a siren.

"Cops are on their way," someone called.

Jack exhaled heavily, but sirens came with implications.

Clementine couldn't fly under the radar after this. Her past would come to light. She could be arrested.

Her eyes drifted closed.

"Clem, honey—stay with me. Help is here. You fucking stay and fight."

She roused slightly and licked her lips. "I lied," she said, each word seeming to pain her. "I do love you. Always did."

His throat closed. "Not as much as I love you, so you don't get to leave me, Clementine. You don't get to give up."

"But I lost your necklace. I lost ev...everything."

Of course she'd worry about that. "I have the necklace, love. And the record. There's nothing for you to worry about. You haven't lost anything at all."

Especially not him. He wouldn't give up on her. His lawyers would earn their retainer, fight to find a loophole in the system, ensure her freedom. She wouldn't end up in prison because a man had lured a child into the criminal underworld.

He heard people rush down the stairs and one of the Elvi explaining Clementine's injury, but he didn't look away from her, could barely force his lungs to inflate.

A gloved hand landed on his shoulder. "Move out of the way, sir. We need space to work."

"Don't you dare give up," he whispered to Clementine again.

He didn't remember standing, or a woman tending to his hand. He couldn't tear his eyes off Clementine's limp body being loaded onto a stretcher, her blood a dark stain on the floor.

He shook off the EMT treating him. "I need to go to the hospital. I need to be with her."

"She's in good hands, sir. Let my team do their job. But is there anyone we should call? Family we should notify?"

The answer only worsened his distress. No one. She had no one.

"Jack!" His mother picked her way through the throng of Elvi, hand clutched to her chest. The second she neared him, tears sprang to her eyes. Because he was her son, because in his world family meant love and worry and support.

"I'm Clementine's family," he told the EMT, and he'd be there for her as long as she'd let him.

EPILOGUE

ONE YEAR LATER

Find Elvis Presley.

JACK'S SCAVENGER hunt habit was adorable. The last one he'd sprung on her had led to a three-legged bearded dragon named Ethel. Unfortunately, this clue unearthed a slew of unpleasant memories.

Stop and breathe, her therapist would say. *Count to ten and remember the good things in your life, the progress you've made.*

Instead of thinking about Lucien's similar text at the start of her fateful Van Gogh job, she focused on her *current* job and how much she loved greasing up her hands under a car's hood, earning her paycheck with sweat and muscle. She thought about her Friday night gossip sessions with Imelda and Tami, family BBQs hosted at Marco's, helping David Industries with their philanthropic work, obstacle-course racing with Chloe, and all the Elvi who'd hugged her at this year's festival, thrilled to see her alive and well.

She thought about her favorite Elvis.

Kind Jack. Sexy as Sin Jack. Patient as a Saint Jack.

She didn't know any other men who'd have stood by her after the lies she'd told and danger she'd caused. And Jack hadn't just stood. He'd worked tirelessly with his lawyers and the cops so Clementine could help track Lucien, her clemency a mercy she still wasn't sure she deserved. Thankfully Lucien hadn't returned to his New York condo. Lucy had been there, unharmed, and Jack had helped reunite them. He had given Clementine space during her therapy, while she'd grappled with newfound trust issues and her even more complicated past.

She inhaled this goodness and let it fill her up, then reread Jack's note. Lucien's phantom thorns didn't cut as deep, and she knew where to find Elvis.

She toed off her boots and padded from the entryway into the open kitchen. Another note was tucked into the frame of Jack's family photo—Elvis with his arm slung around Maxwell David the First's shoulder.

Her greasy fingers had smudged the first clue, but she pocketed it in her jeans. If Jack kept slipping notes into her car and purse and underwear drawer, she'd have a novel's worth soon. Excited, she plucked the latest memento from its home.

Find the place where I learned to let go.

Definitely the bedroom. Although she loved when Jack took charge and possessed her mind and body, he'd allowed her some control, too. He'd released some of the insecurities tethering him to his past while she'd found ways to make him shake and curse. Sending handcuffs to his office had been good fun.

She jogged to their bedroom. A blue box lay in the center of the duvet, tied with a pink bow. She ripped it open like an impatient kid. Another note greeted her.

Find your favorite place.

Easy as pie.

She raced to the reptile shelter and pressed the Open button three times. *Hurry up, already.* The humid air wafted over her as she darted inside, the fly-away hairs from her loosening braid sticking to her face. A yellow box sat by the dragon enclosure.

"He's being an adorable sneak," she told Lucy.

Lucy stared into space. Or was she staring at Ricky? He had been making nice with Ethel lately. Jealousy could ignite. "If he loves you," she told her dragon, "he'll stay faithful."

Jack was the prime example of unfaltering love.

She decimated the box and read Jack's note.

Find the item responsible for our meeting.

Man, he needed to make these clues harder. Paper tucked into her pocket, she zipped through the house, her socked feet sliding out from under her as she careened around a corner. Her T-shirt—which was dirty from greasy cars—earned another sweat stain. She should pause and jump in the shower, change at least, but she could never contain her excitement with Jack, and he never complained about her attire.

She bolted for the three-car garage and flung the door open. She felt around for the wall switch. Lights flared. Clementine's heart skipped a beat.

Jack was in the garage, dressed in his work suit, his hip propped on a stunning wreck of an automobile she'd never seen.

"Took you long enough," he said.

She opened her mouth and closed it, perfecting her impression of a startled goldfish. "This can't be for me."

"It's certainly not for me."

"But it's too much."

"It's a hunk of junk."

The Pontiac Firebird was dented, more rust than paint covering its body, and a couple windows were shattered. It was the type of car you'd find abandoned during a Zombie Apocalypse.

"It's too much," she said again. A total masterpiece from the early seventies, every inch of it begging Clementine to restore its former glory. "You have to stop buying me things."

"You have to stop telling me how to spend my money. Not that you have to worry. This large garbage can didn't break the bank."

He was incorrigible. And sexy as hell with his dress shirt's top few buttons undone. She licked her lips, but the car pulled her attention. "Can I see the inside?"

"Thought you'd never ask." He waved his hand toward the driver's door, and his smirk wavered. He swallowed several times, each drag of his Adam's apple faster. Was that sweat beading on his upper lip?

"If you put a snake in there," she said, "I'll time it so a rat drops from the ceiling while we're having sex."

The corner of his lips kicked back up. "That threat never gets old."

"Neither does my cat burglar nickname."

They both enjoyed this suggestion from her therapist, to treat the past lightly whenever possible, giving it less power to hurt them. Although it worked for them both, it didn't explain why Jack was acting like a weird sneak.

***

IF JACK HAD THOUGHT this scavenger hunt through properly,

he'd be wearing running shorts and a T-shirt, not a full suit. His sweat-a-thon had begun the second Clementine had pulled up to the house. If she didn't get in this trash-heap of a car soon, he was liable to combust.

"Have I ever led you astray, love?"

She chewed her lip, still eyeing him with distrust. "There was that time I dropped off Blue for Imelda and you let me stand in the rain."

He chuckled and dragged a hand through his hair. "You love bringing that up."

And he loved her teasing. He couldn't imagine a day where she didn't make a crack about his jumpsuit collection or call him an idiot, mischief in her cinnamon eyes. The nights she lazily draped her leg over his while falling asleep were his favorite. The handcuffs and dirty packages she sent him at work were a close second, always with cheeky notes like: *In case you're in a frisky mood.*

He was always in a Clementine mood.

And she wasn't ready to relent. "Just saying, most gentlemen would offer shelter, basic human kindness, when the weather turned. Who knows what kind of indecent thing you've stored in the car."

"Guess you'll have to see for yourself."

She tried to glare at him, but it looked more like a cute nose twitch.

When she finally stepped toward the driver door, his heart hitched. If this was too soon, if he set her therapy back, he'd be furious with himself. But Lucien and Yevgen's trials were on the horizon. Clementine was the key witness. He wanted her to know, beyond a doubt, that he was here to stay.

The door groaned as she opened it, the Firebird one mile shy of pushing up daisies. She glanced through the busted window. "There appears to be a gift inside my gift."

Jack rubbed the back of his damp neck. "No clue how that got in there."

She shot him a playful look. "Likely story."

She eased into the driver seat, ran her hand over the dusty dash and whistled, then mumbled something he couldn't hear. Cursing him for another gift? If that was the case, she'd be livid over that box.

She lifted the parcel tentatively and gave it a shake. "Nothing growled, so that's a good sign."

"Maggots don't growl," he said.

"Rats galore," she shot back and ripped the wrapping.

He held his breath. Last time he'd been this nervous, he'd been teaching Clementine to swim. He'd stood at the pool edge, three lifejackets at the ready, that stupid song about her name always in the back of his mind.

She tossed the paper and bow onto the passenger seat, then worked the lid off the box...and screamed.

Not the reaction he'd wanted.

He rushed over and fell to his knees. "Don't freak out."

"I'm freaking out."

"Okay. You can freak out, but only because you're unbelievably excited to be my wife and spend the rest of your life waking up next to me."

Her answering whimper was less distressing than her scream. She lifted the chocolate diamond wedding ring from the box. It shook in her grasp. "How can you love me this much?"

"Because I do." There was no describing the indescribable obsession of love. It was a rainbow on a sunny day, the tiny hairs on your neck that announced a premonition. Love was everything you needed and nothing you didn't.

It was Clementine Abernathy, cat burglar, who'd stolen his heart.

"God, Jack—are you sure?"

He took his grandmother's ring from her hand and held it at the tip of her finger. "I want you forever, Clementine. I want to grow old with you and love you and fight with you so we can make up and do it all over again. I want to sing to you always and do that thing you like with my tongue." Her watery laugh spurred him on. "I want us, baby. I want you to be my wife."

She sniffled, her fingers shaking in his grasp. She didn't reply.

"Clementine? Are you unsure?"

"I'm overwhelmed."

An emotion he wished she didn't still feel with him. At a loss, he said, "I know the ring isn't traditional, but it was my grandmother's. It matches the necklace I gave you." The one she'd worried about while bleeding on his floor. "My mother's thrilled for you to wear it."

"She approves of this...of me?"

If Clementine only knew. "She cried when I told her and is already listing venues."

His mother had cried a lot since losing Dad, these particular tears both happy and sad. Maxwell wouldn't be here for his son's wedding, or the milestones afterward. A fact Jack still struggled with, and Clementine's worries weren't hers alone.

After his mother had regained her composure, Jack had said, "Do you think Dad would approve?"

Maxwell's first instinct after the shooting had been to warn Jack away from Clementine. Advice he had happily ignored. His father had come around eventually, even calling Clementine "his girl" often. "*How's my girl today*?" had become his standard greeting for her.

Jack had immediately regretted asking his mother about Maxwell's approval, feeling like he'd betrayed Clementine.

But Sylvia David had taken Jack's hand in hers and had given him a squeeze. "As a kid, you would cry during those UNICEF commercials. You'd come to me and ask if you could donate your toys and clothes and everything in the house. Then came the Humane Society commercials and more tears and you foraging for injured wildlife. You were born a compassionate soul, and Clementine needs compassion. Your father and I both saw how happy she makes you, and how much she challenges you, as any partner should. Your father recognized that as he got to know her. And the way she was there for all of us, and you, when he passed? You two are each other's center of gravity."

Her words had settled him back then. He wished she were here to settle Clementine now.

"My mother is beyond thrilled for us both," he said. "So I'll ask again, since I'm a slow learner and didn't phrase my last attempt as a question. Clementine, will you marry me?"

Her wobbly smile was the most beautiful thing he'd ever seen. "Part of me still feels like I don't deserve this—deserve *you* —but if I keep thinking like that, I'll have to add a bunch of dollars to my low-self-esteem jar, and I'm tapped out." Her hand steadied and her chin ticked up. "I'm also not letting you get away."

"Is that a yes?"

"That's a hell yes."

He slipped the ring on her finger and cupped her cheeks, drawing her lips to his, needing her in a way he'd never experienced. They kissed slow and deep, every taste of her making him lightheaded. Their kisses always spurred his pulse, but this was different, slower and harder all at once. It was his future. It was a promise, one he would honor until he died.

He pulled back and made enough space to hold out his hand to her. "My name is Maxwell Jack David the Third, fiancé to the most spectacular woman in the world. It's a pleasure to meet you."

Forget that last smile, this one—giddy and mischievous with a dash of awe—was his new favorite. She slipped her hand into his. "I'm Clementine Abernathy, reformed criminal and fiancée to the best Elvis tribute artist to ever live, even though he forfeited last year's final competition and lost to Alistair this year."

"Alistair is the worst," he grumbled, always surprised by his new fondness for his old nemesis. They had wagered the signed gold record in a private bet for this year's competition. Jack should have been livid he'd lost the title and that prize. Secretly, he liked knowing Alistair kept the treasure safe. "And you forgot to add that I'm the man who'll spend his days buying you gifts that will piss you off."

She sputtered a rebuttal, but he silenced his future wife with another kiss.

Want to know what happens when a girl with stage fright is forced to work as a stage magician's assistant? Check out Kelly Siskind's slow-burn romance *New Orleans Rush* today!

And keep reading for a look at her next release: *The Beat Match*.

New Orleans Rush

Falling for your surly boss is a rotten idea. Letting him saw you in half is even worse...

Beatrice Baker may be a struggling artist, but she believes all hardships have silver linings...until she follows her boyfriend to New Orleans and finds him with another woman. Instead of turning those lemons into lemonade, she drinks lemon drop martinis and keys the wrong man's car.

Now she works for Huxley Marlow of the Marvelous Marlow Boys, getting shoved in boxes as an on-stage magician's assistant. A cool job for some, but Bea's been coerced into the role to cover her debt. She also *maybe* fantasizes about her boss's adept hands and what else they can do.

She absolutely will not fall for him, or kiss him senseless. Until she does. The scarred, enigmatic Huxley has unwittingly become her muse, unlocking her artistic dry spell, but his vague nightly activities are highly suspect. The last time

Beatrice trusted a man, her bank account got drained and she almost got arrested. Surely this can't end *that* badly...right?

Buy *New Orleans Rush* today!

Thank you again for reading Jack and Clementine's story. If you enjoyed it, please consider posting a review to help other readers who might be looking for a story just like this one.

Keep reading for an excerpt from Kelly Siskind's next release!

COMING SEPTEMBER 2020

The Beat Match

Two DJs. One beat.
An off-limits romance neither of them expected.

Weston Aldrich is known for his devastating looks and crisp Italian suits. He's been groomed to take over his family business and is on the brink of closing a massive merger. Only two wild cards can derail him.

Wild Card One: If anyone learns he moonlights as a masked DJ, his credibility will be toast. Wild Card Two: Annie *can't-hold-a-job* Ward.

The Annie Ward he promised to help raise after her brother died. The scatterbrained girl who makes it her mission in life to drive him crazy. The gorgeous woman he's not supposed to fantasize about, let alone kiss.

Annie hates Wes's insanely overprotective nature, and how his ridiculous bone structure makes him look like a Greek god. His jokes about her plethora of jobs are beyond irksome. She has no plans to tell him about her latest aspiration, to match beats as a budding DJ. Until she learns what Wes does at night. Now she plans to prove Weston Aldrich has met his match.

Flip the page to read an excerpt!

THE BEAT MATCH EXCERPT

Weston Aldrich always dressed for success, from the shined tips of his Berluti shoes, to the crisp knot of his silk tie. Failure in business was for lesser men. A last-minute fumble when applying for a pharmaceutical patent? Fixed with well-placed phone calls and courtside Knicks or US Open tickets. An investor getting cold feet? He could sweet talk a vegan into buying a cattle ranch. He walked through life prepared, his mental rolodex one flip from solving the unsolvable. Which made his father's shocking statement all the harder to compute.

"Biotrell is entertaining an offer from DLP," Victor S. Aldrich said for the second time.

Weston stared at his father's impenetrable expression as his horrifying words sank in. The prospect was so absurd it was laughable. He'd been working toward the Biotrell merger for two years. Planning. Maneuvering. Clocking more hours than a video game junkie who urinated in a bottle to secure a win. Like hell they'd lose this deal to anyone, let alone those shady bastards at DLP. "You must have heard wrong."

His father straightened to his six-two height, custom-made

suit creasing as he crossed his arms. "Since I heard it from the horse's mouth, I'd say my sources are accurate."

Weston blinked, at a loss for words. An anomaly. His words usually worked just fine. They were pretty damn clever, actually. Up until one minute ago. "We're the right company for this deal," he said, his tie suddenly a boa constrictor around his neck. He jammed his finger into the knot and yanked it down. "Biotrell will remain intact if they merge with us. DLP will tear them apart. They must realize that."

"DLP has promised to keep all their employees on."

"Because they'll say whatever they need to get the deal done." Lie. Steal. Cheat. They made cesspool pond scum look appetizing.

"We both know they've found ways around promises before, but they're saying all the right things. Mr. Farzad still wants Biotrell under our umbrella. Seems he also wants something else, and he's using talks with DLP to entice us to up the ante."

Weston huffed out an incredulous breath, the sprawling Manhattan views doing zilch to calm his rising agitation. They'd been nothing but accommodating with Biotrell, working with their timelines, ensuring their workers wouldn't lose wages, offering them enough cash to keep five generations of Farzads living like kings. This would be one of the largest pharmaceutical mergers in history. Why toss a wrench into their plans now? "If they want more cash, we'll be hard-pressed to find it."

His father joined him by his office window, their polished shoes parallel, matching starched shirts as stiff as their stances. Their resemblance didn't end there, as people never failed to remind him. They both had thick heads of hair—his father's grayer than black these days—and blue-eyed glares that could cut diamonds. The Aldrich jaw was sledgehammer strong.

They had bodies built for athletics and minds sharpened for business. Weston had been groomed to steer their company into the future, exactly as his father had planned.

Their hobbies, however, were a different story. If his father knew Weston moonlighted as a DJ, a scene known for drugs and wild parties, the man would have an embolism, or disown him, or both. If Biotrell knew, they'd have squashed this deal months ago.

Thankfully that secret would never get out. Whatever had Biotrell playing hard to get must be fixable. "There's no derailing this merger," Weston said, unsure why his father was stalling. Victor S. Aldrich was as direct as a compass and twice as obstinate. "We'll close this deal no matter what it takes."

His father nodded once, sharply. "I'm glad you feel that way, son. It seems Mr. Farzad wants a personal favor from you."

Now things were getting downright bizarre. "What do you mean *personal*?"

"You know his daughter Rosanna?"

"Yes," he said slowly, the wheels in his head spinning to get ahead of this quagmire. Rosanna was a few years younger than Weston, founder of some cosmetics business, beautiful with her full mouth, dark hair, and striking eyes. A hellcat on wheels last he heard. Something about a salacious video going viral tickled his memory. "What does Rosanna have to do with a deal that's been negotiated and tentatively agreed upon?"

His father stayed facing the windows, his only movement a gentle tug on his jacket cuff. "Karim Farzad is a proud man, but all men are willing to admit weakness if it means helping their children. It appears Rosanna is heading down a slippery slope and Karim thinks you can help."

He had no doubt Rosanna was one bad decision from landing on a seedy reality show, but his father's "helping children" comment had him biting his tongue. Aside from lavishing his wife with affection before Weston's mother passed away, the man was as sentimental as a slab of granite. "How exactly does Karim think I can help his daughter?"

"He'd like you to ask her out."

Weston sputtered out a laugh. "Excuse me?"

"You're an upstanding man with an impeccable reputation. You have excellent connections and a bright future. Any father would be honored to call you his son-in-law."

Weston searched the streamlined wood cabinets, his contemporary sculpture collection, the leather seating area and glass coffee table, looking for a hidden camera or microphone or any explanation for this insanity. Surely this was some kind of sick joke. "I'm not getting married to some girl I barely know. This merger is a smart business move for both our companies. Karim knows that. His demand is nothing short of ludicrous."

His father faced him, unruffled, serious as ever. "Marriage is the long game, if it suits you both. Karim's only asking for you to be open to the idea. But I'm not asking. I'm telling. Take her on some dates. Spend time together. Rosanna needs a positive, stable presence in her life. She's a beautiful girl. Asking her out is no hardship."

Unbelievable. His own father was pimping him out to secure their financial future and market share.

Weston stalked to his chair and dug his fingers into its leather back. His desk was tidy, papers neatly stacked, pens tucked into unobtrusive holders, keyboard and cell phone parallel with the dark mahogany edge. Everything organized and uncluttered, exactly like his apartment and daily life. Only two framed photos suggested Weston had a beating heart inside his chest: his best friend, Leo, who died nearly thirteen years ago, and his mother, who died the year after that devastating night. They were reminders of why he worked ungodly hours but risked it all with his secret DJ gigs.

The photographs were also a wake-up call now.

Weston had no intention of ever marrying. Losing the people closest to him had taught him one paramount lesson: love always ended in pain. He'd been forced to attend therapy. He knew the drill, why he still kept people at arm's length. Emotional distance, fear of abandonment. He was so textbook the textbooks were jealous of him.

Label him whatever you wanted, Weston planned on a long life of bachelorhood, most of it spent in this towering office. But dating wasn't marriage, and Karim wouldn't force the couple into a union that would end in divorce. Plus, he hadn't been lying when he'd said he'd do whatever it took to seal this deal. This was his chance to make his mark on Aldrich Pharma. Prove he deserved to take over the family business one day and appease shareholders who worried he was being gifted the reins.

"Fine," he told his father, still angry about this change in circumstance. Business should be business. Dating to secure a merger had made this personal. "Tell Karim I'll try—"

His cell phone rang, cutting him short. Anthea Ward's name flashed on the screen. The only person who came before work. "I need to take this. I'll ask Rosanna out in the next couple of weeks, once I get my head around it all."

"See to it that you do, and that you do it soon." Victor's heavy jaw clamped shut.

Weston didn't bother replying or watching him leave. He answered the phone. "What can I do for you, Anthea?"

She growled through the line. "How many times do I have to tell you to stop calling me Anthea?"

"Sorry, *Anthea*, but it's hard to hear you over the whine in your voice. Is there a particular reason you called?"

"Yes, *Weston*, unfortunately there's a reason. Otherwise I wouldn't be calling you."

He chuckled at her irritation. Needling Annie with her full name was the only thing that could amuse him on a day like today. "Well then, *Squirrel*, do fill me in."

Another growl. Something snarky under her breath. She enjoyed his nickname for her as much as her given name. Instead of biting back, she said, "I need a lift."

"Did you forget how to use the subway? Are you allergic to taxis? Did your Uber app malfunction?"

An exasperated sigh slipped through the line. "I lost my apartment keys and accidentally left my purse inside my locked place."

"So ask your landlord to let you in."

"It's more complicated than that, and I need to get to work. So can you or can you not pick me up? This is an emergency."

Everything with Annie was an emergency. The night she ran out of glue for her obsessive scrapbooking hobby and dialed 9-1-1 had been a special level of absurd. The time she spotted a vintage purse she just had to have and made him stop in the middle of the street so she could bolt from his still-moving car had been stroke inducing. Anthea—*Annie*—Ward had the attention span of a fruit fly and was as organized as a Black Friday sale. He had no clue how she made it through each day. "Tell me where you are, and I'll rescue you before the sky falls."

He felt her trademark evil stare as she barked out the address and hung up.

He shook his head at Leo's photo. "When you told me to look out for your little sister, you didn't tell me she'd be this big of a pain in my ass."

He smiled sadly, wishing Leo would bust his gut laughing, or punch Weston's arm and tell him to suck it up. He wished Annie had more people to rely on than Weston, who barely had time to sleep, let alone nag her to stick with a job longer than a month, or go back to school for a useful degree.

He snatched his keys and wallet from his desk drawer and stalked out of his office. After quick instructions to his secretary to divert his calls, he cracked his neck and jabbed the elevator button twice. *Go on a date to secure a merger. Be a son-in-law for hire.* It was unprofessional. Exploitative. His vision turned spotty as he marched inside the opened elevator.

Duncan Ruffolo slipped in before the doors slid shut. He nodded at Weston. "Hey."

Weston grunted.

Duncan rocked on his heels, hands clasped over a new, astronomically expensive suit. Weston of all people would know. Where some father's played ball with their sons or shared laughs and shouts over a sport telecast, Victor S. Aldrich would drag Weston to his tailor to be poked and measured and told to stand straighter. "The suit doesn't make the man," his father would say. "The man uses the suit to reinforce his greatness."

If Weston didn't know better, he'd say Duncan was wearing a Guanashina suit, the luxurious fabric exceeding greatness. The blended mix of guanaco, baby cashmere, and kid pashmina was so fine it felt like silk against the skin. At fifteen thousand dollars a pop, it better feel like heaven.

"Have we given you a raise?" Weston pressed the button for the parking garage. Always best your employees knew you were attuned to details.

Duncan chuckled. "Only you would notice the suit. And no, sadly, you have not given me a raise. My father came into some cash, spread it around his kids. Thought I'd have some fun with it instead of saving." He leaned closer to Weston's ear and dropped his voice. "You should see the new bed I ordered."

Duncan was an exceptional executive assistant. He was

flexible with senior managers and shrewd enough to anticipate needs. He was resourceful and efficient when coordinating events and arranging travel, and was well-liked by the staff. He was also well-liked by most of New York's female population, as he never failed to boast.

"Be careful putting those notches on the bedposts," Weston said. "You wouldn't want to weaken the structure and have the bedframe crash."

"Crashing would only heighten the fun."

Normally Weston would laugh, but he wasn't in a laughing mood. He didn't envy Duncan's player status, either. Weston may not be relationship bound, but he believed in treating women with the respect they deserved. With Duncan's All-American blond hair and quarterback build, his once-and-done attitude often left a trail of unhappy women in his wake. But Duncan was a top-notch employee who worked hard. He was entertaining, quick with a joke, often prodding Weston to join him for post-work drinks. An effort he'd been upping lately.

Duncan had that sharing-is-caring look about him now. "Saw your father leaving your office. He looked pleased about something."

Weston sure as hell wasn't pleased. "You mean he wasn't scowling."

"The man won't be hired for a toothpaste ad anytime soon. But, yeah, he seemed less lethal than usual."

"Well, he shouldn't be. Not when—" He cut himself off before launching into a tirade about Karim Farzad and this merger turning into a Match.com slumber party.

Duncan had proven he could be counted on and was as discreet as employees came, but no one could know how low he was sinking to get this deal done. "Some final things are snagging the merger's momentum, but nothing detrimental. My father was just filling me in."

Duncan studied him as the elevator hit the garage floor. "Care to join me for a Scotch at Leverage tonight? Looks like you need to unload."

What Weston needed was to fit ten hours of work into five, clear his head for tonight's gig, and prep for an unwanted date. Duncan's continued efforts to socialize were still appreciated. "Thanks, but I've got to work."

"All work and no play makes for a dull life," Duncan said as they headed for their cars. "When does the great Weston Aldrich make time for fun?"

"Fun is overrated." Weston waved vaguely as he unlocked his Audi and slid into his seat.

Playing tonight's club would be thrilling. Invigorating. Duncan's version of fun—dating, socializing, relaxing on weekends—was reserved for a different kind of person. Accomplishment drove Weston, professional strides and goals reached, which made the merger's latest obstacle all the more infuriating. His mind kept skittering to Karim's outlandish request, his father's not-so-subtle agreement. Weston's own easy acceptance. Like making Rosanna a pawn in their business merger was no big deal.

His car nearly stalled as he accelerated up the garage ramp. He almost sideswiped one of the support columns. *Date Karim's daughter. Hopefully marry her.* The longer he ruminated, the more erratic his driving became. No. He wouldn't ask her out unless she knew what had driven the request. If she agreed, then he'd do as suggested. Wine and dine her.

Still, he couldn't see her taking kindly to her father's meddling, and the city's gridlock shot Weston's already frazzled nerves.

By the time he pulled up to the curb where Annie should be, he was close to crushing his steering wheel. He searched the busy sidewalk for a girl in layers of vintage clothing, long blond hair tied into a knot on her head. He often told Annie she was one oversized sweater shy of looking like a tree-hugging hippie. She would roll her eyes and tell him he wouldn't know chic style if it bit him in the ass. His designer-filled closet would disagree with her, and there was no sign of Annie or her eccentric wardrobe anywhere on the bustling street.

Then a woman—*not* a tree-hugging hippie—stood from the stair of a pizza shop, and his heart two-stepped. What in the actual hell?

This woman was definitely Annie. The birthmark above the left corner of her upper lip and striking hazel eyes, so much like her brother's, were unmistakable. But this Annie's lace top pushed up her breasts and bared her abdomen. Her black skirt showed more leg than a Radio City Roquette, and her tall black boots had every passing male licking his lips.

This Annie was about to get an earful.

He pushed from his Audi, closing the distance between them as he removed his suit jacket and swung it around her. He tried to usher her toward his car, away from the man who'd just winked at him knowingly. Goddamn creeps in this city.

Annie dug her heels into the sidewalk, nearly toppling them both. "Aggressive much, Wes? Are you trying to break my legs?"

"I'm trying to get you into my car before someone offers you a key to a room that rents by the hour."

She shoved him and his jacket off. "Are you for real?"

Was she trying to give him a coronary? "Since when do you dress like...this?" He motioned to her skimpy outfit, then sneered at a preppy jerk giving her the once-over. "If you value your face, buddy, keep it pointed ahead."

The idiot snickered and walked on. Weston tried to shield Annie with his body.

She tipped her head back and sighed dramatically. "You are such an overbearing asshole sometimes."

Honestly, this girl. He hadn't driven through ungodly traffic instead of poring over this merger disaster for the pure joy of it. "If my memory serves me correctly, and it usually does, you're the one who called me. Something about an emergency."

Her face turned serious. "I was dying for one of those amazing gyros from that place around the block, but when I got to the restaurant I realized I snatched my keys but forgot my purse. And I *may* have left those keys in their bathroom, which were gone when I went back to check. Since there's the teeny, tiny issue of me being late on rent, I can't speak to my landlord today, and when I explained my situation to the nice man waiting for his gyro, he lent me his phone so I could call you. Small mercies, right? So I'll have enough cash for rent after tonight's shift, *but* I'm cashless and cardless until then and can't be late for my new job, so we really need to get a move on. And I'll need to borrow your key to my place."

He counted to five, making sure her verbal deluge had ended. Annie had three settings: Chatty Cathy, sarcastic comedienne, and pit bull. "What do you mean you're late on your rent?"

"It's nothing. Just a small setback. All will be well tomorrow."

"This isn't a small setback. This is irresponsibility."

"I don't need you to lecture me, Wes."

"No. You need me to rescue you."

"I only called you because everyone else I know has a real job."

Well, wasn't that the cherry on this shit-flavored day. "Did you hit your head this morning? Is there some kind of frontal lobe damage I should be aware of?"

It would explain the wardrobe malfunction and asinine comment. Annie knew Weston clocked upwards of eighty hours of work a week. She was well aware he ate, drank, and breathed his job. Aside from fitting in hours at his home gym, squeezing in time with her, and the evening activities she'd never know about, his life revolved around Aldrich Pharma.

She sassed out her hip, a move that hiked her miniskirt farther up her thigh. A bike messenger whistled at her. Weston gave him the finger as the moron plowed into a parked car.

"Let's dissect this, shall we?" Annie said, oblivious to the male chaos she was creating. "Did you have to tell someone, a boss for instance, you had to leave work?"

He glared at her, and she smirked.

"Are you worried," she went on, smug as a Cheshire cat, "you might get in trouble for sneaking off? Be given a warning? Lose your job?"

He curled his lip at the implication. Just because he had freedom to come and go as he pleased didn't make the demands of his job any less real. Or less stressful. He was being told to date, hopefully marry, a woman for God's sake. But there was no point explaining his responsibilities to someone who flitted from job to job, barely making rent, quitting when anything got too tough. "Don't talk about things you don't understand, *Anthea*."

"Come on, Weston Ald*rich*. The word 'rich' is in your freaking name. You don't know from real work." The pit bull unleashed.

"And this outfit you're wearing," he said, unsure why he was getting so angry, "is that for a real job? One that won't have your brother rolling over in his—"

Annie flinched, just enough for shame to silence him.

Mentioning Leo was a low blow. Too low. They never outright fought. Ragged on each other, sure. Went out of their way to tease and torment. Something was different today, though—her outfit, this weird protectiveness that had him wanting to build a castle around her. With a moat. And sharks.

During the thirteen years since her brother's death, he'd watched Annie grow out of her gawky limbs and boyish figure, into this...woman. He wasn't sure when the change had fully struck him. It felt gradual, yet sudden. Expected, yet feared. Forward momentum he was powerless to control. The past year he'd found himself staring at her occasionally as she'd fuss over one of her scrapbooks, her teeth lodged into her bottom lip, T-shirt carelessly slipping off her shoulder. He'd forget himself when she'd laugh, the sound huskier than he remembered, her head tipped back and throat open, so much easy joy in the sound.

Yeah, he'd noticed the burgeoning beauty in Anthea Ward, little sister of Leonardo Ward—*in a totally platonic way*—which meant other men had noticed, too. And here he was, tasked by her brother to ensure some idiot didn't hurt her or take advantage. Near impossible in her current outfit.

"Just...please get in the car, Squirrel. We can yell at each other in there while you tell me about your new job." He didn't want to hear about what sleazy bar had hired her. He didn't want to call Rosanna Farzad and ask her out. He may be free to leave work as he pleased, but this felt a lot like he was being controlled. Governed down to the company he kept. Except for tonight's gig. He spun music for many reasons, but they were *his* reasons.

Annie didn't glower or snark back at him. She said a soft, "Sure," her fierce eyes oddly downcast. A weird ache pinched the center of his chest.

The Beat Match is Available September 2020!

CHECK OUT KELLY SISKIND'S OTHER TITLES!

STANDALONES

New Orleans Rush: "The romance in New Orleans Rush will leave you smiling and filled with optimism." ~ Helen Hoang, author of *The Kiss Quotient*

Chasing Crazy: "...this is one of the best New Adult contemporary romances I've read to date." ~ *USA Today* Bestselling author K.A. Tucker

INTERCONNECTED STANDALONES

Over the Top Series

My Perfect Mistake: "This has easily earned itself a place on my all-time favorites shelf." ~ The Sisterhood of the Traveling Book Boyfriends

A Fine Mess: "Delicious, sizzling chemistry that leapt off the page!" ~ *USA Today* Bestselling Author Jennifer Blackwood

Hooked on Trouble: "...experience the romance, the sexy times, the heartbreak, and the swoons...you can thank me later!!" ~ The Book Hookup

---

One Wild Wish Series

He's Going Down: "An intoxicating romance that lingers like a great Merlot and leaves you with one hell of a book hangover!" ~ author Scarlett Cole

Off-Limits Crush: "...with loads of flirty and witty banter. Siskind knows how to write characters that have off-the-charts chemistry." ~ RT Book Reviews

36 Hour Date: "Kelly has blended a mystery into this compelling love story in a way that keeps the reader flipping pages. I couldn't put it down!" ~ *USA Today* Bestselling Author Ellis Leigh

ACKNOWLEDGMENTS

A common piece of writing advice is to write what you know. While I didn't grow up as an avid Elvis Presley fan, I now live in a small Canadian town that actually hosts an Elvis festival. The fun-filled weekend brings out all sorts of characters. It's the perfect backdrop for a quirky romance. Then, on a visit to Nashville, I saw Elvis memorabilia, early photos of the handsome man, and I heard some of his recordings in the original RCA Studio B. The legendary man came to life for me, and I wanted to create a character who was inspired by his charisma.

When I heard a news story about a family who didn't know they owned a famous painting, the rest began to click. The priceless piece had gone undiscovered because it hadn't been signed. I don't recall the painting or the artist, but the juicy details sparked the beginnings of a plot.

Thank you for reading this story. Jack and Clementine took me on journeys I didn't expect, and I'm thankful to have readers willing to escape to my sometimes offbeat, imagined worlds. My next story will feature Annie, the little foster girl

Clementine once lived with, and I can't wait to share her romance with you!

Thank you to my talented cover designer, Mary Ann Smith. Your work is such a highlight of bringing my stories to life. Thank you to my thorough editor, Tamara Mataya, and to the many writers and friends who've helped me on this book: J.R. Yates, Jamie Howard, Chelly Pike, Tara Wyatt, Michelle Hazen, Shelly Hastings Suhr, Tammy Cole, Sandra Lombardo, Jen DeLuca, Beth Miller, Brenda St. John Brown.

Heartfelt thanks to Robert Maaskant, whose engineering expertise helped me piece together the lens factory struggles and details. He also makes a mean gin and tonic. Any inconsistencies are my errors alone.

To my husband: you have all my love.

Thank you to my Facebook group, Kelly's Gang, for making social media fun. To the blogging community, you do incredible work spreading book love. Thank you times a million. And thank *you*, dear reader. You're the reason I write.

ABOUT THE AUTHOR

A small-town girl at heart, Kelly moved from the city to enjoy the charm of northern Ontario. When she's not out hiking with her husband or home devouring books, you can find her, notepad in hand, scribbling down one of the many plot bunnies bouncing around in her head. Her novels have been published internationally.

For giveaways and early peeks at new work, join Kelly's newsletter: www.kellysiskind.com

If you like to laugh and chat about books, join Kelly in her Facebook group, KELLY'S GANG.

Connect with Kelly on social media:
    Twitter/KellySiskind
    facebook/authorKellySiskind
    Instagram/kellysiskind